DESTINY SEEKER:
THE MESSENGER

Printed in the United States of America

First Printing, 2018

ISBN: 978-0-692-12532-8

Cover design: Garrett Hamon, https://
ghamon.weebly.com/

Editors: Travis McGruder, Hannah Ratliff,
Emily Bates

for Travis

PART ONE

PROLOGUE

"Ilsi, love, what is it?"

"Papa," his little girl gasped between shrill sobs, "Mama is gone!"

"Gone? Where is she? What are you talking about?"

Jonan was relaxing from his recent shift in the mines. He raised an eyebrow when his daughter came into the kitchen where he was heating up the iron stove to start cooking. He looked down at his daughter and noticed that she was extremely pale and pink with melted snowfall on her skin. She left the front door open as a dry, frosty wind wheezed its way in.

He looked at her in puzzlement and then back outside; the summer months were halfway finished—it was not the time for snow. He also just came home an hour ago and didn't see a single flake of snow on the ground.

He smoothed back his hair in alarm. He knelt down next to his shivering daughter and tried to hug her to calm her down. She hiccupped and resisted.

"Papa, you have to go get her! Papa!" she wailed. Her pink face pinched as she started to cry again.

"Ilsi, tell me what happened, why are you hurt? Who did

this to you?" her father pressed. She had bruises on her knees and the side of her head.

"I was playing," she started, "I was playing in the field. Then it got really windy—everyone ran away and I was all by myself. I didn't know what to do! There were a lot of colors and a magic wall came—"

"A magic wall?" her father repeated.

"And Mama is trapped on the other side!" Ilsi finished, trying to shake her father's shirt with her tiny, clenched fists.

"Show me exactly what you saw, love," her father said, thrusting the door all the way open. Everything was white for miles and extremely cold.

"Where did this even come from?" he cried in alarm, scooping his tiny daughter in his arms as he raced out into the cold. He shivered tremendously but didn't care; he couldn't remember a moment in his life where he ever felt cold, but this bizarre weather chilled him to the bone. "I can't get warm. I can't melt it."

Jonan scanned the scene as he stomped through dead, frosted blades of grass. Ilsi directed him through the town streets for about ten minutes until they came to an imposing wall.

The wall stood and stretched in all directions. It was impossible to tell how thick it was, but at the moment, it was transparent like frosted glass. He looked up and could see no end—he looked from side to side and the wall sliced through homes, fields and ocean. No edges in sight.

"Here, Papa!" Ilsi said. "She's on the other side!"

"Good girl," he replied, setting her down. "We'll help her out and hopefully we'll be out of this cold soon."

They knelt together next to a transparent wall. Jonan

knocked on the surface; it sounded thick and permanent. Jonan shook his head; his only concern was freeing the woman with gold curls on the other side.

Despite the length and width of the wall, he could see her through the thick wall; his wife desperately waved to get their attention. He could tell she was yelling but Jonan couldn't hear a thing.

Jonan, despite his cracked lips and dry throat, tried to hum and cast a spell. He looked around and the snow wasn't obeying him. He was using a fairly easy spell, but he couldn't get the chill to leave his body. The feeling was foreign and horrid.

In his tribe of Ice Chanters, controlling the cold was a traditional gift. Whatever curse this wall brought, it was beyond his control. This island was populated by people who never felt cold and formed ice to serve them. This snow and ice was different. He was certain not even the Council could readily explain this. Now he couldn't do anything to stop it. Explanations and thoughts failed.

Ilsi squealed. "Mama!"

"It's alright, love," Jonan said. "We'll help her get through."

Jonan's wife knelt on the gray earth and frantically tried to make a hole in the wall by scraping at it with her nails. She looked up, and her eyes were full of tears. She tried to call out to Jonan but her voice was barely audible.

"Stay calm, Helene," he said, attempting to be calm for all three. "Ilsi, go grab Papa's house tools." The girl, relieved to have an important job, raced home and returned with the tools soon after. The desperate father grabbed for the tools and threw his weight into each blow, but his tools were warped and mangled with every attempt. The wall hardly sported a chip or scratch.

He began charging into it, determined to use every ounce of strength to get through.

Helene clutched herself and bit her lip in frustration. Her hands were red. She tore off her blouse and skirt, revealing her undergarments. She held her clothes to her forehead; she looked like she was dripping with sweat.

"She's burning up," Jonan wondered aloud. "But why? We're freezing to death over here." Jonan sat in the snow, wracking his brain. He knew a few other common spells but they fizzed out and didn't cause any damage.

He was there for hours until he looked at his own hands—beaten, with blues and reds. He wanted to stay until he saw the wall crack enough to get his wife through, but he thought of his daughter, hardly dressed for such sudden weather.

"Jonan!" a man called out for him. "We've been looking everywhere for you!" A group of men with sooty faces approached the strange wall and the desperate man kneeling at its base.

"Jonan," the man said between breaths, his eyes scaling the Wall's height, "what is this?"

"I have no idea, but Helene is trapped on the other side," Jonan said through gritted teeth.

"I'll get my tools," he responded, a few others calling out to draw attention to the foreign, wicked thing. They called for fire or weapons and for help from the Council.

"Jonan?"

"What, Peder?" he replied tersely, grabbing anything and trying to smash it into the wall.

"No one can use their Ice Chanter spells against this snow," Peder replied, "Something is terribly wrong."

"Just help me break this thing down!" Jonan cried. "Helene is on the other side!"

"Papa! Let me try!" Ilsi cried.

"Ilsi—" he replied, but that didn't stop her. She charged with all her strength, and crashed into the wall.

"Ilsi!" her father cried as he watched her smack against the wall. Her small body made a slight thudding sound and she fell into a patch of frozen grass. She didn't reply, so he quickly picked her up and brushed away the snow from her face and hair.

"She's bleeding," Jonan said. "Can you get someone to bandage her hand and head? I have to get Helene."

"By all means, do you what you must. I'll take her to my house," Peder said. "Tyk can entertain her."

"You'll know where to find me."

———⊙———

The Ice Chanters quickly gathered what crops they could to properly store the goods until they could find a new way to sustain themselves. The Council further ordered that until the timeless winter stopped or they could leave the island, they would prepare for winter and take care of any Fire Weavers who couldn't manage to stay alive. The tormenting winter was especially harsh on them.

Jonan routinely visited to the Wall, knowing that he would leave without making a single dent, scratch, or smudge. Quite a few people soon joined Jonan once they realized their kinsmen didn't return that night.

———⊙———

A month after the incident, Ilsi watched from the upstairs window as he schlepped a bag of tools to test their strength against the Wall.

"Tyk, do you think they'll rescue Mama?" Ilsi asked the little boy. He sat next to her, drawing and doodling with charcoal pencils.

"Of course they will," he responded, looking at his parchment and the drawing he just made. "Our Papas have magic; they can do anything."

"But now it's so cold; Papa could make everything warm when it snowed. But I think because Mama is gone, he forgot," Ilsi said sadly.

"The snowfall has the whole place going mad," Tyk's older sister replied, her fingers rhythmically knitting while she sat in a chair. "There have been some Fire Weavers here that can't use their magic to help themselves. They're dying."

"Why can't they just warm themselves up with fire and give us some?" Tyk asked.

"Because *no one's* magic is good against this snow, stupid," the girl said rolling her eyes impatiently. "The Fire Weavers can't melt the snow and we can't make it go away. What's the point of having ice abilities if it's *already* cold?"

"I just want my Mama back," Ilsi said, still looking out the window.

"I want the snow gone," Tyk said. "I thought Ice Chanters were supposed to like snow. I hate wearing mittens and boots."

Hours later, Ilsi saw her father coming back to the house with Peder, Tyk's father.

"Papa!" Ilsi cried, racing down the stairs, "Papa! I want to help! Is she still okay?" Jonan hung up his scarf and cap and ruffled his hair, then rubbed his face.

"Ilsi, love," he said, squatting down so they could talk eye to eye, but he struggled. "I tried. I went there every day for a month to get your mother back. I really tried, my love. But today . . ."

The little girl looked up in her father's face, as his hand slid across her cheek.

"Ilsi," Peder finished, "Your mother wasn't there today." Ilsi's eyes immediately felt heavy as the tears came—more because she was sad to see her father cry for the first time since the Wall first appeared. Jonan took his daughter into his arms, and they both just sat there like that.

Tyk and his sister came down the stairs, and their father motioned for them to follow him home. Jonan picked up his daughter and brought her upstairs. Peder and his children could still hear her cries and hiccups.

"But Papa," Tyk insisted as his father helped him into his winter clothes, "you have Ice Chanter powers. I thought you could do anything."

Peder rubbed his hand over his short beard wearily.

"Tyk," he sighed, "some things just aren't that simple anymore."

CHAPTER 1

Mama, I found your little journal the other day. I wish I got to know you better in person, but I suppose this little book is better than nothing.

I must've been very important to you, because most—if not all—of the book is about me. How you raised me, how I grew up, and how you knew something about me that no one else did. You said in your little book that you had a very special power that only Papa knew about. It must've been dangerous, because I haven't heard of anyone around here having special powers besides our ancestral Ice Chanter spells. Maybe everyone here is full of secrets.

Well, I must be no different. I have a little scar on my wrist that looks like a wave. I got it right when Wall came and took you and almost half of our tribe away from us. Hundreds. After that day, that something strange happened to me.

You wrote Swift a lot in your book, and it wasn't until I said it aloud that I realized it has special meaning to you and me. Mama, every time I say the word Swift, the word alone forces me faster than the birds into whatever direction I need. It's like extra guidance to my feet and I can run. Fast. I see the same line drawn on random pages of your book. I wonder if you are the only one who understands me. I'll never know how I got this *power, but I think I somehow have you to thank for it.*

When did you tell Papa? He must've loved you all the same, because he really tried to save you, Mama. He really did. He loved you. I love you.

I haven't told a single soul about my power, Swift. I've been hoping to get the courage to tell Papa, maybe even Tyk. You must know him—Peder's son.

But I see that you've kept your power a secret and even though I can't imagine why, it must've been for a good reason. Papa never told me about it, and even in your little diary, you don't really make much of an effort to explain it to me.

Eight years ago, you and our kinsmen took all that was warm and bright away with you. We miss you more than you know. I wish your little book explained how to bring you back.

I always wonder what you would say to me if you were alive. Are you proud of the young woman I've become? Was it my fault that you died and I lived? What happened that day, and why was I too young to remember? You've taken all the answers to your grave and I wonder if I'll ever be able to dig them back up. I'm seventeen years old and I think I finally deserve some answers."

———⊷∘⊶———

"What are you writing?" a familiar voice asked. Ilsi looked up and saw Tyk standing above her, already dressed for the outdoors. "Lecture has been over already for a few minutes. You aren't still taking notes are you?"

"I most certainly am not," Ilsi said, snapping the book shut and wrapping it in leather binding before putting it in her satchel.

"Then what were you writing?" Tyk asked.

"It's my journal," Ilsi said. "It's for my private thoughts only."

"You have *secret*, private thoughts?" Tyk smiled, trying to fish out the book from her satchel. "Surely you trust me with your private thoughts, right?"

"They're called *private* for a reason, Tyk," Ilsi said, clamping her satchel shut and putting a protective hand over the flap.

Ilsi rolled her eyes and smiled. Ilsi flipped back her long, dark blond plait as she smoothed out her dark green skirt and made a face at a stray ink stain on her white blouse. She tugged the sleeves down so she could put her dark yellow sweater over it.

She layered her frame with a thick, woolen winter coat, and tied a scarf around her neck. As she stepped outside, she pulled her scarf over her nose and cheeks. She walked on, scrunching her shoulders to protect her face.

"You're coming over to my house today, right?" Tyk asked. He pulled a knitted hat over his thick, black hair and generously wrapped a fat, knitted scarf around his neck.

"I have chores and I promised Papa I'd help him with—"

"I thought you said you had time today to see my latest project."

"Oh! Sorry, Tyk," Ilsi said, shaking her head and gestured her hand quickly over her eyes. Tyk chuckled, as she continued, "I was just thinking about the lecture and the chores I have at home. I forgot that you have something in your shop that might—"

"It'll stay in one piece," Tyk said. "You're my good luck charm, so it'll work."

"I've got no luck to just hand out," Ilsi chuckled.

"Well, I think I'll accept your apology and forget your slight mistake once you take a gander at my latest project," Tyk said, arching his eyebrow, pleased with his offer.

"But didn't the last one—"

"How was I supposed to know it would *explode* like that? I promise, all the bugs are worked out this time, okay?"

Ilsi just laughed and followed him to his home.

"So what about today's lecture was particularly enthralling?" Tyk said, taking Ilsi's books and held them for her. "You're pretty quiet today."

"It was so dull and pointless," she answered, crossing her free arms over her chest and stuffing her hands in her armpits. Tyk snorted.

"I spend more time than just one lecture thinking that," he replied, "and I'm sure I'll be thinking that way in the morning when we have to do it all over again."

"They always say they have something to teach us, but they never do," Ilsi said. "I want to know about the Fire Weavers."

"What's to know about them?" Tyk said. "They play around with fire. People cross them and they get burned."

"But they're on the other side of Wall," Ilsi protested. "What if they made the Wall?"

"Why would they do that?" Tyk said. "We've done nothing to them."

"That's exactly what I'm trying to say," Ilsi said. "What if we don't learn about their history because there's more to the Wall that no one wants to talk about or remember?"

"I'm assuming talking to your father about what happened has run its course?" Tyk asked. Ilsi scrunched her shoulders up, letting the scarf swallow up as much of her face as possible.

"He's never been the same since Mother disappeared," Ilsi said. "I know he hates that Wall. Enough that he takes a longer way to work to avoid even looking at it."

"Someday someone will break down that Wall," Tyk said. "It just takes a will. With enough desire, it won't hold any of us back anymore."

"Don't say that so loudly," Ilsi said, slightly appalled. People made it a point not to talk about the Wall ever—Ilsi only ever mentioned the word itself to Tyk because he wasn't afraid of the Wall. Some were very superstitious about it, and others were just too emotionally scarred by the events.

"Call me crazy, but we'll never last long enough as a people if we're stuck on frozen land without any way of trading with people or getting out of here," Tyk said. "Why do you think I make things?"

Ilsi suddenly realized that they had arrived in front of Tyk's house. Instead of going inside, they went around to a large wooden shed with a sign outside which read, *Warning: Enter at your own risk.*

"Your latest installment?" Ilsi asked, pointing towards the sign.

"Mother made me, especially after patent 87," Tyk said, rolling his eyes.

"Patent? Is someone buying your work?"

"Someday, I'm sure. For now I call them whatever I like," he answered with a smile.

Ilsi loved Tyk's workshop. He had large scrolls of paper flattened and nailed to the walls, even the ceiling held a patchwork of sketches of all his invention ideas, and pages from books that pointed out the anatomy of various types of wings.

Ilsi remembered when he started sketching things that were supposed to hurl rocks and chunks of ice at the Wall. But then he became much more interested in finding out if he could climb or fly over the Wall, and thus the drawings and tinkering began.

She took off her large winter coat, because it was plenty warm inside the workshop after he stoked the small iron stove with coal. Tyk became busy, putting a stained smock over his school clothes and lowering a pair of chunky, homemade goggles over his eyes.

"I'd suggest you do the same," Tyk said, pointing to a pair of spare goggles hanging by a nail on a nearby wall. Ilsi grinned and fitted them over her face. As she was tying a smaller smock around her waist, she noticed a pile of clothes heaped in sawdust.

"Tyk," Ilsi said, picking up a shirt, "what happened to this shirt? It's all ripped up."

"Aw, it's too funny-looking on me anyway," Tyk answered. "It's good for my wing models, though."

"Well, if you need cloth, you could have asked me," Ilsi returned, examining pants and shirts, all severely torn.

"Your material is too thick and woolly," Tyk argued. "I need something light and weightless."

"Fine then, let's see this new monster of yours," Ilsi said, rolling up her sleeves.

"All right," Tyk announced, "it brings me great pleasure to present patent 88!"

He ripped a cloth from the table, revealing a large brown traveler's pack.

"You're inventing travel wear?" Ilsi teased, giving him a questioning look.

"It's not over yet!" Tyk said, still with his announcer voice. "It's *only* fashionable travel wear until you watch what happens next." Tyk took a deep breath and closed his eyes, as if making once last mental plea.

Suddenly, Tyk pushed a lever on the side of it and a large pair of wooden and cloth constructed wings unfurled from the sides of the bag. The wingspan went from wall to wall. Ilsi jumped back a bit in surprise.

"What *is* that thing?" she gasped. Tyk just stood back a bit to watch his creation. He had a crooked and pleased smile on his face.

"It's something I thought of a month ago. It's a pair of wings that you strap onto yourself to make you fly. It even has normal storage, so if you fly up in the air, you can have a snack in midair," Tyk explained, pulling an apple from the large pocket of the sack and took a big bite. "Not sure how one can reach back to get it while in flight, but it's in the works."

"Wow, impressive," Ilsi said, afraid to get near it. "It hasn't fallen apart yet."

"Just give it time," Tyk laughed. He edged under the wings to get to the other side of the backpack, grabbed the sack, and took two straps and latched them securely over his shoulders. He then tightened a belt connected to the lower part of the sack. He checked all the straps carefully and then walked sideways out of his workshop and out into the snow.

"Wait, you're not testing that . . . *thing*, are you?" Ilsi called, following him timidly, "Patent 88 might kill you."

"Relax, Ilsi," Tyk said casually, "I measured everything; the wings should be able to support my weight, promise."

Ilsi gave a doubting look towards the pack that had a pair of wings with thin mesh attached to it. The cloth and wood creating the appearance of wings didn't give her the confidence that he did his calculations twice to check for accuracy.

Tyk pushed the wings back into the old traveler's sack

until they clicked and locked shut. Ilsi followed him out of the shack with her winter clothes and her belongings, when she noticed that her friend with the wings stopped in his tracks. With a panicked look on his face, he turned and ran back to his workshop and Ilsi followed suit.

"What happened?" Ilsi said.

"Shh!" he said. He frantically shoved the wings back into place until they clicked. Ilsi was about to protest, when he suddenly put his hand over her mouth and put a finger to his lips. She strained her ears for any sort of noise or commotion, but looked around with nothing to hear.

Suddenly, she could hear glass breaking, yelling, stomping. She thought she heard the sound of Tyk's neighbors protesting and begging. After what seemed like forever, Tyk removed his hand and began rolling up scrolls of scribbles and sketches. He hid what metal parts were lying around and took off his goggles.

"What's going on?" Ilsi asked, frightened. Tyk craned his neck around the corner for a moment and then turned to her.

"Ilsi," he said, nervously, "There are soldiers here."

"What?" Ilsi whispered loudly. "We . . . we don't have soldiers. We've never *had* soldiers; just the town police."

"Shh! They're coming this way!" Tyk answered, interrupting her. "You should go, *now.*"

"But Tyk, how do you even know they're soldiers?"

"They've got black matching armor and there's a lot of them. Listen, just go home to be safe. I'm going to make sure the neighbors are okay."

"What about *you*?" Ilsi cried, throwing her hands in the air. Tyk threw her own bag into her hands and Ilsi accidentally dropped it. She picked it up and brushed the sawdust off of it and gripped it tightly. He already had his coat on as he pulled his cap over his ruffled black hair.

"Don't worry about me," Tyk said, "The Council will handle it. I'll make sure they come to do something about it."

"But Tyk, they're *outsiders*, how did they find us?" Ilsi whispered loudly. "How did they get *in*?" Tyk widened his eyes, and pressed a finger to his lips firmly to make a point. She stomped in the ground and glared more viciously back. She wound her scarf around her face and shuddered under the harsh wind blowing outside. Tyk stood behind her.

"Tyk," she said, with a glimmer of hope, facing him, "what if they're here to rescue us? To take us away from the island?"

"Ilsi," he said through gritted teeth, grabbing her shoulders, "they're raiding my house right now! I don't think they want to help me or anyone in this clan!" And with that, Tyk ran quickly around his house and out of sight.

CHAPTER 2

Ilsi's heart thumped mightily. *Foreigners*, Ilsi thought. She followed Tyk's direction, but turned right and took winding turns around stores and homes, biting her lip. She wasn't quite sure what to be afraid of, but it'd been a very long time since she'd seen Tyk worry like this.

She finally saw her house, easy to distinguish with its diamond-shaped window placed just under the slanted roof. She was across the cobblestone street, hiding behind another building when the sound of many heavy footfalls startled her back into cover. When the sound was gone and there wasn't a soul in sight, she walked hurriedly back to her house. She made it inside without a fuss, and she sighed with relief.

She gladly locked every door in the house. She closed all the drapes and the house went dark. When she was satisfied, she hung her winter coat and mittens and left her snow-covered boots on her feet. She still shivered with nervousness. Her mind whirled in fright. *How did they get through? Someone passed through the Wall! What do they want with us?*

Just as she thought she could relax, she heard a loud knock at the door. Ilsi knew it wasn't her father because he planned to work late until supper; plus, they both had a key so he could simply let himself in. Ilsi didn't care who it was—she refused to open it. Her mind became even more set when the knocks became loud thumps.

"Is anyone in there?" a man shouted from outside.

"Kick down the door, dammit! I don't care if someone's in there, search the house anyway!" another voice said loudly.

With a loud bang and a grunt, the middle of the door cracked in, wood splinters sticking out. Ilsi bit her tongue to keep from screaming. She quickly darted up the stairs, taking two with each stride. She abandoned nearly everything in the doorway except her mother's book, which she quickly stuffed safely under her sweater.

Her footsteps were drowned out by the sound of the intruders breaking in the front door. By the time she got upstairs, she heard a final bang and feet stomping around. She felt the cold air rise to meet her, like it betrayed her location. At that point, she started to hum.

She was now standing in the small space of her room. She whirled around to see if there was a weapon to use for her defense, but she darted back into her room at the sound of more stomping up the stairs. The intruders began thumping around, occasionally tossing things around.

"Hey!" one man said coming into her room. Ilsi's humming proved true; she extended her arms and fingers in front of her and a rush of ice and snow blew into the soldier's face and hair.

"Ugh, these people!" the man said, grabbing his face, feeling the frostburn quickly eating at it. "I found someone!" Ilsi held up her hands threateningly at the men, each in black uniforms with a jagged lightning bolt across the shoulder armor.

They weren't armed at all, but Ilsi assumed weapons weren't necessary. They had to have something else entirely to get them through the Wall.

"Get out of my house!" she shrieked, as they held up their hands threateningly in return. *I know I shouldn't use it, but it's my only protection*, she thought. *I need to get out of here, now.* She was about to cast a Swift spell, and one of them realized she was about to strike, so he cast a sudden counter-spell. She heard a zap.

Not only were they foreign, but so were their powers. Ilsi crouched and ducked her head. The spell meant for Ilsi broke the diamond window instead. Shards of glass spewed everywhere as Ilsi screamed. She could feel gusts of freezing air coming through the empty space that used to be a window as she scrambled to her feet.

"What do you want? Take whatever it is, but I haven't done anything!" she found herself shouting.

"You ice people don't have much to want," one of the soldiers said, gesturing for her to keep close to the ground. "I order you to come with us and we won't destroy what little you have."

"We don't have all day! If you've got the girl, we need to head to the next house!" another soldier said from downstairs.

"Why do you want me?" she said. "I demand you—"

The nearest soldier from behind gave her a blow in the back of her head in response, saying,

"We're moving out now, girl, so shut up and march!"

Ilsi's eyes watered at the pain coming from her skull. She quickly glanced around to find somewhere to run. She wasn't about to follow them wherever they intended to take her.

There was no way that she could use the stairs or the ladder to escape downstairs, and she knew that others were downstairs awaiting her. She looked around wildly, the soldiers chuckling at her fear.

Time seemed to stand still. She looked out the window and saw the snow falling. Suddenly, to her own amazement, she ran. She ran in her simple boots, school clothes and sweater, and jumped out the window.

"Hey!" one of the soldiers yelled.

She screamed wildly as she fell. She landed on the snowy ground with a crash. The snow was heavily piled up, so her whole body was soon covered in snow. She regained her senses, and the men looked out from the window and searched to see where she landed. They began pointing and yelling.

"She's up to something! She's resisting!" one yelled. "Don't let her out of your sight!" Ilsi turned and ran away from her house, brushing off bits of snow as she went. The wind bit at her cold, wet body. Other neighboring Ice Chanters saw this and began crying out in alarm.

"Who are they?" someone shouted up towards Ilsi's broken window.

"They're outsiders!" a woman shrieked. Out of the crowd emerged her father. He was clad in his winter coat and soot smeared on his face and brown mustache.

"Ilsi!" Jonan cried incredulously, dropping his work sack to put his hands around his daughter's shoulders. "What is going on? What are you doing out here without a decent coat? Did you just jump out the *window*?"

"Outsiders, Papa!" Ilsi cried, wrapping her arms around him. "Some men from outside the Wall are here and they attacked me!"

Despite the cold, Jonan hastily wrapped his scarf around

her neck good and tight around her face. He kissed her forehead.

"Go to Peder's house and keep safe," Jonan said.

"Papa, I can't! They already tore through Peder's place. Papa, they'll hurt you, their magic is—"

A man from the crowd hummed a spell and shards of ice flew towards the window and pelted the walls of the house and through the window. One of the soldiers raised a hand and sent sparks into the crowd. People began to disperse to warn others or to grab weapons.

Jonan's eyes widened as a few men jumped from the same window, and a few more came from the shattered front entry.

"Ilsi!" he roared in a voice she had never heard him use. "Find good shelter. Keep safe and warm. I will come find you when it's over. I love you."

"I love you, Papa," Ilsi said. She knew she needed to go, but she felt glued in position.

"Ilsi, you must run!" Her father yelled above the wind.

He and a few men in the street started humming and preparing spells. Ilsi sighed and started to run, to obey her father's wishes, but turned to watch. She held a hand to her mouth as she saw her father fighting the soldiers off. He received more blows than she could bear to watch. Her heart took courage when she saw Tyk entering the scene to relieve her father.

She ran in the opposite direction as fast as she could, pumping her arms to help her leap across the snow. She began to think about where she could go and who she could ask for help. She immediately thought to go to the Council, the tribe's leaders, who would no doubt know where she could stay; they could protect her if necessary.

She began running through town, darting from one place

to hide to the next. At the moment, no one was really following her, but she was sure that the soldiers wouldn't give up. She kept turning around to ensure she could see in every direction to make sure no one could surprise her from behind.

The Council met in a fortified central structure that held a lot of important historical artifacts and documents. The Council collected everything to the middle of town so any and all could come for help and guidance. She was a ten minute jog away if she ran in plain sight.

All she could see and hear was destruction. Her friends and neighbors were darting out of their homes and fighting back as best as they could. The younger or weaker people were huddled and protecting each other while the stronger who weren't afraid to use their magic were singing and humming, sending ice and snow on their invaders.

That horrible zapping sound. Ilsi remembered that noise— the skies used to crackle and rumble before shedding warm rain. As Ilsi watched the soldiers make their way into each building, she began to hope that the Council's keep was still safe and that her father was still holding his own.

She hid between two brick and stone buildings with her body pressed against the stone. A little boy was huddled there by himself, clutching himself and shivering. He was there first and she hardly noticed him.

"Are you okay?" she whispered. He looked up and shivered, nodding his head yes. Without thinking much, she yanked the boots off of her feet and gave them to him, even though they were several sizes too big.

"Keep warm, little one," she said. "If they come for you, run or throw these big boots at them. Your Mama and Papa will come for you." The boy smiled weakly at the thought. Ilsi on the other hand wanted to keep moving to get to safety sooner and to prevent her from freezing where she stood against the wall. Why hadn't she seen the Council out trying to combat the soldiers? She didn't want to think about the possibilities.

She abandoned her safe area and ran against the wind, and her eyes streamed tears in retaliation. As her legs pumped and her arms flew at her sides, she didn't realize that something was in her way. She suddenly crashed and fell back in the snow with a grunt. She looked up and shrieked as she saw a soldier standing above her.

He wore the crackling symbol down the front of his uniform, but by the way the symbol glowed in the dark gray weather and the furs decorating his sleeves and collar, he was more of a leader figure than a foot soldier.

"You're in a hurry," he growled, holding a hand up menacingly.

"Your men will die here," Ilsi yelled up at him, as she tried to get up on her feet. The man immediately grabbed her by her braid and scarf and yanked her so she was inches from his face.

"And what makes you think that your people are so immortal?" the man hissed into her face. "We're not leaving this place until you are in our custody."

"I don't want to *be* in your custody," Ilsi grunted. Ilsi encased her own hand with enchanted ice after a few quick notes and used it to bash whatever part of his body she could gain access to. Her knee collided with his groin and stomach and he finally grunted and released her.

In her mind, she was aware of the risk, but at that moment, she never wanted to be near that man again. She whispered *Swift* and knocked him over to the side and zoomed off in whichever direction she could. She ran down the row of shops and homes with her gifted speed and skidded to a halt when she saw the Council keep and the center of town on the other side of the blacksmith's place.

She ran with her own speed to find a safer place to hide. She knew that the fur-lined scowl would eventually catch up with her, but hopefully it would be a time where she had the Council to protect her.

Ilsi went through the shelter created by the smithy—a building with tarps to keep the heat in and invite frozen buyers to the wares. The fire was still kept aglow, even though the blacksmith was nowhere to be found. Ilsi sighed generously once her soggy feet walked inside and could feel the noticeable warmth. She kept her breathing shallow so soldiers would pass her by without noticing her. She crept past premature tools and horseshoes to the back of the building. A wooden door with metal framing was between her and the center of town.

A small glass window allowed her to peep out. She rubbed the glass to see better without the condensation. Her heart sank as she felt a booming shake and saw the Council's keep suddenly caught on fire. It had been a while since she had seen so much fire in one place. She didn't know if they were alive inside, or if they were about to be consumed by the flames at their door. All she knew was that the Council would be of no help to her now.

Ilsi suddenly heard frustrated footsteps coming through the store, metal clanking onto the ground, and swearing. She fumbled with the door, but groaned as it was locked. She held the knob tightly and hummed impatiently as the knob froze over and she jerked it free. The door swung open and Ilsi kept the scarf up to her face to meet the cold winds once more.

"It's the window girl!" she heard from the side. She looked and saw soldiers coming in three directions as she hummed through her chapped lips and nostrils. She held up her red hands and shards of ice shot out in diagonal spears all around her.

"These ice people are crazy!" one of them cried out, nearly avoiding being impaled.

Ilsi held her hands out defensively and kept singing. Her voice carried strength as she stepped between the ice shards. She kept the soldiers at bay by sending more shards of pointed ice at her left and right as she turned to run with her own strength.

"Why are you people following me?" she roared in frustration.

Now she was running without a final destination. She stopped singing and instead used her arms to just keep her moving. She had never run so much in her life, and she was wondering if she could possibly take it anymore. She looked over her shoulder and saw a squad of soldiers on her heels.

I'm not going to run around like this forever, Ilsi thought. *I have to stop eventually. They know that. I'm trapped here!* She ran north of town until she saw the huge expanse of the Wall, standing there as if expecting her arrival.

Could leading them here get them out of the city and stop attacking everyone? Ilsi thought again. *If I go with them, will they stop this?*

Despite the cold, she could feel static tingling through her limbs. The soldiers were sending sparks at her. She couldn't run at full speed and ensure that she could fight them off. She saw the man in furs over her shoulder.

"Ilsi!" she heard someone yell. She looked to her right and saw Tyk running in her direction. She turned a sudden corner and ran towards him.

"Tyk!" she answered, hoping her red feet could carry her to him. Just as she was a few feet in front of him, she reached out, just to watch a bolt of lightning fly through the space between them. They both fell back in shock and fell in the snow.

"Ilsi! Are you okay?" he said, crawling frantically towards her.

"Stay away, Tyk!" Ilsi answered. "They're going to hurt you!"

It was too late; a bolt of lightning curved and coiled like a whip and flicked Tyk's left cheek. He fell back, clutching his face. Ilsi looked up to see the man in furs again, and she weakly rose to her knees. Three soldiers pulled Tyk up on his feet and stuffed cloth in his mouth to prevent him from humming a spell. He grunted and struggled as the soldiers formed a semi-circle around Ilsi. She clutched herself, the wind reminding her that she was quickly developing frostbite.

"Surrender yourself, little woman," the man in furs said, holding his hand up to signal to his men not to strike her. "If you come with us, we will leave your pathetic village behind. Surrender yourself and your magic to us, and this boy won't die."

Tyk's eyes widened as he looked at Ilsi, almost accusatory.

"Why? Why have you come?" Ilsi cried, holding up her hands. "What do you want with me?"

"Surrender or he dies!" the man barked. Ilsi looked at Tyk as he struggled. He obviously didn't want her to go with them by the way he shook his head, his hair falling in his face.

The Wall stood all-powerful behind her. She narrowed her eyes, frowning at the man in furs.

"How did you come through this Wall?" she insisted. "How did you know we were here?"

"If you come with us, you won't have to wait long to figure that out."

So it's possible, Ilsi thought. She thought to what Tyk said about having a desire. A desire to break free. *I will it! I want to go beyond the Wall!*

"Keep threatening me!" Ilsi shouted, feeling half-mad. "Keep chasing me! That's all you'll ever do!"

And with that, she shouted her Swift spell. She propelled herself away from Tyk and his captors and disappeared towards the Wall.

"The hell—?"

The man with the furs fill his hands with snow and threw it at the Wall and swore. "After her!"

Tyk groaned and yelled into the cloth, struggling. The only thing left behind was a pair of bloody footprints in new snow.

CHAPTER 3

Ilsi moaned and coughed. Her head throbbed and she massaged it where the pain lingered. As she attempted to rise from the ground, she could only roll onto her knees. She grunted and her arms gave way and her face was covered in sand and dust.

Voices swarmed around her like gnats, but she couldn't make out any words even once they started to crescendo. She wiped the sand from her face and her skin felt hot, coarse, and agitated like one huge rash.

She tried to feel around for something solid to help her into a standing position. Her fingers touched a large, vertical flat surface but the slightest touch against her skin felt like fire. All she could do was scream and pull away.

Her vision started to clear and she looked up and saw a small crowd of children giggling nervously and looking down at her. The kids had brown skin, accented with dark hair and light, piercing eyes. Ilsi tried to extend her arm to ask for water, but they giggled in surprise and fright and ran away.

Ilsi collapsed, her face meeting the dirt. A few moments later, she heard a low hum of people talking and whispering.

She tried to situate herself on her knees so she could see who was coming. The children brought adults with them. They wore clothes in all imaginable colors, but the majority of the people wore reds and oranges. It was like looking at fire. She squinted up to understand who they were. *Why is it so* hot*?*

"Is she an Ice Chanter girl? Is this *possible?*" another asked. "But how did she make it?"

"She's pale just like those soldiers! What if she's one of them?" another said, pointing.

"She looks like she's from a different clan. Her hair is too fair."

"Who are you?" Ilsi asked weakly. "Can someone please help me?"

"What's going on?" one voice shouted above the rest. A girl shouldered her way through the people, many of which moved to allow her to pass. She wore a faded, thin shirt, rolled up at the sleeves, and tied at her waist was a brightly colored sarong. She was wearing bracelets on her arms and legs, and they jangled as she walked. She had thick, black blunted bangs over her forehead and the rest of her hair was cut short.

She was about to ask again, but she immediately saw Ilsi on the ground. "Who is that?"

"Some of the children found her. We don't know if she'll stand the heat, but she's got to be an Ice Chanter girl," one voice answered. "They all go pink like that in the sun."

"Well there's no point in watching her scorch," she insisted.

"But what about the Council? Won't they want to talk to this girl?" a man said, standing in her way, "Let's take her to the Council. She could be dangerous. She arrived just after *they* did."

"I think they'll have an easier time talking to her if she's alive," the girl shot back. "I can help her, and you can send the Council to my door. Just look at her—she needs water and shade."

She lifted Ilsi to her feet and slung one of her weak arms over her own shoulder for support. Ilsi's pink flesh paled compared to the girls' tanned limbs and face. The girl's shaggy black hair stuck to her face and she brushed it away and it spiked everywhere from her forehead.

"That girl's gonna bring us trouble," the man grumbled to himself and the others nearby. It wasn't exactly clear which girl he was referring to.

Ilsi leaned heavily on the girl's shoulders and tried to walk. She turned weakly, so she could see behind her. There was an immense glare from the sun reflecting off the Wall and blinding her. She pinched her eyes shut and shrieked slightly.

"Where am I?" Ilsi cried.

"You need rest and shade, then you get talking time," the girl grunted, as she urgently helped her walk faster and through the crowd. The people all turned to watch the two go, all eyes examining Ilsi's skin. As the girls walked on, their feet kicked up a small cloud of dust that trailed behind them.

They weaved in-between all sorts of clay-walled homes of assorted shapes and sizes. More villagers looked on with curiosity as the girl led Ilsi through the maze of homes and people. Ilsi could barely keep up.

"Please, it hurts," she begged.

"We're almost at my home and you can rest as long as you want, I promise." Ilsi forced herself to close her eyes and let her feet continue walking.

"Watch your head," she heard the girl say between labored breaths. Ilsi followed her command and with her eyes closed, she saw the intense glare of the sun suddenly vanish from behind her eyelids. It suddenly felt degrees cooler and Ilsi sighed in gratitude.

"Be careful, that's good. Now lay here," the girl murmured, her voice a strange mix of empathy and sternness. Ilsi fell to the floor and landed on a thin, soft pad.

"Please, my ankle," was all Ilsi could muster. The girl began peeling away at the layers of heavy wool clothing Ilsi was wearing. She gripped her mother's book tightly, amazed that it lasted the journey. That was the last thing she remembered.

———◦◦———

When she finally opened her eyes, Ilsi moaned softly, smelling food. The same girl brought two small brown cups as Ilsi tried to raise herself to a sitting position. The girl took a swig out of her mug and handed the other to Ilsi.

"The name's Reshma, what's yours?" she asked, wiping her mouth.

"Ilsi," she replied weakly, as she rubbed her eyes, and then her cheek. "Thank you very much for your hospitality."

"No need for that," Reshma grinned, "my mother taught me a lot." Ilsi nodded politely and slurped from her cup.

"So tell me, how did you get through?" Reshma asked, gripping her cup.

"Get through . . . get through what?" Ilsi asked dully.

"You just went *through* the Wall!" Reshma said, her eyes wide, confused, "or you must have, because you are not from here. You're in Tijer!"

"I'm where?" Ilsi sat up and shook her head in disbelief.

"You're in Tijer. It's what we call our side of the Wall."

"Tijer?" Ilsi repeated softly.

"Yeah, we gave up on the name Ravenna and called our side of the island Tijer."

Ilsi sat back for a moment. Her eyebrows furrowed and gave Reshma a look.

"So . . . you're a Fire Weaver?" Ilsi asked. This definitely wasn't Dove, but she knew that she shouldn't have made it across the Wall and survived.

"Yes, I am," Reshma said, slowly. "Are you an Ice Chanter?"

"Well yes, of course I am," Ilsi answered. "Am I still asleep? You can't possibly be a Fire Weaver."

"After I took care of you for *two* days and bandaged your ankle and let you sleep in my house you are going to *argue* with me over whether or not I'm a *real* Fire Weaver?" Reshma laughed incredulously, cocking her head. Ilsi furrowed her eyebrows and stared off out the bright window.

"The real question is, how did you do it? And why?" Reshma insisted. She was equal parts wary and curious.

"Look, I don't know what happened. One minute I'm in Dove, the next I'm in some horribly hot place surrounded by strangers." That in itself was a partial truth; she did know what happened, she just hadn't thought it would work. However, she didn't want Reshma to be the first to know the grim details.

Reshma suddenly let out a great belly laugh.

"Well, happy to meet you. I was worried you wouldn't make it, but you did. Looks like the whole of Tijer will want to meet you fairly soon, nothing much you can do about that," Reshma said, smiling. "I hope you don't plan on returning home any time soon."

"Well, I plan on recovering first, if that is an option," Ilsi sighed. "Where's my book?"

"The little black book?" Reshma said, "It's right next to you." Ilsi looked over her left shoulder and there it was on top of her winter clothes.

"I didn't pry," Reshma said.

"I wouldn't accuse you of that."

"And accuse me of not being a Fire Weaver?" came a chuckle. "Makes me wonder what you Ice Chanters have been doing all this time. We always hoped you all survived, but we had no way of knowing."

"Wait—where's my mother?" Ilsi said suddenly. Reshma crinkled her eyebrows and tilted her head to the side.

"Your mother—?"

"A long time ago, my mother was separated from my family because of the Wall," Ilsi explained, hurriedly, "If I came through alive, maybe she did, too!"

"I don't understand—"

"It was ten years ago," Ilsi exclaimed, sitting up and waving her arms, "Curly blonde hair? Do you remember? You have to know something about her—my father tried to free her from the Wall for weeks. For months."

Reshma gave her a questioning look. Ilsi's eyes widened desperately to hear an answer.

"Anything?"

Reshma sighed, staring at her. She bent her head apologetically, tucking a tuff of bangs behind her ear, knowing it wouldn't stay.

"I can't remember much. I was pretty young, you know? All I remember is that someone found her at the Wall's base, digging.

She wouldn't ever stop digging, not until she just collapsed with exhaustion. It was as if she didn't realize we were there. We tried to help her break the Wall, too, to save our own. But you know how it is. I mean, she wasn't the only one; quite a few of your people didn't make it here; the heat got to them. They just gave up because their powers couldn't save them. I'm very sorry, Ilsi."

Ilsi had barely allowed herself to hope that there was a second chance to have her mother back, but to know that she really was dead, it felt as though she lost her all over again. Her mood sunk into Tijer's dry dust. Not only was she gone, but she couldn't even find consolation from her father. His tight, safe embrace seemed worlds away and she felt lost.

"Ilsi."

"I've already lost her," she said, turning to her side, her back towards Reshma, "I can't bring her back. It's fine."

"So, when are you going to tell me your story?" Reshma asked gently, taking a seat next to her, "I don't mean to be rude, but everyone's been asking me for days how you got here."

"I said I don't—I don't know," Ilsi managed.

"Oh please," Reshma chuckled, "You found a way to break through when no one could. I hate to tell you, but I probably won't be the only one trying to figure you out."

"No, really," Ilsi said, facing Reshma and rubbing her cheeks, "I was chased by these soldiers all dressed in black with symbols on their sleeves and chest. I sung a spell, and I think they cast one in return and I don't remember anything after that."

"The Yildirims," Reshma said.

"Pardon?" Ilsi said, her forehead pinched in confusion.

"Did their symbols look like a zig-zag? Lightning? Right on their shoulder armor?" She lifted her finger in the air and traced the symbol, her finger going left then right but continuing in a downward motion.

"Yes," Ilsi said, mustering a reply.

"Those soldiers go by the name of the Yildirims," Reshma said with a somber face. "We just encountered them a week ago. A few even accompanied you across the wall but we managed to subdue them."

"Who are they? I need to know," Ilsi whispered. She shuddered at the thought; Yildirim were likely crawling all over their lands and could come for her at any moment.

"Don't worry. They came and left before you came. The Council is willing to protect you and all," Reshma answered. "But as to who they are, only a few locals here remember something about them in the time before the Wall."

"What do they do?"

"That's the thing, no one knows exactly," Reshma explained. "They just have really unnatural magic. I mean, everyone can do something, our peoples can do even more, but . . . it's like they can call down the storms out of the heavens. I've never seen anyone do that."

"Yes, I saw it," Ilsi said. "Lightning."

"What I want to know," Reshma said, "is how they managed to get here, and what brought them here. The Council needs to know that not only are they here but there are many of them passing through the Wall to your people. That's serious."

"I hope they find whatever it is they want and leave us be," Ilsi muttered.

She still had the thoughts slithering around in the back of her mind; they seemed so driven to take her captive, and the thought made her fidgety and anxious. Perhaps they thought her dead since they saw her crash through and gave up. It was a very optimistic thought.

She had always imagined one day breaking free from the eternal snow, and she had done it. But it was hard to imagine going alone, leaving her father and Tyk behind. Entering Tijer was a complete accident, but it was maddening now that she was really gone, not knowing what became of her family and people. They were back home, defending their honor. Was it still intact?

"Do you think they will come back? To Tijer?" Ilsi asked. "What if they find out their men were unsuccessful?"

"Haven't the slightest idea," Reshma shrugged as she muttered. "They pillaged, searched, took what they damn well wanted and left."

"Did they take something of yours?" Ilsi asked, daring to look around.

"Yes," Reshma said, jaw clenched. "They took my family."

"What?" Ilsi asked in disbelief. "Do they just kidnap people? Is that what they do?"

"They took our strongest," Reshma said, her throat thick, "Should I be surprised that my family was taken? But you can only imagine what I will do to find them again. I was left behind by some sort of chance. I won't let that go to waste."

CHAPTER 4

"It is quite the rare opportunity and pleasure to meet you," a man said, bowing as he sat on a pallet. His dark skin contrasted greatly with his red robes. He had his long, scruffy black hair braided over his shoulder, much like Ilsi would've fashioned hers. He and five other men and women of the Council were sitting cross-legged in a semi-circle on the floor. "My name is Yossef and I personally welcome you to Tijer."

Ilsi stood still with her hands to her sides, unsure how to act. She was wearing whatever Reshma found in their house that would be remotely presentable. She wore a pair of loose trousers and a thin shirt with a long piece of red fabric that went around her waist, behind her back, and ended across her chest. She had done her best to braid her hair into a crown around her head to keep it off her shoulders.

"Thank you," was all she could manage to say.

"I am not sure if Reshma has told you this," the man said, "but in the past decade since the Wall came, we have only had two disturbances amongst our people: the Yildirim soldiers and you."

"It was an accident—"

"An *accident?*" one of the women said, straightening her

posture. She had a toned frame of a female warrior with the bald head and white tribal tattoos to entertain the suggestion. "There is no possible explanation as to how *anyone* can go through the Wall *by accident*. Are you an Ice Chanter or not?"

"Of course I am!" Ilsi protested, attempting to keep her composure. "I am Ilsi of Dove. I was attacked by the same soldiers that apparently tore through Tijer. I don't know what happened—I cast a spell, then they cast one in return. I think it sent me hurtling towards the Wall but all I remember is waking up here in Tijer. That is really all there is to know."

"What spell did you cast?" the woman asked. Ilsi blanched, knowing that her spell was *Swift*, but she wasn't about to reveal that to just anyone. She didn't even want them to know that she fully intended to have the soldiers follow her through the Wall.

"An Ice Chanter spell," she answered quickly.

"This is a bigger issue that we thought," another man said. "An army attacking a young woman is abnormal."

"They sprung on us yesterday," Ilsi said quietly. "They raided our homes and I tried to run and find shelter."

"Yes, Ilsi, we experienced a very similar traumatic experience," the spokesman of the group answered in return. "It is most alarming and peculiar how they have arrived. There is a Wall that divides and surrounds Ravenna. This much our people have discovered. While we were certain there is no way in or out, there is something about you and the Yildirim soldiers that has proved that not entirely true."

Ilsi's heart quickened; it's been a long time that she'd heard anyone mention the name for the full island, rather than just one side or the other.

"Please believe me when I say there is nothing special about me," Ilsi said, a hand to her heart, "nothing that should alarm you about me. I'm just an Ice Chanter who is separated from my home."

"Yet you haven't died," the woman replied, with a steely glare.

"Pardon?" Ilsi asked, crinkling her brow.

"Do you want her to keel over dead, Uti?" another woman piped up, concerned. Her dark eyes and lips created a look of disgust. "She's just a young girl! How else will we learn about what has happened on the other side? If you ask me, this is a rare opportunity to discover what has happened to the Ice Chanter tribe, and perhaps more of the dealings of these soldiers."

"We saw the other Ice Chanters who were trapped on this side of the Wall and none of them wanted to survive. They hardly got off their pallets. We need to know what exactly the soldiers want with this girl," the woman, Uti answered stiffly. "If these soldiers can just hop from side to side as they please, there is no telling if they will come back for her again. We'll have to fend them off all over again."

The main spokesperson sighed calmly and looked at Ilsi. She trembled slightly, not sure what more she could do to defend herself. She wondered if any of them had the ability to read minds. She had heard of the gift, and some claimed that the Dovian Council had the gift.

"Thank you, Uti, for your observations. For all we know, the soldiers couldn't possibly assume that Ilsi made it through," he said, "And if they wanted her as a prisoner and thought she survived, they would've followed her trail. They would've already sent more soldiers after her. Luckily for us, that is not the case."

Ilsi let out a long breath of air that she didn't realize she had held in. She felt certain that the soldiers must've discovered her

Swift abilities. In her heart, she was beginning to believe that they would come after her if they were that driven to capture her, but she was happy that most of the Council didn't see her as a threat.

Something inside her told her that she couldn't afford to reveal all of her abilities. *The Council would easily feed me to the soldiers to get rid of them,* she thought, *All of my chances of ever returning home would go up in smoke.* Meanwhile, the Council talked amongst themselves and a new speaker arose.

"Ilsi, you are permitted to stay amongst our people so long as your actions are peaceful. We will defend you along with our kinsmen if threats arise," he said, "You will be branded as innocent before our people, should anyone disagree. We will request more meetings with you to ask more about Dove and the fate of those from our tribe that were lost on the other side. I think that is rather decent and fair."

"Yes, thank you," Ilsi said, bowing, even though she wasn't sure what customs here would have her do. "If it is all right, I would request staying with Reshma as she was the first to offer assistance."

"Very well," the speaker responded. "You are dismissed."

———◦———

"So, can you stay?" Reshma asked, once Ilsi left the Council's meeting. "Well, I guess they can't force you out with the Wall and all." Ilsi barely emerged from a large, clay-walled building with a large rug for a door when she met Reshma outside waiting for her.

"Yes, they will let me stay," Ilsi said with a smile, "If that's fine with you."

"Oh, you can stay in Tijer as long as you want," Reshma grinned, "I'm not the Council, girl."

"I actually meant staying with you in your home," Ilsi answered.

"Oh," Reshma said, "well, I could use the company. You can cook, right?"

"Yes, of course," Ilsi answered, as they walked along.

"Then it's decided! You can stay with me."

"I don't intend on staying for long," Ilsi replied, "I have to get back to my father. I'm worried about what the Yildirims might have done to him and the rest of my clan."

"Well, if you don't mind me saying," Reshma said, making eye contact as they walked, "how will you get across if you don't even know how you got here in the first place?"

"I don't know yet," Ilsi said, setting her jaw, "but I have to."

Ilsi followed Reshma as they ambled their way through the streets covered in sand and dirt. The girls, along with the other Fire Weavers they passed, walked barefoot or with thin sandals. The people gawked openly or from behind their clay homes or the thick palm trees as Ilsi walked by.

"What are they staring at?" Ilsi muttered, already aware that she was wearing very little clothing.

"They're staring at your white skin," Reshma replied with a small grin, "and that golden hair." Ilsi tried to ignore everyone's staring as they continued on. It was scorching weather outside and the only remote shade came from inside the squat buildings.

They finally approached Reshma's home and ducked past the large home-spun rug used as a door.

"The Council wants to know about what's happened on the other side of the Wall," Ilsi said, collapsing on her bedmat.

"And is that a problem?" Reshma asked, then said, "Want some water?"

"Oh yes, please," Ilsi sighed, "everything is so *dry* here. How do you stand it?"

"Knowing that we'll figure a way out of this makes it worth the sunburns and sweat," Reshma answered, handing Ilsi a cup of water.

"Anyway, when they asked to know what happened to us, it made me realize just how little I know, or knew about your side of the Wall," Ilsi said, "I suppose I was too worried about getting my mother back. I didn't even care to know if there was a civilization on the other side just as trapped as we were."

Reshma sat next to Ilsi on the floor, wiping a fleck of sweat off her own forehead.

"I don't remember much from that time in particular," Reshma said, "but my parents were well aware of how many of our kinsmen were lost on the other side. Nothing against you Ice Chanters, but when you lose someone of your own kind, it's more difficult to deal with."

"I know the feeling," Ilsi said, thinking of her mother. "Our tribes intermingled without a problem, so it was hard to imagine when the Wall came and we watched all the Fire Weavers die and come to grips with the fact that we were forever severed from others we cared about."

"Everyone is amazed beyond belief that you are here. I think we could only imagine what happened to you and your folk. Now we can start putting those pieces together."

"And when I can return, I will tell my people all that I've seen and learned," Ilsi said.

"Why bother?" Reshma said, "If you can pass through, we

may well find a way to finally break the Wall down."

"That's true," Ilsi mused, her heart pounding.

"Granted, no one from before survived," Reshma said with a hopeful glimmer in her eyes, "but think about how we could make things go back to how they used to be."

"Is that a fight we can win?" Ilsi said, her fingers enjoying the last of the cool touch of the cup.

"Could be," Reshma said, sitting back on her heels. "I've always wondered what Dove looks like."

"It's too cold for you," Ilsi said with a smile, "you would miss the heat instantly."

"Do you miss the cold?" Reshma asked in return.

"I don't think so," Ilsi said. "The heat really gets to me, and it burns, but I fancy something in between. The way things used to be, I suppose. I got sick of the snow years ago."

"Ah, an Ice Chanter sick of snow and ice? You're something."

CHAPTER 5

Ilsi waited until Reshma finally fell asleep after the day was done, or at least until Reshma insisted the day was done. Ilsi was used to gray skies during the day, and ink-blot black skies at night; here, it was almost white-hot colored during the day and a honey orange during the evening. The sun would hang low in the sky but never fully disappear beyond the horizon.

Even in the time they called "night," it was still fairly bright outside. Reshma had to completely block out the light as much as possible when it came time to sleep. As she finally lay on the cot and let out a long sigh, Ilsi slipped away, and slunk past the door flap to the warm outside air.

After a few attempts, she finally found her own way to Tijer's side of the Wall. She felt very much like her mother, taking her place at the Wall's base in an attempt to find her way through. It was like looking into glass or a mirror with a sharp light reflecting on it; it was hard to look at it for very long before it hurt to see.

Ilsi sat cross-legged at the base of the wall, cupping the sand and dirt in her hands and watching it fall between her fingers.

"Mama," she said to the wind, "why was I able to cross

over alive and no one else? Why couldn't you have found your way back to us?" *Did you even try?* Only the rustling sands around her responded. "Do I have what it takes to go back, or are the Yildirims waiting on the other side?" She buried her head in her hands. "I found out that they took the strongest of this tribe. They're looking for strong people, I guess. What makes me one of them? What if they took Tyk?"

She was torn between assuming they would take him because he posed a threat and assuming they killed him in the fight. Either way, her thoughts terrified her and kept her awake.

"If you plan on leaving without me knowing, you're mistaken," said a voice behind her. Ilsi jumped slightly but quickly recognized the voice as Reshma's.

"Reshma, you scared me," she said as she rotated herself to look up at Reshma.

"What are you doing here?" she asked, "alone?"

"I'm just here to think," Ilsi said, pulling her knees to her chest.

"And to burn your eyes out of your head?" Reshma said, avoiding the Wall's glare in her face. "Hardly a place to think straight."

"This is where my mother was," Ilsi replied, "or I'd like to think this was where she was."

"Ah," Reshma said, dropping her posture into a squat next to her. "I'm not trying to tell you what to do, but you *are* the most interesting thing in Tijer right now, and I'm sure if people saw you here, they would think you're up to something."

"Well, I suppose it does seem odd," Ilsi mused, pushing herself back on her feet.

"You're odd all right," Reshma said, "but I like odd."

Ilsi had been in Tijer for almost two weeks. The Council had already requested her a few times and after each meeting, they reassured her that their protection still stood; not a single soldier had come for her, so they took that as a sign that she wasn't as dangerous as she thought she could be.

Ilsi thought about all the questions they had for her, and all the questions she was permitted to ask; the more they met, the more she wanted to go home and share with her people all the wonderful things she had seen and heard. She wouldn't even care if they thought she was delusional; she wanted them to know of their brothers and sisters on the other side. All the while, she wrote what she could on the pages of the book she kept with her.

It made her all the more anxious to find her way back. A few nights before, she tried ramming herself into the Wall, but at the last moment, she veered slightly to the right, just grazing her shoulder against the Wall. Her skin didn't thank her for the scalding. She immediately realized that she might never be able to return to the other side, and not saying good-bye to Reshma beforehand seemed like the worst decision she could make.

She regained awareness of her surroundings once they returned to Reshma's little house. Her eyes caught sight of some portraits hanging on the walls, just before Reshma closed the door-flap. There was a formal painting with the whole family, obviously outdated, because the girl she guessed was Reshma looked five years younger than she did now. Another looked like it came from the hand of another artist, of six children playing with each other. The workmanship was juvenile and homemade but precious. They were painted directly on the walls of the house.

"Reshma," Ilsi said, trying to still look at them from her bed mat on the ground, "have I told you how lovely these pictures are?"

"I'm sure you have," she said, absentmindedly. "You can see everyone, all six of us kids and the proud parents."

"Who's who, again?" Ilsi asked.

"There's the boys, Jaron and Arik," Reshma pointed, then guided their eyes to another, "and there's me with the girls, Ophelia, Mika, and Gilly."

"Who made these?"

"Father. Well, Jaron tried his hand at that one, that much is obvious; he can't paint girls to save his life."

"It's still amazing."

"Yeah," Reshma sighed lying back down on her own bed mat, "They were all here one moment—the next they're gone, just gone."

"That must've been difficult," Ilsi answered solemnly. "How did you get left behind?"

"I *tried* to fight," Reshma returned, as though it stung. "They dragged my mother away, I couldn't let myself take that just sitting down. But I had to also think of the girls. I told them to hide while I tried to find my brothers. Jaron told me to hide, and I did. I can't believe I *did* that!" Reshma said, wrapped up in her own story, "He wanted to hide with the girls to make sure they were quiet and safe. I heard yelling, screaming, until something hit me from behind. I fell, but when I awoke, all was quiet and dark for once. I still have no idea why I'm still here. I've been by myself until you came out of nowhere."

"So, you're saying that they came for them before I came?" Ilsi asked, confused. *Why all of a sudden is Ravenna becoming bombarded with these Yildirim soldiers?* None of it made any sense.

"Loads of people heard them demand people with strange magic. I wish they would've just left us the hell alone," Reshma said, "How dare they? How dare they just come and go when we can't leave this place! How dare they take my parents and my siblings!"

She rubbed her eyes to dry an unwanted stray tear. Ilsi's mind froze. It was if time stopped and her heartbeat quickened. She hadn't really realized it until that moment, but if the Yildirim's sole purpose was to find her and take her away, a lot of people had already suffered because of her. It tore a hole through her.

"Reshma?" Ilsi said nervously, rolling herself, so she was lying on her belly. Reshma propped herself up with her arms and said, "What?"

"I think," Ilsi whispered, "Reshma, I think they really are looking for me."

"Ilsi, don't be daft, why would they be looking for you?" Reshma whispered back. "You've been living at my house and I've taken you to the Council . . . what more do you have to hide?"

"Reshma, I'm not trying to hurt you," Ilsi strained, inching closer. She gripped her sleeve, preparing to show Reshma her scar. "I can explain everything."

"Explain what exactly?" Reshma responded. "I thought you told the Council everything."

"Please understand," Ilsi grunted, "I'm just doing this so I can go back to my father."

"What were you doing just now? With your wrist?" Reshma asked.

"You're more than welcome to look at it," Ilsi retorted.

"What for?"

"Just *look* at it," Ilsi grumbled. When Reshma was close enough, Ilsi sighed. "I wanted you to know the truth, I was just scared to say anything. I didn't know if you would turn me in."

"What does this scar have to do with me or the Wall?"

"I got it when the Wall came, and I think it gave me a different magic. I was too afraid what anyone might think of it, so I didn't tell or show anyone. Whenever I use this spell called *Swift*, I can run really fast. I think that is what allowed me to go through the Wall."

Reshma took a step back.

"Reshma, I know I don't have the right to ask for any favors," Ilsi said, "I just want to leave. I think the soldiers might really be after me, and I can't let anyone get killed anymore because of me. I feel awful that you've done so much for me and I have been a poor friend."

"You'll go back to Dove?" Reshma said. "We'll never know how to break the Wall."

"I promise to help," Ilsi insisted. "I want to break down the Wall that separated my family, too."

Reshma suddenly flattened herself against the wall and slid close to the nearest window and peaked through the curtain blocking out the light.

"Someone is listening," Reshma whispered. She snapped her fingers and in the dark, sparks spat from her fingertips. She motioned for Ilsi to follow her out the door. "Come on!"

Ilsi clenched her fists, and wanted to feel them cool. They ventured to the door as quietly as possible and with Reshma at the lead, they slunk out the door. It was typical, she thought, that the one time she told of her secret that someone could have overheard it.

Reshma turned the corner and disappeared for a slight moment, then Ilsi heard a grunt and a thud. She ran to catch up and she saw a soldier crumpled at Reshma's feet.

"Did you—is he—?"

"No, he's not dead," Reshma said, "He saw me and tried to run, but I cut him off." She held a clenched fist and it was engulfed in flames. Ilsi took a step back.

"He can tell whoever he's working for that we are a force to be reckoned with," she said. Ilsi hummed a spell, and a chunk of ice formed around his feet so they were firmly planted to the ground.

"I don't know how long my spell will last under this heat," Ilsi said, "What should we do now that soldiers are apparently hiding here in Tijer?"

"We need to leave," Reshma said, going back into her home. "He knows about your special power."

"Reshma, if I can cross the Wall, there's no use in going back to Dove; they must be waiting for me to walk into their trap. And I don't know if I can take you with me," Ilsi answered, following her.

"I'm serious, time to go—anywhere. Anywhere but here. With your power, I am willing to bet we can get to Yling faster than by boat, and we can dodge them until it's safe," Reshma said, stopping to face her. "We can't afford to have them find you again here."

"Wait, what is Yling?" Ilsi asked, confused.

"It's a huge port city on the mainland, far from here," Reshma muttered, "Don't you know?"

"Obviously I do not."

Reshma sighed and ruffled her hair. "Why would they be

looking for someone like you?" Ilsi sat on the floor, her long, uncombed hair shielding her shamed face.

"I don't know if they've known about my power all along, but maybe it makes me worthy of kidnapping."

"We'll find people to help us in Yling," Reshma said, "There has to be someone who can help us figure out this mystery."

"But—"

"Ilsi, this is no time to be daft; there's no way I'm letting you go anywhere alone," Reshma said, "I'm going to help you escape."

She stopped and left without waiting for further consent. Reshma held her hand up, and the back door swung open. She went to the back of her house, where she disappeared into an old shed. Ilsi stood outside of the shed, a look of concern on her face.

"Reshma," Ilsi called.

"What?" Reshma yelled from inside, as objects were crashing. She looked back to see Ilsi with rays of sunlight against her back.

"What are you doing?"

"Can you just . . . *help* me with this thing?" Reshma grunted. Ilsi quickly leapt into action and followed after Reshma. Together, they pulled out a canoe onto the parched soil. The canoe was well-made with light wood. It was decorated with multicolored stripes on the edge. At the edge close to the bow a jagged "J & K" was carved into it.

"I just don't know whether I should call you crazy or simply thank you," Ilsi said.

"Well, I am crazy, but a thank you will suffice," Reshma returned.

"Fine then," Ilsi said, "Reshma, I can't guarantee that you

can make it through with me; I don't even know if I will make it through, but I'll do what I can to make sure you find your family."

"Good," Reshma grinned, "because I aim never to return unless I bring them back."

"So, Yling?"

"Of course! I think we went there once when I was much, much younger. You know, before the Wall," Reshma reminded her, "and an old family friend lives there. She'll give us protection until we figure things out."

"How do you know that this 'family friend' is still there? Or if they will even help us?" Ilsi asked, arching an eyebrow.

"Do I look like someone who plans everything?" Reshma returned with a smile and a raised eyebrow.

"No, definitely not," Ilsi sighed, "But how are we going to get off this island?"

"If you could cross over from Dove to Tijer, what *can't* you do?" Reshma asked with a shrug of her shoulders.

———◦◦◦———

Reshma woke Ilsi early the next morning. Reshma had already pulled out a few old dresses from a wooden chest. She told Ilsi they once belonged to Ophelia. They would wear them once they made it to Yling on the off chance they succeeded and made it there. Reshma guessed that the weather would be different in Yling and they had to blend in with the others. For now, Ilsi would continue wearing her Tijerian garb, as the pants would be easier for maneuvering until they reached land. As a result, Ilsi felt restless; the back of her neck and forehead were misty with sweat.

"Should we tell the Council?" Ilsi asked. "It would look suspicious if I just disappeared after being here for just a week."

"I left a note where the right people will find it," Reshma said. "We don't have time to rouse the whole city and like you said, your spell might not last very long."

Reshma's house was about fifteen minutes from the beach area. The girls silently hoisted the canoe over their heads and carried it as quickly as possible to the sandy edge. The sun was already making its way back to the middle of the sky when they finally reached the water. They slowly brought it back down and threw satchels of supplies to the ground as they flipped the canoe right side up, then tossed their bags inside the canoe.

Reshma quietly pushed her wooden canoe out into the water. Ilsi joined her, and felt the wet sand surround her toes. She flinched a bit. The water was very warm; it wasn't very pleasant to stand in. She ignored that fact and turned to look back at the land behind her. Images of winds sweeping into her room, and snow flurries surrounding her heart-broken father filled her mind. She looked back at the sweltering land she was about to leave behind, but she knew somewhere, her father was waiting for her on the other side of the invisible wall. Her memories tugged at her, but knew that heading towards town would not help her reach him any faster.

The girls paddled out about five miles from the shore. Reshma was moving her paddle with rhythmic time and strength, and Ilsi tried to keep time. The canoe suddenly crunched against an invisible object—sending the girls jolting forward.

Reshma, who was sitting in front, was sent forward, and rammed her head against the invisible object. After muttering under her breath, she put a hand to her head, and caressed it gently. She tapped the transparent object with her oar.

"It's the *Wall*, alright. Sheesh! That *hurt!*" Reshma said. Ilsi looked ahead, and noticed the telltale glare of the sun against the wall. It wasn't as harsh as the middle Wall, but it glared all the same. Ilsi hit the heel of her hand on her forehead. *Here is where I come in. How can we escape?*

"What will we do about this?" Ilsi asked, "I could try to use *Swift*, but I'm afraid of what could happen to you." Reshma still had her hand rubbing her head, and shrugged her shoulders. Ilsi bit her bottom lip and thought for a moment.

"Wait, you just said *Swift*, and nothing happened," Reshma said, "You told me earlier that whenever you say *Swift*, you're supposed to go really fast."

"Oh," Ilsi said, touching the wall with her hand, "I can say it normally. I just have to hold out my hand like this and say the word like this: *Swift!*" Suddenly, the whole canoe, with the girls in it, blew straight ahead like an arrow. The girls gripped tightly to whatever was nearby and shrieked. Soon after, the sensation of flying immediately stopped. The sudden speed sent Reshma overboard, Ilsi not far behind. They both splashed into the water. They sputtered and grasped tightly to the canoe. Ilsi was coughing and wiping her eyes.

"Wow," Reshma said with a smile, "I've never seen you do *that* before! Your power is incredible."

"Thanks," Ilsi said sheepishly. They spoke between sputtering gasps and as they kicked with their legs to stay afloat and clung to the canoe, they looked back in the direction they came from.

"Th-this water is fr-freezing!" Reshma laughed, despite herself.

"We must've made it through!" Ilsi said, "I can't believe it worked. I can't believe it *worked*!"

"We're out of Ravenna! We went through the wall, even *I* did!" Reshma said, bursting with excitement. She swam a few feet and held her hand out and tapped the air. She tapped hard enough that Ilsi could hear it, like someone rapping against a window.

"The first time I could touch this damn wall without burning myself," she said once she swam back to the canoe. Reshma pulled herself out of the water and into the canoe. She gave Ilsi a wet hand, and pulled her in, too. She looked at Ilsi with a grand smile. Ilsi smiled radiantly back.

"I can't believe it, it's almost like the Wall wasn't even there!"

"Look," Reshma said, pointing behind them, "not even a skilled sailor could see this island. Now I definitely wonder how those soldiers successfully found us." Reshma was right; the only thing visible was the widespread sea. It was as if the island was cloaked with a blue sheet of sky or as though it was never there in the first place. She sighed, gripping her oar with a slight grin.

"Are you ready?" Reshma grinned.

"Well, I think I would *feel* ready if I knew you had a better idea of how to get there," Ilsi said, scooping sea water in her hand and holding her hand against the back of her neck to enjoy the coolness against her sunburnt neck. The stark coldness faded as she realized that her innate Ice Chanter abilities were keeping her at a pleasant temperature—something she knew her people could always do before the Wall formed. "How I have missed this weather. Warm—but not *too* warm."

"Did you think I would have us go out on the waters without any kind of map?" she said, holding a long, cylindrical box for Ilsi to see.

"You have a map?"

"Of course," Reshma said, "it was my idea, but I'm not about to die at sea." She carefully took a piece of parchment out of the tube and unrolled it, careful to not let it touch her wet clothes.

"So, a friend of the family, huh?" Ilsi said.

"Most definitely. It's been quite a while, but they traded a lot of stuff with my parents and probably had good business with other people my parents knew."

"Well, I hope whoever it is will recognize you," Ilsi said. "I'm sure you've changed a lot since the Wall."

"We've all changed since the Wall," Reshma said, taking her paddle from the bottom of the canoe and started to paddle.

CHAPTER 6

Ilsi continued paddling at a steady beat, despite the fact that her arms stung from the strain. Not only was the paddling demanding work, but she found herself looking back at the stretch of never-ending sea behind her where her home used to be. Her stomach grumbled and she wanted to rest her arms. She looked over at Reshma, who was paddling as if it was as natural as breathing. The two found no words to speak for quite a while.

"What will happen if things don't work out? As in, what if this family friend can't take us in?" Ilsi asked to break the silence.

"The thought of a safe bed and something filling to eat keeps me going. I'm sure there's an inn somewhere with room," Reshma said between breaths. "This paddling thing was a lot more fun as a kid."

"I can imagine that you haven't had to run from soldiers before," Ilsi said, her voice heavy as she gulped. "Sort of makes a lot of things not as enjoyable."

"Well, you blasted us through the Wall," Koksihi said. "Why don't you just do the spell again and we'll be faster than a flying arrow."

"I would," Ilsi said, "Except I don't want to die at sea."

"What are you even talking about?" Reshma said. "Just say the words, do the spell, and get us out of here."

"I can't control it as well as I would like. It's not like I practiced a lot at home," Ilsi began. She shook her head, as fears of somehow disappointing her father ran through her mind. "I'm worried that I would break the canoe or lose all our things."

"Well, my arms are going to fall off if we have to keep paddling on for hours," Reshma said, finally acting as the first to stop paddling. Ilsi stopped too, and her muscles twitched and gave her grief.

"Just do it," Reshma said. "What's there to be afraid over?"

Ilsi let her arms hang limp at her sides as she contemplated her options. She would much rather reach this unknown destination a lot faster, but she felt uncomfortable at the thought of propelling them into danger. What if she accidentally sent them into the ocean and didn't know how to stop?

"Have you at least told me how you came across this spell in the first place?" Reshma asked. "If I knew any powerful spells, I'd use it all the time."

"Even if it was dangerous?" Ilsi asked incredulously.

"It's only dangerous if you use it to hurt people on purpose," Reshma answered, "or if you are afraid of it." Ilsi didn't have anything witty to say in reply. She just wanted to let her tired body rest.

"You said you got your powers when the Wall came," Reshma said, looking at Ilsi expectantly. The Ice Chanter girl looked down at her hands, and fingered her wavy scar on the other hand.

"I'm not sure I can tell you what you want to hear. I was too young to remember anything and I'm not really sure what actually happened," Ilsi murmured. "One moment I was reaching out for my mother's hand and the next I was sitting in snow in the middle of summer. From then on I just had that spell and I guess you could say I *am* afraid of it, because I didn't tell anyone about it."

"What, they would impale you with ice for being a bit quicker than all the other children?" Reshma scoffed.

"No, we're not *violent*," Ilsi chided in reply, "but this whole problem with soldiers invading our lands apparently looking for people like me who can do what I do: if you're different from everyone else, it just haunts you."

"So the Wall came and so did your powers?" Reshma asked. "Odd."

"You could say that, I suppose," Ilsi replied. "I did my own reading, but any reference to my powers were either ripped from books or fairly vague. I suppose all I can do is move with speed." She decided not to mention her mother's mentions in the journal.

"Well, there's no better time to figure out than using it," Reshma replied, shrugging her shoulders. She had a curious look on her face, as if she couldn't understand Ilsi's hesitance.

"Ahoy there!" they heard someone shout. Ilsi had to keep herself calm or else her heart would catapult out through her throat. They whirled around and saw a small fishing boat nearing their small canoe. A young man stood, holding the mast and called out to them,

"C'we take you to shore?" he shouted. Ilsi noted a slight difference in his accent and looked to Reshma. Without missing a beat the Fire Weaver replied,

"Aye, that'd be of most help."

Ilsi realized that Reshma was copying the boy's accent and made a mental note to pay attention. Reshma nodded to Ilsi, and they gave the last bit of energy their arms had to paddle towards the boat. It stank of a fresh catch, and the smell was potent as soon as the tip of the canoe collided with the wooden boat.

"What're you doing out in th' middle of the waters?" the boy asked, as he gave each of the girls his arm and his grip so they could climb in without tipping everyone out of the boat. Ilsi looked into the young man's face. Despite the sweat smeared all over his skin and small beard, he seemed safe.

"Testin' my boat," Reshma put simply, as if that were explanation enough.

"She's a strange thing," the boy replied, looking at the canoe drifting atop the water next to his boat. Ilsi could tell he was sizing it up. "I haven't seen 'ything of its make."

"My brother likes to make new things," Ilsi replied, doing her best to copy the boy's speech. He looked at her as if he finally noticed that she was there.

"How 'bout I take you to shore and we make a deal on it?" he asked with a little grin.

"What are we talkin'?" Ilsi asked, her hands on her hips.

"I've only got fish," the boy said, like it should be obvious. "Whatcha price?"

"Six 'a your fish."

The boy stroked his whiskers like he couldn't believe Ilsi would bid so low, but she didn't really want his fish that badly except as food until they found Reshma's contact, and the ride back to land was far worth the canoe at this point. Reshma pursed her lips but didn't seem bothered by the transaction.

"Sounds like we have a deal?" she said, giving the boy a smile that he seemed to like.

"Aye, I'll take it," he said, "Six fish seems like hardly a price for a new little boat and two lasses to accompany me home."

Ilsi found a place to sit in the ship and rolled her eyes. Her limbs seemed awfully grateful for the change of events, and she just sat with her eyes closed and enjoyed the breeze.

She opened her eyes, and looked at the twinkling waves lulling them back towards land, and further away from her shrouded homeland.

In a few hours, Ilsi and Reshma found themselves standing on a large dock, waving at the smug young man, holding the oars in one arm, and the canoe leaning against a tree. Ilsi readjusted the satchel strap across her shoulder and chest, and Reshma motioned to go. The Ice Chanter only hoped that Reshma had some sort of clue which direction they were going and what the plan was.

"At least the fish are decent," Reshma murmured. "We can probably make a fire and eat them right."

"I can't believe I bartered away your canoe like that," Ilsi said, looking at the wood planks beneath her steps. "How are we ever going to get back now?"

"No worries," Reshma shrugged, "it helped us enough. Besides, I'll find my brothers and we'll make a better one." She glanced over at Ilsi, who still looked upset over her mistake.

"It's not a big deal, Ilsi," she said, gruffly. "We couldn't have carried it around anyway. I was planning on getting rid of it somehow."

"But how are we going to get back home?" Ilsi protested. "No one can see our land. We can't just ask someone to sail us back and drop us off."

"Why are you so anxious to go home when there are people there that are looking for you?"

"Because my father is all I have left of my family," Ilsi sighed.

"We'll be back before you know it," Reshma said quietly. "For now, we need to find our way through this city."

They walked shoulder-to-shoulder along the cobblestone streets amidst the townspeople. Ilsi thought that they dressed fairly similar to Dovians—only with a lot less layers. Ilsi noticed that their clothes were very plain, but quaint. She was happy that their dresses didn't seem so different from the rest.

They heard lots of chatter in the crowds and a fair amount of it was in languages foreign to Ilsi's ears. She looked up at the tall towers. They glistened like tears and stood between the shoreline and rows of homes and stores. Many of the towers had large, yellow flags waving proudly in the blue skies. Cargo ships docked and lined up against the harbor alongside fancy ships owned by the wealthy on display.

"I hope we don't end up like beggars and roam around everywhere," Ilsi murmured. "How long do you think it will take to find your family and get back home?"

"Depends on how good we are at getting information," Reshma answered, "or how desperate they are to find you—that might put a damper on our travels. We might as well find Sebrah or what's-her-name and decide what to do from there."

"That's her name?" Ilsi asked, then continued more to herself, "People have odd names here." Reshma merely grinned and faced forward.

"So you know where we're going?" Ilsi asked, this time with a glance directed towards Reshma.

"I may or may not know," Reshma said softly, grinning. It was as if she was focused on something else entirely. Ilsi made attempts to look around without catching anyone's eye.

"Can you stop that?" Reshma muttered in Ilsi's ear. "You're acting like we just murdered someone the way your face looks."

"I'm *trying* to avoid attracting attention," Ilsi replied matter-of-factly, but she was constantly chewing on her bottom lip and sometimes turning to look over her shoulder. "Besides, what if those soldiers originally came from this city? What if they are still looking for us?"

"Then I'll char-broil them into whatever afterlife they believe in," Reshma muttered.

"We can't do that, people will see us!" Ilsi hissed. "We can't let everyone else know that we're a couple of oddities from out of town. It'll get the wrong attention."

"I don't care what people think of me," Reshma retorted. "Who knows if other people can control fire and ice, but it's not anything to be ashamed of. Besides, if someone is looking for us, they wouldn't attack us when we're surrounded by people."

Reshma seemed set in her thinking, and Ilsi found nothing else more reassuring than to merely walk closer. Her hand went to her satchel, and she could feel the form of a sharp knife still in its place. It silently waited next to her mother's book.

To change the subject, Reshma said, "I remember my papa telling us stories about the people he met in Yling. It shouldn't be a surprise to me that Papa likes to exaggerate to tell a good story."

"What kind of stories?"

"Well, here on the mainland, as he called it, they have these big areas where there are no people, just lots of trees for hundreds of miles. People hardly live there, and sometimes if people go in, they don't come out."

"What about this place?"

"Well, anything imaginable can happen," Reshma replied. "It's wild."

Ilsi looked around and saw something oddly-shaped up ahead. She could've sworn it was a hut of some kind. The place didn't really fit the picture of the lovely towers with their yellow flags. This house was small and a bit apart from the others, along the road leaving the city.

The house was surrounded by a bit of grass but the shoddy lawn was ill-kept and long. The lowly hut looked like it wanted to be left alone; the closed curtains were evidence enough. It was a small one-story thing made of big stone slabs with a wooden door and window frames. A few vines climbed along the walls that served well as natural camouflage. It was as if the owner had left and never came back to take care of it.

"The place looks awful," she commented. Reshma turned to look at her.

"What place?"

"That one," Ilsi emphasized, pointing up ahead at the place a few yards east from the path. The normal path continued on level and straight due northwest, but the hut was off to the opposite side on an elevating slope.

A sharp shiver sprang down her spine. She felt like something was watching her as she pointed, and the feeling bothered her. She wildly turned around, but saw nothing.

"What's wrong?" Reshma asked.

"Nothing's wrong," she said, answered, quaking. "But I don't like the looks of the place."

"I think this place is amazing. It's so strange and wonderful here," Reshma said. "Let's go to that little squatty place. I bet my parents' friend lives there."

"How can you possibly know that—"

They both suddenly felt rough hands on their shoulders. Something looped around Reshma's neck from behind and it squeezed tight against her throat. Reshma screeched, as her hands were held back and the soldier whirled her around to face the opposite direction.

Ilsi ducked and closed her eyes shut as she turned around and held her hands out, shooting sheets of ice from her palms. She opened her eyes and stood face-to-face with a soldier in Yildirim uniform. There was three more behind him, grinning. She realized she'd missed; globs of perpetual ice stuck up in the trees. She stood her ground, petrified.

"You're a long ways from home, ice girl," one of them murmured.

"Who are you?" Ilsi asked, trying to replicate her phony accent once more. She asked even though she already knew the answer. The others just grinned and chuckled at the impish question.

"I think we're more interested in asking you the same thing," another replied. The first one looked at Reshma, "Who're you? You're no Dovian." Reshma struggled with her arms behind her, but the soldier held firm and her movements became more lethargic with each strain of her muscles.

"Leave us . . . leave us *alone*." Reshma spat, holding her head limp. The men chuckled as if embarrassed for her. Ilsi winced; she sounded drunk.

"Always too much for the small ones," the one gripping her commented. Ilsi instinctively gripped her hands into fists and ice quickly encased her tight grip. A few flinched away from her, holding out their hands as if armed with them alone.

"Now you come with us quietly, or we'll kill your friend. Plain and simple," the soldier in front of her stated. "I have no qualms with harming a darkie."

Ilsi grunted, forgot her past qualms with exposing her powers once more and threw the chunks of ice on her hands towards the man, clunking him in the chest and shoulder. The man that held Reshma suddenly squeezed her and Ilsi heard an odd sound. She saw flickers of light dance violently along Reshma's arms and shoulders and she shrieked insanely.

Ilsi threw ice at the man's eye and he released his grip on Reshma and held his face. There would be no point to his trying; the ice wouldn't melt until Ilsi wished it. The Ice Chanter whirled around and crossed her arms above her head and chest and a solid chunk of ice unearthed itself from the ground and shot up in between her and the other soldiers.

The man gained his composure and got up quickly. They attempted to punch through the barrier but only minute fractions flew off. Ilsi took a step back, but Reshma and the other soldier were behind her. Reshma crumpled to the ground as though fatigued.

The other soldier held out a sword. No one had ever pointed a weapon like that at her before, and Ilsi instinctively held up her hands. As he held his arm to strike, he jolted in place. He growled angrily and grabbed his legs, now frozen to the ground. He dropped his weapon and pointed a jagged finger at her, light and energy shooting from it towards her chest.

She thrashed and screamed violently. Her limbs forgot how to hold their strength and she fell to the ground, too. She wanted to move, but her appendages kept twitching and jumping, ignoring her attempts to rise. The other soldiers side-stepped the barrier and Ilsi could sense that all three had the two girls surrounded.

Suddenly, an arrow landed close to their feet. It almost spun into a Yildirim's leg. It quivered slightly in the spot of soil where it rested.

"Who's there?" one cried out.

"Shut up," another soldier barked. He scanned the area, with a stern frown.

A woman approached the area from behind the odd little house. She wore long breeches, and tall boots up to her knees. Along her belt hung five different kinds of knives. Her vest sported frayed edges and a high, open collar. Under the vest was a ripped shirt, torn at her shoulders. Her short, brown-blonde hair flapped against her cheeks, shiny from the lack of washing.

"You leave them innocent girls alone, you mutts," the woman said.

One of the soldiers immediately held out a hand to strike her with his abnormal magic, but she was quicker and ducked. The woman immediately armed herself with her bow and arrow. To Ilsi's horror, she shot the arrow and it went straight for Reshma's neck. The necklace around Reshma's neck broke and fell to the ground and left no injury to the Fire Weaver. The men looked at Reshma, then back to the lady.

"I will tell you once more, *leave 'em alone*," the woman said in a quieter, steely voice. The one above Reshma cowered. They refused to let Reshma go, but there was something about this woman that gave them second thoughts. The woman sighed and reached behind her for another arrow and aimed the poised weapon at him.

She shot the arrow. It flew with great speed, making a whining sound. It punctured the black boot of one Yildirim, and he held a hand to his foot as he fell to the ground. The other two, shocked and surprised, looked down at their comrade, then up at the armed woman.

"Sorry, lads, can't have you getting in trouble," she muttered under her breath as she held two more arrows at once to her bow. She quickly pulled the string back and her hand barely grazed her cheek before the arrows found lodgings in the two soldiers' sides.

"That wasn't too difficult a catch," she said wryly as they crumpled to the ground. She held a hand to the neck of the nearest victim until satisfied. She looked around and motioned to someone unseen by tilting her head towards the three soldiers sprawled on the ground.

A young man wearing a scruffy beard and a large hooded cloak drove a small wagon behind him, pulled by the horse he was riding and trotted lightly and casually around the corner and to the part of the path where the scuffle occurred.

"You know what to do, eh?" she grunted to the boy, as he leapt down from the horse to help her put the bodies in his cart.

"You keep me busy enough," he replied, the hood shadowing his eyes and nose. The woman chuckled to herself in reply. The young man mounted his horse again, the woman gave a slap on the horse's rump and the horse began trotting again with this cargo in tow.

"Who in the blue blazes are you two?" the woman said, her

hands on her hips. She looked squarely at the girls with a raised, arched eyebrow.

"We are looking for," Ilsi began, looking at Reshma for affirmation, "a family friend of hers. We're from Ravenna and we need shelter."

"Ravenna?" the woman asked.

"Do you know Sebrah?" Reshma asked, her gazed timid and unsure.

"The *hell* I know Sebrah," the woman said, wiping the sweat off her hand before offering it, "that'd be me, lassies." Reshma scrambled to her feet, and gave the armed and dangerous woman a hug.

"I haven't seen you in ages!" Reshma exclaimed.

"I was a bit worried you wouldn't recognize me," Sebrah laughed. "I'm not very hard to miss."

"Well, it's been a while."

"You know *her*?" Ilsi asked with surprise.

"Aye, which one are you out of your brood? I haven't heard from your folks for a mighty good while," the woman said with a smile, squeezing Reshma back.

"I'm Reshma, I'm somewhere in the middle," the Fire Weaver replied.

"Good enough answer fer me," Sebrah replied, then nodded her head towards Ilsi. "A friend of yourn?" Reshma nodded, and beckoned Ilsi to come closer.

"Ilsi of Dove, ma'am," she replied, "I'm an Ice Chanter." The woman pshawed and knocked Ilsi lightly on the shoulder.

"I'm not a ma'am," Sebrah said. "That's as seldom said as 'I'm an Ice Chanter.'"

"You said you might know someone here, but I was

starting to wonder," Ilsi said, grinning at Reshma. "Awfully glad we know someone."

"Her father an' I used to be trading partners," Sebrah explained to Ilsi with a wave of her hand, "I knew Reshma when drool came out of her mouth."

"Papa took me here when I was a kid, but I'm surprised that squatty house still looks hazily familiar," Reshma said, laughing at the poor state of Sebrah's house.

"'Tis hard to forget," Sebrah sighed.

"So is this your trade?" Ilsi said, half-gesturing to the ground where the soldiers had lain motionless. "Welcome the newcomers?"

"Oh that? They don't deserve the special treatment," Sebrah said, showing them one of her arrows, "It's drugged. They'll wake up tomorrow with enough pain to make a hangover feel like a good night's sleep. I send my catch of the day to the prime minister and let him decide their fate—let him play God."

"Do the soldiers belong to the prime minister?" Ilsi said, not sure what a prime minister was.

"In a manner of speakin'," Sebrah said. "They started off on their own to keep the peace without the bias or loyalties. They always seemed to be fair and friendly here, but things have changed. Now the Yling prisons are full wif' them."

"I would call hardly those soldiers *peaceful*. They pillaged our towns and made off with my family. They almost got Ilsi here," Reshma answered, rubbing her neck and holding the broken necklace in her hand. "That's why we came. We need your help."

"Your family is gone?" Sebrah asked, a firm grip on her shoulder. She looked around with a brief glance, and pulled Reshma protectively closer to her side. "Let's head to my place. We have some catchin' up to do."

CHAPTER 7

The prime minister of Yling wants me to collect any soldiers I subdue. He and the other representatives believe the soldiers are husbands and brothers of citizens of towns all over the place, meaning they're somehow innocent of their crimes," Sebrah said with distaste. "You mus' understand that this's extra work above my normal tradin' business."

"How does he even know that they're innocent?" Reshma scoffed. "They'll just turn a blind eye because they're related to someone else?"

"That necklace they latched on yeh," Sebrah said, motioning to the silver stone on a leather strap in Reshma's hand, "It apparently does somethin' to whoever wears it. Somewhere, a puppet master is playing with his toys and sending them all over the known world lootin' and plunderin' for who knows what."

"I did feel really strange," Reshma affirmed, "it was like thoughts weren't my own."

"What thoughts were you having?" Ilsi asked cautiously.

"And why were those good-for-nothings followin' after you?" Sebrah said, giving both the girls a glare. "They're the wrong lot to be foolin' wiff."

"I'm not sure if they were searching for me or something else," Ilsi said, "but they saw me and came after me. On our own lands."

"She has extra powers that no one on Ravenna can do," Reshma said, filling in the more important details. "Do you know anyone who can make their body move at great speeds with just a summon of a spell?"

"I know not a soul," Sebrah said, stretching her legs. "I can imagine why someone like them would want to know how to make a quick escape. Or order an army across the globe in a day."

They were sitting in the small house, barely fit for two people. There was only one bed, where Reshma and Ilsi were sitting, and Sebrah was leaning in a wooden chair, sharpening a small knife. Ilsi wasn't at all surprised that the odd-looking house belonged to Sebrah.

Sebrah had some twisted obsession with sharp knives. She had dozens of them lying around, hung on walls and even one laid on a nightstand close to the bed and five or so poking out from under her mattress. She had all kinds of other weapons around as well: sabers, swords, axes, bows and arrows—she even had a small number of slingshots. She wasn't much of a homemaker. The curtains looked poorly assembled and her bed was lumpy. Her wooden floor had bits of wood shavings lying around as if she never owned a broom in her life.

"I've heard talk that those Yildirims are becoming more bold about their plans," Sebrah said. "The prime minister ain't so fine with that. I've tried interrogatin' 'em, but those men and women don't even know what they're being recruited for. It's those amulets."

"Well I feel better already," Ilsi replied with weak sarcasm.

"Sebrah, is it too much to ask to stay here for a while?" Reshma asked. "Just until we figure out the next step in our plans."

"Look, I'm not even plannin' on stayin' so long. I move around—it makes for good business. And they would eventually find you here. Especially since I just took down those soldiers," Sebrah said.

"Well we don't have anywhere else we can go," Reshma explained. "If we can't stay with you we'll probably end up roaming around from one city to another."

Sebrah let out a booming laugh and grabbed her belly with delight. "What do you think you are? Adventurers?" Then between laughs, "You're not even out of school, what do you two know about the rest of the world?"

It's really not that funny, Ilsi thought with equal parts anxiety and annoyance.

"I know enough," Reshma protested.

"No," Ilsi cut in, "We don't. I didn't even know what Yling was, and I bet Reshma doesn't know much more than I do."

"Uh-huh," Sebrah said, wiping a stray tear and letting a laugh escape her lips. She stopped sharpening the knife she held and gestured the blade towards the two as she spoke, "Tell you what, the best place to go is to head for the Woods. It's best to see Ladala. She'll see you a couple nights of good rest. She lives in the woods outside of town. In the middle, there will be what's called the Grove of Elves. Those Yildirims have been trying *forever* to figure out how to take hold of the grove, but those Elves are mighty clever. They've got some way to keep them out."

While she was talking, Ilsi nervously stroked her plaited hair. She read about elves in books and hardly considered them real.

"Oi, I'd suggest going soon," Sebrah said, "They followed you this far, and I'd wager they'll keep puttin' in the effort."

"Hell no will I leave," Reshma said. "What if my family is in the prisons here? I won't leave until I go and—"

"They ain't there, girl," Sebrah interrupted loudly. "I go there all the time. Yeh think I'd not know if I saw yer family there? When I says to go to Ladala, I means it. She knows much more abou' this whole thing. She'll probably know where the leader of this group is hiding. She might know what to do with Ilsi's powers."

Reshma's eyes widened at the thought of finding the leader responsible for her anger and her family's capture. Ilsi's chest pounded at the thought of the potential to get back home.

"Fine, you're right," Reshma said. "If she can really help me and Ilsi, then we'll find her."

Then silently, Sebrah began eyeing Ilsi's long hair with interest. A few awkward moments passed, and Ilsi found herself clutching her braid.

"What are you looking at?" she said.

"That plait might have to go if you don't want them to recognize you," Sebrah said. "If I were you, I'd cut it clean off and change your look, or they'll find you faster next time."

"It'll grow back by the time it's all over," Reshma suggested, trying to be helpful.

"What do you mean, *by the time it's all over?*" Ilsi asked, aggravated. It definitely sounded like she was not going home any time soon.

———◦○◦———

Ilsi held the mirror to her face. Her hair had gone from to her waist, to the tips of her shoulders. Reshma tried not to laugh at the expressions appearing on Ilsi's face. The Ice Chanter kept feeling the crisp, trimmed ends of her hair, wondering how they ever got her to do it.

"I'm pretty good at this stuff, if I do say so myself," Sebrah said casually, twirling her large scissors between her fingers. "And because this is in lieu of a rescue, or other heroic deeds, I won't charge you this time."

"*This* time," Ilsi grumbled to herself. "Both of you have no idea how to tame curly hair. We will all regret this."

"How much do you have on you?" Sebrah continued. "Did you bring anything useful with yeh?"

"Well, we have some food, some extra clothes, but we'll probably need something better to defend ourselves with," Reshma said. "Ilsi wants us to avoid using our Ravenna magic in front of other people." Sebrah smiled and Ilsi's hand went instinctively to her hidden knife.

"Well, haven't *you* come to the right dame?" Sebrah grinned, "After all, I *am* the best weapon dealer there is." She beckoned them closer to a case specially built for holding knives. She held the case open, displaying them with much pleasure. The inside of the case was velvet-lined like a treasure chest, holding five knives that looked like decorative eating utensils by the way they glittered. Each blade was sharped and curved at the tip, and shone like moonlight. The handles were more worn down, but there were signs of delicate repairs.

"I'll give you my hand-me-downs. You won't see much in the way of monsters in the forest in this season," Sebrah said, handing them each a sharp dagger.

"Monsters?" Ilsi asked in disbelief as her fingers fumbled to braid her hair out of her face. "I thought those were stuff of tales, not *real*."

"We call 'em monsters because we don't really have much of a better name for them," Sebrah said. "In the thick woods, you have to kill before you get killed. Don't bother with askin' 'em what they are or what they want."

"You expect *us* to kill monsters?" Ilsi asked, arching her eyebrow.

"We didn't do so bad with those soldiers," Reshma shrugged. "What's a couple of monsters to us?"

Both Sebrah and Ilsi found themselves sharing a laugh.

"I hope you're joking," Ilsi said. "They had me on the ground twitching like a mad witch, and you—"

"Enough with the minor details," Reshma laughed, rolling her eyes.

"Back to the knives, ladies," Sebrah said, gesturing back to her collection. "Now do either of you even know how to use these?"

"Yes," Reshma volunteered quickly, while Ilsi rose from the bed, folded her arms, and walked in what little space the house had to offer.

"I assume you mean beyond preparing food," Ilsi sighed, "So my answer would be no."

Before anyone could add to that, she made a move to step outside of the house. Reshma quickly shot up from the bed.

"Where are you going? Someone could see you!"

Ilsi stood, still facing the door, and crossed her arms.

"Ilsi," Reshma said, placing her hands on her shoulders, "This *isn't* the time to be worrying about—"

"We can't do this!" said Ilsi, turning around defiantly, "We aren't fighters and we're barely survivors, Reshma, and you know it. We almost got captured and we barely made it to the mainland. What makes you think we can keep this up? I just want to go *home*."

"Well, you can't!" Reshma bellowed. Ilsi's eyes widened, and she bit her lip into a remorseful frown. Reshma's shoulders sported smoke to reflect the smoldering look on her face.

"Don't mess with our plans so we get what *you* want and not care about what *I* want," Ilsi said hoarsely. "I got us out here, remember? Or is that all I am in *our* plan?" She quickly turned and left. Reshma flinched, ready to follow her, but Sebrah held out her arm, a blade in her hand.

"She's fine," Sebrah murmured. Reshma heard quiet sounds of crying—sighs and sniffles. Her shoulders sank deeply and let out a sigh of her own. "Let her cry, 'n talk with her when she's ready."

—◦◦◦—

"It sounds like we both want the same thing—to be reunited with our families."

Ilsi put a hand instinctively to the dagger in her satchel with a gasp. It took her a second to recognize the voice so she could release her tense shoulders.

"We don't have to work together, you know. You can go back; I'm not going to stop you. It's not my place," Reshma said, leaning against the side of Sebrah's house. "But I'm not going back to Ravenna—I'm going out there to find my family and I won't go back until I find as many as I can."

"Are you so immortal?" Ilsi said, using the sleeve of the dress to dry her cheeks. "I guess I can't stop you, but . . . why am I the only one who feels like I don't know what I'm doing? I have this stupid little knife in my bag and I only feel confident in my bread slicing abilities."

"I'm sorry I made you cry," Reshma said.

"It's fine," Ilsi said dully, wiping her red cheeks. "Sometimes there's just nothing else to do besides crying. I can't pretend like this isn't the most frightening thing to happen to me."

"You're right," Reshma sighed. "I'm sorry about what I said. I didn't mean for it to sound like I didn't want to help you. I want to go home to Ravenna, too, but I think we both know that things need to change first."

"I just miss my father," Ilsi said, freshly remembering her pain. "I miss him and Tyk so much."

"Tyk?"

"He's my best friend. He's really the only person I can talk to about my mother and the Wall," Ilsi said. "Oh, what if they're dead because of me? I'll never know unless I go back."

"I bet your plans will work," Reshma said. "You wanted to come out here to lure them away from home. Maybe they've found out that you've left for good and they're coming here."

"Why doesn't that sound much better?" Ilsi said.

"It's nice that you have a friend back home," Reshma said, squatting down next to Ilsi. "Back at home, I really only had my siblings. I don't think the other kids my age really liked me."

"How so?"

"Ever have anyone call you Iron Skull?" Reshma said, rolling her eyes and shrugging.

"No, not yet," Ilsi smiled. "But you're fun—all the adventure in the world wants to stick to you. You're much braver than me."

"Eh, you've already out-matched my recklessness," Reshma said. "I can't promise that I'll always know what I'm doing, but I swear on the lives of my parents and siblings that I will defend you."

"You're not going to do a blood oath, are you?" Ilsi said, shrinking a bit away from Reshma. "You sound serious enough."

"Well, what are you going to do, then?" Reshma asked, ruffling her hair in the back. Ilsi noticed she did that a lot out of habit.

"I think we're safer together," Ilsi said. "Of course I'll go with you. You just have to realize that this is a lot to take on so suddenly. A few weeks ago, things were just snow and ice for me."

"Yeah, it would serve me well to not get carried away."

"Oh, if you see any of these beasts or whatever they are," Ilsi said, "you have my permission to get as carried away as you please."

"Perfect. Oh, you didn't mean the Yildirims?" Reshma said, taking Ilsi's hand in her clenched fist and shook it triumphantly. Ilsi giggled.

"I just hope Ladala will actually help us," Ilsi said. "The soldiers can't get in their lands—great for them. What about us? Do we know the magic word to get in?"

"Hopefully," Sebrah said, leaning out the window. Ilsi and Reshma scooted so they could look up behind them. "Sorry, it's not like I couldn't hear you two talking. But as I'll tell yeh this. I try to avoid bettin' on anything, but if there's anything I'd bet on, it's Ladala. She'll help when she's needed. 'Swear on every blade I carry.'"

CHAPTER 8

"Hold the light up a little higher," Reshma insisted. "We need to see the road ahead, not your feet."

Dusk already fell and the girls ventured out of Sebrah's hut and out to the main street out of Yling, the town Ilsi barely knew. The street lamps provided little light, burning the last of its oil, and the stars dotted the sky.

"I look ridiculous," Ilsi mustered. Reshma rolled her eyes and helped Ilsi raise her arm so they could see a few more feet ahead of them.

"You don't look ridiculous," Reshma said with a grin.

"Girls don't wear pants," Ilsi whispered sharply. "It feels so odd."

"Girls can and should wear pants. How else will she run from monsters?" Reshma retorted.

Sebrah insisted they wear pants with leather boots in order to move around in the terrain. In her opinion, skirts were just going to be ruined, and weren't the best for running. Reshma was more than willing to comply. However, this was the first time that Ilsi had ever worn pants and it took getting used to. In Dove, they were worn by men only. It was as odd as if she saw a man wearing a lady's dress.

They both wore long-sleeved white cotton shirts, with belts meant for weapons. Ilsi had a blue tunic and Reshma had a black one. They were both draped in long capes. As the night grew darker, Ilsi gathered the material around her like a blanket.

Ilsi wished the leather boots wouldn't make such a loud sound against the cobblestone. She was sure the whole town could hear her heart pumping and her chattering teeth. She couldn't walk in a way to make her walking any quieter against the cobblestones.

"I dare you to ask Ladala for a dress then," Reshma said. "I'm sure she'll give you something comfortable to run in."

"I'm not going to ask people for clothes," Ilsi returned. "Gad, I didn't ask for *these* in the first place."

"I feel like an adventurer," Reshma said softly. Ilsi looked over at her, wondering if that comment was for her or meant to be private. "I'm just another step closer to finding my family."

Ilsi remained silent, keeping her arm stiff in the air to hold the light up right. The cobblestone road soon became a dirt road, as they entered the forest. The dark, thick trees were busy with nightlife. Sebrah lived at the southeast part of town and she directed them north, away from the docks and into the forest— the great one that Reshma had explained about.

Ilsi couldn't imagine ever seeing such a place. Such large trees that touched each other and edged so close like curtains. Their only means of light was the lantern. The girls edged along, gingerly taking each footfall with care.

"How do we know we're going the right direction?" Ilsi asked. "Why are we even doing this in the middle of the night? We could've stayed a bit longer for a bit of rest."

"We're invisible out here," Reshma answered. "Besides, we

have the advantage of getting a head start. Who knows if the soldiers are trying to find us right now? They probably think we're back at Sebrah's. Luckily for us, we're not."

"We're still roaming around in the dark," Ilsi said. "And we're not invisible. We're holding this stupid lantern in the middle of the night. What about holding a light makes us so hard to see?"

"They'll probably find us with how loud you're talking," Reshma said, half-joking, half-serious.

Ilsi was starting to suspect that Reshma was more excited about doing the adventurous thing rather than thinking about their safety. She wasn't about to get herself killed because Reshma was having a moment of reckless bravery.

"So, monsters," Ilsi whispered. "We already established the fact that they're lethal and I'm not. What are we going to do?"

"Do you not know how to fight with your magic?"

"Yes—"

"Well, then I suddenly feel a lot safer with you here," Reshma said. "It's pretty simple, anyway. Make sure when you fight, stand up most of the time. You're more vulnerable on the ground. Secondly, you have to stab them in the heart," Reshma said, as she pointed to her own, "Their skulls are too thick and their bellies are so fat, if you stab it, they won't feel it."

"You're making that up," Ilsi said, perturbed. "You've never killed anyone or anything, especially monsters."

"Watch out, you might regret those words," Reshma warned pointing at her. She distorted her face next to her lantern and giggled. "Besides, didn't you hear Sebrah explain the rest? She said they only come out on the full moon." They both looked up and noted that the clouds were covering up most of the moon, so they could hardly tell how full it really was.

"Oh, stop. It's like all the tales are coming to life," Ilsi muttered, shoving her arm lightly, and continued staring ahead in the darkness, "Who do you think this Ladala-lady is, anyway? We're really good at looking for people without asking questions."

"I don't know. I haven't ventured in the forests. I was young, remember? Besides, I bet she's like a friend of Sebrah, or something," Reshma answered. "If they're enemies to the Yildirim, they will likely be friendly with us."

Ilsi faced the darkness ahead of them. The lantern only lit a few feet in front of her, so the rest of the path was left to her imagination. From where she was, it looked like there was no end to it. She wondered what kind of things lurked in that forest, and what could happen to her.

"You there?" Reshma said, probing the darkness to find Ilsi's shoulder. "We'll be okay. Just one foot in front of the other is all it takes."

"Sir, I'm getting no word from the Yling post," said a man wearing a mustard yellow uniform. It bore a black jagged streak across the front of the shirt. He stood straight and stiff facing another man sitting comfortably in a large chair. He sat by a large fireplace that brought the only source of warmth and light. The flames and shadows flickered wickedly over the walls. The messenger didn't dare meet the man's eyes with the sound of his unpleasant message ringing in the dusty air.

"Stop blubbering like a child," the second man said slowly and coarsely. "She's right where we want her. Already lulled into a false sense of security. Everyone is scouting and positioned where I need them. In due time, we can proceed with our plan of further attack upon Ravenna."

"What about the boy, sir?" the first man asked.

"Bring him here."

The uniformed man quickly motioned for two wide doors to open allowing light to enter. In no time, two other uniformed men dragged a young man into the dark room. His black hair was matted and sweaty and his heavy winter coats gone, but his long sleeved shirt was soaked through with sweat. His ankles were bare and sported scratches and scrapes.

"You think you're so big and tough," the man in the shadows said, musing, then said to the guards, "Name?"

"He wouldn't say at first. But through … *careful* consideration he told us his name is Tyk, my lord."

"Excellent," the man answered dully. "And he was found with this girl?"

"Yes, he distracted us for a moment and let her leap through the wall," the guard answered, shaking the boy at his shirt collar.

"Ah, so it's true?" the man said quietly, "The little girl does have very unique powers. Your sister is out there all alone and unprotected, boy. How do you cope?"

"Sir," the messenger interrupted nervously, "W-we actually have confirmed information that she is traveling with a companion. We've sent soldiers into the Beast forest after her."

"The little Ice girl doesn't know about the Beast forest?" the man said with derision. "How frightened she must be. This might be easier than expected."

Tyk struggled and growled under his breath, but the guards held him firmly. The man in the chair stoked the fire and sent embers and sparks flying.

"What *is* her name?" the man asked sternly, his question fired at Tyk. Tyk responded by gritting his teeth and firmly stood silent, while resisting the tightening grip the guards had on his arms. The longer he waited, the tighter the pressure.

"I don't . . . know who she is," he struggled to say. His face shook from the swelling heat and pain in his arms. The man in the chair didn't immediately reply.

After a few painful minutes, he ordered, "Bring me her cloak." The messenger saluted hesitantly and went to a large coat rack and brought a large, black woolen cloak. Tyk stared at it, breathing heavily.

"This little coat reeks of the little Ice girl," the man explained, "Well, at least to our hunting dogs and their masters. I plan on using this scent to find her, and it's very hard to catch a prey if it can still run. The soldiers may not be able to stop the dogs as quickly as you would like."

The man listened to Tyk's labored breathing.

"But you wouldn't be too concerned over someone you don't know, correct?" the man mused. Tyk fell weakly to his knees, the guards still holding him by the elbows. The man stared from in his large chair.

"What is her name?" the man asked again, listlessly. Again, Tyk knelt in silence, head hung. The man raised his hands as the flames illuminated his hand snapping lightly.

"No, please!" Tyk protested, but the guard to his left grabbed him by the front of his shirt and shocked him by the power of his bare hand. He twitched violently and fell to the ground, his shirt giving off a burnt odor.

"She is my friend," he croaked. The guards pulled Tyk to his feet by his arms since his legs wouldn't hold him up.

"I could already tell that you *knew* her," the man scoffed.

"If you hurt her, I swear, I'll—"

"I wouldn't breathe any threats, boy," the man interrupted hotly. He finally stood up and made a few steps towards Tyk, his arms folded.

"You're looking at two choices: more time with my soldiers," his muttered quietly, nodding his head to surrounding guards, one of them playing with a few sparks in his hand, "or you join in the search yourself and become a soldier."

"Join your army? I won't fight for a man who sets out to kill innocent girls!" Tyk fired back. The guards struggled more to keep him still, but he fought with renewed anger.

"I haven't harmed the girl, nor do I plan to, but that doesn't stop my soldiers. Besides, I don't need her dead, you fool. She is a vital to my plans like everyone else," the man muttered darkly.

"What plans? What are you going to do to her?" Tyk cried angrily.

"There's no telling what that girl faces, boy," the man said. "However, I'm sure she won't live to see the extent of what she's capable of destroying." There was a long pause.

"I'll give it time for you to mull over in your mind," the man said, and motioned in the darkness. Tyk scowled and shuffled his feet against his guard's grip. He screamed in frustration that rang through the room and halls like the howling of a beast.

"My lord," the assistant in uniform said, daring to near the chair, "May I ask what purpose we have in keeping the boy?"

"We put a uniform on him, put the amulet around his neck, and he'll become ten times better than our hunters and their mutts," the man in the chair said, more to the flames than his assistant. "He's a young Ice Chanter. A rare addition to my forces. You know well enough that I don't kill people until they become useless to me."

CHAPTER 9

Mama, it's me again.

We're hopefully one more step closer to finding some answers. It's been frustrating, because with each step, it seems like the path only lengthens. Mama, I wonder how you found out about Swift. Who told you about how special it was? Have you ever had a huge army follow you to have it? I have to find out more about what this power really is, and what I have to do to protect myself and my new friend. You would've liked her.

———◦◦———

"Okay, are you ready to keep moving?" Reshma asked. Ilsi put down her crude pencil and nodded.

"I could probably use another day or two of sitting, but I'd much rather get out of this forest someday," Ilsi answered, tucking her mother's book back in her satchel.

"Couldn't agree more," Reshma said. "It's so cold and damp in here. Gives me the creeps."

"Are you kidding?" Ilsi said. "You must still be used to the dry Tijerian heat, because it feels so moist and warm. The air is just so heavy."

"The sooner we find this impenetrable territory, the less we have to debate over the weather," Reshma grinned, offering her hand. Ilsi took it and used it to raise herself to her feet.

Reshma pulled out the map that she brought with her from home, and pointed to what looked like a cloud of uncertainty. It was marked as Beast Forest. The mapmaker took the time to draw tiny trees sporadically throughout the mass labeled as the forest. The map itself looked like a large wheel; the forest was a large mass in the middle, and all the towns, villages, and cities circled around it like spokes. Yling was at the very southwest point, and drawn to look like a decent-sized city. There was a small island off that coast without a name. The whole east side of the map faded in detail, and Ilsi could only imagine that the mapmaker had yet to discover what could possible extend to the east.

"At least we have something," Ilsi said. "It would be more helpful if this forest had some kind of path for riding, or if the map had some kind of helpful landmarks."

"You're right about that," Reshma said.

"Sebrah didn't mention much about where Ladala would be," Ilsi said as they rolled up the map and started walking. "I feel like we're on a fool's errand."

"I'm hoping Sebrah sent us out here because she thought we had what it took to find the place," Reshma said. "Just a hope, a wish."

"I sort of fancy the idea of being in a place that the Yildirims can't get into," Ilsi mused.

"Didn't we used to think that about Ravenna?" Reshma said. "I find it ironic that we go from one walled-in society to another."

"This one seems to have answers," Ilsi said, determined. "Elves are supposed to know a lot of things, right? That's what the tales tell us. I can find a way to be safe and you can find your family."

"I definitely hope you're right."

"So we're traveling northeast then?" Ilsi said. "Maybe we should travel west and get out of the forest for a moment and ask for directions?"

"That should help, actually," Reshma said. "We could use an updated map. I don't even know how old this thing is."

"The evidence that we are ill-prepared for this task is just piling high right now," Ilsi grumbled.

"If we weren't on the run from soldiers, I'd be a bit harsh on us, too," Reshma said. "But we can hardly catch our breath before someone else tries to put their witchy necklaces on you."

"Hey," Ilsi hissed, pulling out one of Sebrah's knives. Reshma quickly shut up and armed herself as well.

"What do you hear?" Reshma asked. Ilsi quickly jumped in the nearest bush and crouched down, and Reshma had no choice but to follow suit. After a few seconds of silence, they could hear the sound of zapping in the distance. Lightning. Reshma shuddered mightily at the recognition of the sound.

"They're here," Ilsi said through gritted teeth. "Dammit."

Reshma's eyebrow shot up at Ilsi's language and tried to suppress a grin before she heard the cracks of lightning.

"We can get out of this," Reshma whispered.

"What do we do, climb a tree?" Ilsi said.

"They sound like they're too far away to even know that we're so close," Reshma said. "In fact, a good climb can give us the perspective that we need."

"Okay, let's use that one over there," Ilsi said, pointing to a tall tree a few feet away. It had thick branches and pine needles that provided ample protection and covering.

They ducked and headed towards the tree. As they tried to climb and scale the tree, they could hear something approaching.

"Get the dogs around," a voice yelled. "Perhaps that'll speed things up a bit."

"They're . . . no longer dogs, sir," another younger voice said. It was a woman's voice. The other voice swore.

"The girls are no longer in Yling, that's for certain," the first voice said. "This forest has a way of helping people get very lost. Lock up the wicked changelings and we'll find the girls once they decide to stop running in circles."

"Of course," the other voice replied wearily. The girls in the tree heard the footsteps slowly disappear into the distant foliage. Once they were sure that the other people were gone, Ilsi sighed.

"If it's all right with you, I'd prefer to rest up here for the night."

"You're a forest creature now?" Reshma replied with a smile.

"Far from it," Ilsi said. "There's people down there that want us for reasons still unknown. I also hate to admit that I don't know the first thing about climbing down a tree."

"Ah," Reshma answered. "Well, you'll learn fast once you have to pee. Or anything else."

"I can gracefully fall out of the tree tomorrow morning," Ilsi said, "I've fallen from high places before." She remembered her escape through her bedroom window with derision.

"Sounds fine by me," Reshma said. She left her satchel and weapons on the branch she was sitting on and said, "I'm going to try and get any higher to see if I can see where we are."

"Enjoy the view," Ilsi said, as she drank from her water pouch. Reshma began grappling for branches nearby and soon she was scaling the tree and out of sight. Ilsi laid her head against the rough trunk and closed her eyes, wondering if she could get a decent night's sleep in a sitting position high up in a tree knowing that unwanted enemies could be lurking below. After quite a while, Ilsi could hear Reshma making her careful descent.

"Ilsi," Reshma said, coming down the tree, "It's incredible. It's just trees in every direction. I don't even see anything of stone or man-made. It's just . . . trees forever until the horizon."

"You didn't see anything that looked like a place that Ladala would live?" Ilsi asked.

"She would have to have towers that touch the clouds in order for me to see them," Reshma said, breathing heavily in awe and out of exertion.

"Did you hear what they said about their dogs?" Ilsi said as Reshma found a stable sitting position.

"Yeah," Reshma said quietly. "Did you hear right when they said the dogs were no longer dogs?"

"Is that a euphemism?" Ilsi asked.

"They called them changelings," Reshma said. "They're definitely using some weird stuff to find us."

"To them, we're probably weird girls," Ilsi said.

⸺◈⸺

The next day, the girls slowly but carefully inched their way down the tree. Ilsi just decided to jump once she was a foot or two from the ground, tired of hurting her hands. She fell and tumbled to the ground.

"Hopefully no one heard that," Reshma said.

"Agreed," Ilsi said, as she got to her feed and headed onward.

"So it sounds like they've got this forest surrounded," Reshma said. "It's either find a town and potentially be surrounded, or wander around on our own to find Ladala."

"What do you want to do?" Ilsi asked, unsure if she wanted to hear the answer.

"We've made the bed and now we have to sleep in it, as Mama would say," Reshma said. "Up in the trees, it looks like it would take much longer to get out. I know we've only been out here for a few days, but it looked like we've been venturing out here for months."

"So I guess we're going to keep going," Ilsi said. "Onward ever onward, then."

They cautiously made their way through the forest, attempting to have quieter yet quicker steps. As they kept moving, the only light they had was their weak lantern, and the glow of a large, full moon making its way into the night sky.

"Should we find shelter somewhere?" Ilsi asked. "Might as well get some sleep."

"I'm beat," Reshma replied. "Let's find a decent tree before my legs fall off."

They felt their way through the dark and found what they hoped would be a decent tree.

"I can't even see the next branch up," Ilsi said. "You might as well use your fire so we can see."

"I thought you insisted on keeping our powers a secret," Reshma said, amused.

"It's just for a moment," Ilsi said. "We've had a long day, and I'd like to see our new sleeping quarters."

Reshma didn't waste a moment. She held out her hand and a tiny ball of fire danced a few inches above her palm. It lit up her whole face and she smiled. She held up her hand and the glow showed some promising, thick branches overhead.

Suddenly, they heard a strange noise—a low growl. The hairs on the back of Ilsi's neck stood on end. Ilsi tried to ignore it, remembering that they were in a forest that was full of unusual noises. She let her gaze wander and could hear all sorts of birds squawking, insects humming and leaves rustling. The same growl felt closer and Ilsi flinched.

"Re-Reshma," Ilsi quivered, "W-what is that?"

Reshma was about to comment, but when she turned to face the Ice Chanter, she froze in her place. She thought she saw a pair of eyes flicker as her flame moved with her.

"I think something is close," Reshma said, the growling a bit more distinct and louder. She whispered shakily, "Don't worry. Just . . . *don't* make any sudden movements or loud—"

Ilsi screamed as something jumped on her from behind. Reshma's flame—a large, furry wolf snapping its jaws. It looked large and sinister, like it had already won some earlier scuffles. Reshma threw her fire and it caught hold of the beast's coat. It whined and barked as the creature rolled away, clawing Ilsi and anything else in its way. Ilsi scrambled to her feet, realizing that the creature was entangled in her bag.

"Hey!" Ilsi protested. The beast managed to get on all fours with the flame out and the smell of singed hair in the air.

"Ilsi, it's a wolf," Reshma whispered, holding up a new flame so they could see. Suddenly, they could hear growling and panting from several directions. Reshma held up a second flame and saw several pairs of eyes surrounding them.

"I didn't come all the way out here to get eaten alive," Reshma grunted. Ilsi trained her eyes on the wolf with her bag.

"I'm not going to let anyone take my mother's book," Ilsi whispered. She whispered *Swift* under her breath before she ran straight at the wolf. She was able to snatch the bag, and run with it.

Reshma looked around, realizing that Ilsi was suddenly gone, as well as the wolf. She held out the fire in defense as the wolves neared her.

"Go away or I'll singe all of you," Reshma said aloud. The wolves growled, not fearing the fire. One of them came close and just sniffed at her like a curious puppy. Reshma froze in fear and confusion. The wolf looked up like an obedient dog and whined as it trotted away, almost guiltily.

Dumbfounded, Reshma lowered her aching arms and looked around.

"What just happened exactly?" Reshma said aloud. The wolves didn't even put up a fight. It was if they recognized her as a human and left her alone.

Guess we'll look for another tree once I find you, Ilsi, Reshma thought to herself, gathering up their things. *Before something else does.*

⸺◦◦⸺

Light crept out from behind the trees. Ilsi opened her eyes and saw a large tree stretching up to the sky. She realized she was lying on her back, and she tried to prop herself up with her arms. The ground was soggy and the leaves above her head held small beads of rainwater. Ilsi shivered, realizing that she was lying on cold dirt.

Once she felt that she was fully awake, she was able to calm down and resort to a comfortable warmth as she tried to remember how she got there. She remembered the wolf and reaching for the bag. She remembered running with *Swift* through the dark trees. The wolf behind her didn't make it long, as it collided with some other tree. Ilsi remembered not making it much further before she hit something. She could only guess it was the tree she slept under.

How far did I go? Ilsi thought to herself. *How will I find Reshma now?*

Ilsi rolled up her sleeves and dug through her bag for any form of food. She found meager slices of hard-crusted bread and she nibbled nervously. It was the last of her food rations. She thought that if she stayed put, Reshma could have a decent chance of finding her. It didn't stop her from wondering just how lost she was.

While she was deep in thought, a sound began to reverberate in her ears. It came quietly. Her thoughts froze, as she stood up to hear the sound. It was a whisper. Her bread fell from her fingers, half eaten. Her eyes refused to blink and all thoughts cleared her mind as she was stood up. She steadily walked, with vacant eyes and a closed mouth. She continued, until the whisper, became a voice.

"*Ilsi*," a soft, gentle voice purred. "*Come, Ice Chanter.*"

She staggered towards the voice. As her vision grew dimmer and her mind wavered, she sank to her knees and felt the weight pulling her closer to the earth.

Tiny vines twirled and slunk from the soil like silent snakes and grew in size in seconds like they were sprouting in rushed time. They intertwined themselves sneakily around her ankles, wrists, and shoulders, pulling her closer and tighter to the ground. Her body silently obeyed as her torso slowly fell to the earth, her stomach covered in dead leaves and dirt. All the while, more strands coiled around her waist, ankles, and legs until she was almost covered in a green web. As the final strand came slowly to wrap itself around her neck, Ilsi's wrist lit up brightly and tore a hole through the empty darkness of Ilsi's mind.

Ilsi screamed aloud, and her muscles twitched and tightened. As though the vines could understand her desperation, they frantically pulled her limbs to the ground so she couldn't escape. The vines felt like thick, coarse ropes, and Ilsi screamed in surprise and pain.

Suddenly, Ilsi thrashed her hand out, gripping a dagger. She squirmed to cut at the vines at her wrist and they flinched at the slighted cut. She sawed violently at the thick vine coiling at her throat. It thrashed around like an angry snake and coiled again over her neck, sharper and tighter than before. Ilsi struggled to breath, and felt sharp pain all over.

"*Swift!*" Ilsi choked out. Immediately, the spell propelled her into the air and onto her feet. She collapsed into the nearest tree, and any vines that were still around her snapped like twigs and screeched. Ilsi rolled over on her belly and scrambled to her knees, watching the vines writhe in pain. They dove back down into the earth where they came from. She held her throat as she began to cough.

Ilsi felt the burns lingering on her wrists and a shiver rolled down her spine. She blinked her eyes as her senses came back into focus, and shook her head. She heard wailing and screaming, and the sound of glass continuously breaking and shattering. The sounds gradually ceased, and Ilsi was left alone.

"What was that all about?" Ilsi thought aloud. She looked towards her wrist. *Swift's* brand glowed softly and then faded back to normal. Ilsi noticed her things were scattered all over, so she crawled on the ground and gathered them. While doing so, she noticed something sparkle in the grass.

She moved her head back and forth as her eye caught the reflected light a couple times. She brushed the grass away and between her hands lay a simple rose gold band. She almost didn't see it, but a sudden glint of light made it sparkle in the midst of the grass. One of Ilsi's dirt encrusted hands picked it up and brought it towards her face.

Ilsi casually slipped it on to marvel how it looked on her finger. She held up her hand, wondering, "Who do you belong to?" As she pondered, she felt dizzy and tired, when she blinked, her eyelids were heavy. Everything looked so fuzzy and dark. Her eyes closed and her mind faded, and Ilsi collapsed back down to the ground.

CHAPTER 10

Reshma continued her way through the forest, stepping over rotted logs, and brushing by long branches in her way. She would occasionally call out Ilsi's name, but she couldn't hear an answer in return. She glanced at the sky above and wrinkled her brow.

It's almost morning—how long have I been at this? Reshma thought. She stopped to fill her mouth with water. When she put her water pouch away, she heard an unearthly scream. It rang through the trees and sent flocks of birds to scattering from the treetops and soar into the morning sun.

Oh, no, please don't let it be Ilsi, anything but that! she thought, as she sprang into a run. She tried her best to run quickly with little light. She called a spell, and she formed a small ball of fire, acting as a guide along her way, not caring if anyone or anything was watching. Not long after, she heard the wailing stop. She heard the movement of leaves. Everything muted.

Reshma's mind whirled as she stopped for a moment for any audible clues. She decided to keep going, even though she felt like she was running in circles. An hour later, she found what she was looking for: Ilsi, lying in a patch of crunchy leaves, with a small grin on her face and a glittery object fitted around her finger. Sparkling glass was spewed all around Ilsi, glinting in the faint moonlight and early morning sun. Reshma, hardly bothered to wonder where the glass came from, brushed it away so she could kneel next to her.

"Ilsi, wake up, c'mon, Ilsi! Get up!" she said, shaking her. Ilsi arose in fright, whirling her head frantically.

"What! What's going on?" Ilsi cried, and caught sight of Reshma, "Oh, thank the gods you found me!" The two friends embraced, as Reshma's ball of fire encircled them. Reshma picked up Ilsi's lantern and whispered a spell. The ball of fire immediately disappeared into the lamp, offering more light.

"What's that thing on your finger?" Reshma said, pointing at Ilsi's hand. "Looks valuable."

"I'm not sure," Ilsi said, bemused, holding her hand out to allow both to admire the ring, "I was under some sort of spell, I think. I can't remember much of what happened, but I saw this ring, I picked it up, and everything else is all just a blur."

"A spell?" Reshma said.

"I *think* so, I just heard a strange voice and it took control of my mind," Ilsi said, breathing heavily. "Then something happened and next thing I realize, I was pinned down to the ground by vines—"

"Well, let's get out of here before something else happens to us," Reshma said, helping Ilsi to her feet. "I'm not waiting around for that to happen again."

"Agreed," Ilsi said, and the two set off.

"We should be extra careful, though," Reshma murmured, "That spell wasn't an accident. It could've been a trap set by someone who lives here. Or even the Yildirims. I'm getting real suspicious of that ring."

Ilsi shivered. "Or maybe it means we're getting closer," she suggested hopefully. "Sebrah said that the Yildirims couldn't get in. Perhaps it's because the elves set too many booby traps." Ilsi looked back towards the ground where she was almost choked to death, then clutched her own hand closer to her, looking down at the ring.

They continued on their way, even until the sun had finally awoken. It became visible enough to walk without the lantern, and it became more frequent that Ilsi's stomach growled with hunger. Ilsi and Reshma walked out of the shade of trees and out into a large, open clearing. The trees were dead and the grass was scorched yellow and in need of watering. Swarms of large flies scanned the area for anything alive to eat, and noticed that the girls were the best options. Ilsi swatted them away in disgust. Their feet crunched large clumps of grass, when something pushed them back.

They stumbled backwards, feeling dazed and slightly confused. Ilsi rubbed her nose and gritted her teeth. After shutting her eyes in pain, she opened them to see nothing. The largest obstacle was a decaying tree to her far left. It was just air before her.

"What was that?" Ilsi said, feeling the air in front of her. Her fingertips stopped, as if she was hitting a wall. Reshma felt it, too.

"I think we found something," Reshma rubbing her forehead with a sly grin.

"Is this another Wall? Another spell?" Ilsi asked. She spread out her hands and felt the invisible solid, trying to find any holes. The barrier exceeded her height, and touched the ground and stretched quite a ways away from their first contact.

"Well, we have to think of something. We can't go back the way we came," Reshma said.

"Wait, maybe this wall needs *Swift*, too," Ilsi said, "that was how we left Ravenna."

"Valid," Reshma replied, hooking her hand around Ilsi's belt. "Give it a shot."

Ilsi braced herself, not knowing what could possibly wait beyond the invisible shield but feeling secretly happy that she was good for something. She gripped Reshma's hand and gritted her teeth.

"*Swift!*" she finally cried. She wasn't sure of what to expect, but she felt her body rush towards the wall and the same amount of force push her back again. Reshma sputtered and wheezed as she too crashed into the barrier and flew backwards. When Ilsi's vision came back to her, she looked up and saw the same withering scene.

"Oh," Reshma groaned, her bones making cracking noises as she arose, "I wish that had worked. Good thing I'm still the Iron Skull, eh?" Ilsi groaned in reply and remained on the ground, staring up at the sky. She felt pain everywhere and wanted to do anything but stand up.

"Get up, lazy bones," Reshma said, offering a hand.

"More like broken bones," Ilsi said, but raised a limp arm to grab Reshma's hand. Ilsi took another look at the barrier once she was on her feet and her eyes could focus again.

"Well, I suppose if *Swift* didn't do the trick, I highly doubt that any other powers will work," Ilsi thought aloud. Reshma lightly traced a circle, touching the wall, her finger was yellow and orange from the flames flickering and dancing on her fingertip.

"Nope," she said, "Fire won't cut through. Maybe a weapon?"

"Knives wouldn't work," Ilsi answered, discouraged. "Sebrah said the Elves were protected, they wouldn't create a defense susceptible to man-made swords or arrows."

"True."

The girls thought silently to themselves, trying to come up with a good idea, but secretly waiting for the other to suggest something first.

Ilsi looked back down at her hand resting on her knee while she sat on a rock, and admired how the ring it shined in the light. She gently pulled it off her thumb and held it between her other thumb and pointer finger, and spun it with her other pointer finger to admire it from all angles. As it spun in her hands, she saw something peculiar about the inside of the ring.

She suddenly had the idea to hold it up to her eye. She closed her right eye and looked through the ring like it was a telescope. Though her vision blurred at the far left and right, she could see a noticeable difference between what she saw through the ring and outside the curve of its shape. Through the hole, everything was the same, only full of life, dark green grass and trees that held their branches sturdily instead of sagging under dead weight. She quickly lowered the ring from her eyesight and saw dead, yellow grass again. She held up the ring again, and saw the thick, tall grass once more.

"Reshma," she said. "This ring is amazing, look!"

She held it up so Reshma could look through it. Reshma

held out a finger to steady it near her face, but she hissed and retracted her hand.

"The thing burned me!" she cried. "Why do you keep it on your finger?"

"What?" Ilsi said. "It feels like regular metal to me." She held it in her hand to prove her point.

"Did your parents teach you to pick up just anything in a forest?" Reshma countered. "A forest that probably has a lot of eerie things in it that are trying to kill us, apparently?"

"Well, I just held it up to my eye and everything was living and beautiful," Ilsi retorted. "I wonder if it could do something to this barrier."

She stood up, still gripping the ring with her thumb and pointer finger. Before she really thought about what she was trying to do, she held out the ring and pressed it against the invisible surface. She pushed hard to make sure it would keep its position.

"What are you—?"

Waves of color suddenly burst straight through trees and grass and stretched as far as Ilsi could see. Like a pebble thrown into still water, small ripples of rich hues circled about the area where Ilsi held the ring against the wall. Suddenly the colors whitened into a bright light and the girls covered their eyes from the sight. The light faded, and sparkles drifted to the ground.

Ilsi slowly lowered her arm and the two looked before them in wonder. There was a visible division between the decaying vegetation they stood in and lush green grass swaying like ocean waves that reached to their waists. Trees reached for the skies with their branches, bursting with life, as if housing thousands of creatures. The branches were heavy with fruit and blossoms and created a straight path before them. Everything was exactly how Ilsi saw it through the ring's hole.

The girls looked at each other and cautiously crossed over to the transformed growth and walked briskly through the small field. Nothing impeded their path and they kept walking.

"Look! Apples and oranges!" Reshma pointed, and didn't wait a moment to scramble up the tree. She plucked fruits from several branches, dropping them to the ground below. When their bags were expanded to the limit with food, they ventured onward, hungrily biting into the juicy fruit. Ilsi laughed as juice dribbled down her chin and tried to rub it away with her hand.

"This is so delicious," Ilsi said with relish. "I'm so glad we're out of that forest."

"We should build a huge cottage and just stay here forever," Reshma suggested.

"You can build the cottage," Ilsi returned, "and I'll take a nap for you."

They came across a small stream and joyfully knelt at the edge and drenched their faces with cool water.

"This is amazing," Ilsi smiled, "Do you think Ladala lives here?"

"If I were Ladala," Reshma answered, "I would."

They followed a dirt path over a large hill and stood at the very top to admire the scenery below. There was a large, deep, round valley bordered by roaring waterfalls pouring into it. A cloud of rising mist made it hard to see the just how deep the waterfalls went.

"Where *are* we?" Ilsi breathed.

"Incredible," Reshma whispered. The path snaked through trees and fields, pointing towards the valley.

"Let's go and find Ladala," Ilsi said and walked on briskly and happily, Reshma following behind.

"What do you want with Ladala?" a voice asked sternly. The girls whirled to see a pair of figures standing behind them. They wore matching uniforms of green tunics tucked under green jackets buttoned at the front. They both wore brown britches and thick brown boots laced up to their shins. One was a man, his hair black, bushy and curly, his sword wielded defensively; the other, a blond woman with short, straight blond hair, her arms folded smugly.

Each had long, pointy ears protruding out of their hair, but their long slender noses and almond-shaped eyes captured Ilsi's attention. She flinched and realized two more were behind her. Another man and woman stood behind the girls, both aiming arrows at the center of the girls' foreheads. The woman had short, coiled brown curls and the man had short spiky red hair shooting off behind him as though a harsh wind was blowing them back.

The four figures edged closer, and Reshma unsheathed a dagger and Ilsi gripped her own tightly and pointed the tip at the closest one to her.

"You have no business being here," the elf with red spikes warned. "Who are you and how did you get here?"

"Which one of you has the ring?" the blond elf questioned. "Hand it over if it hasn't already burned your stubby fingers."

"It's right here," Ilsi said, showing the ring snug on her middle finger. The blond elf flinched and took a few steps back, her blond side-swept, bangs shielding one of her eyes, and the black haired elf stepped closer to Ilsi.

"Why hasn't it burned you?" the red spiked elf asked

bewilderedly from behind. Ilsi turned to look at his dazed expression.

"She must be a Transformist," the brown-haired woman suggested, still poised to strike. One small flick and the arrow would surely strike true between Ilsi's eyes.

"Don't be daft," the blond snapped, unsheathing her own dagger. "She looks just as confused as we are."

"But a little girl with *that*?" the woman with brown locks returned. "Impossible."

Reshma suddenly hummed an alto note and her fingers burst into flames. Her hands looked like fierce and deadly talons of a dragon and as she held them defensively before her.

"Step back and give my companion and me some room. And stop pointing all those weapons in our faces!"

The four elves looked at each other, then at Reshma's blazing hands and Ilsi's unblemished hand curled into a fist around her dagger, the ring twinkling. The two equipped with arrows loosened their grip and pointed the tips to the dirt, while the black-haired male sheathed his sword and the blond followed suit. She pointedly stared at Reshma's hands.

"Thank you," Reshma retorted. "Ilsi, please give them their stupid ring."

Ilsi pulled it off, held it in her palm and stepped forward to hand it to them. They all recoiled as though Ilsi was offering poison.

"What are you trying to do?" the blond exclaimed.

"You wanted it," Ilsi said, confused. "Did you change your mind?"

"She doesn't know what it does," the black-haired man mused, grinning knowingly.

"Thank you, Basim," a voice called, "I can take it from here."

Ilsi turned around. She was face-to-face with a stunning woman draped with mint green fabric. A long flowing dress swathed her figure, embellished with green gems. Her sleeves were silky, long, and gathered at her fingers. She had a headpiece made of silver fitted across her forehead and under a long strand of brown hair in front of her face.

Her long, dark brown hair snaked down her back as curls, with a portion pulled back into an elaborate bun at the back of her head. Her hair matched her equally dark skin and round eyes. Ilsi noticed that she had a long gold chain around her neck and she had a pair of noticeable pointy ears with a large hoop earrings dangling from them.

"Milady," Basim breathed.

The woman flicked her hair off her shoulders and smiled. As she took silent steps forward, the four elves fell to one knee and bowed in respect. The girls glanced quickly at the elves then back at the beautiful woman. They shakily copied the elves and sank to their knees, staring at the grass beneath their feet. Reshma silently extinguished her fingers and they gave off a little smoke.

"Who are you, and what are you doing here?" the woman asked softly.

"We're here to see Ladala," Ilsi said in the bravest voice possible, "If you could just tell us where she lives, that would be—"

Ilsi broke off her speech at the sound of one of the elves stifling a snort under their breath.

"Now, now, Liselotte," The woman chided slightly, "This is no way to treat our guests. Please, stand on your feet."

Ilsi looked up into the woman's face and rose to her feet. Reshma following suit, brushed off her knees.

"I'm afraid I didn't have the chance to introduce myself immediately and have slightly deceived you," the woman smiled, her headpiece sparkling. "I am Ladala."

Ilsi and Reshma stood motionless, feeling color rise to their cheeks in awkwardness.

"It's—it's nice to meet you," Reshma murmured, holding her hand out to shake hands with Ladala.

"Why are you looking for me?" Ladala said, not reaching for Reshma's extended hand.

"Well, my friend Sebrah told me—"

"Ahh, Sebrah sent you, did she?" Ladala laughed merrily, then faced the four elves. "In that case, you can leave us be, I have much to discuss with our visitors. Any friend of hers is most certainly someone I should meet for myself."

CHAPTER 11

Ilsi and Reshma looked hesitantly at each other as Ladala walked in between them and lead them towards the city surrounded by waterfalls. The closer they came, the louder the crashing water became.

"I hope my personal guards didn't give you *too* much trouble," Ladala said with a smile, "It's been ages since they've been able to interrogate intruders."

"It's fine," Ilsi chirped hesitantly.

"But we aren't really intruders," Reshma protested, "Sebrah sent us here for protection."

"Yes, you said that you know Sebrah," Ladala said. "What are your names so I can address you properly?"

"Oh, forgive us," Ilsi said, stopping her gait to awkwardly bend her knees in a slight curtsy, "I am Ilsi of Dove and this is Reshma of Tijer." Reshma quickly nodded her head in a gesture of a bow.

"No need for such formalities here," Ladala said, smiling gracefully, "we're no longer strangers. But Dove and Tijer? Where is that exactly?"

"Ever heard of a place called Ravenna?" Reshma offered.

"The island Ravenna?" Ladala said, her eyebrows arched with interest. "You've come quite the distance."

"You could say that," Reshma said. "We're the first two to people to leave the island because of the wall put there. The Yildirims were the first to come through."

"We came because Sebrah said that you would be able to help us," Ilsi said. "The Yildirims attacked our people."

Ladala kept walking, but looked down at Ilsi curiously, then looked forward.

"What serious circumstances," Ladala replied, shaking her head. "How they would know where to find an invisible island is strange indeed."

Reshma gestured to Ilsi. "They went all the way to Dove to find her and people like her."

"I haven't done anything," Ilsi said quickly. "I'm a good person."

"You'll be safe here," Ladala smiled, still looking ahead. "We know the Yildirims are up to something, but they won't get to you here."

Ilsi breathed out a sigh of relief. It felt good to be somewhere safe for once. She looked over at Reshma, who seemed to share the same sentiment. She looked ahead of them, with a smile on her face.

"Sebrah was right to send you here," Ladala said, "and for now, this is probably the safest place for you two. Lately we haven't been taking in visitors. We've been busy with keeping the Yildirims at bay."

"Have they succeeded?" Reshma asked.

"Not at all," Ladala answered. "They come and go, trying to hack away at the barrier and skulk away when they fail."

111

"So how did we manage to enter when the Yildirims couldn't?" Ilsi asked, her brows furrowed.

Ladala simply smiled gracefully and looked to her four soldiers, then the girls.

"I can tell you that enemies try to break in all the time, but only the deserving may enter here. My soldiers here will assure that you find a comfortable place to rest," Ladala said. "You ought to recuperate from your travels and then we can talk."

"Thank you, that's very generous of you," Ilsi said, bowing quickly. She supposed that they could afford to wait. She felt as if her neck was aching from constantly looking over her shoulder. It was a good time to rest and be patient. Reshma also bowed, and Ladala just smiled.

"Thank you," Reshma said. "I'm not sure how we can return any favors, but we will."

"It will happen sooner than you think," Ladala said with a twinkle in her eye.

———⋘∘⋙———

Ilsi could see green for miles. Along the path, long grass swayed in the breeze; it reminded her of the fields by her home before the Great Chill came. There were large trees that stood every so often on both sides, full of white blossoms. The green stretched on forever until they approached the massive waterfalls, feeling the air full of moisture. Through the curtain of mist, she could see a carriage waiting for them and a driver poised with the reins in his hand, as though anticipating their arrival.

Ladala climbed into one of the seats and the two girls followed suit. With a snap of the reigns, the carriage flew down the winding road slinking and spiraling down until Ilsi began to see buildings nestled safely in the valley.

"This is absolutely incredible," Ilsi breathed. Her eyes traced the waterfalls; there were seven of them. She noticed how their gushing waters emptied into a large ring that hugged the entire city. Ilsi could see the path they would take ahead; it descended down into a valley surrounded by the waterfalls. It zig-zagged in between homes and fields like canals, with small bridges connecting the land together. The area was absolutely massive with patches of forests, vineyards, and homes; from their vantage point, it seemed hard to imagine all of these things fit inside the Beast Forest.

"It's a relief that you were able to come to us," Ladala said. "We suspected that the Yildirims were making another attack. You could've run into a bit of trouble."

"Do you really think they would come through?" Reshma asked.

"They've been constantly trying for the past year or so," Ladala sighed. "They've hardly made progress, but it's a bit naive to think that they will stop trying."

"We thought they might use you to get to us," Basim said. He was riding a horse next to the carriage. "If you could get through our barrier, then perhaps they would use you as their way in. They need people like you to get to all the places they cannot go."

"You have *Swift*, don't you?" Ladala said, as her body swayed to the rocking of the carriage.

"Yes, I do," Ilsi said quietly, almost drowned out by the noise of the carriage wheels grinding the dirt path. "How did you know?"

Ladala shrugged. "There is a narrow list of ways to enter here and your abilities is one of them."

"*Swift* seems like the way to get places," Reshma murmured light-heartedly. "But it was that ring you found that really did the trick."

"Another means of entering. Which is why the Yildirim are probably looking for you," Ladala said. "They have been tracking you since you left home, haven't they?"

"Yes, they have," Ilsi answered. "But if it's so important, why can't they find someone else? I can't be the only one with *Swift*."

"*Swift* is quite rare. I've heard of other people conjuring it, but you're the only one I've met in person."

"You mean that Ilsi isn't the only one?" Reshma said, gripping the edge of the carriage seat.

"Well . . . yes. I'd like to think that there are people everywhere that have such abilities. But none have made themselves known."

"So why *Swift*? Why is it so important?" Ilsi asked. "I just want to use them to go back home and protect my father. We need your help."

Ladala's body swayed with the carriage's motion and sighed. She pursed her lips and replied, "I'm sure there's something I can do."

CHAPTER 12

Within an hour or so, they arrived at a pair of sleek ivory doors that were twice the height of a normal man. The building had windows just as long. It was circular in shape and was surrounded by lush bushes with flowers. Ladala exited the carriage, and Basim was waiting there to take her hand and gently lead her the very short distance from the carriage to the ground.

"This is my home. It is a safe place to stay and talk," Ladala said, gesturing to the doors. "Follow me, won't you?"

Ilsi and Reshma jumped out, not wanting to take Basim's hand, even though he didn't offer it. They collected their things and quickly followed her footsteps.

"Dear Reshma," Ladala said, "I wish to speak with Ilsi alone for a moment. My attendants will show you around and make sure you're comfortable."

Reshma looked at Ilsi with hard eyes, not wanting to separate but nodded and offered a slim smile. Liselotte came to her side and offered to direct her in the opposite direction.

"Why just the two of us?" Ilsi protested. "Reshma can be trusted."

"This isn't out of trust," Ladala said. She didn't continue and Ilsi couldn't find any words to respond with. She followed the woman through a hall with natural light pouring through windows along the left wall. Everything about the place was warm and bright.

Ladala finally brought her to a room filled with books. The light spilled through a round wall that had no window; a natural breeze blew right through. Ilsi noticed there was hardly anything hanging from the walls or the ceiling to provide light.

"I know what it is you want," Ilsi said, looking at all the books. They reminded her of her father.

"And what is that?"

"Here, milady," Ilsi said, taking off the ring and holding it out towards Ladala. "I found it in the forest, and your soldiers asked for it. It must belong to your people, am I correct?" At first, Ladala didn't respond, but just stared at Ilsi's cupped hand and the rose gold twinkling on her palm.

"If it hasn't harmed you," Ladala said quietly, "then it is not mine to take."

"Then why did your soldiers ask for it?" Ilsi said. "They knew I had it and asked for it, but they didn't dare take it. Is this a weapon?"

"Depends on how you use the word, dear girl," Ladala replied. "It is of no use to many of the people you know or will chance to meet. It only works for those with rare gifts, such as *Swift*."

"So what do I use the ring for? Branding?" Ilsi asked. It brought to mind the moment Reshma touched it and felt it burn her hand. Ladala chuckled as if it were a joke; Ilsi didn't smile or laugh.

116

"You could possibly do that, but from what I know, it was crafted to empower you, or anyone with powers like you," Ladala explained. "When someone like you wears the ring, it adds not just to your magical strength, but to your natural strength, too. It's generally nasty towards anyone who doesn't deserve its enormous assistance. That's why it was found in the wild forest; there's no telling what it will do, and it helps keep away the wrong people."

"I was attacked by vines," Ilsi said, her pulse quickening at the memory. "Only *Swift* could save me."

"Ah yes, magical items in the forest like their little tests," Ladala said.

"I am just full of questions and hardly any answers," Ilsi said. "How would we have made it to your home without that ring? We would still be lost in the forest without it."

"I know many things, but I can only answer where I can," Ladala sighed.

"What *do* you know, milady?" Ilsi said. She wanted to stomp her foot like an impatient child. "I've read stories about the Elven people. They say that you are as beautiful as you are wise and ancient. Do you know who put up the Wall? Do you know what the Yildirims want with me?" Ilsi became flustered; she came this whole way because Ladala was said to know things, but she wasn't delivering on the process.

"If you are looking for a being who knows all, has seen all, and can see all that is to come, then I am not that person," Ladala answered. She looked displeased with the need to explain herself. "What I know, I know from my fair share of studying and pondering. I can safely admit that I know a thing or two about this life and the creatures that surround our lands, but I am no fortune teller or prophetess, nor can I tell you what you want to know about the Wall.

"I do know this. We caught wind of the Wall when the world was very fascinated by your people. You could say that your abilities to use the ice and never feel the cold are the stuff of fairy tales to people in Yling, the Pearl Mountains, and even this vast forest. People wanted to trade and learn about Ravenna's curious lineage. Then you disappeared. Almost like the mapmaker blotted you out from his map. We haven't seen or heard anything about your people since."

"It wasn't our doing," Ilsi protested. "We were trapped there. Reshma and I are the only ones who were able to leave our home."

"And you wish to return?"

"Yes," Ilsi said desperately. "I miss my Papa. He's the only family I have. My mother was separated from us," Ilsi said. "I have her diary. I think she had the same powers as me. That's all I know."

Ladala looked at Ilsi as if to gauge just how she was taking this conversation. Ladala was lounging on the couch, while Ilsi stood there, about ready to tear the room and all of its books apart.

"Do you know why they call me 'Lady'?" she asked.

"No," Ilsi said, shifting her feet and questioning the sudden change of conversation. "I could only imagine that you a part of a royal family of some kind."

"That's a decent guess," Ladala smiled, "but in this part of the woods, there are no royalty. You won't find a single drop of royal blood here."

"Then how did you become a leader? You have your own soldiers," Ilsi asked, gesturing towards the door where they knew a guard was standing watch.

"People listen to me," Ladala said. "I unite them. People trust my judgments. I can sense what a person or creature is capable of. They come and ask me what kind of person they are and they trust my replies."

"You said you weren't a prophetess," Ilsi stated flatly, her brows furrowed.

"If only! I just observe," Ladala said. "I see how people talk and carry themselves and I just give them suggestions. However, it's become a kind of tradition that people come to me when they're faced with heavy decisions."

"And this makes you a leader?"

"I put the best of the best where they can succeed. It makes for a happy people when each and every soul believes they are wanted and needed."

"What does this have to do with the Wall?" Ilsi said, her arms folded. "What does your position have to do with me and Reshma?"

Ladala sighed before continuing, "I may not have some immediate answers, but I will find them." She gestured to the curved walls that held thousands of books. "I see a look of leadership and bravery about you. You've traveled farther than most who have come for my counsel. That says much. If I am to help you, the best I can do is give you a good direction and insight on who you're dealing with. But give it time—I'll be able to give you a sufficient answer when the time is right."

"Pardon me asking," Ilsi said, then closed her eyes and

quickly shook her head. "I mean, thank you for offering your help. We appreciate it. I just want to know how much time you think this will take."

"Well, you barely got here," Ladala laughed. "I'll have assistants gather to help us—my librarian and some of the city readers—to help me narrow down the search once you've properly rested. You and Reshma are allowed to stay as long as you see fit, but I don't plan on wasting your time."

"It is flattering that you think me a leader," Ilsi said, even though in her mind she firmly disagreed with the interpretation, "but I don't know what to make of this."

"No one knows what to do right now," Ladala said. "People can't trust each other. Everywhere they look, their father, mother, or sibling is going away to join this elusive Yildirim force. They need a leader, and I have my suspicions that you could fill that position."

"And you can't?" Ilsi asked. She felt like she was being flattered into a corner to do something she wasn't happy to do.

"I could, but you would do better," Ladala said, looking her in the face. "A leader can oppose chaos and bring people together. People are preparing to fight a battle and they don't know why. Because you have *Swift* and now this power-enhancing ring— you can go places and do things that I or my people can't."

"This is far from the answer I was looking for," Ilsi said. She looked out the window and knew that her frustration was about to turn into tears. She tried to hold her emotion in check. "I wanted to know more about my past, not this future you think I should have."

For a few moments, no one said anything. Ilsi looked out

the window and blinked away a few disgruntled tears. Ladala sat in thought.

"I feel as though I've worn you thin before you've had your chance to rest," she murmured quietly. "Why don't you go rest. My associates and I will start preparing. Come and find me when you're ready. Hopefully soon we will have a better explanation for you."

The last thing Ilsi wanted to do was force herself to sleep. She wanted to be in here reading as well—if these books were written in a language she knew. But she knew that Ladala was right; she needed rest, and hopefully with time Ladala will be more forthcoming with whatever was on her mind.

In answer, Ilsi nodded.

"The guest rooms are further down this hallway. One of the guards can lead you there."

"Thank you," Ilsi said, bowing her head, "I'm just trying to piece things together."

Ladala rose and put a soft hand on Ilsi's shoulder.

"Everyone comes to me for answers," Ladala said. "I won't let you down."

———◇———

"What kind of help is she looking for exactly?" Reshma said sleepily. She stirred when Ilsi arrived and wanted to hear about their conversation. "You're just going to run around everywhere?"

"What kind of help is she looking for exactly?" Reshma said sleepily. She stirred when Ilsi arrived and wanted to hear about their conversation. "You're just going to run around everywhere?"

"We didn't get to that," Ilsi said, giving her a look. "She just told me that she likes telling people the potential futures they can have and told me I am some kind of leader."

"Ahh, the stench of responsibility," Reshma murmured, her forearms stretched over her eyes.

"I feel like I'm being forced into something I don't want to do," Ilsi said, looking over at Reshma. "like she will exchange her research for my services." She cringed slightly at the thought. It sounded harsh, but she wondered if Ladala was only being so accommodating because Ilsi was useful.

"You don't owe them anything that big. Not your life," Reshma said. "And why do they need you? Because you can use their ring?"

"Because *Swift* can apparently help them stop the Yildirims. Or help the people stop the Yildirims."

Reshma gave her a long look, then thought to herself as she stared at her lap.

"I know you want to go home," Reshma said. "It must've been hard to hear that you've barely met the lady and all of a sudden she wants you to help her with the Yildirims."

Ilsi sighed and nodded. "Yeah. Not exactly what I want to hear."

"So what did you tell her? Did you tell her to go find someone else?"

"I didn't tell her anything," Ilsi said. "And to be fair, she didn't have much to say, either."

Reshma rolled over on her stomach and groaned into her pillow. Ilsi laughed despite herself. She closed her eyes and tried to piece together what she had learned and what she had demanded to know. She started to wonder if Ladala had been planning for their arrival the whole time; Sebrah told them to go visit Ladala for help, and even the forest itself helped them find the land that no else one could find or enter. She didn't like the idea of being someone else's game piece.

"But what if I help them to stop the Yildirims?" Ilsi thought out loud. "I help them, and they help us. Our families will be safe from those soldiers."

"This doesn't sound like a short-term plan," Reshma said cautiously. "You realize you might not see your father or home for a very long time, right? If what Ladala said is true, there could be big things coming. Like a war."

"A war?"

"Don't ask me, I'm just speculating," Reshma said holding up her hands. "Apparently a lot has happened since the Wall came. The Yildirim problem being one of those things. They're more widespread than I ever would have thought. A lot of people are confused, afraid, and angry. Those three things never really lead to anything peaceful."

Ilsi's shoulders sagged.

"We're just islanders," Ilsi said, "what do we know of battling?"

"We know that you have ice and I have fire," Reshma said. "I'm just going to set the world on fire until I find my family."

"I've tried to fight it," Ilsi said, "but it's true. I'm not going to be able to go home and act like this was all a bad dream. They'll only find me."

"Ladala has guards," Reshma offered. "I'm sure Ladala will protect us if we do what we can to help."

"You're right," Ilsi mused. "I just hope we, you know, don't get killed."

"We've managed this long," Reshma said, snuggling deeper in her bed. "Has to be a sign, right?"

"Hardly," Ilsi retorted. She looked over at the large mass that was Reshma covered in downy blankets. She nestled herself in her own blankets and said softly, "You can hardly stave off sleep, let alone a Yildirim soldier."

CHAPTER 13

Ilsi got off her bed and looked out the window. She had repeated this routine for what she guessed was a few days. The house servants knocked politely on the door, brought them food, and left without a word. They ate their fill and slept or lounged around. Ilsi felt more exhausted from the extra sleep, rather than rejuvenated. She looked out the window and each day was just as lovely and bright.

She finally decided that she was done with resting and walked out of the room barefoot. She left everything, except her mother's book (stuffed in the back of her trousers). It was a fairly short trip back to the room full of books. The books must've been old, but they hardly looked dusty. The shelves appeared freshly stocked.

"Glad to see you again, Ilsi said," Ladala said from behind. "It appears as if you've caught us on a short . . . break."

"It's not a problem," Ilsi answered, turning, trying to pretend that she wasn't incredibly alarmed by Ladala's sudden entrance. "I'm hoping you've found something for us." She glanced over to Ladala, and noticed her clothes. She had apparently changed into a simple cream cotton gown with a brown vest laced over her chest.

"And I hoped I would find you here," Ladala smiled. "I thought you and Reshma would take advantage of the quiet to sleep, but . . ."

"We still need to talk," Ilsi said, running a finger over her ring absentmindedly.

"That we do," Ladala said. Ilsi stood in silence and realized that Ladala was waiting for her to continue.

"What kind of help do you need from me?" she said, her fists tight. "What can I do that you can't?"

"Since you have a rare gift, you can give people hope," Ladala said. She motioned for the both of them to take a seat. They sat again on the long couch in the middle of the room and Ilsi took her place. "If the people see that someone can match the Yildirims in power, they will rally and unite. They need to see that hope isn't lost."

"Why is this even your concern?" Ilsi said. "Why are you asking for my help when your people are safe? You could live here forever and be happy."

"Because I choose to defend our walls," Ladala said. "We had quite the scare yesterday. One soldier almost made it through. It's the closest they've come yet."

Ilsi's heart pounded at the thought of their sudden intrusion. She didn't like sleeping when she could be figuring things out, but if the Yildirims came again, she wouldn't have another peaceful rest for a long time.

"But I see the future with optimism, and luckily, the elves here trust me," Ladala said. "We could watch the whole world burn around us, but that wouldn't make us happy. Eventually whatever was left would turn against us."

"So," Ilsi said quietly. "If I'm to act like some unifier, than what do I do exactly? Send them to your gates?"

"You will tell your story to leaders and countrymen alike," Ladala said. "You can tell them that if they want help against the Yildirims, they can come see me. When they are desperate enough, they will want powerful friends like us to save their people from whatever the Yildirims want."

"Would we have to fight?"

"Yes," Ladala replied. "I can't guarantee anything except we will help you stay as safe as possible."

"But we can't fight. We just can't. And now if we go home or if we stay to help, we'll die," Ilsi said. She looked out the window and wearily added, "What would life be like if the Yildirims never attacked?"

"You would still be under the belief that the Wall could keep you in," Ladala said gently. Ilsi nodded, knowing the elf was right in that sense. She sniffed back the tears as she put her head in her hands.

"Do you know how to fight?" Ilsi asked quietly. "Have you killed people before?"

"Yes," Ladala said. "But we have the finest teachers. They know every weapon ever made and know a thing or two about conflict."

"Have them teach us," Ilsi said. "We need to know."

"You can stay and learn," Ladala said, "But I'm afraid that we all need to brush up. Our men and women on the border are predicting an ambush based on the rate and passion with which the Yildirims are attacking our borders." Ilsi nodded, looking up from her lap.

"I suppose that means I will help you," she found herself saying. "I will help spread the word."

"I have something for you," Ladala murmured, as she rose from her spot. She made her way towards the bookshelf. The room itself curved like a large egg, and the bookshelf began its curve right by the double doors. She took a book from the shelf in an arbitrary place and brought it to Ilsi's side.

"You're giving me a book?" Ilsi questioned, glancing at the book.

"I'm gifting what's inside," Ladala answered. She flipped it open. Inside there was a hole carved from the pages all the way down to the cover on the other end. It was a thick book. As Ilsi glance inside, she could see another ring sitting in there.

"You're the only one here who can touch it, so I will ask you to pull it out if that's all right," Ladala said, holding the book open patiently. Ilsi stuck her finger inside the hole and pulled the ring out. It was a bright silvery shine and Ilsi held it up for closer inspection.

Ilsi wanted to laugh. "Why keep it here in a book?"

"We weren't sure what to do with it," Ladala confessed. "It ate through a lot of other options. At the time, it was a safe place and it has worked for us."

Ilsi put the silver ring on her middle finger since the width suggested that it would fit there best. She felt a sudden rush that hit her like the roll of a drum. She was taken over, and she felt a strange feeling creeping up her spine and erupting in her brain. She felt so overwhelmed, yet so strong.

She closed her eyes. When she thought it wouldn't ever stop, it slowly died down. She breathed slowly, trying to calm her excited heart. She opened her eyes, and faced Ladala, who smiled.

"Are you all right?" Ladala asked, putting cautious hands on Ilsi's shoulders. "You look like it took your breathing air from you."

"I just feel really strong," Ilsi said, in a tone she hardly recognized as her own.

"Sounds like it was good that I remembered where I put that thing," Ladala chuckled.

"Thank you, milady," Ilsi murmured, still in awe in spite of herself. "Thank you. I must ask you why these rings are even here and why they help me but no one else."

"I know little of them," Ladala began, "but, I have fortunately come across some materials that helped me remember the story."

"Story?" Ilsi repeated.

"Every good relic has its legend," Ladala smiled. "*Swift* belongs in a class of magic once called the Powers of the Elite. Whole tribes of people possessed *Swift, Understanding, Fortune* and *Entice*. Each individual tribe had their own individual powers, and no one possessed more than one. These tribes had much more power than you do now. They all lived away from the rest of civilization. They all lived in relative harmony.

"A young boy from one of the tribes found two rings while playing in the mountains. He brought them to his tribal leader. Everyone was astonished by their power. It amplified their gifts beyond imagination. However, each tribe wanted the rings for themselves. They went into a long and bloody battle, all over a pair of rings. As it turns out, the people were decimated and only a small number survived. Weary of battle, the few decided that they would leave the troublesome trinkets in the forest and vowed never to gaze upon them ever again.

"They kept that promise. Eons later, we found one of them within the Elven realm. Because of their power, I forbade anyone to touch them. They are quite strong together, so we sent one of the rings as far as we could into the forest, and kept the other in this book. It broke the strong bond they shared when near to each other.

"The day the ring finally moved from the forest ground was the day you found it yourself. Since you already had *Swift*, the rings readily respond to you. Otherwise, you would have been burned, just like the rest of us."

"So my mother is . . . a descendant from one of these tribes?" Ilsi asked. "Is this what I'm to believe?" The idea intrigued her.

"It seems as that could be the only way. The few who survived the war decided to separate and wander into civilizations that knew little about them. Where they really went is lost in history. These powers give the wielder the ability to leap through barriers like you have already done. It takes a lot to create them, though," Ladala said. "It encourages my suspicions that the leader of the Yildirims must have one of these powers . . ."

"Otherwise, how could they come into Ravenna?" Ilsi said, finishing the thought. Ladala nodded her agreement. Ilsi wondered if the leader himself came or not. It made her cringe.

"So they could come in," Ilsi said. "I came in, and they're on the brink of breaking in, too."

"We're preparing a massive attack for whenever disasters strikes. The rest of us will have to find a new place to live if it comes to that."

"How awful," Ilsi said. This was no longer a safe haven. Instead, it seemed a disastrous slaughter waiting to happen.

"This is why you can step in to help," Ladala said. "How

can we compare to a leader who potentially have one of the Powers of the Elite?"

"Do you even know why they are like this? Why they're attacking?"

"Any soldier we capture gives us useless information," Ladala sighed. "They literally don't know what they're doing. Once their amulets are broken from their necks it's like they're totally different people. The oddest thing."

"That's what Sebrah has said. She's been tasked with finding them and interrogating them," Ilsi said. "I guess we had better get learning. We can help with what we know, but we need help ourselves."

"The three of us will start meeting more often," Ladala said. "I can afford to give you more guidance on where to go from here. Maybe we can sneak you safely off before they finally breach us."

"I have a feeling Reshma is way more excited to swing a sword," Ilsi said. "She makes for a fiercely loyal ally."

CHAPTER 14

Reshma, may I take a moment's time?" they heard. Reshma turned her head quickly to see Ladala scaling the hill to greet them. Reshma suddenly lowered her sword and shield, and Ilsi motioned to Diedre that she was stopping her fight, too.

"I only need Reshma," Ladala said, glancing at everyone. Reshma grunted that she would return and left her tools on the ground where she originally stood. She wiped the sweat from her brow as she walked quickly to meet Ladala's stride.

"Do you need water, or can we keep going?" Deidre said, breathing heavily.

"I'm fine," Ilsi said, raising her shield. She was insanely curious to know the nature of their private conversation. She wondered if it was a special job just for Reshma. What would Ladala have in mind for Reshma? What if Reshma was meant to be a leader, too? She was a warrior at heart; she only needed the opportunity to prove it.

She shook her head, determined to bury herself in her training. Reshma would be back eventually, and she didn't know how long they would have the luxury to train and rest—not with the impending Yildirim threat.

"Eyes on the prize, Ilsi," Deidre called. "You're anything but focused." Ilsi grunted and continued their mock duel. Deidre was the kindest of the four in the way she reminded her of her form and ways that she could expose herself to danger.

"Reshma is not in trouble," Basim tried to remind her gently.

Ilsi tried to ignore their observations and show that she was at least learning something. They were probably used to training elves who were born and willing to fight—Elven men and women who were hand-selected by Lady Ladala. She fought and practiced drills for another hour or so before Reshma trotted up the hill.

"Sorry for taking so long," she said. She picked up her sword and shield and said, "I'm ready to finish for the day."

"You can stay and finish up," Liselotte said, picking up her gear. "Ilsi's done for the day, that much is certain."

Ilsi let out a breath of air that she didn't know she had kept inside of her. Each day they had been training harder and longer, so she was relieved when her day was over. Reshma gave her a look that she didn't understand. She looked sad.

"I'll talk to you when I'm done," she said, then faced Liselotte to begin their duel. Ilsi walked alone to Ladala's home. She was certain that she could lie down and let sleep take the stress off her back. She had never trained so hard in her life.

But it wasn't just the physical strain—the mental also bogged her down. It was hard to perform as well as they asked of her. They never seemed satisfied with her progress. Reshma seemed like a natural. She probably thought it was enjoyable—just as much as Sebrah loved collecting and trading anything with a sharp point.

———∞———

Ilsi didn't remember falling asleep; she only remembered waking up. Reshma pushed at her arm gently and Ilsi awoke to the touch.

"How was training? While I was gone?" Reshma said. She was changing out of her sweaty training clothes and into something dry and fresh.

"Just about the same," Ilsi murmured as she pulled herself to a sitting position.

"Sounds better than my day," Reshma said. She sighed as she dressed in a light, airy shirt and a loose light brown shift over it. She collapsed in bed and splayed her limbs out to soak in the moment.

"I could sleep through supper if I wasn't so hungry," she moaned. "Ilsi, what am I gonna do?"

"Do about what?"

"I can't . . . I can't kill the Yildirims anymore." She closed her eyes like it was painful to hear herself.

"Why?"

"Ladala's soldiers came in with news from the outside," she replied, "about my family."

"They know where your family is?" Ilsi said. "That has to be good. It means they're alive, aren't they?"

"From what they said, yes, for the most part," Reshma said, pulling herself up to face Ilsi. "They saw most of my family. But not as prisoners. They were dressed like Yildirim soldiers."

"They have those," Ilsi paused, motioning to her neck, "those necklace things. Surely they didn't join because they wanted to."

"It's so strange," Reshma replied. She hopped off the bed to pace for a bit. "Do Yildirims really take no prisoners?"

"And why would they bring your family all the way out here?" Ilsi said. "They're probably really good at Fire Weaving. Enough to be 'groomed' into being soldiers." Ilsi felt in her heart that no matter what side they could be on, it was all about collecting the talented, the strong, and the eager.

"But I don't want to fight and realize my siblings are standing right there, poised to kill me like they never knew me," Reshma said, her body shaking. She let herself drop to the floor and held herself in a kneeling position, her arms bracing herself. Her shoulders shook and she wept quietly as Ilsi knelt and wrapped her arms around her.

"They're alive," Ilsi said softly. "That means that we can still save them."

Reshma nodding and sniffed, and solemnly vowed, "We will save them and the Yildirims will suffer fire and brimstone."

CHAPTER 15

"Y ou should be trained to fight like everyone else," Liselotte had told them a few weeks ago. "If you want to slip past guards and Yildirim soldiers, your unique talents could give you away. Lady Ladala has instructed us to help you learn these other tools. Sometimes you just have to resort to your fists."

At the time, Ilsi agreed with a grimace. While she didn't want to resort to violence, she didn't want the Yildirims to find them. She didn't want someone to turn them in because they stood out too much. She didn't want to stick out at all.

But she didn't want to be a monster.

Weeks later, Ilsi found herself hunting for practice. Ilsi's arms quaked slightly. Her arms were lifted up to her chest and she was holding that position for longer than she thought she could handle. She held a simple bow in her left fist and her right hand pulled back an arrow. She was poised to strike. Suddenly, she loosened her grip and relaxed her arms as she crouched down. She knew that her movement rustled the leaves and branches around her too much and she tried not to voice her frustration.

She instead held her bow horizontally. She scowled as her

target scampered away. She picked herself up and scuttled off to find a better vantage point.

There wasn't a single sound in the forest. Ilsi wondered how far away Reshma was from her and the goal. Reshma caught on quite quickly how to stalk in silence. Ilsi was catching on; it was just difficult to keep quiet and try to shoot the arrow as well. She knew her target would've already been done for if she just gave in and used her Ice Chanter gifts. Ilsi put such thoughts away and instead focused on how she could find higher ground.

She kept low and did her best to weave between trees and straggly branches. It was dank and muggy in the forest; she could tell they'd been at it for at least an hour.

Up ahead, Ilsi caught sight of a small flame. It flickered for a few seconds and then went out. It was a message. Ilsi ran faster to meet the signal flame, assuming that her footfalls would be evidence enough that she understood the flame. Soon, she approached Reshma.

She blended into her surroundings well enough; her dark skin and muted green garb made her almost impossible to tell apart from the moss covered tree trunks. She didn't look, but instead signaled for Ilsi to crouch down.

"You need to trust yourself more," Reshma whispered. "You had him."

"I don't have very many arrows left," Ilsi replied softly. "I didn't want to waste them in vain."

"I got the one from yesterday," Reshma insisted, "Today is your kill."

Today is your kill, Ilsi thought to herself. Probably because Reshma ended up getting the last six or so. *I'm only here because I want to defend myself, not kill soldiers.* She was about to reply, but they both hushed as they finally got a full view of their target.

It was a deer. It pit-patted around the forest, trying to nibble on leaves in the shadows. A hint of sun shone on the creature's coat. The coat was light brown; the back and tail were speckled with gold spots. They had waited long enough that perhaps the deer thought it was safe.

"He's right there," Reshma said. "I know you have the aim."

She was right; Ilsi hit the practice targets with much more ease than Reshma, but it was her hesitation that made it difficult to strike true. With as little time as possible, Ilsi aimed, closed her eyes, and let her arrow fly. Her eyes remained shut as she heard the beast give an exhale of life before she loosened her grip on the bow.

Ilsi opened her eyes to see Reshma get up from her position and head over to the creature. The arrow was stopped right between the creature's dead eyes.

"I would prefer to stay with my ice powers," Ilsi said quietly. "At least I can make it go away if I change my mind."

"You did great," Reshma said, as if not hearing. "You were brave for closing your eyes like that."

"Where's Basim?" Ilsi said. "He's usually here by now."

"Yeah," Reshma said. "It's too quiet in here when we're not being criticized or something." They went to the deer, half expecting their Elven instructors to come out of nowhere to analyze their performance.

The forest became horrifyingly quiet. It felt like the trees were trying to hold every last leaf still. Ilsi was sure that if the deer were still alive, it would've already left the deafening scene.

"Is this part of our training?" Ilsi whispered.

"If it is, we need to disappear," Reshma returned. Her

hands were already tingling and snapping with flickering flames. Ilsi could tell Reshma missed her fire. As they headed back a few feet into a space wild bushes and thick trees, they felt a hand on their shoulders.

"Get out of here!" Liselotte hissed.

"What? What's going on?" Ilsi whispered her demand.

"Grab your gear and get out of here," Roan said gruffly. "We came to find you and tell you that the Yildirims have finally breached the wall. You two need to leave immediately and never attempt to return."

"This is madness," Reshma said. "I thought we had more time!" The girls hastily picked up their remaining arrows and secured everything for travel.

"You can meet Diedre at the other side of this forest," Liselotte said, as she started to walk in the direction and pointed for emphasis. "Basim, Roan, and I will meet you and escort you somewhere safe."

"What about our things at Ladala's home?" Ilsi asked. Her thoughts instantly went to her mother's journal. Of all days to leave it at her bedside. She couldn't be parted with it.

"There's no time—"

Ilsi suddenly cast the *Swift* spell and in a whirlwind, she quickly found herself at Ladala's gates. The heavy doors were already open and she ran with her normal strength into the home. She tried to run as quietly as she could through the hallway, but the marble made it difficult for her to mask her frantic steps.

She ran passed the library room and noticed a few soldiers were rummaging through books; opening them and tossing them aside. *Are they looking for the ring?* Ilsi thought suddenly. She kept running and heard a voice protest behind her.

She picked up speed once she heard thunderous footfalls and shouting. Running was difficult with the shield and quiver of arrows on her back, but she made it to their room. It looked like someone was already there; the beds were mutilated and feathers were everywhere.

"You there!" a female soldier shouted right behind her. "On your knees! Hands behind your head! Start pledging your allegiance!"

Ilsi instead swung her fist in the soldier's face. Her knuckles were crusted over with ice and her blow drew blood.

"I'm not bowing to the likes of you," Ilsi retorted as she turned away. She headed to her bed and grabbed her book from its hiding place under a floorboard as the soldier recoiled.

"Stop and kneel!" the soldier said again, blearily. She was already on her feet and held a sword poised in her direction. Ilsi briefly glanced over her shoulder. The woman was dressed exactly like the soldiers that she met in Yling and the sight was like a reoccurring nightmare. She had a large black shield that had the image of crackling lightning raining down on a tree. It made the shield look ragged and broken. In her other hand, lightning was already hissing and crackling around the woman's fingers and palm.

Ilsi didn't want to waste time, and she didn't care what happened as long as she got out alive with her mother's book. She leapt out of the window without hesitation and tumbled to the ground as lightning sprayed out the window. It pricked and sent spasms through her limbs, but it didn't injure. She used *Swift* to return back to the forest. By the time the soldier and her comrades got to the window, the girl was gone.

Ilsi caught up with the others who were waiting at the border of the forest. She stopped by means of collapsing into a tree, but didn't waste time to get on her feet.

"What did you—" Deidre began. Ilsi realized that they hadn't seen her use *Swift* before. The elves gave each other guarded and confused looks as they kept going.

"They're looking for us in Ladala's home," Ilsi said, her breath catching up to her, "I didn't see her there."

"She's most likely at the border," Basim said. "She always spearheads an attack."

"Ilsi, they could've seen you," Reshma said, pinching her arm. "Don't get yourself killed already."

"It was worth it," Ilsi said, tucking her mother's book in her traveler's pack, and handed Reshma her own bag from home.

"Run with us to the grass ahead," Basim called over his shoulder, "There could be soldiers on the other side. We need to leave with as little evidence of absence as possible." Silence met his request as they followed him. Just as if from a dream, Ilsi and Reshma could see yellow and wilted grass up ahead.

Even though they had little training, the physical exercises helped them to at least keep up with the other elves while carrying the weight of what supplies they had, plus their weapons. As the others ran, Deidre ran up ahead and scaled a tree. Ilsi looked up briefly and saw that she was already high up and had arrows ready at her fingers.

Deidre shot a few arrows and for each arrow, a Yildirim fell out of the trees they were about to pass. Reshma yelled out in terror, wanting to stop and check the bodies.

"Fire Weavers never cower in trees!" Ilsi tried to yell out in comfort.

"What do you think we did in the forest before we found this place?" Reshma yelled back over her shoulder. A few soldiers jumped from the trees, spreading lighting with their hands. It spread onto the trees, and a few branches fell off from the shock. A few flames picked up as a result and Deidre jumped down from her position with an injured grunt.

With a sweeping hand, Reshma moved the flames in an arc and created a scorching circle in front of them as a shield. The soldiers couldn't come closer, but a few attempted to climb the trees around them, or shoot them with arrows. Reshma hoisted up her shield and walked through her own wall of flames like it was a curtain. She was gone for a few minutes while Ilsi and Basim attempted to pick out the soldiers that were scaling the trees. Ilsi tried to aim for people that didn't look a thing like Reshma or the other Fire Weavers.

The fiery wall soon disappeared with Reshma still in front and in combat with a soldier.

"Fire at will!" Reshma cried. She jabbed her shield towards the young boy who was fighting her. His amulet caught onto her shield and she snagged it away until the cord snapped. When the amulet fell, the young man realized where he was and fear struck his eye.

"Milady, I yield!" he cried, kneeling. He exposed his back. Reshma lowered her weapons, relieved at the sight. Suddenly, another Yildirim came from behind and hacked at the young man's back with a double ax.

"We bow to no one but our great leader!" the soldier cried— an older woman. The boy choked and collapsed onto the ground. Reshma felt like she was the one struck down, but immediately snapped back into the fray with her sword and shield ready. Deidre came to her aid, and took the woman's attention.

"Ilsi is already up ahead!" Deidre said. "Join her so we can get going!"

Ilsi was a few yards up ahead, running with Liselotte in front, and Roan and Basim behind her. Reshma joined them, realizing that the handful of soldiers were all either retreating or dead on the ground. She fancied herself a warrior, but it was hard seeing death for the first time.

As they reached the yellowed grass, it seemed like the fighting wasn't happening from their side of the city. While still in the Elven territory, they could see smoke rising above the trees. If the elves were in any way sad or otherwise affected by the sight, they showed no sign.

"You're going to take a path in Beast Forest and head towards Karno," Roan said to the girls. "We can leave you there per our Lady's instructions. We will then join Ladala in finding suitable lands for our people, as well as for our soldiers."

"At least you all have a plan from Ladala," Ilsi said, trying to take a brief moment to drink water from her flask. "She was going to go over it with us today, but I guess we won't have that chance anytime soon."

"You may not see her for a while," Basim said, "But she will watch the steps you make and ensure you as much safety as she can guarantee."

"Thank you. Thank you for everything," Reshma said, quieter than normal. "We wouldn't have made it out alive without your training."

"You'll get a lot of practice from now on," Deidre said. She continued as they found themselves back in the canopy of the forest once more. "Although you'll find that the world is a lot less forgiving."

CHAPTER 16

The wall still shimmered, like the film of a bubble. Ilsi instinctively held up her arms in front of her face as if to react to the brunt of the wall, when really it felt like walking through mist. Everyone passed with ease and gathered together in the thick, yellow weeds.

"A horse? We have a horse?" Reshma suddenly asked. Sure enough, as they turned around the way they came, a brown horse trotted through. It looked like it materialized out of nowhere as the horse and the rider came through the Elven border. A normal Elven foot soldier dismounted and saluted.

"Much appreciated," Basim said quietly. "May you subdue the enemy with grace and agility."

And with that, the soldier ran into the grass and disappeared.

"Probably to fight the Yildirims," Ilsi said. "You people think of everything."

"We elves think of everything," Liselotte corrected. "It's time you get going."

"Where exactly should we go?" Ilsi said. "We weren't officially briefed."

"Here," Deidre said, handing them a small scroll. It was about the length of her outstretched hand. "Ladala wrote this for you to read. Otherwise, make your way towards Karno. It's one of the closest cities. You'll probably pass a few hamlets to get there. None of us have really been there before, but I trust the scroll will tell you more. Try to lie low and keep quiet. One of us will probably come to ensure you both are safe."

"One of us will *always* ensure you're safe," Roan bowed his head quietly. Reshma stepped forward and they gripped each other's hands tightly.

"Thank you," Reshma said. "We owe you."

"Don't lose too much sleep over it," he grinned slightly, then put a hand on Ilsi's shoulders. "Keep swinging your swords. Just be careful. We really must go."

"Where are you going?" Ilsi asked, eying their silvery helmets with peacock plumes.

"We're tasked with finding safe lands for the survivors," Basim answered. "And anything that Ladala needs of us."

The girls nodded as the four elves put on their helmets and trotted in the same direction as the anonymous soldier.

"Never have I met anyone more dedicated to a cause," Reshma murmured as she mounted the horse.

"Says the fire girl who wants to burn down the whole world to find her family," Ilsi returned as she tried to mount behind Reshma.

"This saddle isn't exactly big enough for the both of us," Ilsi said, as she brought a foot back down to the ground.

"You're the fast one," Reshma said. "For now, I'll ride and you keep up. We'll switch when we're not fleeing for our lives."

"Then I have a feeling that I'll never get my turn," Ilsi muttered, as Reshma directed the horse into a full gallop. Ilsi ran with her own speed, her bow at the ready.

The woods were quiet in an eerie way. They remembered what it was like to make their way through Beast Forest and how unnatural it felt.

"How do people get around in woods like this?" Reshma asked.

"Are you asking me this now?" Ilsi said, still running. "Because if you are, you'll have to wait until I have my breath to answer."

"I mean," Reshma said, "They seemed so confident that we would make it to the hamlet-village thing. We hardly know how to get there."

"Use the map!" Ilsi shrieked. She sighed, and stopped running. "Just, pull out the map and see. I don't know how you expect me to keep up with a horse."

Reshma directed the beast back a few feet where Ilsi sat on the ground.

"What's wrong, Dash?" Reshma cooed, leaning against his neck and stroked his neck. The horse whinnied and shook its mane. As it clopped and stomped on the leaves nervously, Ilsi suddenly looked up.

"Oh, its name is Dash now?"

"I'm hoping it's a fast horse," Reshma shrugged.

KA-ZAAP! A streak of lightning skidded out of a thick area. Ilsi scrambled to one knee with her bow poised.

The horse reared back in fright. Reshma held on tightly to Dash's neck, and Ilsi rolled away to avoid the hooves. Two Yildirims stepped out of their hiding spots. Reshma cautiously took out a dagger from her belt and gripped the reins with the other hand.

"Woah, Dash," Reshma said. "Don't go mad on me."

"Keep the horse mum," one soldier barked.

"Give us the girl and we'll leave you to your business," the other said, motioning with the blade of his sword for Reshma to steer the horse away. The other kept his hands bare except for the sparks that flashed and orbed around them.

"She doesn't belong to anyone," Reshma growled.

"I said move!" the second one spat.

"I'll go with you if you tell us of any Fire Weavers," Ilsi cut in. They looked at her, as if stunned that she could speak. "Do you know of any Fire Weavers?" Out of the corner of her eye, she knew that Reshma shifted uncomfortably in the saddle.

"I ain't seen one," the first one said, pointing a spitting and sparking finger at her, "But I'm sure to remember to tell you when I do."

"*Swift!*" Ilsi suddenly circled the two men like a mini cyclone. Reshma and Dash pulled back to avoid the winds. Ilsi was at a speed so fast, the two inside only see a blur of Ilsi's blue attire. Without warning, Ilsi charged through her circle, and aimed her dagger at the second man. His eyes bugged out like a fish, and clutched his chest. She stopped herself completely. One man was clutching his body for air, and the other was sprawled on the ground.

"What the—"

Before the first man could finish, Ilsi quickly aimed her arrow at him, and kept it pointing at his forehead.

"I'd like to introduce you to my friend," Ilsi said in a low voice. "She wants to know about the Fire Weavers."

Reshma's whole arm flared up into flames as she hummed darkly. She had already dismounted and took a few quick steps towards the soldier. His own sparks vanished out of fear as she held out her hand a few inches from his neck.

"Have you seen fire like this?" she asked the soldier. She turned to Ilsi and said, "Yank off that bloody necklace to loosen his tongue."

Ilsi reached out to do the job, when the man suddenly raised his hand and shot a web of lightning into the sky. Reshma growled and gripped his neck with her fiery arm, and stuck him with the dagger in her other hand.

He crumbled next to his comrade. Ilsi stood there stunned. The flames suddenly disappeared from Reshma's arm as they both looked at their handiwork.

"We killed them," Ilsi said.

"We did," Reshma replied slowly. "I'm sorry. It's all I can think to say."

"I'm sorry, too," Ilsi said as she put away her arrow and crawled away.

"Were you really going to turn yourself in for information?" Reshma asked. "About my family?"

"I knew you wouldn't let them get very far," Ilsi said. She thought of the beautiful deer she shot. The same vacant look in the soldiers' eyes. She retched.

———◦❧◦———

KA-ZAP!

The sounds echoed from a distance, sending flocks of birds fluttering in chaos out of the forest. A man leaned against the wall of a building and he cocked his head slightly at the familiar sound. He lifted his chin to see the forest. He saw the spell.

"Wake up, you mutt!" the man said suddenly, and kicked a nearby soldier at the leg.

"I'm up, I'm up," he growled. He was young for a Yildirim, between child and man, although he looked strong enough to hold his own. His chin was coarse with young stubble. His black uniform was covered in earth and dust, but he otherwise looked like a shadow.

"I saw the signal," the man said. His uniform matched the boy's. The boy merely grunted in reply, as he brought himself to his feet.

"We should report it immediately," the boy said. "That signal is pretty far away. It'll take us a few days to even get close."

"You go, and get us some breakfast and hurry, boy!" the other barked. "We can eat first and wait. If she's in those trees, might as well wait until she comes closer to us."

"Or she will travel farther from the signal and we'll lose her in the forest," the boy replied, frustrated.

"Look, we've being doing this shit for a lot longer than you have," the first soldier said, popping his hand against the back of the boy's head. "Let the other yuppies get lost in those tangled woods, and we'll pick up whatever's left." The young man grumbled, running his hand through his black hair. He stood and stretched and then headed deeper the village.

He didn't like the idea of being bossed around by a coward. If they were really the veterans they claimed to be, they would know that their leader wanted nothing more than loyalty. At the moment, it was all the boy had.

He approached the local bakery. He could see a blond-haired lass inside, elbow deep in flour and dough. She was working next to the window to let out the unbearable heat, as well as the smell of her fine work. As if the girl could notice someone staring, she began,

"I have a huge order today and Papa—"

"Can I get the usual?"

The girl looked up, her round cheeks coloring.

"Oh hello, it's you," she said quickly, wiping her hands clean on her apron. The young man leaned against the wall as she peeked out.

"You've been gone for a while," she said, absentmindedly trying to clean the flour smear off her neck, "I was beginning to think you didn't like my pastries anymore."

"Haven't stopped thinking about them once," the boy said, transferring his posture, so one arm leaned against the wall of the bakery, and the other ruffling his hair.

"Come inside," she motioned with a wink and she disappeared. The boy smiled and followed through the door.

Later, the lad left the bakery with a few jelly pastries and a satisfied smirk. People clad in gray clothes murmured and avoided the boy. He thought it was probably because of the lightning bolt streaked across his uniform. He didn't see why they feared him. He sighed at the ignorance of the onlookers.

He carried a few for his crew, when one of the other soldiers in his group approached him.

"I've got the—"

"It's our lucky day, boy, that dame we've been searching for is in there!" the man said, slapping the boy's back triumphantly, "I got word from some others, so let's get going!"

"What about the others?" the boy asked. "It sounded like Geron wanted to—"

"Ahh, he doesn't matter to me! Give the others their pastries and let's go in there like real men. Surely we could earn higher ranks for doing what these other morons won't."

The man got his gear together, and tossed the boy's load to him. He dropped one of his bundle of pastries and they fell onto the ground. The lad still slung the gear over his shoulder, looked once at the soiled food, and grinned. He hastily met his other comrades and took a triumphant bite out of a clean and hot roll.

CHAPTER 17

Ilsi's heart hammered in her chest as she shakily drank out of her water flask.

"We should start moving, the village shouldn't be all too far," Reshma said as they packed up the remains of their silent lunch.

Ilsi couldn't think of anything to say for some time as she rode on Dash's back. She just let her body sway from left to right with Dash's gait. Her mind was still upon what she had done. She took a swig of water from her flask, and then spoke.

"I can't believe I killed a man," Ilsi said, with a touch of disgust. It's all she could think to say during the past few days.

"I understand. I feel bad too. But we just barely left the Elven territory a week ago. I highly doubt that will be the last time you will have to defend yourself."

While Reshma had a point, Ilsi still found it difficult sleeping at night, with the nightmares of the dead soldiers or their loyal friends coming back for her. She knew the cost of protecting her own life, but it still stayed with her. She wondered what Tyk or her father would think of her with blood on her hands.

"How do you keep your emotions in check all the time?" she asked quietly.

"I would rather them not see how much it hurts," Reshma said. "My emotions are none of my enemies' business." She made her way to untie Dash and his reins from a nearby tree when she noticed her own hairs rising up from her arms. Gooseflesh.

"Stay quiet," Reshma said, taking large, crouching steps away from Dash. She instinctively snapped her fingers and a few flames licked her fingertips, but then she quickly waved her hand and they disappeared.

"Sorry, old habits," Reshma said, shrugging at Ilsi. Ilsi understood; if she weren't trying to hide her abilities, she would be planning where she would create ice stakes from the ground.

"Something feels odd," Ilsi said, recognizing the same sensation on her skin. She hear and felt the shock again as her whole body seemed to go numb. She had been holding her bow, but suddenly felt her body twitch and her grip falter. Reshma fell over on her side and started to twitch. *More soldiers,* Ilsi thought to herself.

A young soldier with a medium build jump into the clearing from atop a tree. Ilsi wanted to react, call a spell, or anything that make him go away. Unlike the other soldiers, he wasn't wearing a helmet or hood. She could see his disheveled black hair and budding beard.

"Who is she?" the boy said, pointing at Reshma, "Who is this brown girl?"

Of course, Ilsi couldn't respond, with the paralyzing feeling in the air. Did the soldiers do this all the time? Was he gifted? Ilsi felt herself fall over, too, and gravity embraced her as she collapsed.

"Since when do you travel with a protector?" the young man said.

Zaps of light shot from his fingertips and towards Ilsi. The sensation freed her muscles oddly enough, as if to snap them back into normal function. Ilsi used the opportunity to move her limbs and her lips.

"Do I know you?" Ilsi said, pulling herself steadily to her feet.

"Get him!" Reshma said, holding her own bow and arrow poised. She rolled to her knees just as Ilsi was getting to her feet. "What are you standing there for?"

"I think I recognize him," Ilsi cried.

Before the young soldier or Reshma could respond, another soldier entered the clearing with his own sword and shield.

"Let's get her and get going already," he said. "What are you interrogating her for? This isn't your job."

"My job was to stay behind, but I thought better of it," the young soldier said.

"No need to get testy, boy," the older soldier said. "Or do I need to do this myself?"

"I've had enough of this!" Reshma said, curling flames forming in her hands. "If you think we're going with you, then think again."

"No! Don't hurt them," Ilsi said firmly, holding up a hand to stay Reshma's. "It's Tyk. He's my friend."

"What?" the older soldier protested. "You know her? What is the meaning of this?"

"Of course I know her," the soldier said. "She's the reason why we're here! She's why I'm out here with no way of going home. If she didn't keep running away and making life hell for us, none of this would've happened. He said so. We take her to Althod and then I can be free."

Althod? Ilsi thought to herself.

"Tyk, what are you doing out here?" she yelled in exasperation. The more she studied his face, the more that she couldn't deny that he had to be Tyk. However, she didn't know if it was really him, or if she was fooling herself.

"He's obviously a clever look-alike," Reshma said. "I hardly count him as a friend if he wants to turn you in."

"Leaving me and the rest of your people to suffer doesn't sound redeemable, either," Tyk spat. Ilsi looked at him with glossy eyes with a mixture of shock and disgust. *What happened to him?*

"I have no time for—" the older soldier began.

"No, we do this my way!" Tyk said, directing his focus on his partner.

"You're crazy!" the soldier said, pushing Tyk back with his shield. "You're just a foot soldier, telling me what you want to do! This isn't about you, you—"

"No!" Tyk shrieked. He grabbed the soldier's face and showered him with waves of lighting. The man convulsed and screamed until he dropped his weapons and sunk to the ground. He twitched and flailed until his whole body went limp.

"You . . . you killed him," Reshma said.

Tyk gave Ilsi a look to gauge her reaction. She just stared at him.

"Ilsi, it's not him," Reshma said. "He couldn't possibly be your friend, let's move on." She was making her way towards Dash who was shrieking and stomping.

"No, you're running away like a coward," Tyk said. He suddenly hummed a familiar spell, and Ilsi held out her hands to stop it. Spikes of ice shot up from the ground and headed in Reshma's direction. Ilsi's counter-spell deviated the course, creating a divide that separated Resham from the two Ice Chanters.

"Give me your necklace," Ilsi said quickly.

"What?" Tyk protested.

"*Give* me that stupid thing around your neck!" Ilsi replied with gritted teeth. She suddenly used her *Swift* spell, sending them both a few feet forward, and driving them onto a fallen tree. Ilsi had enough time to grab the amulet and the leather band. She yanked it off and tried to run away with her own strength. Tyk responded by clawing at her face and hair to snatch it back.

Ilsi turned and threw the amulet away from the both of them. It landed on the ground a few feet away, and Reshma torched the particular spot on the ground for a good few seconds.

"There," Ilsi said. "You should be back to your normal self." She was breathing heavily as Tyk got up. He responded by pushing her away and taking large strides towards his associate. His breath was haggard and rough.

"You just," Tyk began. "I just—"

"Talk to me, Tyk," Ilsi said, following him. "It's going to be okay."

"This," he said, gesturing towards the dead soldier, "is not okay."

He stared for a moment at the blackened patch of grass where his amulet used to be, then met Reshma with hard eyes. She returned the gesture. After a few moments of clenching his fists, Tyk suddenly darted away and into the trees.

"Don't go after him," Reshma said through gritted teeth. "I won't let you."

"You don't have to worry," Ilsi said. She sighed and collapsed to the ground and just lay there.

CHAPTER 18

It took them two weeks since the Yildirim ambush to finally see signs of life beyond the forest. The little village wasn't too far, judging by the telltale sign of smoke rising into the air from squatty chimneys. Ilsi and Reshma guessed that they would make it in time for supper. It unfortunately gave Ilsi a few more hours to think about Tyk. She was fairly sure that she just confronted him, but she wasn't sure if his attitude was the result of the amulet. She wanted to believe that was the truth.

"At least you know he's alive," Reshma said after an hour or so of silence. Though she didn't sound particularly happy with her statement, Ilsi knew that she genuinely meant it. Controlled by an amulet or not, Tyk was alive, and out of Dove of all places. It made her wonder if many more Ice Chanters would cross her path.

"True," was all Ilsi could say. At that moment, she wanted to gag; the back of her throat closed and she clamped a hand to her mouth. "What *is* that smell?"

"Smells like manure," Reshma said with a shudder. "I really hope we don't have to stay here for too long."

Ilsi shook her head. Reshma, hand over nose, shrugged it off, and prompted Dash to keep going. Well, the directional signs were correct, because just over the shrouded area, appeared Karno, clouded in a questionable and sickening smell. Reshma unwillingly guided Dash into the village.

The roads were ill-kept. The people roaming about were loud and boisterous, yelling, laughing and talking with one another. They tried to make way for Dash as he went by, not particularly happy to do so. There were small houses along a cobblestone street, which led to the heart of Karno: the market.

As Ilsi, Reshma and Dash moved along, Ilsi looked disgusted, and Reshma looked entertained by Ilsi's face. A man carrying a barrel swarming with flies noticed her disgusted looks, too.

"It's not like your shit smells any better," he muttered as he elbowed passed.

"Maybe we were sent here because no Yildirim would come here, and smell all of this."

"There's a lot of people," Reshma murmured. "After a week or so, we'll have no problems blending in."

Ilsi groaned in reply. She suddenly felt something gently shoved into her hand. She recoiled as a natural reaction and looked around her for a sign of someone familiar. She just saw people chattering and yelling at each other. A young messenger boy thrust something in her hand and hurried off.

She held up her hand and saw that she was clenching a piece of parchment. The message was written in small, hurried strokes.

We'll find you in two weeks. Stay low and relax for a while. Ladala sends her greetings.

"Well, word travels fast," Ilsi said, handing Reshma the note. "It has her seal, so I guess that means that they know how to communicate with us if they need to."

"How do you know it's her seal? This leaf symbol?" Reshma asked, examining the small wax circle stamped on the note.

"Looks like the image on their shields," Ilsi shrugged.

"Hopefully they keep talking," Reshma said. "I don't like the idea of sitting on my bum until they come to hold my hand."

"Doing nothing will only make it harder for the Yildirims to find us again," Ilsi said. "Maybe while we're here, we can find out if anyone has seen your siblings or parents."

"Sounds good to me," Reshma said. "Thanks. I see something that looks like an inn up ahead. Maybe they wipe themselves after they're finished doing their business."

"Reshma!" Ilsi scolded.

<hr />

After circling the town a few times, the girls had to resort to the only inn available. It sat tightly in the fork of the street, with one street splitting to its left and right, thus lending to the inn's triangular shape. The right path looked as if it led lower down to the docks, and the inn leaned slightly to the left to avoid sinking with the descending path. To the girls, it looked like a child's toy tower that was threatening to topple over.

"It has what we need," Ilsi shrugged. Reshma eyed the fish market that lined the road below it and the fishing boats in sight to the right.

"Ladala is testing us," Reshma said. "I'm sure of it. Dash will be fine at least—looks like the inn might have a decent stable. Smells like piss, but what can you do."

They entered the inn and asked for a room. A frail little lady gave them their key and a snaggletooth grin and directed them up the stairs. Once the girls made it to the first floor, they could already feel the tilt of the building.

"So," the little lady began, "How long 'r yeh stayin' with us?"

"Probably a few weeks," Reshma said, looking around.

"Oooh," the innkeeper crooned, "that's longer than most, I'd admit. Travelin'? Just th' two of you?"

"Just visiting friends," Ilsi tried.

"Oh-wee! I probably know them!" the lady answered excitedly. "Who're they?"

"Oh, just—"

"We're actually really starving right now. What is the house specialty?" Reshma cut in.

"That'll be the fish. We eat a lot of fish here," the lady answered happily. "Here is your room."

Ilsi sighed as the lady took back their key, opened the door for them, and gestured inside.

"I'll be lookin' forward to seeing you later this evening," the woman chattered on cheerfully, "Give my hello to yer friends from me. I'm Frita in case you need to know."

"I'm Ilsi and this is Reshma," Ilsi answered, gesturing between the two of them.

"Oh how lovely. Nice to meet you," she smiled sweetly. She sauntered off with small, quick steps and giggled to herself, "People give their children the oddest names nowadays."

The girls entered and Reshma closed the door behind them. The room had two pallets on the ground, a simple washbasin and a pot.

"Well, I'm surprised that this door has a working lock. And the room has four walls."

"It'll grow on you, I'm sure," Ilsi answered, rolling her eyes. "At least we have a great view of most of the city from here." They had one of the rooms with a window facing the fish market. If they leaned a certain way, they had a view of the main road before the fork.

"Frita's a friendly one," Reshma said.

"See, always thinking positively," Ilsi patted Reshma's shoulder.

"So we lie low," Reshma murmured. "How about we find some clothes to help us blend in? I'm sure the chipper lady knows where to go."

Ilsi nodded in agreement. The innkeeper was so excited to meet her new guests that she didn't have time to comment on how they were nearly armed to the teeth and wearing light, quality armor. Not to mention they were wearing trousers.

"What can we leave here?" Ilsi asked. Reshma was already removing most of her armor, sliding what she could underneath the pallet. There was a small, dingy closet in the corner and she was stuffing larger items in there.

"I'm taking a knife in my belt," Reshma replied. Ilsi stripped everything off except her shirt and trousers, and did her best to hide her belongings. She slung her bag back onto her shoulder, keeping her knife and mother's book close.

After consulting with Frita, the innkeeper, they were directed to a small shop. They were able to find some simple clothes, paying a lot more than they expected in the process.

"We can keep these along the way," Ilsi said. "I have a feeling that we'll be doing this a lot."

"Dresses," Reshma muttered. "You can do so much more in short trousers, I'm only saying."

They headed back to the inn and changed. They both wore simple, light brown and blue dresses that reached their ankles. The neckline was a bit low to Ilsi's liking, but the humidity was a tad more bearable. Reshma kept a scarf tied around her head and knotted at the top of her crown.

Ilsi's hair was beginning to grow again since Sebrah had cut it, and was inching its way just past her shoulders. She was able to braid her hair close to her head in a circular pattern so it arced over the crown of her head much like Reshma's scarf. She folded a kerchief into a triangle and tied it over her head with the knot tucked under her chin.

"You look like a regular fisherman's wife," Reshma said. "Once we get pit stains, we'll blend in for sure."

"How many more of those remarks do you have?" Ilsi said, raising an eyebrow.

"Enough to last us the two weeks," Reshma shrugged with a grin.

———◦◦◦———

Over a few days, Ilsi and Reshma trained themselves to walk slowly and calmly to blend in with the pace and lifestyle of the fishing people around them. Ilsi still took random occasions to look over her shoulder whenever she overheard someone talking about Yildirim sightings or attacks.

Ilsi was able to get work at the inn as a dish scrubber and Reshma got a post herding cows with Frita's grown daughter. They got used to people's friendliness; they recognized the two pretty girls as friends and didn't think anything of it.

"This is torture," Ilsi said. They were sitting in candlelight in their room after another long day. "I just want to know what we need to do. It's hard to pretend like no one wants to kidnap or kill us."

"Tell me about it," Reshma said, rubbing a wet cloth on her muddy, bare shoulders.

"Wait," Ilsi said to no one in particular. Hastily throwing a shawl over her shoulders, she lifted her skirts to put on her slippers before racing out.

By the time she returned, Reshma had already put a fresh shirt on and was stretched out on her pallet. Her eyes barely glanced over as she said, "What were you going on about?"

Ilsi was breathing hard like she had run the whole way. She tossed something towards Reshma and it rolled and wobbled to a stop.

"The scroll?" Reshma said. "We had this the whole time and we didn't bother to read it?"

"We knew to go to Karno," Ilsi said, allowing herself to collapse onto the floor, "and we thought they would arrive sooner to help us."

"Well maybe we can do a little something about helping ourselves," Reshma answered. The parchment was rolled up and sealed with Ladala's seal, as well as a sheet of leather for protection. They were so concerned about escaping and finding refuge in Karno, that Reshma wasn't surprised at their forgetfulness. She unraveled the parchment and read aloud:

If you're reading this parchment, then the Yildirims are currently giving us grief. I am probably off attacking them as we speak. It also means that you made it out alive. I trust my soldiers with my life, so it comes as little surprise that they were able to preserve yours. You were sent to Karno because its beaches and harbors border the great ocean of the North. You can very well go anywhere you wish from this location. You must visit the Sea King. He rules much of the North and South Ocean and the mermaids that inhabit those waters. He would make a powerful ally. We wouldn't want the Yildirims to get to them first. You will find that the king is very powerful. You will be able to match his with the rings that only you can touch. They will help you reach them.

Stay safe. We shall meet again—either in person or via my soldiers.

Lady Ladala

"Is she serious?" Ilsi asked.

"Says right here. Sea King," Reshma said. "And he is the king of the mermaids." They just lay there on their pallets and stared up at the wooden planks that lined the ceiling. For a while, they couldn't think of anything to say and just continued to stare.

"Did you know that mermaids existed?" Ilsi said.

"Heard of stories," Reshma said. "But they were only tales."

"I'd only heard of elves from tales, too," Ilsi murmured. She suddenly had no desire to leave their room; just thinking about Ladala's "mission" made Ilsi feel even more overwhelmed than she thought possible.

"So it's a good thing you have those rings, even though they singe like the devil," Reshma began, "but I don't see what she really has in mind here. Are you just going to sprint along the ocean floor or whatever is down there?"

"Well, I want to see what happens," Ilsi said. "She wouldn't send us here to do something we couldn't do."

"Your optimism is unrivaled," Reshma said. She put her boots back on her feet and slipped a dress over her shirt and skirt.

They walked from the village to the docks, following the

gentle downward slope as they went. They walked along long wooden planks propped up high above the lapping water. Ilsi sat on the dock, and Reshma continued to stand. The sky was shifting from blue to warm colors of red, orange, and purple. The ocean's blue sparkled like armor, making the smelly place actually pleasant. Ilsi just sat, looking at the water.

"How do you think we'll do it?" Ilsi asked.

"Don't know, my plan for tonight was to lay on my back and not do a thing. You're in charge," Reshma sighed. Ilsi didn't answer. She took of her boots, and let her feet dangle off the edge, and they didn't even skim the surface. She stood up, and flexed her arms, about to dive.

"What are you *doing?*" Reshma asked, not sure if she should be alarmed. It was almost night; the water would be freezing. Not to mention, everyone was cleaning their nets and finishing their work for the day. It wasn't like they were alone on the docks. Ilsi quickly flashed a smile, then turned and dove into the water. Reshma's mouth went agape.

Ilsi swam a few feet in below the surface. Feeling the weight of her clothes, she ventured deeper under the water. She noticed that the deeper she swam, the more her ears began to pop with the pressure. She felt her lungs begin to ache, like they were being squeezed more than possible. The pain began to throb in her head. She was set to prove something; but she couldn't even keep her eyes open.

Just as she thought her lungs would shrivel up like sun-dried fruits, she was tugged upwards around her torso. She looked up to see Reshma pulling her up, bubbles shooting from her nose angrily. Ilsi gave up swimming further down and reluctantly started back for air.

Ilsi and Reshma rose to outside air and choked on it harshly. Reshma rubbed water off her face roughly with her fists and shook her wet hair. Ilsi smoothed her hair back and out of her face and kept herself afloat.

"What were you trying to do?" Reshma cried, "And why did you try to go without me? I wasn't planning on keeping watch all night!"

Ilsi mumbled, "I thought the rings would do the rest, somehow. I'm supposed to go where others can't."

"Well, let's express our inner thoughts next time so we can discuss them and shoot them down, alright?" Reshma said. She tried popping her ears and then motioned to swim to shore.

"I guess I was waiting for something to happen," Ilsi said. "I was waiting for the rings to do something to help us, but they didn't."

"Let's dry off and try something else tomorrow," Reshma said. "And a time where the whole village won't be around to watch us."

Ilsi silently agreed, making attempts to avoid eye contact with anyone as their clothes dripped with dirty seawater. Ilsi followed, but couldn't find it in herself to smile.

CHAPTER 19

"Ilsi, turn down the lamp," Reshma moaned as she squeezed her eyes shut. Through her eyelids she could sense light gently pulsating; bright, dim, bright, dim. She grunted slightly in satisfaction when it became dark again and she slowly slipped back to sleep.

She heard a faint click and recognized it as a door clicking shut. Furrowing her brows, she rolled herself sluggishly in a sitting position to look at the front door. It wasn't shut all the way.

Reshma looked to Ilsi's pallet and it was vacant with her blankets in disarray. She shielded her sleepy eyes again with her hand as the pulsating light pierced them. It wasn't in the room, but coming from the window. She quickly got up and made her way to the window. She shook her head to move her hair from her eyes—the skies above showed swirls of lilac and pink as the sun was slowly opening his eyes, too. It was still early; no one had gone around and lit the lamps yet, so the streets were still dark. It made the pulsating light stand out even more as it illuminated houses and shops.

For a few minutes the source of the light wasn't visible, but the rays were still traceable. Once the source turned towards the water, Reshma could see what was making all that light.

"Confound it, Ilsi!" she barked. She scooped up a pair of boots, her cloak, and her dagger and ran out the room, slamming the door behind her. She thundered down the stairs like a storm and flew out the inn's front door.

Making a sharp turn out into the street, she looked towards the light's rays that reached past the rooftops surrounding it. She could finally see Ilsi, who was walking only in her nightgown. Reshma scowled and ran at full speed to catch up to her.

Her cloak spun behind her like sheets hanging up to dry as she twisted and turned to catch up with Ilsi. She finally saw Ilsi making her way to the beach. With her in sight, she pumped her legs harder into a sprint. She grunted under the effort until she got to the edge of town and jump down into the sand. The sand made it hard for her to move, but she was gaining on Ilsi.

"Ilsi!" she called, "What do you think you're doing? Are you crazy?"

Ilsi didn't respond to the question but kept walking, her pace quickening. Her arm was outstretched in front of her body, as if tugging towards her destination. It was her hand, or something on her hand, that produced the light.

She finally got close enough to Ilsi where she could grab her by the waist and stop her. Ilsi's head tilted back from the wind from the ocean and Reshma could see that her eyes where closed as though still in sleep, but her feet were kicking against Reshma and her hand making light stretched to go further, as though tugged by an invisible rope.

At first Reshma dismissed it on the account they were standing in sand, but she realized that her grip on Ilsi was weaker than expected. She planted her boots into the sand, but she felt herself moving with Ilsi as she began walking again.

"Ilsi! Stop! What are you doing?" Reshma cried. She flinched once she felt tide water sloshing in her boots. Ilsi was barefoot, but her face showed no recognition of what was going on. She waded steadily into the water until it soaked her nightgown up to her waist; the Ice Chanter shivered uncontrollably.

"Wake up, Ilsi! You've got to *wake up!*" Reshma yelled. Ilsi couldn't walk any more, but her legs kicked Reshma as she started to swim. Reshma tried to kick to keep up with Ilsi, still trying to stop.

"This is probably the *worst* case of sleep walking I've ever seen," Reshma said. She smacked Ilsi's face to see if she would register, but she was still unresponsive. Ilsi was suddenly jerked under water and her body slipped under the waves. Reshma felt the tug, too and she was pulled under. She held her breath and tried to pull Ilsi up towards air, but it was like being tied to an anchor. Reshma frantically kicked but Ilsi felt like lead.

The light was still flashing on and off, and Reshma realized that it was Ilsi's ring. She tried to reach them to pull them off and wake Ilsi up before they were too deep. Reshma grunted under breath trying to pry the ring off her finger, but Ilsi clenched tightly and jabbed Reshma in the jaw with her shoulder.

The light broke through darkness like sun through a tree's ample leaves and became bright and unbearable. Just as Reshma was about to close her eyes as well, the light revealed a menacing creature and quickly died away. Her mind was filled with images of hungry eyes and she stopped breathing.

Reshma slowly opened her eyes and noticed brighter colors surrounding her. She could see streams of bubbles chasing each other to the surface and fishes swimming mindlessly around her head.

She discovered she was lying on her back and tried to scramble to her feet, but felt her legs tied together. She pushed herself into a sitting position with her arms and looked down at her legs and shrieked. Her voice echoed and vibrated in a way that felt strange to Reshma and a hand automatically clutched her throat in panic. There was sound but no pain, no air.

She looked at her hands, front and back and touched her face in shock. Her skin was a light pink tint, pearly and shiny. Her feet had disappeared and instead she saw a large fin flapping against a rock impatiently.

Reshma looked over to Ilsi and she was sleeping comfortably in the sand, curled up like a kitten. Her blond curls were spilled all over her face and swayed with the current. She also had a fin that sparkled a deep turquoise shade. Her skin was a bluish shade and it twinkled slightly. The light was gone, but the ring still remained.

"Ilsi, wake up!" Reshma said. She couldn't move herself well without legs, so she threw herself onto the sand and pulled herself with her arms towards Ilsi and shoved her arm into Ilsi's side in attempt to roll her over and wake her. Ilsi moaned and bubbles rose from her lips as she flopped over on her back. She turned herself back to her stomach by herself, the first few movements done on her own accord, coughed slightly. Puffs of sand swirled in her face like smoke.

"I'm starving. Do you think they'll have some bread downstairs?" Ilsi mumbled.

"For cryin' out loud, Ilsi, you're a mess!" Reshma said, propping herself up by her elbows. "We're nowhere near land."

"Reshma, you have this weird rash, aren't you itchy?" Ilsi asked, prodding Reshma's cheek, "That shirt you're wearing looks odd." Reshma looked at herself and she had some sort of bright red cloth wrapped around her chest. Something like she would wear at home. She shook Ilsi's shoulder impatiently and Ilsi collapsed back in the sand.

"We're underwater, girl!" Reshma cried. "Your rings turned us into fish people!"

"That's right, you *do* look like a mermaid now that you mention it," Ilsi exclaimed, bubbles protruding her mouth. Ilsi was taken aback, because she spoke with a clear voice under the water. She propped herself up with her arms and stared in childlike interest at her sparkling fin flapping slowly back and forth. She put her support on one arm and massaged her forehead.

"Wait," Ilsi said, starting to stare at herself in horror, "I'm awake, aren't I?"

"Yes, you are!" Reshma said, smacking her forehead in impatience. "One minute you were sleeping sweet dreams, and the next you were sleepwalking out into the water."

"I could've killed us both," Ilsi whispered, looking at her rings and then her surroundings, "I'm sorry, I didn't realize what was happening. Why did Ladala not tell me we could just turn into fish?"

"We'll ask her the next time we have a quill and parchment," Reshma said, looking around.

"Okay," Ilsi said, looking around, trying not to lose her

cool, "So we're mermaids. We're mermaids. We are literally underwater, not dead, and I have no idea how this just happened. I guess this is an easy way to meet the Sea King. Of course it's not something I *planned*—"

"Shh!" Reshma cautioned. She fell back and dumped sand over herself. "I hear something coming!" She tried keeping her fin still and covered it heavily with sand and dug herself into the sand quickly to bury herself further and kept hiding her figure. Ilsi did the same until they blended in with their surroundings. They waited patiently for what they expected to come.

A large shadow darkened the scene above them and swam over the twin heaps of sand. They watched silently, noticing that the approaching creature looked a lot like them. The creature looked like a young woman with light brown hair that swayed around her face and back in large knotty curls like tentacles. It complemented her pinkish-purple fin and skin.

From where Ilsi lay hidden, she thought to maybe ask her for help and figure out what they could do besides laying around in the sand. The young mermaid must know where the Sea King is. She shifted her body slightly and clouds of sand puffed up and coiled in the water.

The mermaid turned and saw Ilsi's fin swerve like a cat's tail. She reeled back and she screeched. The girls flinched at the high-pitched alarm. She swam over them quickly and disappeared from their view.

Before they could react, they felt sharp shoves as sand flew everywhere. Once the sand subsided, Ilsi could see that a few broad male figures that were bare-chested except for breastplates. They reached out and swept away the sand and lifted the girls from their hiding places. They were holding what looked like ancient harpoons. Whatever they did say to Ilsi and Reshma, the girls couldn't understand.

Ilsi only complained and shrieked at the prodding.

"Hey!" she screamed. "Let us go! We're humans—we're friendly!"

The mermen in response bound their hands behind their backs and hoisted them over their broad shoulders. Ilsi had no choice but to stop moving. She breathed heavily and gave Reshma a wary glance.

"You wanted to see the Sea King," Reshma said, breathing heavily. "So we're going to meet the Sea King."

The mermen swam on and the young mermaid who had discovered them darted back and forth, as if frightened. Reshma scowled at her. The mermaid shuddered and darted off behind a large growth of coral. They entered a cave and there was darkness for a few minutes and a heartbeat.

When they came out of the darkness, Ilsi scrunched her eyes from the light pouring in. Rays of light cut through the water like long ribbons, causing everything in sight to glitter and sparkle. Ilsi could only see behind the merman carrying her, but she was still able to admire the kaleidoscope of colors. Fish were swimming in schools, and everything was in different colors and sizes.

Ilsi admired the sun's rays that lit the area; everything glittered brightly in the rippling current. She met the stares of mermaids and mermen who were swimming past. The two guards dragged the girls on through crowds of merfolk, which parted as they approached—some of them screeching and making high-pitched hissing noises.

They halted at the foot of a lengthy coral patch, where a large merman sat. There were more mermen armed in the same fashion as their captors, harpoons at the ready. The merman sported a long turquoise beard, and clenched a large staff in hand, with a majestic crown on his head decorated with sparkling stones and pearls. On his forehead, was a picture of an open eye, and it seemed to be staring at Ilsi from where the soldiers held her.

He was joined by a dazzling mermaid, with dark turquoise hair with pearls and diamonds dotting her hair. Dozens of mermaids swarmed her affectionately, adding more treasures to her hair, neck and tail fins.

The soldiers halted before the couple, as more guards surrounded them and the mermaids fled and swarmed behind the couple. The area became quieter and quieter with the sight of Ilsi and Reshma being carried.

The Sea King waved his hand casually and the mermen pushed their captors off their shoulders and Ilsi and Reshma couldn't do anything but fall into the sand. People around them giggled nervously at them. They girls flipped around like fish left to die on a dock. The merman spoke again in their mertongue, and Ilsi let her shoulders sag. She had barely sworn herself to help Ladala and it seemed like she was already failing.

The mermaid king furrowed his brows in thought, then raised his arm and called for someone. Swimming gracefully, a younger mermaid approached them, her light turquoise hair trailing behind her. She looked just as adorned and fancy as the mermaid sitting beside the merman. The merman, whom Ilsi started to assume this had to be the Sea King, began speaking, and pointed at Ilsi. The mermaid grinned, and to their astonishment, began speaking.

"Having trouble swimming?"

Chapter 20

"You can understand us? And you've been carrying on like this all this time?" Reshma blurted. The queen flinched, and looked slightly offended.

"We can perfectly understand everything you say in your garbly language, but you cannot understand us. Most of us won't speak to you in your language," the mermaid said, the large merman nodding quietly in approval. The mermaid gestured to the couple on the thrones. "This is my beloved father and mother, who reign over us all, and I am Gürsel. What it is that you want with us?"

"Your highness, we don't want any trouble. We are humans, I promise. When we dove into your . . . waters, my rings just—"

"Your rings?" Gürsel said, grabbing Ilsi's hand to examine it. The other mermaid trilled with awe. The king's eyes widened, as he strained his neck to see them. Gürsel tried to touch them, but immediately pulled her hand away and hissed.

"They are very much like the tales say," Gürsel said, examining the rings closely, but not reaching to touch them again, "Who gave them to you? And how are you able to wear them?"

"They belong to me," Ilsi said, pulling her hand back. Her

speech was followed by an amount of hissing and scowling. She tried again, "I need them to help Ladala."

"What does she want with us?" Gürsel hissed. The king's eyes narrowed.

"She's the one that sent us here," Reshma said.

"We ave to stop the Yildirims," Ilsi added quickly. At this the queen arose from her sitting place and began yelling at her husband, which Ilsi was glad she couldn't understand. She kept pointing accusingly at her right between her eyes. The guards grabbed Ilsi and Reshma again and lifted them by their arms. The king tried to patiently lead his queen back to her seat and wearily leaned his chin into his hand.

Ilsi wished she could bury herself in sand again. The warriors around them stiffened, awaited command and the mermaids attendants fled in the wake of their queen's ferocious fury.

"If there was any group of people that deserves to be destroyed mercilessly, it is those fiends. What I wouldn't give to slaughter one or two myself," Gürsel hissed, "And that's just what I feel—you should be glad you cannot understand what everyone else feels. If not for their gill-less necks, they would raid and kill us all."

"They *did* raid my homeland. They tried to kill my clan. I think I know a bit about wanting revenge and so does Reshma," Ilsi pressed. "And now they are trying to find me, because I can wear these rings. We've come for your help to stop the Yildirim from getting too powerful."

"I think you're much mistaken," Gürsel countered, "for we have good reasons to believe that they are looking for my father, the king. Not a normal human girl."

"The king?" Ilsi said, trying to avoid staring at the eye on his forehead. "But he doesn't have *Swift*. Does he?"

"Silly girl, you couldn't possibly know what you're talking about," Gürsel returned, folding her arms and clenching her jaw.

However, the king spoke and Gürsel turned in surprise. She protested vehemently but her father just shook his head. He held his wife's hand and calmly spoke with his daughter. Her shoulders sagged a bit and glowered at Ilsi and Reshma.

"My father wishes to hear your message," Gürsel said quietly. She slapped her fin in the water as she swam towards her mother and sat next to her with a stiff and cold posture, not taking her eyes off Ilsi.

Ilsi suddenly felt the grip on her arms loosen and she sank slowly in the water like an anchor. She landed on a large rock before the king and queen, but felt that her view made them look larger and taller.

She timidly began her story, starting with how she discovered her powers. She told them about the Yildirim's doings. She told them about Ravenna. She explained enough to prove she had nothing to hide. The queen looked pleadingly towards the king as he instead looked at Ilsi in thought.

The king began staring straight into Ilsi's eyes and she couldn't turn away. He murmured something, and the "eye" on his forehead suddenly blinked and flashed brightly for a brief moment. Ilsi suddenly felt an unnatural feeling go through her spine, as if her thoughts were being examined, like someone leafing through a book. She finally broke eye contact with the king before looking at Gürsel for an explanation.

"My father has the gift of *Understanding*, one of the four Elite Powers. My father is the only merman with the power to decipher truth from lies," Gürsel tried to explain "He says that your story is true, which is amazing considering your race."

Reshma rolled her eyes at the remark.

"Why have you come here?" Gürsel shrugged. "Why help us if you don't know us?"

"The Yildirims collect people," Ilsi said, gripping the rock. "They put people in their army that are special. I don't know why. They use their minds and ungodly magic to control people. They've already raided the Elven realm. They'll come for you."

"Ladala and her little wall?" Gürsel scoffed.

"If you think water and pointy forks will protect you, you're sadly mistaken," Ilsi found herself saying. "If you support Ladala, she can help you."

"Help us how?" Gürsel shrugged. "She has her own problems and her own people to worry about. Her city was just invaded as you said. And she can help *us*? Why send two young humans to give her own message?"

"Do you not remember?" Ilsi said, gesturing to her own hand.

"My father would do many better things with those rings than you," Gürsel replied once she noticed the shine. "He will take them from you if he so chooses."

"So you accept?" Ilsi asked, her voice unnaturally shrill. "Your father is willing to help stop the Yildirim? Because I plan to help stop them with these rings. I don't know if there's a better cause than that."

"How dare you, two-legged—"

"Stop," a deep voice interrupted. Gürsel turned around and realized that voice belonged to her father. Ilsi snapped her mouth shut, forgetting that she was the only one needing translating. He said simply, "They are guests. Be kind."

"Your Majesty," Ilsi began, not sure how to address him,

"Will you consider our offer? To be allies?"

He stared at her again, the piercing eye focused on her. He groaned and muttered and looked to his daughter beseechingly. She sighed in annoyance and looked to Ilsi and said tartly, "If we want to consider your offer, we will call on you. You can leave us in peace until then."

"Is that a no?" Ilsi replied tersely.

"Yes! Now leave," Gürsel said before excusing herself.

⊷⊶

Ilsi curled up against a large rock protruding out of the sand and tried to control her fin. She tried lifting her lower body to make it flap against the sand but it slinked back and forth instead. It was useless to try; she was lost without her legs. She let go of the rock and her arms rested weakly at her sides.

"This is so stupid," she moaned loudly. "We get transformed into mermaids and we can't even swim. We've been sent here on Ladala's ridiculous errand, and Gürsel is the only one who can talk to us. This isn't what I expected."

"Well," Reshma answered, "At least I haven't seen a Yildirim for days, or however long we've been here. What's wrong?"

Ilsi felt lumps of frustration in her throat, threatening to surface and explode.

"I just thought this would be easier. I thought Ladala would be able to help us take care of this. Now we're just two lame mermaids trying to convince the *Sea King* that he's stupid if he doesn't join our side," Ilsi said through gritted teeth. "What am I going to say or do to get them to reconsider? They deserve what they get." Her fists shook slightly and she tried to calm down and swallow her anger.

"You both are much too young," Gürsel's soft voice murmured. Reshma turned her head to see Gürsel gliding smoothly towards them.

"What are you doing here?" Reshma muttered.

Gürsel glared at her, and Reshma paused. Gürsel was treading water slightly and loomed over Reshma and Ilsi.

"If you let me talk, I might try to help you, you know," she replied coldly. Reshma frowned slightly in contempt and waited for Gürsel to continue.

"Help us how, exactly?" Ilsi asked. "We're only here to try and help *you*."

"That remains to be seen. You have quite the load on your shoulder. I am sure you two won't even understand the extent of it," Gürsel continued, looking at Reshma, "You're the second person I've met that has one of the Four Elite Powers."

"The Four Elite Powers?" Reshma asked incredulously. Gürsel rolled her eyes at Reshma.

"You love the sound of your voice, don't you? My father and Ilsi here possess two of the four powers. They are *Fortune, Understanding, Swift,* and *Entice*. There is a man, named Althod, the leader over all of the Yildirims, who wishes to possess all four powers to add to his strength," Gürsel said.

"Lady Ladala already told me a bit about this," Ilsi said. "But why would he even try?"

"To have all four, it would make you more powerful than every living creature. To be able to possess all four would be," Gürsel explained, "like being what you humans call a god."

"A god?" Reshma whispered, "But people can't become gods, can they?"

"You're asking one who doesn't believe in a deity in the sky, but in the ocean," Gürsel replied smugly. "Besides, those powers are dangerous enough alone, to combine all four is foolish."

"How is it even possible for one person to have all four? Isn't it passed down in the family?" Ilsi asked.

Gürsel rolled her eyes and began plucking sea weed blades out of the sand. "We don't know that. We hope he's running after a foolish desire."

Reshma snorted. The mermaid definitely preferred to know things rather than admit lack of information.

"As for you," Gürsel said, smoothly, smiling at Reshma, "Why exactly are you traveling with her, anyway? In it for the scenic route?"

"No," Reshma answered defensively and hastily, "Unlike most, I'd like to help my friends, even if there's no visible reward on hand. Plus my family is in danger. The royal family has compassion on protecting one's family, am I right?"

"Hmmm," Gürsel returned, "Well, you'll be doing a lot of 'helping' with no sight of any form of reward for a long time, if you live that long."

Ilsi shot her friend a look as if to reassure her of the opposite. Reshma just stood there with a set jaw.

"Why are you telling us all this?" Reshma said.

"To prove to you just how ridiculously little you know about what you've promised to do for your Lady," Gürsel returned. "You're both mad if you think that you know enough or can do enough to help *us*."

"We should just go," Ilsi muttered. "They don't deserve our help if this is how they'll treat us." After Gürsel excused herself once more, Ilsi collapsed in their private space away from the rest of the court.

"It was rough, but they didn't exactly reject you," Reshma said.

"Why are you not as angry as I am?" Ilsi said. "We're risking a lot just to come here to send them a message and they won't take it."

"This is a battle we're talking to them about, not a guild or secret society," Reshma responded. "Besides, I *am* mad, but I'm more stubborn than they are. We can keep talking to them at least until we figure out how to get our legs back."

"You're right," Ilsi sighed. She looked at her hand as they swam. She wondered how long the fin would stay there and when the rings would somehow decide to change them into something else. Despite their usefulness, she had no idea how to control them.

"I just wish they weren't so stubborn."

"Well, how did Ladala convince you?" Reshma asked. Ilsi shot her a quick look, her eyebrows pinned together in annoyance.

"You make it sound like I was fooled into this responsibility," she said. "I believe that she can really help. She seems to have a lot of power herself and know a lot of powerful people who could do something. They just need more people to join them rather than fight them."

"So you were impressed by her skill set?"

"Stop that," Ilsi returned, pounding her hand on the rock. Her claw-like nails drove into her flesh and she muffled a remark.

"She can help me. She can help me help my father and whoever else is hopefully still alive."

"Okay," Reshma said. "That's exactly why I'm for it, too. It's personal. So, you got to get personal with *them*."

Ilsi paused and reflected on the notion. "I have to make them feel uncomfortable. Like, they would lose something precious if they don't join us."

"Don't threaten them," Reshma scoffed, "They already don't think we should be taken seriously."

"The king does, a little," Ilsi answered. "or, he at least believes me."

"Then maybe you should appeal to him, rather than Gürsel or whoever doesn't want to understand."

Chapter 21

Ilsi and Reshma couldn't really move or function unless they tamed their tales. As a result, they learned quickly. They still had to rely on their arms for guidance while the others kept their arms calmly at their sides. But they managed to get themselves back into the Sea King's court once again the next day.

"Do you think he just sits there all day?" Reshma mutters. "Or does he wait for crazy stuff like this to happen?"

"You can ask him," Ilsi teased. "He seems like quite the talker."

Gürsel looked minutely surprised at their arrival. Her face pinched into a small smile—something Ilsi was sure took more effort than it appeared—and cocked an eyebrow.

Ilsi briefly glanced around, taking in the scene. If she ever stuck her head in a beehive, she was sure it would look similar to what was happening before them. Mermaids and mermen were swarming the area; some would enter the large expanse and others would leave. Despite the fact that thousands of souls were present, she was sure that none of them were really paying attention to the two of them. She wondered how far some of them traveled to come this way. Did the Sea King rule all the waters?

It probably explained why only Gürsel was the one to notice Ilsi and Reshma's approach; everyone else was preoccupied with themselves.

"Interesting," Reshma muttered, leaning towards Ilsi, "They had an army of merpeople armed to the tooth when they brought us here. Now there's not a single one." Reshma was right; no one was wearing armor and, at least in the vicinity of the king, no one was wielding a single weapon.

"So they *are* afraid of outsiders," Ilsi murmured aloud. She tucked the idea away as she looked at Gürsel and said, "We'd like audience with the royal family. May we speak?"

"You may speak," came the formal reply. "What is it that you wish to inform the royal family?"

"I wish to inform the family what they already know but might be too blind to see," Ilsi said icily. "The Yildirims have some kind of power that allows them to break barriers. They invaded my homeland through a wall that none of us could break with mortal or magical strength. They came in and kidnapped people. They're probably still there.

"If you think you're safe just because of how deep in the ocean you reside, you should consider what lengths this group will take to do the same to you," she finished. It hurt her personally to talk so much of what they did to Dove and what they might still be doing.

A flicker of recognition passed over their faces as they listened. Probably because they understood her words but hadn't formed an opinion about yet.

"And what will joining Ladala do for us against them if they have this power?" Gürsel asked.

"A splash of water might get a man wet," Ilsi said, "But a wave could drown him. They are growing in numbers because of how they use their power to control innocent people. If enough of us gather together, we can stop them. There's no point to idly stand aside."

"Is it possible that Ladala is seeking favors because we would make a worse enemy?" Gürsel said. "She trusts that they would use our numbers and influence to foil her plans."

"They're after the king, your father," Ilsi insisted. "They just want him for his *Understanding* ability, not the power he possesses over the seas and the merpeople. If you or he cared about that, it would be in your favor to consider the offer. I would know since they tried to come for me."

"Leave us," Gürsel said quietly. "The Yildirims will want to collect you, Ladala will want to collect you, but they won't collect us."

"What?" Ilsi cried incredulously. She looked to the king, almost wishing for him to read her thoughts and her heart once more just to prove her intentions.

"We refuse to be allies. You can stop wasting your mortal breath convincing us. Ladala's threats or prophecies don't hold weight to us," Gürsel answered. "You must go now or we will send for our guards."

Ilsi and Reshma stared dumbly at the royal family, earning a stern, somber stare from all three of them. Reshma sighed and looked down. Her fists clenched.

"We've shared the warning twice," Ilsi said. "I hope you're right and you're strong enough to withstand what's coming."

Gürsel shook her head. "You have so much to learn."

With that, Ilsi used her arms to leave as quickly and

gracefully as possible. Once she wasn't facing anyone, her face hardened and twisted into an enraged frown.

"Don't worry about it," Reshma murmured right next to her, "Ladala didn't guarantee that everyone would listen and accept. Let's just get out of here and get on with our lives. Other people will listen and get a chance to do something."

Ilsi didn't immediately respond, although she could feel biting words leaping to her tongue. She just set her jaw and nodded.

———◦○◦———

After a while, they were both far enough from the crowd that all they could hear and feel was the gentle swaying of the tide. Ilsi swam towards a clean patch of sand on the ocean floor and looked up at the water and fish above. Reshma joined her, except she rolled over on her stomach and groaned.

"How do I get this fin off?" she said, her face cradled in her hands. "I don't like mermaids anymore. Not like I formed an opinion beforehand, but now I think I've picked a side."

"As soon as I figure it out, we'll get back home," Ilsi said. "I don't even know where we are. And to think, I was so close to turning Gürsel's tail fins into a block of ice."

Reshma laughed right out and said, "That would be so low. Not to mention dangerous, seeing as how we're completely surrounded in water. But I like your thinking."

"Shall we swim to the surface and get our bearings?" Ilsi said.

"Sounds easier than climbing a tree," Reshma answered.

They looked up and began sweeping their arms in large arch motions and tried to swim as straight up as they could. It took them quite a while, but they eventually surfaced.

Ilsi was first to gasp for air; not because she needed it, but she was surprised at how cold and loud it was. She could hear everything; birds calling, the waves, the wind guiding them. Reshma gasped too.

"This is so odd," Reshma said, shivering. She dipped her head so only her eyes peeked above the water. "But we're definitely still mermaids."

They turned themselves around to get a sense of where each direction headed. They surfaced during the evening time, so it was almost too dark to see. Ilsi realized that their eyes were changed to not be as hindered by the nighttime. She could make out shapes but very little detail.

"We're very far from shore," she said.

"Can you see land?"

"Barely. Does that count?" Ilsi said, pointing. She had no idea as to the direction.

"I think it's a ship," Reshma said, "Or my eyes are tricking me into thinking that weird shape is moving away from us."

"Are you tired?" Ilsi asked.

"From swimming? Hell yes," Reshma replied.

"Can we try to swim for a bit to start making our way home?" Ilsi tried. "We can rest on a rock or reef below and then keep going."

"Sure, yes," Reshma answered. "Are you all right?"

"No, not really," Ilsi bristled. "But I will be happy to report to Ladala that we tried, even though I thought *Swift* was supposed to help us. And I'll be asking her what my 'ancestry' has to do with them hissing and acting all deranged."

"Tell me about it."

———◦◦◦———

They surfaced again to better understand their surroundings. It was much brighter outside, but with the light came the realization that any form of land they thought they saw wasn't real. It was just blue waves in every direction.

"How do we know which direction to take?" Ilsi said. "How did we ever get this far, anyway?"

"It could be those weird rings. But I wouldn't be surprised if mermaids had anything to do with this," Reshma replied. Ilsi responded with a dubious frown. Reshma continued, "You hear the stories of mermaids singing and otherwise luring sailors to their death. What if they somehow got us lost?"

"I'd like to think that when they asked us to leave, they wanted us to leave the water, not dwell in it," Ilsi muttered. "Maybe we can retrace our path by going underwater again."

"You know it all looks the same down there," Reshma sighed. "Maybe we can focus on finding some kind of land, changing ourselves back into our original selves, and hopefully flag down a boat or ship that can take us back to the fishy village."

"Or I help," someone said behind them. They splashed and turned to see another mermaid bobbing just above water. She was the same girl with brown, flowing hair. It strung over her face but she didn't seem bothered by it.

"You, we've seen you before," Ilsi said, startled by the mermaid's attempt to communicate with them. "Who are you?"

"Dalit," came the simple reply. "You lost."

"Yes we're lost," Reshma said calmly. "Do you know where we are?"

"A day swim to fish people."

"The people who eat fish?"

"Yes."

"Well, we need to swim to people," Ilsi said, nodding encouragingly. "Can you guide us?"

This was met with a blank stare.

"Swim . . . with us? Go to people?" Ilsi tried again.

"I take you to people," the mermaid smiled, pleased with herself.

"This is great," Ilsi whispered to Reshma as Dalit dove underwater. Her fin flopped up almost as a beckoning gesture before she completely submerged.

"If something bad happens, let it be known that I don't care for mermaids," Reshma said.

"Maybe it's just the royalty that's a bit sour," Ilsi said, starting to follow Dalit. "This one may save our lives."

CHAPTER 22

Ilsi's arms and belly hurt from swimming for so long, but definitely because they were traveling at a faster pace. She lagged just behind Reshma and both of them were a foot or so behind Dalit's fin. Ilsi kept moving her arms, hips, and fin since her fears of being left behind were greater than the exhaustion.

They kept a few feet under the water surface, which allowed them to better see the creatures around them, as well as any oncoming vessels to avoid. Every once and a while, the waters shadowed a bit as large fishing boats hovered and dangled their large nets into the waters.

"You are not mermaids," Dalit stated simply.

Ilsi and Reshma looked to each other with confused expressions before Ilsi answered for them, "We are human girls. You know we are humans. You saw that we needed help."

"I know this," Dalit replied, as if proud. "Humans don't understand water at all."

"Thank you for helping us," Reshma said gently.

There was a long pause and Ilsi wondered if the meaningless conversation was over. However, Dalit turned and began swimming backwards and said, "They tell me that I should get you lost." She wasn't smiling or showing any kind of emotion; she just stated it like it was a fact.

"Are we . . . lost?" Reshma said. Both Ravennians looked up at the surface, tempted to check for any sign of security or direction. Reshma began clenching and releasing her hands, which matched the tension of her jaw.

"No, not lost. Never lost," Dalit said, shaking her head. Her hair lazily followed her motions. "They told me to make you lost. But you want to still help us. That is very odd. It is why I asked you if you were a mermaid or not. Not many creatures are nice to mermaids, unless they are afraid."

"We're not afraid," Ilsi said, "Or we would have never come here."

"You don't seem afraid," Dalit announced again. "I like you two. Will you show me people?"

"Uh," Ilsi said, filling the space as her mind whirled in confusion. "Why do you want to see the people?"

"Curious," was her answer. Ilsi blanched at the idea. They were going to a market where they made money by catching and selling fish. They wouldn't exactly be the friendliest lot to anything or anyone with a fin.

"Why are you nice humans?" Dalit continued. Ilsi felt like it was talking and reasoning with a child.

"We like to be different," was Reshma's simple reply. "Not all humans are nice. Some are very mean. They want to hurt others that don't want to be mean. So we help the nice people live and be happy."

"That's like the King," Dalit said. "He helps everyone."

Ilsi wanted to grumble a reply, but remembered they hoped

to reach some kind of alliance and how guilty she felt that it didn't work out.

The light was doing odd things to Ilsi's mind. They were slowly approaching shallow water and it showed by the gradual, smooth incline. However, it was getting darker as the day was coming to a close.

"How far away are we from the people?" Reshma asked Dalit. She was doing a great job of being patient with their guide, now that they weren't afraid of being led astray. Ilsi figured Reshma's moments of understanding and gentleness came from having younger siblings.

"Not far for mermaids," Dalit replied. "Look at the moon; it moves for us to know if the day is almost done."

———⚬✦⚬———

The last of the town torches were put out by the time Ilsi and Reshma surfaced. They breathed in the grimy air and each took a turn of sighing in relief. Their maddening task was over. They turned to look at Dalit who cautiously peeked her head out a few feet away.

"The people are sleeping," Dalit stated. "I better come back when they are not sleeping."

"We'll come to see you tomorrow if you'd like," Ilsi smiled, relieved that Dalit had temporarily given up on her request.

"The air is cold above," Dalit said again with a touch of sadness on her face. "I come back. I meet you here later."

"We'll watch for you," Reshma smiled. Dalit quickly turned and arched her back. She used her face and shoulders to dive back into the water and disappear.

"I'm surprised she flat out told us that she was instructed to get us lost out here," Reshma said once she was really gone.

"It's not that hard to imagine," Ilsi shrugged. "I would probably be used to telling the truth all the time if my king could tell if I was lying. It was nice of her to still help us."

"Speaking of help," Reshma said, gesturing to herself, "We need some kind of coverings to make it back to the hotel." As soon as they approached the boats and shoreline, it was as if they entered a new territory. Their gills and fins began to disappear from their neck, hands, and legs.

The night wind swirled around the girls and they began raiding small fishing boats for any kind of cloth. Besides lots of nets, the girls didn't find much in the way of warmth or coverings.

"Should you just use *Swift* to zip us back to our room?" Reshma asked.

"And risk making a lot of noise?" Ilsi questioned in return. "I'm pretty good at sprints, but that's mainly when I know where I'm going. I could knock us into a building and think of how the neighbors would react."

"Right," Reshma grunted. She climbed into a boat and then snorted. "Brilliant. I can't believe it."

"What?"

"There's a parcel in here with our names on it," Reshma said. Ilsi could tell by her tone that she was pleased by that. "Someone's left us our clothes here. Ladala's seal and everything."

"They must be here already," Ilsi's mood already brightening. "Let's get these on and get inside."

They giggled at their embarrassing fortune, got dressed, and then lifted their skirts as they waded to shore.

———◦◦◦———

Ilsi woke up, looked up at a wooden ceiling and sighed. She gathered her blanket closer to her, then realized that there were two other blankets on top.

"It's for the chill," she heard someone say. "Except you probably aren't cold, aren't you?"

Ilsi turned and propped herself up to see Liselotte sitting on the floor with her boots off, whittling at a small stick. She was wearing simple traveling pants and a tunic over a cotton shirt—she had a tattered scarf tied over her head and knotted at her neck to pin back and hide the tips of her ears. She looked nothing like one of Ladala's right-hand fighters.

"Liselotte!" Ilsi cried, "You made it."

"Aye, we did, about a week ago," she said, still looking at her little project. "Didn't think you'd be back so soon."

"So soon?" Ilsi repeated.

"They couldn't kick us out fast enough," Reshma grumbled, slowly shifting around, keeping the blankets about her. Ilsi looked sheepishly back at Liselotte.

"We tried talking with them, but as soon as they discovered that I had *Swift*, they practically banished us," Ilsi said. "Why didn't any of you tell us that the rings would turn us into mermaids, anyway?"

Liselotte laughed. "If I had any clue, I would've informed you immediately. I don't know anything about them except they burn at the touch and Ladala lets you learn a lot of things on your own."

"I'll be sure to let her know my opinions on waking up on the ocean floor," Ilsi said, rubbing sleep from her eyes, "and that we failed our first task." Reshma put a reassuring hand on Ilsi's upper arm.

"We didn't expect a whole lot," Lotte said, finally looking at the two. "We haven't spoken to them in decades. They make it hard to access, really. I'm sure you couldn't even point out their kingdom on a map, and you've been there."

Ilsi nodded in acknowledgment.

"Ladala picks well," Liselotte said. "I can imagine you got real nice and cozy, threatening them in the face. I can count only a few people that have had such the honor."

Ilsi smiled a bit at the joke, still regretful of the sour experience, but relieved that no one else was as disappointed.

"I'll wait for you downstairs with the others," Liselotte said as she put her knife and wood away and stood up. "We can talk about your time with the merfolk once you are both properly awake."

"We should meet by the docks," Ilsi added. "Our guide, Dalit, hopes to see us there. Or at least, the fishermen."

"She would be ideal to talk to," Liselotte smiled, then left. Once the door clicked shut, Ilsi rolled over so she was lying flat on her back.

"They don't hate me," Ilsi said. "They don't think I'm a failure."

"Why would they hate you? You know they can't do what we can do," Reshma mumbled, pulling the blankets over her face.

"You look like a corpse," Ilsi joked.

"I want to sleep like one," came the voice under the blankets.

—◦◦◦—

"Glad to see you're back in the land of the living," Roan said as Ilsi and Reshma approached. The two kept to their fishing village attire while the Elves draped themselves in ambiguous traveling attire. Roan himself had a floppy traveler's hat to cover his red, spiky hair; he tipped the edge a bit as a salutation.

"As opposed to the land of the dead?" Reshma asked, as they all exchanged hearty handshakes and hugs.

"He's teasing," Deidre said, rolling her eyes at him. "We've got a bit of a common joke that mermaids don't get enough sun. Sunshine helps things grow and all. Don't make me explain the rest of it or it sounds silly."

"Do you normally get along with them?" Ilsi asked.

"Usually. Never any wars," Deidre shrugged. "We obviously don't talk much. Would've been terrifically surprising if they agreed to help."

"Liselotte told you?"

"Yes, she gave us your report," Basim nodded, giving an encouraging smile. "What you did was fine and exactly what we hoped would happen."

"You hoped we would somehow make it down there and get rejected?" Ilsi asked.

"We didn't want to get our hopes too high," Basim explained. "But they are properly warned. They'll come looking for an alliance once things go from bad to worse. Althod has done a lot of damage in every city in a way that there are people missing and joining their ranks by the day, but no city officials even know there's a problem."

"So we're messengers," Reshma said. The four Elven soldiers looked to each other then back at the girls.

"Perhaps this setting in the middle of town isn't suitable for this kind of talk," Basim said. "I think we can go to the shore, talk to your guide, and then better explain what we're trying to do."

"What is there to discuss?" Ilsi said.

"We can talk about the next places for you to go and what we hope to achieve," Deidre said. She put a reassuring hand on her shoulder and they all casually walked towards the shoreline.

Straight ahead lay the constructed docks and boats coming in and out of the city. Ilsi and Reshma led them off to the right where the terrain became full of sand and rocks. Pretty soon, they reached rugged cliffs that rose up a mile or so above their heads.

"Do you think she'll come?" Ilsi heard one of them say.

"These creatures are not humans," Dalit concluded, out of nowhere. Only her head and shoulders were above the water. The water was clear enough that Ilsi could see that she propped herself up out of the water at her elbows.

"How could you even tell?" Reshma asked as her immediate reaction.

"They aren't afraid of me," Dalit shrugged. "Humans always like to carry around pointy things in case they meet someone that isn't a human."

"You'reright," Deidre said, lowering herself so she was squatting in the sand. "We're Elves. We live in the woods." Dalit wrinkled her nose and smiled.

"You are all very strange," Dalit said. "Elves and humans. Very strange."

"On land, a lot of strange things are happening," Deidre continued, adopting a calm, gentle tone similar to the one Reshma used while they were navigating their way home. "Could you tell us more about what life is like for the mermaids?"

Dalit propelled herself closer as everyone sat down in the sand and listened. As Dalit went on to explain what Ilsi and Reshma had already seen and witnessed, Ilsi thought about their exchange with Ladala's soldiers.

Her brow furrowed, accompanied by a small scowl on her face as she thought about it. It seemed like everyone was reminding her of how little time there was to explain what she needed to know, or they weren't in the ideal location to divulge more information, or just the plain fact that she agreed whole-heartedly to a cause that she admitted she didn't fully understand.

Her enemy was Althod. She hardly knew anything about the man except his name.

She was supposed to use *Swift* somehow to do good and oppose the Yildirims. Apparently turning into a mermaid fit into that scheme.

It wasn't long before Reshma nudged her and brought her back to the present moment. She said to Ilsi, "I already told Dalit that we don't know anyone here that we could safely introduce her to."

Ilsi shook her head, as if to clear her mind of her frustrations. "Yeah. We're only in this village for a short time. We haven't made any friends."

Dalit didn't look sad or remotely frustrated, but smiled softly and said, "I meet you two. Very peculiar. I hope more human girls are like you. Maybe I see you again."

"Where are you going?" Ilsi asked. Did she miss something?

Dalit arched her body again to turn herself around the way she came. They heard a plunk and Dalit disappeared. Ilsi whirled around and saw a few medium-sized ships coming to the dock.

They were far enough away that they probably didn't hear

anything that happened, but those on board could probably notice that four adults and two teenagers were sitting together in the sand. Ilsi was tired of worrying about people watching her already.

Without saying anything, the group collectively stood up and walked away.

"Having a private conversation is so much easier to do in the trees," Basim muttered.

"Then let's go in the forest then," Liselotte said. "We'll strike up an official meeting. We owe it to these two to know what they're really supposed to do. We might as well leave anyway—our business is done here."

CHAPTER 23

Well, I would've kicked myself if I put this journal in further disrepair. Through dumb luck, we made it to the mermaid territories and by dumb luck I didn't bring this with me.

Mama, did you and Papa ever argue? And if so, how did you win? It's so frustrating trying to reason with people—mermaids most of all. I hope this is the last I speak of them. I just wished I knew how to show people how much this all means to me. I want to tear down that Wall. Otherwise, I don't know how much longer our people can survive.

But I can't help but be selfish. I knew that the school teachers were never going to tell me what happened and why. I'd like to think that you would join me in escaping so we could figure out the truth together.

❦

Ilsi's entire body stiffened as she sat miles above the forest ground. In fear of being found (and in hopes of having some privacy), the four Elves set up camp high in the tall trees—back in Beast Forest.

"How well do you even know this forest?" Reshma asked. "Every tree looks the same. It's maddening."

"We use that to our advantage," Deidre smiled. She sat

patiently on her own piece of hide that was stretched tightly in all four directions. She swayed slightly as thick ropes each fastened extensively to a thick branch. The others had their bearings as well, while Ilsi's belly hurt from keeping herself from swinging too far to either side.

Reshma laughed. "You must laugh at the travelers that walk in circles down below."

"Oh yes," Basim smiled. "All the time. They give us plenty of opportunity to do so."

"Okay," Ilsi said, her voice wavering, "now that we're all comfy-cozy, do tell us what you intend for us to do. Or should I say, what Ladala intends for us."

"I think you were slightly mistaken about what we expected and we apologize," Roan began. "It seems as though you were shaken up by what the Sea King had to say—or didn't say— about our hopes for an alliance. We should all be worried that they wish to stay out of this, as they don't fully understand what the Yildirims are capable of doing. But we had realistic expectations."

"Yes, we already have an idea of who is for and against the Yildirim, and it doesn't make them wicked," Deidre continued. "We sent you to the Sea King because no one has been able to reach him in decades, but you did that with ease. We hoped you would change his mind, but we don't blame you for his decision."

"Your mission is just to find the toughest allies and give them a chance to join," Liselotte said, looking straight at Ilsi. "And right now, we have to focus on the next huge player that could help us unite the other cities. We need you to find Giselle."

"Giselle?" Ilsi asked. "Is there a title with that? Queen, empress?"

"She is a lady of the woods, just like Ladala," Liselotte answered, "except she lives alone and she isn't an elf. We suspect she's a shapeshifter."

"So . . . we're looking for a lady who lives alone in the woods, and she's a shapeshifter, so no one probably knows what she looks like," Reshma mused aloud, "And she's going to help us in what way?"

"She's fairly powerful," Liselotte said. "Just like the Sea King, she's very difficult to get a hold of. She shows herself when people really need her most and, to be put bluntly, if Althod somehow finds her first or if she is swayed on their side, there's nothing much we can do to defend ourselves."

"Wait, she's powerful enough to tip the scales like that?" Ilsi said incredulously. "What exactly does she do?"

"We don't really know," Diedre said. "I know how it sounds. Ladala knows little about her and yet she specifically requested that you seek her out. Ladala thinks she'd know how to find your family." She looked at Reshma as she finished.

Reshma answered by looking up and saying, "She's not just saying that, is she?"

"If this Giselle is a shapeshifter, she can use that power to either find them or extract them," Roan answered. "If she likes you well enough, I'm sure she'd perform a favor."

Reshma kept her legs crossed as she lay back and stared up at the rest of the branches above. She gave no clue in her expression if she had a strong opinion on the situation.

"So what do we do when or if we find Giselle? Will you find us and tell us what to do next?"

"You'll have to find her and bring her back," Basim said. "We're sure that the last time anyone thought they saw her it was fairly close to the Pearl Mountains."

When they received blank stares from the two young women, Roan said, "Our spies report that the kingdom in the valley is sympathetic to the Yildirim cause. So you don't want to get too close in case they are harboring a lot of soldiers. We're thinking more of your safety than Giselle's."

"The more people see you or hear about you," Liselotte warned, "the more often you're going to run into the Yildirim. So just do whatever you can to get them off your trail. There is a small team of our stealthiest warriors that will do what they can to protect you while you're on your search."

They were met with silence as Ilsi closed her eyes and Reshma kept looking up. Their tree tents swayed and creaked as everyone suddenly sat in thought.

"Where will you go?" Ilsi asked softly.

"We'll be likely going the opposite way," Deidre smiled sadly. "We'll be wherever Ladala needs us. Probably to defend smaller villages that the Yildirims are targeting for soldiers."

"You take down a soldier and they raise two more," Reshma murmured.

"Any advice on navigating the forest in one piece?" Ilsi asked. Roan grinned as he fished something out of his belt pocket.

"Should I toss it over?"

Reshma held up her hands in anticipation and Roan tossed a small item into her waiting hands. She turned the small thing around in her hands to examine it.

"The spindles point north," he explained. "You can at least

know which direction you're going in. It doesn't find a path, but it does what it can."

"Elf-invented, huh?" Reshma grinned.

"Don't worry, you'll catch up soon enough," Basim smiled. "If your horse doesn't frighten too easily, we can probably rest up here for the night and then go our separate ways."

"Ilsi, look how far away our steed is," Reshma goaded.

"I refuse to look down, Reshma! Lay off already!"

———⟡———

The next morning, Ilsi woke up to find that Reshma was already to her left, hugging the trunk of the tree and fidgeting with her tent.

"How did you manage that?" Ilsi asked. She rolled over to her side, to get a better look. The other suspended pallets were gone as were the elves that slept on them.

"As if I *only* manage things," Reshma rolled her eyes with a smile. "Try to swing yourself towards me and don't look down and I'll pull you towards me."

Still wondering how Reshma did the same on her own, she tried to ignore the creaking sound the branch above her made as she swung herself closer and closer to Reshma. She was only a few feet away, so it didn't take too long. Once Ilsi could confirm that she had a full grip on the tree, she let go of Reshma and looked around and found a branch to stand on.

"Well that was a big deal," Reshma teased as she let Ilsi's pallet—ropes and all—tumble to the ground below.

"As long as you don't let me fall down like that," Ilsi muttered to herself.

It took a lot longer to descend than it had for the elves to take her up the tree and into her hanging pallet. Her legs and arms ached and her hands throbbed by the time both feet reached the ground. Reshma only beat her by a few moments and was soon feeding Dash and preparing them for travel.

"You know where to go?" Reshma said, tossing the compass to Ilsi.

"The Pearl Mountains are northeast from here, if I read Ladala's maps right. I have no idea how long it will take us to get there, but I will be happy so long as we don't lose this thing."

They soon came upon a dirt trail where a few people were in front and behind them with animals and carts. They seemed to know their way and many were men on their own or traveling with their sons, so Ilsi assumed they were traders who had made and knew the path.

The dirt—now mud—path wove through curtains of tall pine trees. The humid sun all but disappeared except for a few rare peeks through branches of pine needles. Wind blew through the branches, causing needles to lazily flutter to the ground below.

"I think someone is following us."

"Normally, I would be grateful for the paranoia, but we just barely found a trail," Reshma answered in a low tone, "Let's just get through and keep our eyes open. Hopefully there are safe paths and people to travel with to the next village." The two kept to the road for once, trying not to give too many sideways glances at the other travelers.

⌐∘⌐

"We need to find some water," Reshma said, "We're already out." Ilsi asked for directions to a nearby body of water, and then they took a deeper, muddier path that forked left of the road. No one followed after them and they traveled down the path until they found a nice pond surrounded by patches of tall grass.

Reshma slid off Dash's back and led the horse to the water to drink. Ilsi took this opportunity to wash the fish stench out of her shirt. She also rolled up her pants to wade in a bit and continued washing her arms and face, but couldn't erase the sickening feeling that someone could be following them.

A shiver ran down her spine. A large branch cracked, followed by absolute silence. She looked and saw nothing. She wrung the water out of her shirt and hastily put it back over her head and nervously stuck her arms through the sleeves. She sloshed out of the water and sat on the side of the pond, unrolling her pants and lacing her boots again.

Ilsi looked around and Reshma was patting Dash's nose and between his ears as he stood patiently. She looked to her laces to continue tying them and stood up when she finished. She looked up and about choked on her rising heart.

Without any warning, a strange creature stood nose to nose with her. She was met with large, round eyes with slitted pupils belonging to a round, furry face. With smooth, slow movement, it slowly rose to its full height and maintained its intense stare. Ilsi craned her head to see clearly and noted that the furry creature towered a full two feet above her.

Ilsi immediately flicked out a dagger and pointed it between its eyes defensively. With one eye squinted, her other eye saw a savage, yet elegant, sleek creature. The figure had the face, tail and feet of a cat, but the hands, breasts and curvy figure of a woman. The creature's figure was wrapped it a torn dress with one strap over her shoulder, revealing tense, toned arms. Along with being fully covered in light beige fur, she had a tangled mass of human-like hair swept to the side in a ponytail resting on her shoulder.

The creature looked intently at Ilsi, as though Ilsi was the wild creature. She crouched closer to Ilsi to continue staring with her round, green eyes. Ilsi took a step back, her eyes darting back and forth, noticing more similar creatures hiding in nearby trees and bushes, hiding in the shadows or daring to slink closer to the pond's bank to circle around Ilsi.

"Ilsi!" Reshma cried from a distance. Dash whinnied and caught Ilsi's attention. Her feet finally uprooted from her shocked stance and she tried running towards Reshma and Dash. She didn't want to risk killing the creature and angering its friends or family.

Her attempts at escape were futile; while the figure didn't move, the others surrounding them ran with silent speed to surround Ilsi, and a few surrounded Reshma, baring their teeth clawing the air, or holding spears. They came from behind the tall trees; some jumped from higher branches and gracefully landed on the ground on their feet. Dozens more came about, and they all circled around Ilsi.

They began to push and prod her deeper into the forest. She turned to face the one that was nudging her—and noticed they were doing so with their upper arms or faces rather than their clawed hands.

"Where are you taking me?" Ilsi tried to ask. "What do you want?" They pushed in closer to her, providing no escape.

She heard Reshma protest behind her, so she knew her friend was trailing behind. She heard excited voices mingled with the overpowering thundering and vibration of a pack of purring creatures.

<hr />

Just when Ilsi thought she had seen the same distinct tree a few dozen time, she noticed that a few male-looking creatures were guiding Dash ahead of the pack. She worried for the horse, but also for all of their worldly possessions, which were strapped to him. They brought Reshma closer to her and they exchanged looks.

The creatures took her to a small village made up of crudely built huts. The huts were constructed everywhere; some of them were scattered over the grounds, but many had been constructed high up in the trees with vines dangling from them. Those were the ones she could see easily.

They took Ilsi, and later Reshma, to the hut of a larger creature that resembled a fat tabby cat. He was wearing a tunic that wasn't large enough to cover his bulky stomach. As soon as they entered, his ears perked up at the sight or possibly the smell of them.

"I see we have visitors," he purred.

"We did no harm . . . sir," Ilsi said, surprised at his ability to speak.

"We are beasts, and hunting is what we do best," he purred again. "My agents tell me that you were in our lands. What were you doing?"

"We barely strayed from the marked path for water,"

Reshma interjected. The band went into uproar, many of them crying out for meat. The female creature that first approached the girls suddenly bore her long fangs and let out a bone-chilling roar that made everyone quiet.

"You know our vow not to eat humans," she growled.

"But they smell of fish! Strongly of fish!" one cried.

"Just because they smell of fish, doesn't mean they *are* fish," she said again, and the creatures hissed again, but stayed still.

"Why exactly are they here then?" the tabby asked, looking at their defender and captor. "They don't look interested in joining us."

"They're young, but they can help us," she answered.

"Saqui—"

"I brought them here for personal reasons," she interrupted. "They will be under my care."

The tabby looked away wearily and gestured with his paw that they were free to leave. The female grunted in satisfaction and motioned to those closest to Ilsi and Reshma to pull them out of the hut.

"What are these personal reasons?" Reshma was the first to ask. "Do you know us?"

The female looked long and hard at her before saying, "You are my decoys. These trees are littered with sky callers and they track you whenever you're in these trees."

"Sky callers?" Ilsi repeated.

"Surely you know them," the creature explained. "They call the crackle from the clouds and kill the innocent with it."

"Yildirims."

"Everyone has their own name for them," the woman said, putting her large hands on her hips. "As for my name, I'm Saqui.

210

I will be your guide and protector in these trees. I know you're traveling. I'll take you through the forest to wherever you plan to go. Of course, in exchange, you will help me lure the sky callers here to be slaughtered."

"Wow, to the point," Reshma murmured. "You said this was personal. So what's your problem with the Yildirim?"

"Where do I start?" she said, gesturing to herself. "Come, the Beast Teacher will explain all."

"Why not tell us yourself?" Ilsi asked.

"He is the keeper of our history," was all she said. "He tells it better."

CHAPTER 24

It was so warm in the leather hut that Ilsi needed to hum a soft cooling spell. She created a gentle and relieving breeze that consistently blew on the back of her neck and other areas like the crook of her elbows and knees. Reshma seemed fairly accustomed to sporting beads of sweat but not feeling the heat. Ilsi looked at all the figures around her and how they relaxed. While Reshma and Ilsi were sitting with their legs crossed, everyone around them lounged very close to each other in various poses.

The younger creatures—almost as tall as Ilsi—cuddled so close to their mothers they were almost like extra appendages. The mothers themselves were either grooming their young ones or themselves. In general, they squatted on their hind legs, or lay on their sides with their tails curled around them, very much like normal felines.

Ilsi, annoyed that everyone decided to cramp up against her instead of spread out, finally asked, "So how did your clan come to be . . . Beast Teacher?"

Her question startled just about all those present. It was as if they were never introduced to noise before. The thickest one—the one with white whiskers on his chin—looked at her, heard that the question was directed at him. He didn't appear decrepit or aged, but he seemed to be the oldest in the group.

"Saqui has told you of my role. Everyone here is not of the same family you know," he answered. "We were once prisoners. Yet, now we are family."

"Prisoners?" Reshma asked. "Of whom?"

"The ones who call upon the skies to threaten other creatures," came the reply. *Ah, the Yildirims—a big surprise,* Ilsi thought.

"At one point or another," the old feline continued sluggishly, "each of us was a captive. It's what we have in common."

"Did they capture you because you're good hunters?" Reshma asked. She assumed these creatures would be fairly useful as spies or warriors if chained to Althod's cause.

He shook his head. "When they first captured us, we were humans," Beast Teacher replied. "It's a life that most of us don't remember and we try to forget. You see, the forest changed our form."

They're half-breeds, Ilsi thought, frightened at the thought.

"A curious notion, I'm sure," the cat nodded. The others pretended not to pay attention, but Ilsi could feel a lot of eyes watching her to gauge her reaction. "All we know is this: There are some strange beasts that hide and hunt in these trees. I remember . . . one of them attacked me. I attempted escape and one of them found me before the captor did. The thing almost killed me. When I awoke, I was no longer a man but part beast."

Ilsi and Reshma looked back in awe.

"It was a blessing. I would rather be a beast than a slave. That creature gave me the strength and agility to kill my captors," the old cat sighed. "We offer that same gift to anyone who wishes it."

Ilsi and Reshma looked around, uneasy. Ilsi said, "Oh, you mean us? We're fine as humans, thanks. We have our own gifts." She hoped it was a gift of free will. The idea of all of them pouncing on them made her grow uneasy.

"This is a sanctuary of the lost and stolen," Beast Teacher continued. "Everyone has escaped by shedding their human flesh in exchange for fur and claws. We will do whatever it takes to protect anyone here from those men and women who think to take control of us. Does that answer your question, young one?"

<hr />

Much to Ilsi's discomfort, they stayed with the cat-creatures for a week. They didn't do much, except help with the hunting. Ilsi wasn't sure why they were invited since the half-breeds were the better hunters. Much like regular street cats, they were able to pass through the forests without so much as a sound or any tools to guide them. Too often, she lost sight of them during such hunts. Ilsi hated the thought of being separated from the hunting party and being lost; the forest had its usual charm of lacking obvious landmarks.

"How can you be so good at hunting with only a small dagger?" Reshma said to Saqui. Saqui grinned as she flashed her sharp claws. Ilsi flinched at the sound of her retracting claws and with a swish of Saqui's tail they were off.

When Ilsi thought of the expansive forest—that she now realized connected to every city like the center of a spider web—she wondered if it was an advantage to hide. After all, she had been lost in the forest with Reshma before—if the half-breeds knew their way around the forest, wouldn't that give her the upper hand? Or did the Yildirims know their way around the trees, too? Because of this dilemma, she wasn't sure whether she should be on her guard or not.

Saqui then motioned for them to be silent. Ilsi crept quietly behind Saqui, as she crouched down close to the ground. *I wonder what she is hearing?* Ilsi thought.

Suddenly, Saqui pounced. Ilsi leaped behind her, bow and arrow poised and ready to back her up. What she found through the bushes was startling. Saqui was struggling to stab a young man. He had black hair was soaked with sweat—his arm quaking mightily as he attempted to force the blade away from his chest.

He was just a young man, and clearly not an equal for the large cat creature. He wore a faded, worn Yildirim insignia, and Ilsi almost let her arrow go, but paused when she saw his face.

"*No!* Stop!" Ilsi said. Saqui, who still had her dagger poised, whirled around to look at her. The young man kept his focus on the dagger, pushing it back.

From her crouched position over him, Saqui stood up, holding the boy aloft by the scruff of his neck. He winced sharply as his toes lifted slightly off the ground.

"Why do you tell me to stop? He is *hunting* us!" she snarled, pointing at his Yildirim emblem with her blade.

"No," Ilsi said softly, "not in that way." She got a good look at his face and knew it was the young man they saw earlier—Tyk. She couldn't bring herself to kill someone who was or could look like her best friend from home.

Saqui stood back, appalled. She loosened her grip on the

young man, and he fell to his knees. He was panting heavily, and they all stood there, not knowing what to do next. Reshma finally caught up with them, only to find Ilsi and the boy in his Yildirim uniform.

"Ilsi, it's one of them! Stand back!" Reshma said, poising an arrow, but Ilsi stopped her by putting her hand on the bow-shaft. Reshma was just as shocked as Saqui, if not more so.

"No, Reshma," Ilsi said, looking at the boy, "It's the one who looks like Tyk. Let him talk for himself first. We can at least take this amulet off." They all stood back as Saqui loosened her grip and the boy clutched his abdomen and vomited.

"Well, that's quite the hairball," Saqui said, amused. Tyk simply collapsed on the ground and passed out. Ilsi ran and knelt by his side.

"Ilsi, he's on the side that likes to kidnap people like my parents," Reshma said. "Some of these people are on their side because they want to. We should've gotten rid of him the last time he attacked us. I'll do it." She clenched a dagger and held it poised.

"That's not fair!" Ilsi said sharply, making a point to stand directly in the way of the blade. "We'll question him. He must know where they keep their prisoners or where they train them. Ask him everything you can think of and if he doesn't prove useful . . . then I won't stand in the way again."

Ilsi's lips formed a determined, hard line even though she hated what came out of her mouth. Reshma sighed and sheathed her dagger; without a word, she turned and headed towards the others.

"You wish to help your *enemy?*" Saqui asked, surprised as

well. "You're not a very good hunter, and you're certainly not a smart prey."

"Please, I think he's someone I know," Ilsi said. "I just need to know he's the same friend I used to know."

CHAPTER 25

Saqui placed her knife safely back in its leather pouch and helped Ilsi drag Tyk to better shelter. They stopped by a large tree, and set his body close to its base. Saqui told Ilsi she would continue to hunt with the party and come back for them in a few hours. Ilsi was thus left to treat her patient.

She noticed a tear through the front of his uniform. She opened his shirt to reveal a horrible gash that stretched across his torso and stopped at about the middle, below his breastbone. He wasn't wearing the odd amulet and it was nowhere on his person.

"Who could've done this?" Reshma asked gruffly, approaching the tree.

"I thought you went back to the hunting party," Ilsi replied, her voice flat.

"Saqui told me you were here and I thought I shouldn't leave you alone," Reshma replied with a drawn-out sigh, "in case the bastard wakes up and goes for your throat." Ilsi said nothing, and began tearing a spare shirt.

"Ilsi, what are you doing?"

"What does it look like? I'm making a bandage," Ilsi replied smartly.

"If he's that badly wounded and alone, he obviously has enemies."

Ilsi looked pointedly at Reshma and raised an eyebrow. Reshma just rolled her eyes, set her jaw firm, and helped Ilsi remove the armor and heavy uniform material to finish their work.

"Your family members aren't the only Yildirims that shouldn't have to die," Ilsi murmured sourly.

"I'd like to stay alive to see the day they're freed."

Saqui sometime later came, carrying bundles of raw meat. By that time, the two had finished wrapping the makeshift bandage around his chest and draped a cloak over him. He was breathing normally and appeared to be sleeping peacefully.

"I know you humans might not like the sight of creatures tearing one another apart, so I did it already. I wouldn't want you to vomit like the boy," Saqui said.

"Thank you," Ilsi said, "Although we're used to that sort of thing for cooking. Thanks for the food."

Reshma murmured something to herself, then stood up and said, "I guess I'll get some wood for a fire. I can tell we will be staying for the night." She carefully made her way through the forest, and disappeared from Ilsi's view. Ilsi looked up and realized that it was getting late in the day.

"I will stay with you, do not worry," Saqui smiled, sensing Ilsi's anxiety. Ilsi smiled back and nodded her thanks.

"Are we safe by sleeping here?" Ilsi asked, gesturing to the forest ground. She wondered if they would have to move everything up the tree for the night.

"I'll keep us safe," Saqui replied. "This is our hunting territory. A lot of beasts in the forest understand that and keep their distance."

———◦◦◦———

"Reshma?"

"*What?*" Reshma said icily, scrubbing harder at her face.

"Are you still mad at me?"

"I just hate being in this dank and eerie place," Reshma shivered. "And yes, still pissed off."

"Look, how else are we going to find your family? It's not like prisons or training camps are easy to find or easy to access."

"Yes, but why this one? I bet he knows nothing. You're just saving him because it looks like—"

"We both know a thing or two about personal desires," Ilsi said over Reshma. "We're all out here looking after ourselves and what we're after. Sorry that I can't bring myself to kill Tyk, good or bad."

"I just don't trust him."

"Maybe I'm overly trusting," Ilsi sighed. "But it's him against the three of us. What do we have to lose?"

Reshma was ready with a reply when they heard a cry in the distance.

"Come on, someone could've heard that!" Reshma said. They quickly dried their faces and necks and made a run for it. Ilsi followed Reshma into the bushes, and they hurriedly made their way back to where they had rested. They wouldn't have found their way back without the visual markers they nicked into the tree.

Ilsi moved aside some branches to reveal Saqui and her captive. She had him pinned against the tree in the same stance when they first caught him but this time he was trying to put up more of a fight. The boy stared at Ilsi in alarm, and he tried to quickly stand up.

"Keep him down, Saqui," Ilsi said, worried this young man might actually be as ruthless as Reshma predicted. She told him, "If you want to be mended you should stay down."

"She's gonna kill me!" he cried.

"Hell yeah she'll kill you if you cross us," Reshma said, unsheathing her sword with the blade directed at his throat. "Who the hell are you and how did you find us?"

"Ilsi? Don't you *remember* me? It's me, Tyk!" the young man said firmly.

"You sure as hell better be Tyk," Ilsi snapped. "I will send you to whatever gods you believe in if you're not really Tyk." Her fists were encrusted and frozen over with ice.

"Ilsi!" Tyk said, his turn to be alarmed.

"Tell me something that only Tyk would know," Ilsi said through gritted teeth.

"Well I didn't know you had *Swift* for one thing—"

"That wasn't my question!"

"I'm an inventor!" Tyk bellowed back. "Patent 89, remember? Just let me explain what's going on! Get this woman off of me."

"Please let him go, Saqui," Ilsi said. She rubbed her hands and the ice melted away. She rubbed her wet hands over her face in exhaustion. Saqui didn't seem bothered, but her eyes kept turning towards Reshma, who leaned against another tree, fingering her dagger holster.

"Tyk," Ilsi said quietly, "Are you really a Yildirim?"

"Well," Tyk replied, slightly embarrassed, "Yeah. It's a long story, really."

"Oh, don't worry about taking up our time," Reshma said tartly.

"When you left Dove, they held me hostage and took me away from Ravenna. They took me to Althod, the leader. The 'boss' said that he would kill me and the rest of the Ice Chanters, but if I decided to be a Yildirim, I could live. I only did it so I could find you, and warn you—"

"So what was all that the last time I saw you," Ilsi said, biting her lip at the memory. "Just . . . acting?"

"No, it wasn't acting. It's the amulet," Tyk said. "It turns you into your worst self. It takes the parts that are already bad and uses them against you. I'm glad one of you broke it.

"Everyone who wears those amulets hates you, Ilsi," Tyk continued. "Everyone knows they're enlisted to fight for Althod because of you. Most don't even know why, but they still have you as their common enemy."

"How did you find out so much?"

"I think it's because I've been so hell-bent on finding you. Maybe they want you to know."

"Know what exactly?" Reshma said.

"I know, Tyk. He's got a huge army and I'm sure he wants me in it because I'm an Ice Chanter and I have *Swift*," Ilsi said. The words were bitter and hard to say. "He's like a toy collector that wants anyone special to be his warrior."

"I don't think you understand," Tyk said. "This isn't about making you his soldier. He just wants your powers. He doesn't want you. He will keep you alive and take what he wants. He doesn't want Ice Chanter powers or else he'd keep me on a tighter leash. He wants *Swift*."

After a few seconds of silence, Ilsi murmured, "Well he's certainly not the first."

Chapter 26

S o, what happened after I . . . left?"

Tyk and Ilsi sat next to a small lake, staring into the clear water. They were a five minute's stumble through the woods to where they set up camp. Tyk still wore his bandage, but had donned the old, billowing black shirt and his uniform jacket. Ilsi tried not to stare at the abundance of bruises.

"I saw you go through the Wall, and it was absolutely amazing. I was waiting my whole life to get out of Dove, and you finally did it. Only, I thought you were dead."

"*Tyk.*" Ilsi put a hand on his arm and looked up at him expectantly. "What happened? Is my father alive? Did they kill him?"

"I don't know how much comfort I can give. I was taken across the Wall with their strange magic immediately after. I worry about my family, too."

"To Tijer?"

"What is Tijer?"

"Where the Fire Weavers live. It's really hot—the complete opposite of Dove. It's where I met Reshma."

"Nope. We headed straight for blue ocean water."

223

He stared at the water and sighed; he absentmindedly chucked pebbles into the water to do something in the silence. Ilsi silently wondered what prevented them from immediately following. It was like they wanted her to have a false sense of security.

"You haven't changed a bit. Except you're wearing pants," Tyk said with a small smile. Ilsi cocked her eyebrow and opened her mouth as if to say something back.

"I mean, it looks good! I've never seen you with your hair cut that short. Who convinced you to unravel that long braid? I'd almost forgotten you inherited such curly hair."

Ilsi laughed when he wound his finger on a stray curl.

"I needed a new look to throw off the Yildirim. It's clearly working."

"Well, with these *Swift* powers, I'm sure you get by."

Ilsi shifted uncomfortably, trying to pick at the right words.

"I was too ashamed to tell you. I know better now," Ilsi murmured.

"Ashamed? Think of what would happen if I actually knew. The Yildirims would've spilled my guts by now. I understand. I would've probably done the same thing." He put a reassuring hand on her shoulder and gave it a squeeze.

"No, I really should have. It was something that my mother never told me about while she was alive. I wonder if my father had any idea," Ilsi said. "I just don't like keeping secrets from you. I probably would've felt much happier if someone else knew."

"Your mother had this power?"

"Oh yeah. She wrote about it in a journal. I think she wanted to tell me someday. She just didn't get the chance."

"Ilsi, you had the power to cross the Wall all on your own.

We can go back home and help everyone leave! They're stuck on the island with nowhere to go without you." Ilsi wanted to cry at the look of his sheer excitement.

"I want to go home, but I can't. I've sworn my allegiance to Lady Ladala. I'm helping the resistance against the Yildirims. Reshma too," Ilsi sighed. "She won't drop a toe on home soil until she brings her family back in one piece. We can't."

"You're fighting the Yildirims?"

"And you're dressed like one?" Ilsi wanted to scoff. Tyk threw a small rock and it plunked with a deeper tone into the water.

"Ilsi, I didn't have a choice. I did what I did to protect you."

"I *had* a choice and I decided to protect everyone else but myself." Ilsi looked down at her knees and flexed her hands. "The question is, are you going to come with us?"

"Why would I go back to the Yildirims? Besides, I'm surprisingly more afraid of them than I am of your friend. Reshma is her name?"

"Yes. Without her, I wouldn't have made it this far."

"Well, you will need my help. We can find Reshma's family—"

"Where would you even begin to look?"

"Try everywhere and anywhere. Althod likes to scatter his playing pieces. But I can talk to people who might know where they're stationed."

"What exactly . . . was your job?"

Tyk opened his mouth but words didn't come out. He shook his head and ran his hands through his hair. Ilsi felt her heart drop as she watched the struggle. She didn't let him squirm longer than necessary.

"It's okay. I understand. I think."

"I'm not really sure what I was, really," Tyk sighed. "I thought in my deranged mind that by turning you in, it would stop an unnecessary war. I wouldn't let them hurt you, but I hoped it would prevent any more harm done to our people."

"So you're saying I should go to him?"

"No!" he cried, putting both hands on his shoulders. "What Althod does to people I wouldn't wish on my worst enemy, let alone you. He searches for your weakness and twists it against you. I don't know why he wants *Swift*, but he doesn't deserve it."

Ilsi was about to answer, when she heard shouting through the trees. The two looked at each other and Ilsi gasped

"Let's check to see if everything is okay!" she said, getting up frantically and helping Tyk to his feet.

Ilsi ran across the rugged terrain, leaping over decaying logs and branches and brushing leaves out of her way. Tyk followed closely behind but then ran past her at the last moment. He entered the camp area first and Ilsi could hear the high-pitched screech of a blade leaving its sheath. She muttered slightly and realized she was weaponless.

"Get your hands off of me!" she heard Reshma exclaim. Ilsi grimaced and peeked into the camp site to see six soldiers fighting her friends. Saqui effortlessly sent her attacker scurrying with her gleaming claws and teeth and her keen eyes fixated on the fear in his eyes. Reshma freed herself from another soldier by warming up her body enough to scorch the soldier's hands and arms.

Tyk soon joined in, using one arm to cast ice against his confused opponent and the other to hold his abdomen. The soldiers paused and glanced momentarily at the lightning bolt on Tyk's pant leg.

"Ilsi! Help us fight them!" Reshma said over her shoulder. Before Ilsi could locate a weapon, a soldier clung to her neck from behind. Ilsi took a swing and knocked his jaw, and he reeled back. Reshma fired an arrow at the wounded man's back. Tyk lashed out and knocked out another one coming from behind by forming ice over his fist. The man fell, and Tyk stabbed him in the chest with a long piece of ice.

Saqui used her sharp, thick claws and slashed a man coming at her, leaving three men down. Reshma kicked a man from behind. She swerved around, and stabbed him quickly. Ilsi got a few more with her ice.

One more stood in the forest, his five bloody comrades slain on the ground. He held his wounded, slumped shoulder and stared coldly at Tyk.

"You've helped the wrong side!" he exclaimed. "You will pay for your betrayal."

Reshma didn't wait for him to say anymore and instead shot him with an arrow. The soldier fell down, hardly noticing her move. All was silent, save their whinnying horse. The group stood silent.

"Look out!" Saqui cried, waving her arms, blocking Reshma. In a split second, an arrow spun into Saqui's back. Reshma screamed as Saqui fell onto her. They both fell to the ground and Reshma shoved the heavy body off her own and Saqui's body rolled so her face dug into the earth; the arrow in her back was stiff and fatal.

She no longer looked feline; her skin suddenly rippled under her clothing and she suddenly sported the same brown skin and dark black hair as Reshma.

"Ophelia?" Reshma gasped. She turned the body to get

a better look at the face. Her hands shook as she went into a frantic shock that Ilsi had never before seen.

"Reshma?" Saqui asked.

"You look like Ophelia, my oldest sister," Reshma choked out. "Why do you look like my sister?"

"Because I am your sister," the woman said. Her accent was twin to Reshma's, only lower and weary. "I joined that tribe because I wanted those soldiers to pay. I'm a monster because of them."

"But you're *you* again, you're human!"

"I meant to explain everything. I just didn't want to disappoint you. I love you." Her body became limp, and her face fell to the earth. Reshma dropped Ophelia's hand in shocked defeat and shielded her eyes with her fists.

"No!" she screamed furiously, more terrifying than anything Ilsi had ever heard. Reshma's face was pinched in anger, her face flaming red with steaming tears on her cheeks.

She suddenly reached for an arrow behind her, and fired from where the deadly arrow came from. A sudden cry was heard, and another Yildirim fell from his hiding place in the bushes.

"You think you can just kill people like that, huh?" Reshma shouted in the same direction. "Huh?"

"Can we save her?" Ilsi said as Reshma put a few shaky fingers to Ophelia's neck.

"She doesn't have a pulse, I don't know what to do," Reshma said, the tears returning.

"Keep her warm, maybe that will help," Ilsi encouraged.

"I'm going to scout for any others still hiding," Tyk said, taking a set of bow and arrows.

"Try not to get lost," Ilsi called back.

"I can't lose her," Reshma said. "We weren't always close since I'm much younger than her, but she's here. What would my parents think?"

"*When* you see them again, they will understand that you both did what you could to survive," Ilsi said. She put her ear to Ophelia's heart to see if she could feel any changes. Her whole body felt warm and soothing like she was sitting in a warm bath.

"Still no heartbeat."

Ilsi slowly sat next to Reshma, although Reshma made no attempt to acknowledge her presence.

"Can I just be alone?" Reshma said with a tiny, gruff voice.

———⚬◦⚬———

As they watched over Ophelia's human form, Ilsi looked across the fire to Tyk with her brows knitted.

"Do you hear that?" she whispered. The forest still continued its soft evening chatter.

"More like, do you *feel* that," Tyk corrected, looking around. It felt like heavy, warm air settled on them. Ilsi felt as if the air were pushing down on her, demanding to be noticed. Reshma felt it too, at least Ilsi assumed so, since she swooped her right arm out and away from her and scooped up the fire from the camp. She held it like a ball she was waiting to throw.

Through the dark, figures approached the light, illuminated only by the fire in Reshma's palm. Reshma took a few steps back and looked around as her flame flared. Ilsi looked over to where Tyk should be sitting but couldn't even make out the shape of his silhouette. She looked back to Reshma and realized that her flame illuminated some familiar faces.

"It's the tribe," Ilsi whispered. Reshma let the flame fall back on the pile of wood and it crackled and spit. They were completely surrounded by the half-breeds.

"We're hardly the most frightening thing you'll find in these trees," Beast Teacher said. "We came because we felt a loss. Something amiss."

"In the whole forest?" Ilsi thought wildly. She wondered for a moment if they would be blamed for Ophelia's death. "That loss is probably Ophelia. She fell by an arrow to save us."

"She had a fondness for you," the cat smiled. Or, it appeared as if he smiled. "We were proud to have her in our midst."

"The Yildirims," was all Reshma could say.

"Too many of them are still alive," Beast Teacher purred.

"We'll stop them," Reshma said, clenching her fists. "We have to."

The tabby stood firm, folding his arms over his chest. Ilsi felt as though his gaze could still penetrate.

"You have an army?" he asked.

"We know of one," Ilsi said. She reached in her bag and pulled out a small stone. She fumbled her way around the fire and away from Ophelia's body towards the Beast. She held out her hand and the leader took it.

"You must know Lady Ladala since you share the same forest," Ilsi began. "She and her people have left their sanctuary and are gathering anyone willing to fight. If you take this, you agree to help and be helped."

"If she's fled her nest, then a battle truly is coming," Beast Teacher said, taking the stone.

"This will glow when they need you most," Ilsi said, recalling what Ladala's soldiers taught her. "I'm not sure how, but I don't pretend to know Elven ways." The round cat purred and chuckled.

"You're not too far behind the rest of us," he shook his head. "Revenge will taste sweet." He clutched the stone for emphasis and put it in a pouch that hung around his neck.

"Milady would be," Ilsi began, her heart pumping, "honored." It felt like the war was already won, knowing that the Beasts agreed to help them. It was like having the whole forest on their side.

"We will find a safe place for Saqui to rest," Beast Teacher nodded. "She will only hinder you now from whatever it is you plan to do."

"We're looking for Giselle," Tyk said softly, behind them. Something akin to a snort came from the tabby.

"The Beasts will be prompt when this calling stone awakens," he said. "I hope the witch won't make you late for your own war."

With that, the leader signaled to a few others near him and they quickly picked up Ophelia disappeared into the woods. The leader then held up the stone and nodded before he too disappeared with the half-breeds. The trio was left to their fire and their horse.

Reshma sat still next to where they had scooped Saqui off the ground, staring off into the inky darkness before her. Ilsi knelt down next to her and put a hand on her shoulder.

"They've taken good care of her," Ilsi murmured. "Now we should go take care of the rest of your clan."

CHAPTER 27

The fire crackled in the night, illuminating Reshma's face. Ilsi glanced over a few times at her as she nibbled at their meal of bread and rabbit meat. She was worried. The forest made her antsy; she wanted to find Giselle the sorceress so they could figure out their next steps. She hoped that she would be understanding to the cause like the Beasts were, but there was no telling. Reshma's expression however was that of a bed of dying embers and Tyk hardly said anything so as not to say the wrong thing.

"Reshma, when should we head out?" Ilsi asked quietly.

"I'd like to leave soon," she murmured. "I need to get this place out of my head. Is he coming?" She looked at Tyk with the most neutral face imaginable.

"Why would he not come?"

"Because he's one of them. I don't know why I should trust him at all."

"Do you trust my judgment?"

"Look, you can understand her point," Tyk said. "But you two don't have to talk about me like I'm not here. You can search me or whatever, but I'm no longer under the influence of that amulet, necklace-thing."

"What are your skills?" Reshma asked, jutting out her chin.

"I'm an Ice Chanter, so I can do that. I was trained in using a great sword, too."

"You got one of those?"

"No. I just have a normal sword at the moment, as you could tell with my effects right here in camp." Tyk didn't look the least bit bothered. In fact, the campfire betrayed a bit of amusement in his expression.

"Do you use the Yildirim lightning?"

"Not anymore," came the quiet reply. "I refuse."

There was a moment's pause where Ilsi looked at her two friends, wondering if Reshma was satisfied with her little interview.

"Well, seems clean to me."

"Oh, that's it? No quest to prove his loyalty?" Ilsi said, trying to make things light-hearted but really wanting to give Reshma a piece of her mind.

"He's *fine*. He's your best friend from home. I just wanted to give you guys a hard time," Reshma shrugged. Tyk smiled and shook his head while Ilsi laughed.

"Are you kidding me? Reshma!"

"You two were just solemn like trees," Reshma rolled her eyes. "I know I just lost my sister and I won't be over it that soon, but I can't go about letting that weigh me down. I at least believe she's in a better place. Except I *will* throttle the next Yildirim to cross me, so watch out, Tyk. You're either on our side, or you're dead."

"Are all Tijerians like you?" Tyk chuckled.

"Don't even doubt it for a second," Reshma grinned.

"Reshma, don't be funny for our sake," Ilsi murmured. "We know she was important to you."

Reshma nodded and looked down at her hands.

"What's that?" Ilsi asked. She noticed Reshma had been moving something small and thin between her fingers.

"She wore this on her wrist I think," she replied, holding up a long string of woven threads and beads. She then wrapped it three times around her own wrist. "We often keep things of the dead with us to remind us they are always with us."

Ilsi smiled softly as she pulled a blanket up over her shoulders, lay down, and stared into their small campfire.

———⊙⊂———

The next morning, the area was hazy with new fog. The three continued on through the woods, and Reshma took the lead with the small compass and map in hand. After a few days of trekking, they saw what looked like the start of a new trail. They continued down the path through the forest, and noticed the path creating a gradual incline.

"Are we going up a mountain now?" Ilsi asked.

"The map shows some kind of hills and a stretch of nothing . . ." Reshma said, her face in the map.

Ilsi snapped the reigns and Dash trotted a bit forward. Ilsi took Dash into a light gallop and ascended the hill. Soon, the trees parted and the path widened and deepened to show extensive use.

"Come see!" Ilsi cried, pulling Dash to stop. As Dash paced a bit, Reshma and Tyk caught up and took in the sight. Below, they saw a flat stretch of land, the earth a deep, rich, reddish color. They saw a few homes and shops lining small roads that crawled and squirmed their way up a large dark mountain. Its peaks were shrouded in thick clouds.

"Nice view," Tyk murmured. Ilsi, Reshma and Tyk continued down the trail, making a gradual descent that veered to their right. The path hugged against the hill and gradually curved down towards town. They finally made it to a small, neatly written sign that read, *Charcoal Ridge*.

"I say we should stay here for a while," Reshma said. "We're out of the forest, at least. We better get somewhere warm or I might set myself on fire."

"Yes, let's find a place to stay," Tyk said. "Wouldn't want a spectacle."

"So is this a good place to stay because it's close to where Giselle might be?" Ilsi asked. She felt impatient about their delay but it was true: they had managed to worm their way out of Beast Forest and it would do her some good to let her mind rest from the maddening and limitless trees. She'd never been more relieved to be around other people.

"I don't know her location any more than you two, but if you look here, it's a good starting point," Reshma said, gesturing to the map. "We're fairly east of where we started in Yling. We're completely east from that forest, too."

"Sure, we could all use some rest." Ilsi sighed.

"It's like I can taste the air," Reshma said. "It's so damp and humid." She had already taken off her shoes to feel the red clay dirt under her feet.

"Does it feel good to have red feet again?" Ilsi asked, grinning. Tyk looked down and noticed the rim of his shoes were already red.

They started to walk in the village streets. The closer they came to town, the more the buzz of people grew. From Ilsi's view, she felt like she was in a red sea, because just about everyone except Reshma, Ilsi and Tyk had different shades of red hair. The people walked around on the dark reddish dirt roads and also walked barefoot, many with the red stuff up to their knees.

"Do you see an inn or something from way up there?" Reshma said. Ilsi looked around to see a building that might've looked bigger than the others. Up ahead, she saw lots of two-story, light wood buildings all building alongside each other, but nothing stood out.

"I just see buildings," Ilsi shrugged.

"I need a bed," Reshma moaned. She looked down as a few kids—practically covered in red dust—giggled and squeezed between Reshma and Dash.

"Woah, hey there!" she said to the kids as well as Dash, who seemed very agitated by all the people pressing at every side. Reshma looked up just as she accidentally bumped into a young man.

"Oh, I'm sorry!" Reshma said, trying to look anywhere than his ears. They stuck out like thick, squatty Elf ears. He smiled, tilted his head, and said something back as the crowd pushed him in one direction and them in another. It was like staying afloat in a river.

"We need a place to stay!" Ilsi said. "Can you help us?"

"Ohhhh!" the young man smiled, showing gleaming white teeth. "You are tired! Sleep?"

Ilsi nodded vigorously as the young man fought against the crowd and put his hand out towards Tyk.

"I'm called Berg," he said. Tyk took his hand and replied by saying his own name. Berg continued, "My father owns beds, he can help all of you."

"What are the chances?" Reshma shrugged and smirked. Berg took the reins from Ilsi's hands with care and gentleness as he led them slightly to the right, which proved slightly less painful than walking directly against the current of the people.

"Why are so many people on the roads?" Tyk asked over the din.

"Time to go home," Berg said. "Workers come from the mountains. Time to go home to wife and kiddies."

Ilsi smiled at Berg's accent. She could tell that their language wasn't his first, but he did fairly well switching over.

He took them to a quaint building that sat at the corner of a four-way street, with the east street taking a sudden incline towards a trail that snaked up to a small mountain range. It was decorated beautifully with spirals and mixtures of red, brown and orange colors. Instead of being tall, it was wide. There were kids playing with a farm dog in the first patch of grass Ilsi had seen since they got into town. It had a family touch to it that made it feel inviting. They had to hike up a slope to go around the building to access what looked like a modest stable.

"The horse will love this place. Dry and warm," Berg said. "May I take the horse?"

"Oh yes," Ilsi said, flustered. He looked up at her with bright blue eyes. It wasn't until she got off the horse that she realized he was only dressed in trousers that went to his knees, a thin shirt without sleeves, and a scarf tied around his neck.

When Ilsi took what they needed, he made a big gesture to the front two doors and said, "Father is inside. He will help you find a room to sleep. I take care of horse." He bowed slightly and led Dash to the stalls. The three bowed back and thanked him.

"I swear, everything here is red," Reshma said. "Their skin can't be red like their hair."

"It's the dust," Tyk grinned.

There was a mat by the door and Reshma tried to wipe her feet, as Ilsi and Tyk tried to kick away loose dust from their boots. It seemed like it wouldn't matter much, since a light red dust coated the floorboards inside.

When they first stepped through the doors, they were greeted with a deep, rich scent of that evening's supper. Ilsi's stomach growled. It was meats and *lots* of spices. The main room had wooden tables scattered about, and the people occupying them were loud and talking happily with each other.

Lights and open windows brightened the decorated walls. A girl collecting empty mugs made her way to a pleasantly plump woman standing around and chatting with a few women at a table. With a few exchanged words, the same round woman came to greet them.

"*Welcome*, strangers!" she said merrily. She held both of Ilsi's hands in her own and glanced at Tyk, then back to Ilsi. "So very nice to see you. You need a bed?"

"Three, *three* beds," Ilsi answered, her cheeks burning.

The woman laughed merrily and grabbed a large ring of keys. "Three beds she says! Three beds I have!" Reshma laughed at this as they all followed the woman up a flight of wooden stairs.

All the while, the woman chatted lightly to them about the rooms and the food, but Ilsi only paid attention to the part about food. She also appreciated that the woman didn't ask them very many questions. They were led to two neighboring rooms.

When the woman finally left them, Ilsi dropped her

belongings and she collapsed on a simple bed. It sat next to a large window, which revealed the outside streets and the people walking about. A simple closet sat across from the bed next to a small bathroom.

With another knock, Berg arrived with some bundles under an arm.

"We have clothes for you," he smiled, holding it out.

"This is very thoughtful of you," Ilsi said. "We must smell awful." She smiled so he knew she was teasing. He kept his smile and shook his head.

"Mother insists. She wants you to be happy here."

"These look really nice," Reshma murmured, fingering the material. *Maybe they want to run up the tab,* Ilsi thought as Berg turned to leave.

"Mother told you about dinner, yes?"

"How could we forget?" Reshma said.

"The family would be honored to have you to eat at our table," he said before actually leaving. Ilsi and Reshma looked at each other, then back at the clothes. They heard a knock and murmuring next door and Ilsi figured Tyk was hearing the same information.

"Time to blend in," Reshma said, taking some of the top pieces and held them up. "Tell me, why does everyone wear dresses out here?"

"Foreigners," Ilsi winked as she peeled away her clothes and weapons.

Just before supper, she hid her weapons wherever possible. She was on her hands and knees, hiding her bow and arrow last just behind her bed.

She stood up and brushed at her skirts. She wore a thin

brown shirt with long sleeves, and a sash around her waist. She had the shirt tucked under a skirt that had other multicolored material layers underneath, and the top layer was scrunched at the sides. She wore slippers, which was a relief after she slipped off her worn and mud-caked boots. Best of all, she wore a long piece of cloth that wrapped around her head like the innkeeper's wife; the cloth concealed most of her blonde hair. Reshma had a red dress fashioned like Ilsi's, and let her short hair hang free as usual.

"Hungry?"

"Yes," Ilsi answered excitedly. They headed out their room and down the stairs. Ilsi didn't even think of Tyk while they were cleaning themselves and resting until she saw him already surrounded by a family of redheads, smiling sheepishly as they approached the table.

Tyk smiled as Ilsi glanced his way. He looked practically part of the family—it looked like he was wearing something that once belonged to Berg or one of his brothers: brown leather breeches and a light olive green shirt. It was open to show his collarbones and a scar snaking over them. He looked much different than the inventor or the ex-Yilidirim.

"Mama!" Berg cried. "All here!"

The summoning worked and she brought out large platters on her hefty right shoulder and her left arm, followed by a boy and girl carrying platters with mugs of various shapes and sizes.

Once the boisterous family made room for Ilsi and Reshma next to Tyk, the three handed out the food and mugs and hands took what they could greedily. If Ilsi didn't grab for something, she was handed things. A mug filled with warm cider, meat still on the bone, and a bowl of something piping hot.

She then heard a screech, and she saw something coming at her. She involuntarily put a hand on a knife on the table, thinking it was an arrow. She was greatly mistaken. Ilsi thought her eyes were failing her. Two creatures just flew over her head. *Dragons?* she thought.

A slim, gold colored dragon, landed gracefully on Berg's shoulder. Berg nonchalantly held up a smaller chunk of meat clinging to a bone and the creature ate quickly and greedily. Ilsi tried to get up but was squished so tightly between Reshma and Tyk that it was nearly impossible.

"Is that a dragon?" Ilsi asked, horrified. Those who noticed her panic laughed, which sent the golden creature shrieking and flying away, only to be replaced by the other sleek-scaled creature, this one dark gray.

"Just as common as birds of prey," the inkeeper's wife said, waving her hand. "Berg here feeds them well enough that they have no reason or desire to leave."

Three pairs of eyes trained on Berg as he shrugged. "Make for great lifelong companions if you're into that sort of thing."

"You outta to show them the rest of your brood," one of the girls said, raising a big spoon of soup to her lips. She laughed as the hot mess dribbled down her chin. Reshma brightened at the idea and Tyk grabbed a hard crusted roll and chomped with enthusiasm.

Ilsi smiled as she ate her weight in bread and meats. It's been a while since a decent meal and a roof over their heads. After this meal, she could finally sleep without worry.

CHAPTER 28

A lot of things met the senses as soon as the three entered Berg's dragon sanctuary. Ilsi figured he let them enter first so they could get a full view. It meant that he didn't see the honest mixture of wonder and disgust that crossed his visitors' faces.

It was a structure similar to a two-story barn, except there were large windows through which creatures could fly in and out of the building. There were also a lot of posts and wooden columns placed throughout to keep the building sound.

The walls were covered in thick scrapes, and dung and straw lined the loft and sprinkled to the ground with every intense shaking. To Ilsi, it looked like a large, dangerous chicken coop. Many of the younger creatures were crawling on the floors, up the posts, or against the walls, and the adolescents were flying or wrestling with their siblings.

The disgust came more from the smell. They could tell that the floors were as well-kept as Berg could manage, but not enough breeze or clean water could clear out the natural smells. It definitely reeked like dung and urine, but it deepened and worsened with the smell of fresh raw meat that was heaped into a long trough that lined the circumference of the structure.

It was a madhouse and Berg seemed highly content being its keeper.

"What is that smell?" Tyk managed. Ilsi looked at him with a squint in her eye.

"That's the hatchlings!" Berg replied happily. He moved easily around the mess to take his spot back in the lead. "They should be easier on the eyes by now. They're still figuring out their breath, so give good distance."

He maneuvered in between Reshma and Ilsi to get by. As soon as he entered, a few nearby dragons flew or crawled towards him, like children greeting their father after a long day's work. As the three followed him, the other dragons dared to approach their visitors with glances, half-mature roars, and good-natured shoe-nibbling.

"Each week is something new," Berg continued. He gestured to a small nest of dragons that slithered like winged lizards. There were a few eggs still unhatched and they served as extra terrain for the newborns. "I mean, new breeds. Mums and dads come and go and do what they like. It's a bit of fun to decide how big they'll eventually get and what comes out of their mouths."

"Do they live here forever?" Reshma asked, looking around, ducking as a red beast swooped passed where her head used to be.

"Easy come and go," Berg shrugged. "Many take off as soon as they're big and maybe come back if they're about to be mamas. Some come when wounded and they leave when they're mended. I don't mind either way. I'm just here if they need me."

"They must have a need to seek shelter," Ilsi mused. "There's so many here."

"This are quite a few more than I usually tend," Berg said.

"But there's a big population of them around this part of the world. Sort of like rabbits with how many of them there are."

Ilsi looked over to Tyk to gauge his interest. He was quiet lately and it was starting to show—and get on her nerves. He looked around without really *looking*. Like he wasn't impressed being surrounded by *dragons*. He stood there, waiting to leave. Ilsi couldn't quite justify it, but it irked her; he was being rude after everything Berg and his family did to welcome them and make them feel safe.

"Do people train them to . . . fight?" Reshma asked. Ilsi started to pay attention at that.

"Good luck," Berg said. "We know what they're capable of and it's not worth trying to tame something that doesn't have the nature to be so."

Reshma looked pointedly at Ilsi as if she was trying to communicate something to her. Was Reshma possibly thinking of enlisting dragons to fight the Yildirim? Or prevent the Yildirim from getting the same idea? Ilsi shuddered at the idea, but deep down she figured it would be easier to persuade a dragon to fight with her than a mermaid—by a long shot.

Reshma and Ilsi fired a few more questions at Berg before the stench really got to them. Ilsi suggested they move on and follow Berg as he showed them around town. They mentioned that they would be staying for a while and Berg happily volunteered to take them around and potentially look for work.

Berg and Reshma took the lead, and Ilsi pinched Tyk's arm to get his attention.

"What did you think of Berg's dragon farm?" Ilsi asked. She could think of a thousand more pointed ways to bring up the topic of Tyk's stoic silence but opted to try for a subtle, light approach.

"It was decent."

"I bet you would want to draw some of those dragon wings up close to remember for your next project," Ilsi tried. He used to be obsessed with wings and studied all kinds to get a grasp of which one could best hold human weight.

"They probably wouldn't survive the trip home," was his reply. Ilsi fumed inwardly. She'd known him for almost his whole life and he was acting like a complete stranger. He was always happy to learn and be polite to others. Now he was acting stuck-up and unbearable.

Perhaps something was bothering him about this place. As eccentric Berg was, it was hard for her to imagine anyone not liking him. He was too nice and generous. She wanted to ask him what his problem was. But she thought maybe another time would be better.

She still glowered inwardly, crafting the ideal conversation to get to the bottom of Tyk's off-putting behavior.

———— ⊰◦⊱ ————

"Hey, Tyk," Ilsi said, looking at him, "are you okay?" She arrived from Berg's farmhouse and stood in the doorway of Tyk's room, smelling of hay. She had been working there for a few days and came back to the inn after a long day for a bath and supper.

"Oh yeah," he replied, offering a small smile. "Better now that I look less like a soldier. Reshma offered to torch my old Yildirim uniform to remove all traces. She was particularly eager about that."

"I'll say. You can relax, trust me," Ilsi said.

"I'm relaxed."

He now wore his own comfortable brown pants, with hunting boots. He wore a long-sleeved white cotton shirt and a dark navy blue vest.

"Well, you look nice," Ilsi said, smiling. "You hardly look like you've been at the blacksmith's all day."

"It's working out nicely," Tyk shrugged. "You seem happy as a dragon farmer."

Ilsi laughed. "Yeah, Berg and his whole family are borderline obsessed with us. They're so willing to tell us everything about this place, it's worth working close by. The smell is getting better since I've decided to clean up the place," Ilsi smiled. "But it'll be nice to do something while we figure out our next step. If we work, we won't have to pay for our rooms, so it all works out. Besides, hatching dragons seems like more fun than washing and mending."

"I didn't know dragons fascinated you so much."

"I've been fascinated by a lot of new and interesting things since leaving Dove," Ilsi said, folding her arms. "Are you . . . well?"

Tyk gulped and gritted his teeth into a smile. He was sweating mildly when looked at her and said, "I've been better."

"You look like you're having a fever—"

"It's fine," Tyk interrupted, balking from her attempt to touch him. "I know there's sweat on my face."

Ilsi held up her hands in mock defeat and walked out of his room.

"Hey, I didn't mean to sound like that," Tyk said, following. He tried to grab her arm, but she already turned around and sighed.

"You just seem jumpy since we got in this village. I'm sure you're worried about getting caught, but we've been here for a few days and we haven't seen a single soldier," Ilsi said. "I just hoped you were feeling comfortable by now."

"What are you doing right now?"

"Well, I came to check on you," Ilsi said. "Reshma is spending time with Berg and the dragon eggs and I thought I might go back."

"There is, urm, something I want to show you," he said. "Something much more fascinating than dragons." She looked curiously at him, and laughed.

"What do you mean?"

"Just come and see, it's really important," he said. He gently took her hand and motioned to the stairs. Ilsi just followed, giving him a glance of uncertainty. He wove through the throng of people, and guided her out of the inn and out of the village.

"Where are you taking me?" she asked. "Or is this all some kind of surprise?" She looked back, as the inn was growing smaller and smaller. She didn't think to bring a weapon since she didn't know he was going to take her out of the village but up the bordering mountain.

"Just wait," he said, smiling mysteriously.

"Can't you just tell me what this is all about?"

"Just a bit further, Ilsi. It'll be worth it," Tyk said again, flashing a quick smile. Ilsi smiled back, but hesitantly.

They ventured on a small trail that zig-zagged up the slope. The trees stood tall, allowing rays of the setting sun to escape into the clearing. He took her up a ways to the top of a steep hill to look at the scenery.

"It's so beautiful!" she said, between gulps of air. She could see the tiny village below with its red, lush sands spread like jam on bread. The entrances and streets were lit with torches as everyone was finding their way home. Dragons flapped their wings and either swooped into the village or left the quaint place.

"See over there? There's the Crescent Mountains," Tyk said pointing at the faded mountains with snow and clouds covering the peaks, "And there are the Charcoal Volcanoes."

"It's very lovely."

"I told you at one point I'd find a way to get us off that island. I'm just sorry that the only escape route was for you to fly through and for me to become a Yildirim." Tyk said. Ilsi smiled and shook her head, gazing into the distance.

"Well, if this was the important thing to show me, then we better head back for supper," Ilsi said. "I'm starving. You could use some stew I bet."

"Let's stay out a little longer. Would you care if we took a stroll in the forest?" he said a bit excited. Ilsi looked at him for a moment with a puzzled expression. He was sweating profusely when Ilsi knew full well that he was capable of cooling himself with a simple spell.

"I want to go back. I don't like walking out of the village weaponless. We didn't even tell Reshma where we were going. Plus I don't think you know where *you're* going."

Tyk didn't answer and Ilsi followed him as he ventured ahead. Ilsi found this more than odd. He was skipping around like a grade school child and then started to run in between the trees. Ilsi walked behind him, gazing at the trees as it became darker. Tyk turned quickly.

"Let's race!" he said, almost panting with excitement.

"*What*—"

"Go!" he called and ran back the way they came. Ilsi watched him run, and decided to follow him. She began running. She wasn't used to running in a dress. She was tempted to use *Swift*, to catch up, but didn't want to careen into a tree in the dark. She began mumbling different things under her breath.

"Ha! I won!" he called out cheerfully a few yards away.

"Tyk! Are you mental?" she called. She found him, atop a hill, frozen where he stood. He was gazing in the sky again. She was starting to become irritated. She breathed heavily and leaned against a nearby tree.

"Answer me! What's with you? You've been all funny since we got here. I feel like you don't like Berg and his family. So tell me what is so wrong about the village and the nice people."

She was surprised when he suddenly turned and faced her. His eyes flickered red for a short, fleeting moment. He had a small frown on his face, and his eyes twitched. He had changed his mood, and *fast*.

Ilsi took a step back. He just stood there. She was about to speak, when he suddenly stomped away. He was waving his hands in frustration.

"What's *wrong*? It won't stop! That stupid voice in my head won't stop—it's telling me to do things I don't want to do," Tyk said, raging and storming. Ilsi just stood there, confused. He went from calm, to energetic, to suddenly very dangerous. She hurriedly followed him, afraid of what he would do.

"Just let me try to understand—"

Tyk suddenly grabbed her close by her arms and pressed his lips against hers. Ilsi's eyes fluttered. She wrestled out of his grip and backed away. She was breathing heavily, tears threatening.

"What is wrong with you? What was *that*?" she cried, as

she quickly stormed off. She didn't care if she would leave Tyk alone in the trees; she felt more concerned about being safe at home. She suddenly didn't feel safe around him and was tired of playing along with his mental antics. Tyk grabbed her arm.

"Let go!" she screamed, and pulled away, "Stop! Stop it, or I'll—"

"Or you'll do *what?*" he growled, very close to her face. She instinctively slapped his face with an icy hand, the first time she had really hit him to hurt him.

He growled with a tone of voice she had never heard before, as a sliver opened and oozed blood. She dodged his glare and took a few steps back. Tyk growled and shook his head in frustration. He suddenly fell to his knees and cried out in pain.

"Tyk!"

His face was hidden with his shaggy hair, which looked thicker with each moment. He looked up at Ilsi's confused face with hair covering his eyes. She screamed when she saw him suddenly grow fangs.

"Get away from me!" he moaned. She didn't need to be told twice. She ran into the safety of the trees, but turned to see what was happening to him. She wanted to help him, but he was . . . dangerous. He was completely engulfed in moonlight on the side of the mountain and she was still under the trees.

The full moon shone in full glory over the hillside in the black sky. Ilsi looked back at Tyk and held back her stifled scream. Moonlight spilled over his crouching figure. Thick hair grew all over his body. He curled his body with his knees to his chest as he howled in pain. A long wispy tail sprouted out as he tore at his clothes and satchel with large paws. Within moments he had transformed into a full-grown wolf.

Ilsi ran down the path as fast as her slippers would allow. She tripped on a branch and she tumbled to the ground. As she tried to get up, she heard eager and angry grunts behind her and an enormous weight on her back. She squirmed and screamed at a sharp pain behind her neck.

"Go away, leave me alone!" she exclaimed. She sang a spell that shielded the back of her body with ice. She stood up and the beast recoiled at the touch. She drew a line of ice on the ground, putting distance between her and the wolf. It gave her a head start down the mountain.

She didn't remember when she lost her shoes, but she abandoned them for the sake of getting off the mountain and back to something she could understand. As she was running, she looked over her shoulder, and saw him running, chasing her with blood-red eyes.

Tears blinded her vision. Her neck and back pained her. The last thing she remembered was creating a cooling and protective shield over her pain as she tripped and fell.

CHAPTER 29

When Ilsi came to, her shoulders, neck, and back felt heavy and sore. She slowly and haggardly pulled herself to her feet, brushed off some leaves, and put a hand to her unsteady heart. She remembered Tyk suddenly transforming into a wolf and her heart raced again. *First a Yildirim and now a shapeshifter?* she thought. She didn't know if the wild animal was waiting close by or not, but thought that it would be best to get herself back to the inn; she could tell her sore back wasn't just soreness.

Ilsi walked hesitantly and hunched over, bending her knees to keep her footfalls quiet. She gazed up at the sky, and saw the large, full moon hidden from her, behind the thick gray clouds. *What if I never find him, or what if he finds me?* She thought of Tyk, lost in the woods with half a mind.

She came to the beginning of the forest and began retracing her footsteps. She continued walking until she reached the hill where she and Tyk were a few hours ago. If she made a run for it, she could probably be safe and warm in the inn in half an hour.

Then, she suddenly heard something breathing heavily behind her. Ilsi didn't know what to expect, but the breathing wasn't Tyk's. A man grabbed her by the shoulders, and she let out a stifled gasp—from surprise and pain.

"If you run, I'll bash your knees," a male voice said. Ilsi felt a thick hand grip on her shoulder. As he pulled his hood down, she didn't recognize him at all. He was far older than she, with dark, charcoal-colored hair. He had a small beard at his chin, which ran along his jaw and connected with his sideburns.

"Did you know that I've been following you?" he said.

"Get away from me," she said through gritted teeth. She tried to step back, weighing her options. He'd be easy to deter with magic, especially with an Ice Chanter spell, but she felt it would give too much away to her mysterious stalker.

"I can see you're thinking of running," he said quietly. He quickly unsheathed a long knife. It glinted devilishly in the moonlight. He held it close to her face so she could feel its coldness against her cheek. "Why not use your abilities to confirm what I already know?"

"Who *are* you, Yildirim scum?" Ilsi cried. Ilsi whimpered, only to throw him off while she tried to think. Hopefully he'd think she was scared rather than royally pissed off. She made weak pleas for her life, but he just kicked her in the stomach to get her to stop. She wheezed a bit and it wasn't theatrical in the least.

"I met your father," the cloaked man said. "Didn't find your mother. Was she dead before we met?" If Ilsi was trying to be calm and cautious, she gave up. She gritted her teeth and screamed in frustration at the man's taunting.

She suddenly resorted to making a swipe at his face with her iced-over hand. It only grazed him slightly, but it gave her a small window to back away and try again since he let go of her shoulder. She used her other arm to upper cut him in the jaw, which met its intended mark.

Suddenly, she felt wild; she wanted to tear him to pieces

for threatening her and throwing around words about her father and mother. In fact, she wanted so badly to scratch at his face, she could almost imagine it. She shook her head wildly and staggered a few steps away from the man. She then felt a surge of energy in her head. She screamed.

The pain in her head trickled down her spine, down to the ends of her toes. She looked up, and found that the moon had come out from behind the thick clouds. She felt as though the moon had been searching for her and found her with its luminous stare. Ilsi wanted to give the moon its satisfaction. She wanted to expose herself to the light but she realized it was already shining down on her.

There was a tug, a connection with the moon that she had never before experienced. For a few seconds she forgot about everything. She forgot who she was and anyone else she had known. The moon was the only thing she knew.

Suddenly, hair shot out and grew like grass all over her body. She felt pain in her teeth as she felt them sharpen and lengthen. She bent her head back, and let out a long howl. Bones sharpened and moved, and she fell to her knees, to clutch her skull.

With one final snarl, her beast form snarled and stood over the cloaked man with drool rolling and dripping from her jaw. Her jaws snapped in his face and she made attempts to tear at him arm. He used it to block his face, but also called a spell of his own.

Her beast form felt a rolling shock that shook her frame. She whined and ran away. She remembered that feeling and remembered that bad people knew that bad spell. Like trying to interpret a dream, she tried to piece together what she knew and who he might be, but all she could think of was satisfying her hunger.

⸻◦◦◦⸻

She felt free. The cool, night air went through her glossy fur, as she sprinted into the thick forest. It was some time during the deep night that she fully realized what was going on. She found herself far from Charcoal Ridge and up in the mountains. She could sense that other creatures—potential meals—around her were burrowing or otherwise dodging her. She didn't feel hungry anymore but instead felt alone.

Suddenly, she realized what she was. She was an animal. She vaguely remembered the sensation and felt grateful for her forgetfulness. It came together that Tyk was an animal and now she was one, too. She nodded firmly to herself, confirming to herself that this was indeed the first time this has happened, as if the extra assurance helped keep her mind clear.

Maybe, if she was calm and in her right senses, maybe Tyk was the same. It didn't matter if he about mauled her; she wanted to find him and figure out how this happened and how she could be herself again. She also reminded herself of that man that talked about her father. She didn't want to forget that detail. It had to mean he was a Yildirim. He *wanted* to know he was part of the raid on Dove.

Like smelling fresh bread or cooked meat, she picked out a distinct scent that her instincts told her belonged to Tyk. She followed the scent deeper into the forest. It was like his distinct smell drifted higher than all others in the air.

She stopped at a moonlit river, and she looked at what she had become. Her fur looked like shiny silver in the moonlight. She was thirsty, and so she used her long nose and tongue to drink from the river and the cool water felt good against her fur.

When she worried she would lose the scent, but then she saw him. He raised his long nose to howl to the moon that bound him in his wolf form. His fur was dark gray, and it rippled slightly with the wind. Even from a few meters away, he looked to her and somehow recognized her; he made no gesture to attack or flee.

"Not bad for your first time," Tyk said. *"You found me in no time."*

His maw didn't move; it was like he was talking to her with his mind and his eyes. He looked away, pawing at the ground as if he wasn't looking forward to this meeting.

"You stink," Ilsi tried to tease. *"Your scent was as strong as my resolve to find you."*

Ilsi wished she had this sharp vision in the dark as a human. She could see him clear as day, as well as the trees around her. They were probably a three hour's hike north of where Tyk initially met the moonlight and transformed.

She could see that Tyk wasn't going to meet her in the middle so she trotted her way up to him. She looked at him nose-to-nose, wondering what would happen next.

"How long does this form last? Days?" Ilsi asked.

"Once the full moon goes away," Tyk said, *"and the sun takes her place."*

"Who did this to you?"

"You're not cross with me?"

"Answer my questions or I will be."

"This isn't anyone's fault. Mother's an Animan."

"A what?"

"A person that takes the form of an animal at a full moon," Tyk explained. *"You could be just about anything—Beast Forest got its name from animals that turn humans into themselves. But it's the Animen who are the real monsters."*

"You're not a monster. Your mother was never a monster," Ilsi corrected. *"How long?"*

"It didn't get to be a big problem until I . . . well, you know, got tall, a deep voice, a huge appetite, and lots of hair."

"I see."

"This isn't me," Tyk said, shaking his head like a wet dog. *"All this fur and violence. First you meet me as a Yildirim, and now I'm an Animan."*

"But Tyk," Ilsi prodded. He turned to her as she rolled to face him and motioned to her heart with her hands. *"Why didn't you tell me? Am I such a shallow friend that you never thought to tell me?"*

"Ilsi, I was doing well in school, working on getting an apprenticeship, and didn't want the whole town to know," he answered passionately. *"I was hoping one day I would escape over the Wall and fix myself so no one would ever have to know."*

"Well, that didn't work," Ilsi merely replied. She made a snuffling sound and jutted out her jaw as she adjusted herself. She rested on the forest floor and looked anywhere but Tyk's face.

"There was always more to you than the nice inventor that lived next door," she mused.

"Why are you so calm? You're going to become a wolf with every full moon for the rest of your life," Tyk asked. His voice was bitter; Ilsi could tell that he was extremely cross with himself.

"What should I do right now? Bite your head off?" Ilsi said. *"Do you want me to leave you in the forest alone while I leave and live my life? Hardly seems like a solution. Come back with me to the village. Let's talk. Let's . . ."*

"Lie down and sleep for a bit," Tyk said, raising a forepaw to the space behind her neck. It was like he was gently pushing her to the ground. *"You look exhausted. I'll watch over you."*

"Don't run away," Ilsi said, agreeing on the exhausted part. *"Promise."*

"I'll be right here." The voice was soothing and assuring. As she lay on her stomach, she rested her head on her forepaws and felt Tyk's wolf form lay down right next to her.

CHAPTER 30

Ilsi woke up lying face down and sweating profusely. She was on her bed, she realized, and as she turned her head, light came to her eyes. She had made it back to the inn. It was daytime. She was in a heap of trouble.

"Stay still, girl," Reshma said. Ilsi obeyed, but sighed and groaned.

"What are you doing?" she got out.

"Stitching you up so I can knock some sense back into you," Reshma murmured. "You and Tyk just disappeared a few nights ago, then I found you here naked like the day you were born and oozing your blood everywhere."

Reshma's voice was calm and level; Ilsi knew it meant she was livid.

"Tyk," Ilsi began, "has been odd for the past few weeks and I found out why. He's a shape-shifter. An Animan."

"Like Giselle?" Reshma said. "Tyk did *this* to you?"

"I don't know, I promise," Ilsi said, hissing in pain as Reshma kept tightening the stitches. "It was a very confusing evening."

"You've been like this for a few days," Reshma said. "Berg's family thinks you've fallen ill and they are beside themselves with worry—wanting to help and all. Keeping this a secret was half the battle. Not killing Tyk was the other."

"You're a gem," Ilsi grunted. "I mean it. I feel awful. As in this is extremely painful."

"Almost done fixing these stitches. Just . . . go back to the beginning. Where were you and what happened?"

"I just found out that Tyk can turn into a wolf. It's not by choice. But the moon messed with his mind and that's what has made him all weird lately. You've seen it the past few days, right?"

"Oh yeah," Reshma murmured. "Thought he had a bit of a jealousy vein in him. He doesn't like Berg as much as Berg tries to like Tyk."

"He changed into a wolf and somehow . . . so did I."

Reshma momentarily stopped her work. Ilsi could hear her sigh. "Seriously, Ilsi, you're a catastrophe waiting to happen. How are we going to ever find Giselle? This is just another setback to deal with when we're supposed to be looking for this Giselle lady. All we've done is pretend like we're a part of this town. We haven't done any looking."

"Should I make Tyk leave?" Ilsi asked softly, afraid of the answer.

"Do what you want—I know he's your best friend," Reshma said, putting a blanket over Ilsi's exposed back, "But it sounds like there's a lot more to learn here. He might have access to the Yildirims we wouldn't have on our own—or a way to find Giselle if they're both in the shape-shifting business."

"He is my best friend—or maybe was," Ilsi said, staring at the wall. "He could've killed me."

"He won't stick around long enough for me to ask," Reshma said, laying on her stomach to make eye contact. "Most of his things are gone. I haven't seen him. Didn't leave any message as to what he's doing or where. I'd like to think he's more afraid of me than you."

Ilsi growled in response. "How long until I can sit or stand?"

"Give it time. I hope a few days," Reshma said. "I'm not good at letting myself heal, either, but you won't be in a condition to raise your arms or function on your own if you don't rest."

"Just . . . tell Tyk to see me if he does show his face," Ilsi said.

"I hope you sort this all out," Reshma sighed, lying on her back. "And I'd prefer to know what is going on as we go, rather than after the fact."

"You're right," Ilsi said, squeezing her eyes shut. "The sooner we can find Giselle the better. We can find your family and get back home to mine."

⸺◦∞◦⸺

"She's right here. You've made her wait long enough."

Ilsi was asleep again and thought she heard Reshma say something. She felt the bed shift a bit as someone sat next to her. A hand brushed through her unruly blond curls, which actually woke her up.

"Tell me what the hell just happened," she croaked once her vision cleared; she was still resting on her belly. Someone sighed and she knew it was Tyk.

"You're an Animan now," Tyk said, "thanks to me."

"I imagined so," Ilsi said, scoffing, "I saw it myself. I *felt* it myself. What you aren't telling me is how this shape-shifter business started. Your mother got it? How even?"

Tyk folded his arms. "My father was bitten by one while

261

traveling around and apparently there's certain bite wounds that do that to people. My mother got it soon after they were married. Father was able to buy some expensive antidote to cure her, but with the Wall, there was no way to get out and find any for me or my father."

"That must've been frustrating. I wish I could've helped somehow," Ilsi said, with a moan. "We're best friends—why did we keep secrets from each other?"

"You're talking about *Swift*?" Tyk said, raising an eyebrow, "or are you talking about some other secret I ought to know?"

"Yes, *Swift*," Ilsi rolled her eyes. "But you *know* what I mean. We should've trusted each other. We could've helped another. We could've felt less . . . alone."

"I'm . . . I'm sorry that I messed up," Tyk said, rubbing his face with his hands. "I always meant to tell you, but I was afraid."

"Apparently you weren't last night," Ilsi said. "You wanted me see you transform, didn't you?"

"Partially, yes, deep down," Tyk said. "I wanted you to know all of me. But I had no intentions of harming you. I thought it might help you, you know, with your cause. A lot of people are Animen because they were captured by Althod's men and terrorized by creatures in Beast Forest. I thought I could help with connections. I want to help reach out the Animen. Like the beast people in the forest, the Animen will gladly fight for revenge."

"I bet Ladala won't turn away any extra help," Ilsi grinned. "So explain this to me at least. Is this a whenever-I-want sort of ability or what?"

"It's all around the full moon," Tyk said. "It messes with your mind and when you're exposed to the light it transforms you. By the time it came last night, I couldn't get myself away, nor could I tell in my right mind that I was about to—" He averted his gaze, clearly not pleased to explain.

"You kissed me," Ilsi interrupted. "In case you were too delusional to notice, that's how you brought this on me."

Tyk colored a bit, shaking his head.

"That's ridiculous," Tyk answered, "you can't pass a curse like this just with a *kiss*."

"Well, then how did I end up like this?"

"Let's start with why you're recovering in bed," Tyk said, pulling Ilsi up off the bed. Ilsi pulled her wrist away as Tyk looked her over. "Did I scrape you or something? Don't give me that look."

"You're just spinning me around," Ilsi grumbled, holding her tangled hair up and away from her neck to help. Tyk hissed, sucking his breath in. "What is it?"

"You've got a gash down your spine. I truly am an epic asshole."

"It doesn't *hurt*," Ilsi retorted. Her back felt sore but she knew it was probably due to healing and getting up from bed for the first time that day.

"Are you out of it? It's purple and black! And it looks like Reshma gave you stitches."

"Are you peeking down my nightshirt?" Ilsi shrieked, turning around to sit and face him.

"It starts between your shoulder blades and I don't know how long it goes down. Just calm down," Tyk said, throwing his hands up in the air.

"Did you even want to kiss me?" Ilsi asked, balling her fists, "or do you blame all your faults on the Animan, Tyk?"

"Dammit, Ilsi!" Tyk yelled. "And you're wondering why I waited so long to tell you!"

He was already wearing his boots, so he only threw his satchel over his shoulder before making his way towards the door.

"Wait! You can't just leave!" Ilsi cried. She had no idea when she'd see him again. "This conversation is far from over."

"I know," Tyk said gruffly, "But I am too cross with you and myself right now. I need some fresh air. Stay and rest."

Like that will happen, Ilsi thought. She sat there wide awake for what felt like a few hours, frustrated with how things went and how everything seemed to go wrong. She didn't want him to go away. She didn't want to be angry with him, but they kept taking turns putting distance between themselves.

She rolled into a sitting position and gingerly sat up. She then pushed herself up with her legs and put on some extra clothes. The day was getting on and Ilsi figured it best to cover up her weakened state.

As she gingerly made her way down the steps, Ilsi offered a small wave and smile at the innkeeper's wife, and headed towards the horse stalls. Tyk at least made it easier to be found; she didn't even need Dash to carry her around town.

"You didn't venture too far it seems," Ilsi said, peeking her head inside. Tyk was whittling something with a piece of wood.

She peeked inside and had to take a few steps inside to get a better look at him. It didn't make sense why he was here, but he looked up when it seemed like she was venturing too close.

"You can walk?"

"I wasn't given much of a choice," Ilsi said, leaning against a post. She didn't like resorting to moving slowly. "Can we just talk this out?"

"Are you afraid of me?"

Ilsi sighed. "When you're a wolf trying to chase me, then

yes I'm afraid. But I'm not afraid of *you*," Ilsi answered. "I've seen the worst in you. And if this is the worst, then it says a lot about the overwhelming good."

"I don't need you to tell me I'm a good person," Tyk muttered.

"Then what should I say?" Ilsi asked. "I came here because I wanted to apologize for upsetting you. I could've said things better and I could've listened to you. I felt hurt because . . ."

She had to stop because she could feel a roll of emotion rise to her throat. She blinked back unwanted tears, hoping she could do this without crying.

"What's wrong?" Tyk said, finally getting up.

"The kiss."

"Am I that bad of a kisser?"

"Do you have feelings for me?" Ilsi said, looking up with glassy eyes. "Because I'm starting to think I have feelings for you. And . . . I know that the Yildirims have and will use my affections for you against me."

"You're upset about them more than the Animan thing?" Tyk said, his ears reddening under his hair.

"If they do something to you to get to me, I would never forgive myself," Ilsi said, letting a few tears fall. "I guess when you kissed me and then acted like you were sorry about it . . . I just don't know if I wanted you to like me or not."

"You're talking nonsense," Tyk answered.

"Well, you explain to me what the kiss was about," Ilsi began, "because I can forgive you hurting me since I knew you were crazy and thinking with half a brain. But if your affections aren't real—"

"May I kiss you now?" Tyk interrupted. Ilsi's breath hitched as she quickly nodded. Tyk wasted no time giving her an actual kiss. It was softer and gentler. He put a warm hand around the base of her head and kept her close with the other hand gently on her back. He kissed her a few more times before pulling his lips away. Ilsi bit after them to keep them there and kissed him back before they pulled away.

"I *do* have feelings for you, and they've been there for a good while. It just seemed like you were more focused on helping the elf lady than seeing where things could go with me," Tyk said, resting his forehead against hers. "I'm sorry I was so misleading."

"I understand," Ilsi said, smiling softly. "I haven't been clear, either. I really do need your help and I'm here if you need me."

Tyk let her lean against him as he pulled her close. "Then let's find Giselle and finally get ourselves home."

------◈------

"Bring in the lieutenant," a man commanded. One of his uniformed officers opened the large metal door, and another man stepped into the dim room. He entered with a brisk pace, stopped before the man in the chair and bowed, sweeping his cloak away.

"You summoned me, my lord?" he said, his head bent low.

"What are your updates on capturing the Ice Chanter girl, Reubens?" Althod said, his yellow eye staring in fury.

"She's already killed off over twenty-five of my men. Not to mention she has enlisted the favor of the cat people," the Captain said. "I've tracked her down in the Charcoal Ridge hamlet and I've located her sleeping quarters. I also recently discovered she is an Animan."

"Happens to the best of us I'm sure," Althod replied gruffly. "What you have failed to report is what you're doing letting her nap like a dog rather than having her bark like one about Ladala's whereabouts and war plans."

"Forgive me, my lord," Reubens said, "But I thought I was already carrying out your orders. You asked me to *follow* the girl and study her along with whatever plans Lady Ladala has shared with her."

Althod sat there, swirling his drink in a thick mug.

"Have I misinterpreted your instructions, my lord?" Reubens tried. A hand went to his beard as he stroked it absentmindedly.

"Don't patronize me," Althod retorted. "You should be focusing your efforts on organizing the hunt for Ladala's camp while capturing villages and cities. The girl will have little influence if Ladala is out of the picture. Something I've reminded you of, and yet you seem hell-bent on finding this young witch."

Reubens bowed his head with as much humility as he could muster. "It is my will to serve your will. I know how much the girl means to your future plans."

"There will be no future plans if you keep focusing on the wrong player," Althod barked. "Must I find someone else who uses their ears correctly?" Reubens scowled, thinking of a handful of people who would love to see him demoted.

"No, my lord," he answered demurely. "I am yours to command."

"Then see to your next assignment," Althod said, as his assistant gave Reubens a leather-bound message. Reubens frowned as he untied it and read it through quickly. He looked up and said,

"Should I capture their stock of dragons, my lord?"

"Sure, sure," Althod waved the question away. "The dragon trainer is no doubt more important than the beasts."

"And I see that the Ice Chanter boy is still a prime target that must be captured."

"Most certainly," Althod replied. "He's just the man I need to see. You're dismissed. Lucky for you this was more pleasant than your last report."

CHAPTER 31

After about a month of staying in Charcoal Ridge, Ilsi began to slip into a pattern of waking up early, eating a small breakfast, and following Berg to the dragon sanctuary. She picked a new section of the farm to clean up and stayed with it until feeding time. When it seemed like her task was never-ending, she would look up and see the young dragons napping peacefully in patches of light sketched on the clean floor and see that her hard work was well appreciated.

Berg appreciated the help—of course he didn't see much wrong with letting the dragons leave messes all over the place. With Ilsi's help, they were able to clear larger patches of ground to create individual nests for mothers to come and lay their eggs or to patch up older, worn beasts.

Berg beamed with pride, "You have the heart for dragons."

Ilsi realized Crescent, an older male dragon, was already at her side and nestling against her entire right side like an overgrown, scaly cat. The dragon got its nickname from his pearly white scales and his large purple eyes. He wasn't the biggest creature that had visited the barn but he'd stayed long after they fed and tended to him.

"They are fascinating," Ilsi said with a shrug. "You must understand that I come from a very small town and didn't venture away until less than five months ago. I've got a lot to learn."

"You already know all the simple stuff about us," Berg shrugged, taking a handkerchief from his back pocket to wipe his face. "Just a clan of simple farmers and miners."

"And dragon tamers," Ilsi added. "Can't forget that. Are there other creatures like dragons around here?"

"If you're talking animals, then I wouldn't know for sure," Berg said. "Leave that to the Beast Forest. The only other creature that comes to mind is the Earth Witch."

"Earth Witch?" Ilsi repeated.

"Well, it's a tale to tell the kiddies before bed, nothing serious," Berg said, sweeping up soiled hay. "Not sure if she's a woman made of earth or if she is a woman who commands the earth. The mommas like to say that she plays tricks on those who are not kind to animals and trees, but she heals complete strangers. She doesn't bother us. It's not like she comes to say hello."

"She's a legend, then?" Ilsi said, her eyebrows furrowing.

"More like a tradition," Berg said. "We have a holiday where we thank her for all she does. We're not sure if it works, but it does no harm."

"What do you do?"

"We leave a meal of our finest dishes in the forest," Berg shrugged.

"The Beast Forest, you mean?" Ilsi said, pointing in the direction of the foreboding landscape.

"Nah, up east," Berg answered, pointing opposite to the mountains covered in trees—where Tyk took Ilsi to show her the view. She nodded thoughtfully.

"What does she . . . look like? Would you know?"

He shook his head. "Like I said, she's a mystery. We don't know much about her but we do what we can to not upset her . . . just in case."

"Hmm, interesting," Ilsi murmured as they slowly got back to work.

—◦—

"My boy tells me you're asking for the Tree Lady," said the innkeeper's wife, Pia, as the table was covered in hot food. Reshma and Tyk's heads popped up and glanced at the woman as she made herself comfortable on the bench.

"What about a tree lady?" Tyk said.

"Oh, she's a legend here," the innkeeper loudly replied, waving the comment off. "My wife will tell you kiddie tales but no one has seen her for a very long time."

"But you can feel her *influence*," Pia stressed. "We live close to the volcanoes and like this Lady, they are violent yet blessed. The years we give good gifts and offerings are when our bounty is the sweetest. You agree, Rolf, you must."

"It's better to be prepared, right?" Tyk smiled kindly, spooning a hearty amount of stew into his mouth.

"You ought to see her Burning Tree," Berg's sister said excitedly. "It is the proof we have that she walks among us."

"Burning tree?" Reshma repeated. "Where is it?"

"It's not hard to miss, but it's a perilous pilgrimage," Pia began, mopping her bowl with bread.

"Who here doesn't know about the Wood Witch?" guffawed another guest a few tables over. Ilsi blanched at the thought of someone overhearing their conversation. She glanced around while taking a swig from her mug and sighed into her cup. For a moment, she wondered if the man from the woods was here to overhear the conversation.

"I think we'd know more about her if you all would decide on a name!" Reshma blurted. Her retort was met with a chorus of laughs. Berg's family thought that just about anything Reshma said was funny and amusing.

"These young folks are newcomers, they're just learning how backwards we really are, eh?" Rolf explained loudly.

"You didn't tell me you were housing Ylingians!" the other guest exclaimed, and the other men at his table laughed as if he told a good joke. *They must not think much of Yling,* Ilsi thought with a grin.

"Apologies, miss, but maybe you oughta tell us where you're from so we can be more polite," the other guest said, this time without the intent to joke.

"We live close to Yling, so maybe you're onto something," Ilsi smiled.

"I'm an islander," Reshma said, gesturing to her brown face. "Although I get mistaken for a desert girl everywhere we go."

"You definitely look the part," the innkeeper's wife nodded. "But in the best way, sweetie." Reshma smiled lopsidedly and mildly rolled her eyes.

"We're from a colder climate, basically," Tyk said, gesturing between himself and Ilsi. "We used to be neighbors."

"Colder climate? Never heard of anything like that on the other side of the Beast Forest," Berg said.

"Well, it's more like bad luck with weather," Ilsi said. "It's usually nothing to complain about."

"So how did you decide to come out here?"

"We lost our families," Tyk said simply. The room hushed immediately. "We've all lost something and we're out here looking for them."

The innkeeper's wife dropped her spoon and it clattered onto her plate. Ilsi thought she looked like she was about to burst with tears or emotion or both. Pia held a hand to her heart and said in a hushed voice, "So far from home to find your family? How hard it must be!"

Berg and his younger sister instinctively inched closer, looking at the three with sad faces. Pia pulled them close like she was suddenly afraid to lose her own.

"You must let us help you," Pia said, looking to her husband for support, "it's the least we can do. You've come so far!"

"But you've helped us so much as it is," Ilsi insisted, feeling overwhelmed. She gestured at her mug that refused to stay empty and her belly full of warm food. "We have felt so safe and welcome in this place. It's like a home away from home."

Ilsi suddenly realized how much Reshma must miss her big family by the way Berg's family were loud and often talked over each other, but they were all so happy. Ilsi never experienced a loud supper until she came here. She looked to Reshma and squeezed her hand under the table.

"Your kindness will make it easy for us to have hope that we'll one day be reunited with our loved ones," was all Reshma had to say.

Needless to say, Pia and Rolf fretted over the three the rest of the evening, daring to ask more questions about what they used to do back home and what their families were like. Ilsi crawled into bed later that night with a heavy stomach and a heavy heart. It was getting more difficult to leave the longer they stayed there.

———⊶∘⊷———

"I have to write a message to Ladala," Ilsi said. "It's urgent."

"What's going on?" Reshma said. "We haven't exactly made much progress and unless you want to inform her that you're an Animan, there's nothing terrible going on."

Ilsi pulled out a small sheet of parchment from her satchel, along with a simple quill and inkblot she'd borrowed from the innkeepers.

"I have to tell her about the man that tried to attack me in the woods," Ilsi said. "He said he knew my father. I don't know if he was doing that to play with me, but I'm not taking any chances. He knows too much about where we really come from."

"What? A man in the woods?" Reshma repeated. "Were you planning on telling us?"

"Who was it?" Tyk added, getting up from his leaning position against the wall. "A soldier?"

"He was alone and wasn't clearly marked," Ilsi said. "He wasn't even wearing one of those amulets. He just said things that made it sound like he was *there* in Dove when I escaped passed the Wall. It was after, well . . . the rough night as Animen."

"Physical features?" Tyk said. "Be specific, Illy." Ilsi glanced at him for a split second at the recollection of an old nickname she hadn't heard in a long time.

"He looked pretty beaten up, like he had a lot of battle scars or something," Ilsi said. "I noticed his pinky finger was nothing but a nub when he grabbed my shoulder."

Tyk looked searchingly, clearly expecting more information. Reshma looked absolutely clueless and shrugged.

"I don't know, he was a hefty build. Could probably snap me in half. Had a small beard, dark hair," Ilsi trailed off. "It was dark and I dealt with him swiftly before changing into a wolf myself. He threatened me with a knife or dagger at some point, but I don't know what happened to him once I transformed."

At the mention of the weapon, Tyk stopped blinking and looked down at the ground.

"Reubens," he said quietly.

"Huh?" Reshma blurted.

"He doesn't look much different than most men I met on the Yildirim side," Tyk began, "but his knives are unmistakable. They were plain, right? I know of them. He's well-trained in torture, so I've seen him pull them out."

"So he's Yildirim then?" Reshma said. "That's not good. But not all surprising."

"Ilsi, you need to write that note," Tyk said with a low voice, pointing at the blank parchment, then continued with a quieter voice, "and we need to get the hell out of here. He isn't a Yildirim pup like I was. He's high up in the ranks. He led the attack on Ravenna."

Ilsi's mouth gaped open and then she shut it again. Her mind suddenly went back to that day and remembered him as the man in the mass amount of furs. She bumped into him and escaped his wrath through the Wall. Reshma got up from the bed and cracked her knuckles for good measure.

"It's revenge time," Reshma said.

"No," Ilsi blurted. They locked eye contact for a moment and Ilsi continued, "If we fight here, we fight on neutral, friendly

275

soil. These people have been good to us. I'd rather leave and draw the conflict away than see Yildirims destroy these people to get to us."

"You're right," Reshma nodded. "Spoke too soon. I'll start packing the gear. Tyk, take care of the bill for our stay, and write that note, Ilsi. Tell Ladala they *need* to protect this place."

"I think we should split up, but just temporarily, since the Yildirims have likely caught on that we're traveling in a trio," Tyk said. "Ilsi better go first and get a head start on the trail."

"I'm going to find that burning tree," Ilsi said, determined. "It'll lead us closer to Giselle." The other two nodded.

"If we split up and gradually disappear," Reshma said, "it hopefully won't look as suspicious if Yildirims are lurking around. We'll meet back at the edge of Beast Forest due west by the path signs in two weeks as our backup plan." Tyk squeezed Ilsi's hand and she squeezed back.

<hr />

To be delivered to and read by Lady Ladala at once:

Currently looking for Giselle. May have some idea as to where to start looking. Being tracked by Reubens and will have to change positions. Send soldiers to protect these people in Charcoal Ridge. They've been so good to us and would sympathize with our cause. Better yet—Reubens needs to go. He knows too much about us.

Ilsi

CHAPTER 32

Mama, when did you know that you loved Papa? Was it the sickening sadness that sits in your stomach at the thought of being separated yet again? Was it putting your body between him and his worst nightmares? I've always loved Tyk as a friend, which is probably why I would soon rather face Althod myself than see him go back to the Yildirim for my sake.

It always seems like I learn what I cherish most when it's too late. Otherwise, I don't think I would miss you as much as I do right now.

———◦◦———

Ilsi slung her pack over her left shoulder and secured a cloak around her neck and over her shoulders. She wore some of the darker travel clothing they had accumulated with their earnings and turned to face Reshma and Tyk, both dressed for travel but not armed and prepared to leave so soon.

"We'll meet together soon, right?" Ilsi asked nervously. She clasped her hands together in front of her body. She was only separated from Reshma once and was worried about traveling alone.

"As long as we stick to the plan," Reshma said. She approached Ilsi and gave her a big hug—something Ilsi wasn't prepared for.

"That hug suggests it'll be longer than planned," Ilsi joked. Reshma rolled her eyes but didn't smile.

"I'll walk you to your horse," Tyk murmured, taking Ilsi's hand.

She took it and looked once more over her shoulder at Reshma as she said, "Be careful out there."

They went down the hall and quietly down the stairs. There were a few people in the dining area of the inn, but they slumped over their tables; hardly anyone was even present to see them leave.

Once they quietly closed the inn doors behind them, Ilsi and Tyk made their way to the stables. The summer sun was too stubborn to set, although it was finally getting dark enough to rely on torches and lanterns. Ilsi gave Tyk's hand a squeeze and said, "I have a feeling you're not going to meet us after our short separation."

Tyk smiled sadly and looked to the ground. He nodded.

"Sorry," was all he said.

"I want you to stay," Ilsi sighed. "The idea of going home seems more real when you're here. Where are you going?"

"I can't say because I know you'll follow," Tyk said. "As much as it helps to follow you around to find people to fight, I can help you more this way. Trust me. Even though Althod leads the Yildirim, it's Reubens that taught me the meaning of hell.

"He was the one that forced me to be a soldier. You know I'm a creator, not a destroyer. He's using me to get to you, and I can't let that happen. So a bit of distance will help you find the lady you're looking for . . . and it'll help me destroy him from the inside out."

"You're going to kill him?" Ilsi whispered. "What was that bit about not being a destroyer?"

"A leader like him only needs a few brutes to follow him," Tyk murmured. "If I help the others escape the influence of the amulet, then maybe I can scrape together a few men and women who want their own piece of revenge, too."

Ilsi silently looked up at Tyk in defeat and took both hands into hers.

"I'll miss you while you're gone."

Tyk kissed her softly on the lips before she used her hands to hold his face to kiss him back.

"I pray I'll soon be able to do this again," Tyk smiled. "Now go while the night is on your side."

"Promise me you'll find me again," Ilsi said, "or I'll tell your mother."

Tyk snorted and nodded in defeat. He gave her one last kiss on the forehead, then turned her around and gently nudged her in the direction of the stables. She walked quietly to the stalls and looked over her shoulder to see Tyk noiselessly disappear behind the inn doors and back inside.

She went down the first row of horses, pulling down a lantern left in the stall and lighting it to guide her. Most of the horses were settling down to sleep. There were a few stable hands tending to the horses and putting blankets over them. Dash didn't exactly sense Ilsi, but became aware that someone was approaching.

Dash still had his halter over his back as Ilsi grabbed the saddle and straps to saddle him. As she tried to soothe and coax him away from the stall, she caught a figure out of the corner of her eye and turned and flinched simultaneously.

"Berg," Ilsi gasped. "Hello there." Ilsi tried to mask her surprise, while Berg made no attempts to mask his own emotions.

"You're leaving." His features were downcast and flat, completely devoid of his usual good-natured charm.

"Yes," was the reply.

"Can I help you get safely out of the town?"

"Sure, of course," Ilsi said, guiding Dash along.

"Maybe you should leave your horse here," Berg said, taking the reins and guiding Dash back to the stall.

"But—"

"Come to the sanctuary!" Berg whispered, and Ilsi dared to follow. After a few minutes of brisk running, they made it inside the barn, which felt similar to the horse stalls, except the sleep sounds came from every inch of the barn and the air was thicker and warmer.

"Whoever is after you will think twice if you are riding a dragon like this one," Berg said, gesturing towards Crescent. Ilsi's mouth gaped as the creature obeyed the hand gestures and sharp whistle by coming towards them. Ilsi dared to look the beast in the eye as it brought its face close to Berg's to receive a gentle stroke between its pearly nostrils.

"You want me to fly on Crescent?" Ilsi whispered incredulously. "And what do you mean, 'whoever is after you'?"

"I've been worried about you three since dinner," Berg said. "The way you talked about your families being taken . . . I don't need three guesses on who might've taken your family, Ilsi."

Ilsi's eyes widened and bit her lip. Surely Berg was no idiot.

"You're clever, Berg," Ilsi said. "We want to go find who

attacked our clans and we don't want them to come here to meddle with yours."

"It's appreciated," Berg nodded. "We would gladly help. Not just the family, but everyone here. We don't like bullies but we are simple."

"Then hang onto this," Ilsi said, giving Berg a stone from her pouch. "The lady I serve will defend you if you take good care of this."

"Seems not as messy as a dragon—I'll manage," Berg smiled at his own joke. He gave the stone a funny look and put it in the pocket in his trousers

"Quite," Ilsi said, smiling back. She and Berg both looked at Crescent who was nudging for more scratches and rubs on his snout.

"He is safe, I swear it," Berg said. "I've seen the way he takes a liking to you. I fully believe he'll protect you like one of his own, just like he'd do for me."

"If you think he'll help," Ilsi sighed, feeling suddenly nauseous. It felt like her stomach dropped down into her boots. However, she was sure that the trek to finding the burning tree would be easy and incredibly short if she could see it from the air.

Berg whistled again for Crescent, and the dragon moved slowly behind him on his clawed back legs and wings, with Ilsi following behind after the last of Crescent's tail slunk out of the barn.

"Up, up," Berg said, motioning to Crescent. Ilsi sprang up at bit and swung her leg over to sit on Crescent's back. She hadn't realized how big Crescent was until she could comfortably sit on his back. Her boots barely touched the ground.

"You must nudge him at her sides to steer, like a horse,

but be gentle with the scales," Berg instructed. Ilsi nodded, with a forced smile, wishing away thoughts of sudden death. When Ilsi was about to wrap her arms around Crescent's neck, Berg handed her a small, thin whistle on a small chain.

"This is for you. To tell Crescent to lift off or to land, you must use this. I have trained him to listen to it, so he will react to it," Berg said, and Ilsi situated the chain around her neck.

"I owe you my life," Ilsi said, "if I don't lose it while flying on this dragon." She smiled to show she was joking. Berg just smiled in shyness and meekness as he took a few spaces back to give them berth.

Ilsi took the compass and looked for north. The trees of Beast Forest were to the northwest and the red mountains were to the east. The very last rays of purples and reds were sinking behind the trees to the west when Ilsi put the whistle to her lips and wrapped her arms tightly around Crescent's neck. She clamped her eyes shut, blew a clear note, and gripped firmly as Crescent's wings unfolded and flapped.

As Ilsi began to rise from the spot on the ground, she felt a slight jerk as Crescent began his flight. The Ice Chanter yelped in fright and excitement as Crescent gained some air and didn't wait long to zoom ahead. Ilsi dared to look back down and waved down to Berg who waved back from his spot below.

—◦—

Ilsi looked ahead, feeling every muscle tense in her body to keep herself latched onto the dragon. Crescent probably wasn't used to her weight; it showed in the way they would randomly drop a foot or so in the air, or they would gradually sink if

Crescent coasted. This started to happen about an hour into their flight.

She was starting to wonder why Berg thought this was such a good idea; instead, she thought to maybe try her luck at directing Crescent down to the forest below to let him rest. They were flying above a large river bordered by dark sands and grasslands. As much as it was thrilling and convenient to have him, she would understand if he naturally wanted to find his way back to wherever he came from.

Her potential plans came to a halt when she saw the sudden gather of gray clouds. The winds increased, and Ilsi was afraid for them both. The breeze was pushing them away from the mountains where they were heading. She turned her head to get a better view of her surroundings as Crescent circled and descended on his own. They had drifted more towards the edge of Beast Forest. It would still be a few day's flying by her guess to even reach them, but they still instilled anxiety. Just the thought of being lost in the trees again made flying a dragon seem like the more enjoyable option.

She guided Crescent verbally and physically to turn.

"Come on, you're *right*," Ilsi grunted. "A-*way* from the mental trees. Good boy!"

Ilsi thought that if they could make it to the mountains, Crescent could get a break and Ilsi could be closer to the burning tree. Suddenly, a fierce *crack* sounded over the immense sky.

Crescent let out a roar that rang in Ilsi's ears. Ilsi felt herself falling much faster to the ground than she would like and screamed loudly to prove it. The dragon must've been struck by lightning by the smell of burning flesh that rose to Ilsi's nostrils.

Her first thought was Yildirims were involved. The storm

came out of nowhere and there wasn't a cloud in the sky when they departed. A soldier must've seen them and tried to shoot them down. They commanded lightning without a single cloud; Ilsi hoped Yildirims couldn't control the skies, too.

Crescent wasn't flapping anymore to maintain control, and they were making a beeline towards the trees. Ilsi buried her face into Crescent's neck, ready to feel the sudden pain she expected. She went with her gut and cast a *Swift* spell to guide them sure towards the mountains. She did so and was soon embraced into the darkness of the terrain below.

CHAPTER 33

Reshma was just about finished with her packing when she heard an urgent knock at the door. She hastily put a blanket over her things on the floor and wiped her hands on her pants before opening the door. She cracked it open just a bit and realized both Tyk and Berg were standing there. In the dark, only the simple flame of a candle illuminated their faces.

Without saying much, she let them in and the men quickly side-stepped inside. Reshma went back and took away the ridiculous attempt at hiding her things.

"No sense in hiding much," she murmured as she began strapping her travel pack and weapons over her shoulder. "Something wrong?" Berg looked tired but was fully dressed and carrying a candle in a holder; he'd been awake for a while now.

"Someone's coming to the village," Tyk said quietly. "I think it's the Yildirims. There's a dozen or so torches coming. We have to help."

"What? Snuff their lights out?" Reshma asked, raising an eyebrow.

"Literally or . . .?" Berg said in confusion and looked at the two.

"Both senses," Reshma said. "Fire does not harm me in the

same way ice doesn't harm Tyk or Ilsi." Berg didn't stop to ask more questions, but instead guided them quietly out of the inn.

"We have to warn the town," Tyk said. "Whether Yildirim or not, they don't seem friendly. These people will need to hide or fight—"

He was interrupted by a loud boom and crash. The trio just barely closed the door and felt the evening air when they saw the roof splinter and crash. Someone had felled a tree close by and it leaned into the roof. They could already hear screams inside.

"I'll help people get out," Reshma said. "You better wake everyone else up! Hurry!"

She was already gone before the other two could say anything in return. She was armed to the tooth and had a lot of extra weight on her, so she made a quick trip to the horse stalls and dumped as much of her gear as possible and hastily threw a horse blanket and some hay over it. She looked up and saw Dash was still in his usual stall. Her mind brimmed with questions and confusion but shook her head and ran out again to get back into the inn.

People were already filing out in small groups, huddling and looking back at the inn's condition. The tree's trunk continued to splinter violently and sank deeper into the roof. Screaming and yelling filled the whole building.

Reshma entered as Rolf and Pia were still inside, guiding people towards the front door. They looked up at Reshma and ushered quickly for her to join the people.

"I'm here to help!" she answered before they could protest. Another crash and another scream. "I'll go help up there!"

"No, young lady! Stay outside!" Pia cried up the stairs. Reshma didn't listen long but went against the current of people in bedclothes and traveling gear, trying to tote as many of their belongings as they could carry. The building had two full stories of rooms and she kindly helped those who came her way, but Reshma also had her mind on those who might've been stuck or injured from the tree.

She reached the top floor and suddenly felt a warm gush of air blow past her. She shielded her eyes since the gust came with sparks and ash. She looked up and saw smoke billowing and flames growing.

Reshma could always tell the difference in smell between certain fires. It helped to know how to cure wayward flames. Looking at the flames stung her eyes—not because of the sheer amounts of heat and sparks, but it smelled exactly of home.

Without further hesitation, she rushed straight towards the flames. There was hardly anyone left on the floor as Reshma looked in each room for any survivors. She heard cries of distress from the mangled mess of wood chips and soot.

She licked her lips and hummed an alto tune. She raised her hands above her head and clenched her fists like she was lifting and pulling something towards her face. The flames were strong, but after a few minutes, she was able to pull out and suffocate the flames. All that was left was rubble.

Ilsi used her hands to dig through to get to the doors. She kicked one down and it revealed a sick man looking out the window and up at the roof in astonishment. He turned as soon as Reshma entered.

"The flames are put out, use the stairs while they are still there," Reshma said through her heavy breathing. The man was pale and looked as if the thought of leaving was too daunting a task. She went to the window and started shouting for someone to come up and help her carry the man.

She turned to him and looked into his face and said, "I hear more people trapped. Just go to the stairs and someone will help lift you. I have to get the others!" Then she was off again.

There were three more rooms to check, but there were many branches and ash everywhere that made it difficult to navigate.

"Can you hear me?" Reshma cried. "Is someone still up here?" Suddenly, the tree in front of her exploded with flames again, not much to her surprise.

"Who the hell is down there?"

Reshma's heart ignited with a similar flame as it started to beat faster.

"Come down here and face me, you coward!" she yelled back. She hoped her voice would bring quick recollection. Two male patrons came clambering up the stairs from behind and Reshma turned around, the flames behind her.

"Woman, get out!" they cried.

"Get the man in that room!" Reshma barked, pointing at the room. They covered their faces with their arms and burst into the room and carried the man away behind her.

"Hey—"

"No, *you* get out, now!" Reshma said, shooing them away angrily. She turned to face the fire again and saw none other than her older brother standing in his own doing. The flames licked up his Yildirim armor like excited dogs greeting their master as he kept them at bay.

"Sister?"

"*Jarom?* You're alive!" Reshma cried. "Is setting a building on fire any way to greet your favorite sister?"

"What are you doing here?" he asked. If it were possible, Reshma could sense he was both angry and embarrassed to see her. His dark hair looked like hers except longer and wavier. He had a small, pointed beard that made him look much older than she remembered.

"Saving these people you're trying to destroy," Reshma said. "What are you doing with that phony necklace on? Take it off and see what you've really just done."

"My orders," Jarom answered. "It's also my orders to take you into custody. You're asking what *I'm* doing? I should be asking you, traitorous sister!"

"Take that trinket off or you're not my brother," Reshma said. She was already making movements and singing notes to kill the fire again. "Jarom, this is wrong."

He looked at her as she snuffed out the fire again. His throne of flames disappeared. So did the screaming. Either the people escaped through the windows or they were no longer alive. Reshma stared up at her brother. She knew that the amulet made him someone that he wasn't, but couldn't believe he would so willingly kill strangers to obey orders.

"Where's Mama and Papa? Where is everyone?" Reshma said. "Are they safe?"

Jarom looked coldly down at his sister from the scorched pile of branches.

"No one is safe as long as that Ice Chanter girl walks free," he said.

"Is our family *alive?*" Reshma grunted and started running up to the waist-high pile, making an effort to climb up. She grabbed hold and swung her foot up, but Jarom anticipated it and climbed up the broken tree and made it outside of the building before Reshma could get close enough.

"Come back, Jarom!" Reshma cried. "I want my *real* brother

back!" She roared back in frustration and collapsed on the pile. She screamed as if she could actually feel the flames that were once alive. She was doused in it again as Jarom set the tree on fire once more.

⌐◦⌐

Reshma walked away from the still-burning inn, clutching her arm. Physically, she was scraped up and sore, but otherwise sported no burns. Emotionally, she felt raw and drained.

Once she joined the crowd gathering outside of the inn, Pia rushed right to her and began fussing over her wounds and asking questions a million times over.

"Missy, that was good and brave, but you could've gotten yourself trapped and killed!" she kept saying with multiple variations.

"Did . . . did everyone get out?" Reshma asked between heavy breaths and coughs.

"A family made it out of the window between the two fire blasts," Rolf said. "The sick fellow is being tended to. Everyone but three people are accounted for. There's not much you could've done to get them out."

Reshma's body quaked as she felt someone put a blanket over her shoulders. She just sat there and stared into the red dirt. *My brother just killed those people.*

"Reshma! Reshma!" she heard. She looked up and saw Berg approaching her and crouching down. "You're all right!"

He put his arms around her and she let him, sinking into his chest and squeezing her eyes shut to pinch away tears. Parts of the inn began to collapse and crumble into the earth. Reshma turned and saw townspeople heaping their own dirt and sand from the ground and up towards the flames to snuff it out.

Reshma quietly began humming to herself and Berg loosened his grip on her. He watched the inn crumble, but at the same time witnessed the flames, smoke, and heat slowly ebb away. To anyone watching, it just looked like the people's efforts to douse the flames were actually working.

"Tyk is long gone," Berg murmured. "He was very afraid of the Yildirims but helped a lot of people today."

"That was smart of him," Reshma replied. "So what's going on? Did the Yildirim leave?"

As if to answer her own question, a soldier approached the group with a whip secured to his belt and a shield hoisted on his forearm. Berg and the others stood straight while he gently pushed Reshma towards the ground. She crouched down and maneuvered her way towards the middle of the group and towards the back.

"This town is under our command until further notice," the soldier said. "Any resistance large or small will result in befitting consequences."

"No sir! This is my property you just destroyed and you have no business being here!" Rolf cried out. She could hear the sound of a slap or strike across the face.

"We have strict permission to enter as we wish," a man countered.

"You can't just barge in!" a female voice cried out. "It's the middle of the night! Could you have picked a more *convenient* time to come burn down our livelihoods?"

"Get out! Now!" another man roared.

Suddenly light flashed in the near-darkness and Reshma

felt an unfortunately familiar jolt in her body. The soldier had shocked everyone present and they all fell down in surprise and pain. She joined them and tried to overcome twitching muscles as she crawled to get away.

"That is *one* form of a befitting consequence," the soldier said tersely. "You are to bring forth anyone that is not native to this village. That is, any people with *normal* hair colors."

"We refuse to join you," Reshma could hear Pia murmur shakily. It was like hearing her own mother—the way her voice struggled to not sound weak almost made Reshma want to hug her close in comfort.

"We aren't here to make recruits out of you," the soldier said. "We're here looking for stowaways. You cater to outsiders, don't you?"

"The nice ones," the woman replied bitterly. She gasped and sputtered as she was shocked again. Reshma looked around for the clearest way to the stables. It was to her right and behind the soldier in question.

"I'm not nice," the soldier muttered.

Reshma surveyed her surroundings and her options. She needed to get out of there and considered making a scene to draw the soldiers away. The only question was how close she could get to the stable before she got shocked.

She flinched when she heard a terrible roar coming from her left. A swarm of dragons burst and clawed their way out of their shelter and descended like devils onto the buildings and soldiers. A few small ones tackled the soldier that faced them and he fell on his back. Reshma looked to Berg and realized he had a small pipe still held between his lips and he looked like he was blowing furiously into it although it didn't make a sound she could hear.

In the dark, she scrambled to her feet and dodged oncoming soldiers or dragons. Many of the dragons swooped and flew past her but never directly at her. Her short time in town and around the shelter seemed to instill some kind of loyalty that at that moment she was grateful for.

Reshma clambered inside the horse stall and realized all her things were still with Dash. He looked all saddled and ready to go, so she quickly led him out and hoisted herself and her things on his back and rode off.

As she rode out of town, Berg looked to the girl riding like mad. He gasped as she suddenly burst into flames. She was like human torch and somehow she didn't seem to be in pain or to injure her steed. She rode off into the mountains and the soldiers quickly took notice.

Berg and the others took courage and cheered as half of the soldiers marched off into the darkness to catch up with the fire girl.

"The Wood Witch will lead you to your doom, gents!" one woman cried—and whether or not the people agreed with her, they still cheered their support. Someone powerful stuck her neck out to help them.

A dozen or so soldiers stayed where they were and used their power over lightning to strike down the dragons in flight that attempted to maim them. Once a handful were struck down the others took the hint and flew off—either back to the shelter or off into any direction, never to be seen again.

Berg put his pipe back in his pocket and sighed as he watched them take wing into the night while he was on the ground below in the middle of chaos. A soldier held his hand up and cast sparks like flint on stone and the people recovering from the crumbling inn crouched down to the ground, humbly muting their courage.

"Someone here should start talking about that girl and her friends," the female soldier commanded.

"She's gone already, what more do you want from us?" Berg piped up. The soldier took a few steps and kicked him, landing a blow on his upper arm as he fell back.

"Where is she going? Where is Ladala?" the soldier tried again through gritted teeth. "That's what I want from you."

"The Wood Witch and the Wood Elf working together?" Berg wheezed. "I don't know where you come from, but that's bad news for you if it's true."

CHAPTER 34

Thunderclaps. Sheets and sheets of rain. Ilsi opened her eyes and wiped her face with a cold, soaked sleeve. Everything was cold and wet, and she couldn't stop shivering. She heard several unearthly shrieks of pain and realized it had to be Crescent. She pushed herself to a sitting position and tried to stand but quickly decided against it; horrid pain shot up from her ankle to her waist. Lightning stretched across the sky and Ilsi could see her surroundings more clearly for a split second; she could see Crescent's large, scaly body framed by lush trees dripping with rain.

Ilsi used her arms to pull herself towards Crescent's direction and avoided splitting her hands open on twigs or thorns. She finally made it over there and she kindly ran her hand across Crescent's scaly face. He growled and she could feel his scales rush past her skin as he rolled his head to the side. A large patch of scales felt heavily damaged and ripped off; she felt blood. Crescent roared at the touch and the scales twitched; Ilsi guessed it was the joint where his right wing protruded out of his back.

Ilsi ripped off part of her sleeve and tried to patch up his stray wounds. It felt thick and hot as she tried to contain it with soaked-through fabric. Crescent growled low and deep, but Ilsi was grateful that he sat obediently rather than thrash at her.

"Easy," Ilsi soothed. "We'll find shelter soon and you can bite my leg off then."

It might make my leg hurt less than it does now, she thought. Her leg felt like something was stabbing it repeatedly. She knew she shouldn't stand or bend her leg, but she still felt the responsibility to find them safe shelter.

They both rested under a large tree and Ilsi used every uninjured muscle she had left to hoist herself up and fiercely hug the tree trunk. She vainly hoped that at any moment, Berg would find her and the pain would immediately disappear.

Ilsi heard the thunder booming across the sky again. The forest became darker, and the shapes of trees, branches, and leaves became fuzzy as colors blended together. The rain fell harder and harder as time moved on.

"Goodness," Ilsi said to herself aloud, "How did I get used to cold weather in Dove?" She wearily began to hum, hoping the notes would pull and tug at the cold and pull it away from their bodies and only leave warmth. It helped, but her shaky voice couldn't make them dry.

Thunder crashed again, and for a faint moment, Ilsi saw an abandoned cabin. At least that's what she thought she saw. It seemed like the safest place to be at the moment and any space that was void of constant rain was considered blessed. It looked like a ten minute walk away from her tree; she knew it would take a lot longer with her injured leg.

She edged slowly forward, waiting for a flash of light to help her see, and she would inch more. She stepped on a fallen branch, and the snap startled her. It was hard enough as it is to walk with one good leg, but she was now paranoid that she could bust the other.

More twigs snapped behind her and she quickly turned and unsheathed a sword with a free hand. A flash of lightning revealed that it was merely Crescent trying to follow her. She let her muscles relax and she put her sword away before she lost her grip on the tree. She slowly and painstakingly went from tree to tree trying to hold herself up with her two badly bruised arms and her overworked left leg.

It seemed like an eternity before Ilsi felt the door. Long wisps of ivy dangled about it, and Ilsi tore them away. She felt around and recognized grooves of thick wood and thought it could be the door. She felt part of the door cave in a bit about half up her height, like it was carved or scooped out. She gripped it and found the handle. She could see a faint light seeping through the cracks of the door.

She was surprised when she began to hear muffled voices on the other side. She held onto the vines with one hand and unsheathed her sword again, and then slammed the hilt into the door as hard as she could.

"Hello?" an elderly woman's voice called, "Is there someone out there? Hello?" A wrinkly old woman supported by a walking stick opened the door, and let a bright light shine on Ilsi's shivering face.

"Goodness gracious—"

"Let me in now, I beg you!" Ilsi said through gulps of desperate air. The old woman's eyes suddenly widened and motioned with her free hand for someone to hurry to the door.

"Hurry, Gilly! I think she's—"

———◦◦◦———

Ilsi opened her eyes and blinked in a soft light, and immediately jackknifed into a sitting position. She immediately regretted that, however, because shots of pain soared up and down her body. Moaning, she tried to prop herself up with her elbows looking quickly around at her foreign surroundings.

Things slowly came into focus. She blinked a few times and moaned, wiping her eyes to help them focus faster. She thought she was in the small cabin, and when she felt she was totally conscious she discovered she was right. There were stacks of disorganized books all in various heights with potted plants on top of them. Ivy, leaves, twisted branches, and flowers twisted and grew wherever they pleased along the walls and ceiling. Ilsi pulled the blanket strewn across her up and saw that she was wearing a large white nightgown and smooth wooden boards were strapped to her injured leg.

"By the heavens, you've awakened!" the elderly voice rang. Ilsi quickly laid the blanket back over her legs, wanting to leap out of the bed, but even moving her leg an inch was torture. An elderly, bent-over woman hobbled into the cabin. Her light gray hair was pulled back in a bun, yet there were many curly strands poking in every direction. She also had green streaks in her hair, to match her attire: a simple green dress and long, elegant, forest green robes. She came in carrying a basket of what looked like herbs and leaves.

Ilsi tried rearranging herself to look like the perfect patient. The woman tsked and chuckled.

"Now, dearie. You've bashed that leg of yours quite thoroughly. I would suggest you give it time to mend," she said cheerfully, "Whatever it was that you were up to will just have to wait." She smiled and the creases lining her eyes and lips becoming apparent. As she talked, two small dimples were visible in her rosy and pleasant cheeks.

"Where is my sword? And Crescent—"

"So *that's* what you call him! I didn't know *what* to do when I saw that thing munching in my garden! He's just outside," the aged lady explained with a smile, waving her hand absently, as if Ilsi's concern was of little consequence.

"So do you just live here in this cabin all by yourself away from everyone else?" Ilsi asked. The woman chuckled at this.

"No, dear child. I'm only a walking distance away from the local village. And besides, little Gillian keeps me company. We make *quite* the team. We're used to interesting strangers like yourself coming with problems," the elderly woman giggled.

"I'm sure your herbs and what-not couldn't make my problems disappear," Ilsi murmured. The aged lady laughed again, which sort of agitated Ilsi; she just kept *giggling*. The woman scratched her back while using her other hand to walk with her cane a few paces closer to Ilsi.

"Now I feel that you are bubbling with questions, but I have a few for you," the woman said, sitting at the edge of the bed on the right side, or opposite of her injured leg. "What's your name and who are you running from?" she asked cocking her head to the side.

"How do you know?"

"A girl your age with that lovely sword? And your question-of-an-answer does little to deny it," the woman smiled with her eyes. "Not to mention you seem a little far from home. Your accent is quite lovely and fascinating."

"I—I am very grateful for your hospitality and shelter," Ilsi murmured, "My name is Ilsi . . . from Ravenna."

"Ahh, no wonder your accent sounds so fresh," the woman said, "It's been *ages* since I've run into your people. That was back in the day when I could actually walk around without this old thing."

"You know about my homeland? Have you been there?" Ilsi suddenly asked.

The aged lady shrugged. "It's been years since I've been on a good adventure, but I've paid your island a visit."

"Did you hear about the Wall? It's like everyone has forgotten us for a decade. Well, except the Yildirims."

"Sound like your clan's been down on its luck. Yildirims are a nasty bunch. They have a penchant for poking their noses where they don't belong." It was the first time the lady made any kind of face besides a cheery one. "I haven't heard of any wall, but I haven't been listening for news."

"I and two others were able to escape this wall that keeps us in," Ilsi said. "It's been very nice to meet you but I just don't have time to sit around when I'm getting closer to finding something that will help them."

"Well I can't force you to stay in bed, impatient Ilsi," giggled the woman at her own alliteration, "But your leg bones were broken and they need lots of time before you can walk on your own."

Ilsi sat back and the pillow behind her head as she puffed out air from her cheeks.

"My friends will wonder where I've gone," Ilsi said. "Remind me to think twice about riding a wild dragon during a storm."

"Ah, sounds like the start of a good story," the aged lady

chuckled again, "I'm sorry about your friends, but I'm sure you'll be reunited once more."

"Can you help me walk?" Ilsi asked, "I just want some fresh air and see if Crescent's okay. His wing—"

"Come here, child. Let me help you. He's just outside enjoying some sun," the woman said, helping Ilsi to her feet. The aged woman led her out of the cabin and Ilsi hobbled along with her.

"Gracious child! Your gait is almost as bad as mine!" Ilsi hesitantly laughed but tried not to fall over. Then she gazed out and saw the forest in a new light. It wasn't so terrible and cold anymore, and the sun's rays caused the fresh leaves and trees to light up around her.

The trees were close together, but there was a clear path that led past the doorway that Ilsi felt stupid for not noticing in the dark. To the left of the cottage, there was a small clearing; half of it was a well-manicured garden and the other half was grass with a few goats grazing. Crescent lay next to them, as if pondering what they might taste like.

"Hey, looks like someone's still in one piece," Ilsi chuckled, as Crescent grumbled and found his way towards her and rested at her feet. She stroked his neck as though he was an over-sized house cat. His wing was bandaged up but he seemed in higher spirits now that she was there.

"Sorry about the tumble," Ilsi told him, "I promise to be a better driver." She heard the mistress cackling to herself from behind again.

"He has a liking for you," she said, "Where did you find him?"

"Oh he's not mine," Ilsi said. "I helped a friend train him

in exchange for rooming. But it's nice to run into someone who doesn't want me dead on the spot."

She realized what she just said and couldn't take it back. She tried to look at just about everything but the old woman.

"How long have I been here?" Ilsi asked, trying to avoid her blunder.

"Oh, about three days," the woman sighed.

"Three days?"

"You went through a lot of pain. However, thanks to Gilly's strength and my remedies you should be walking normally and by yourself fairly soon."

"Thank you so much, I sound impatient but I'm truly grateful. Where's this girl?"

"Oh, just doing my morning errands for me, I'm not as young as I used to be," the woman answered, smiling as she placed her hands on her round hips, then gazed out into the forest, "Here she comes, says I."

Then, a girl came into the clearing pulling a small handcart behind her full of vegetables, bread, fabric, and small, lumpy sacks. She wore a simple brown skirt and an oatmeal-colored blouse with a black corseted cincher. Ilsi thought based on her looks that she was maybe twelve or thirteen years old.

Her real first impression of the girl was thinking of how out-of-place she looked. Her skin was a deep brown and her black hair was hid behind a shawl that covered the crown and back of her head then hung over her chest. She was fairly exotic-looking compared to the other fair-skinned or tanned folk Ilsi came across. *What's a girl like her doing in the woods with this old lady?* Ilsi thought.

"Milady," the girl said, noticing Ilsi standing before her and rushing to curtsy, "A pleasure to see that you're on your feet."

"You must be Gilly? There's no need for formalities, since I'm of no great importance," Ilsi said with a small smile. She noticed that Gilly's accent was a bit different—like she was using one that wasn't her own.

"How did you two meet?" Ilsi said, gesturing between to the two enigmas that bandaged her leg.

"She took me in a while ago," Gilly said, parking the cart right up against the small cottage. "I was lost and she let me stay here."

"Such a sweet child. I found her alone in the forest, and I gladly took her in. The poor child suffered from a bad wing, and I felt sorry for her. I didn't have it in me to send her away," the lady explained, then motioned for all three women to return into the cabin. Gilly shook her head and rolled her eyes; she smiled at Ilsi as she motioned for Ilsi to lean on her to go back inside.

The old lady took out some herbs and spices from Gilly's bundle, and began chopping and mixing. Gilly led their patient back to the slightly raised bed and made sure she was comfortable.

"Mistress, you're old, right?" Ilsi said, then blushed. "I mean, you probably know about a lot of old things, like legends and such, right?"

"Don't be ridiculous, of course I'm old enough to remember—"

"Do you know about the Wood Witch?" Ilsi said. "Is that you? I haven't even asked for your name."

Gilly looked to her mistress as the old woman said, "That's a name, yes. I assume they're talking about me. As for my name, it's simply Giselle."

"*Giselle?*" Ilsi blurted. "You could've told me you were Giselle!"

"You didn't ask for my name until just now!" the lady shrugged. Ilsi's shoulders slumped as if she was exhausted and she laughed a bit.

"Mistress, I am looking for *you*," Ilsi explained. "At least, I'm looking for a woman named Giselle on behalf of Lady Ladala. We need your help to stop the Yildirim before they get out of control. They're the reason I'm running. They ransacked my people's lands while looking for me specifically."

Gilly looked down at Giselle, who was a head shorter than her, with concern across her face. Giselle brought a flask over to Ilsi and said, "It's time for you to rest. Take a few swigs to help dull the pain. After that, we can talk more."

She winked as Ilsi took the bottle and swallowed the liquid inside before laying heavily in bed like she was molded out of marble.

CHAPTER 35

Helene stood at a podium. A crowd of people met in a secret building in the dead of night. They each carried their own candle. She raised her fist and her blonde curls bounced with fury as she spoke to the large group.

"We cannot live in the shadow a day longer!" she cried. It's a voice that Ilsi remembered as soon as she heard it. This was her mother. Helene raised her fist again. Her sleeve was drawn back, and a small wave print was on her wrist. Some people in her audience shouted their echoes, but some stayed quiet.

"What if it is not the time?" one called from the crowd.

"Is centuries upon centuries enough time for you?" she exclaimed. "Soon, my daughter shall know who she really is, and I do not want her to live in shame of such honor!"

"We cannot allow everyone to know our secret," a man said, just loud enough for the people to hear. All eyes turned to a figure standing in the shadows of the doorway. The woman at the podium kept her stance.

"Come now, no need for concealment. We are all descendants in this meeting," she said, referring to his long draped hood covering his face. He raised it to reveal his two bright green eyes. The symbol of a third eye lay on his shaved chin. Everyone stared openly at him.

"Another tribe," the woman at the podium whispered in awe. Ilsi imagined that her mother hadn't met anyone like this man before.

"I come to speak for my brothers and sisters. We have foreseen a terrible occurrence in the future. If you continue to meet and talk of sharing your past—our past—with the world, we will have no choice but to stop you. It is unwise for you to question us," he said, as a rise of whispers filled the room.

The flames began to flicker with excitement. Helene raised a hand, and silence filled the room. Everyone looked to see what Ilsi's mother would say. She raised her head and stuck her chin out.

"We are not all one joined tribe. We of the Swift tribe will act as we wish," she said.

"Very well," the man grunted. He raises his hood, turns and leaves. Then, quietly, yet heard by many he said, *"While you live in ignorance, your last moments will be full of horror. You will know that your children and neighbors will be the one to pay for what you wish to do."* The woman frowned at the mysterious man's exit. Her face suddenly contorted and swirled into a new image . . .

It suddenly became the image of a vast and beautiful field. Ilsi realized she was herself. She was reliving her moments as a child. She looked at herself and realized she was wearing her favorite dress that day.

The vision swirled again, and Ilsi followed her mother as her normal grown self as her mother walked home from yet another meeting. Ilsi didn't know how she knew, but she was sure of it. The sun shone brightly and everyone was about like normal. Helene's blonde curls bounced up and down. She looked like she was hurrying home, as though she was upset by something.

Suddenly, dark clouds began to form. Ilsi looked down at her feet, *because she saw Helene do the same. It is not winter, yet, Ilsi muttered to herself. She just knew it to be true.*

Ilsi suddenly saw the light in her mother's eyes. Realization. She saw a glimpse of her mother's mind. She saw her mother's nightmares. The hooded man appeared in her dreams every night since she saw him, and he told her what would happen. On one side of the island everything would die of hunger, the other of thirst. Both would die together, yet apart. They would be divided forever, to stop the meetings, to stop what would soon come.

Her mother ran hard and fast. Ilsi ran along with her mother, and suddenly saw herself again—the young version of herself. Ilsi cried with Helene in unison,

"Ilsi, it is happening!"

In her dream, the hooded man, along with members of his clan called a terrible and ancient spell—one that could not be undone without great power. Ilsi ran to the small version of herself to comfort the girl. She couldn't remember if she was herself, the small one, or the mother in the dream, but at that moment she was holding the little girl and rubbing her stiff hands against the two small bare feet. Helene came running, but the wall shot up a few inches in front of where she stood. As Ilsi watched the Wall shoot up the sky, she held the little girl and shivered. Her eyes circled about and saw a world that she grew used to; a world full of ice and cold.

Ilsi cried out for her father, in harmony with the little one. She waited for him to fix everything.

Ilsi woke up with tears in her eyes as they fluttered open. It took her a second to recognize that she was still at the cottage and her leg was still on the mend. Gilly and Giselle were already out of the cottage and working; she could hear them humming together.

This dream kept coming to her, even after weeks of being in the cottage. She grabbed her mother's journal and a quill and ink placed nearby and furiously wrote down everything she remembered from the dream before the images melted away. With each time, a new detail surfaced and she struggled to connect all the pieces into a great whole.

She then included:

It's impossible. I've tried talking to her, bribing her (with what little I can promise), and begging her to help. Maybe it is my own selfishness, but if she is who everyone says she is, who's to say she could end this war within a year? Or what about a day? She's supposed to have the power to do something and she just laughs. Mama, her laughter is infuriating.

It was by a major miracle that I was even able to find her so quickly and now she's refusing to join Ladala so the war can end and I can go rescue Papa. I hate depending on people to get where I want to be. And I hate being lame at the moment—I don't have a moment's chance if we're attacked.

———◦◦◦———

"So what's keeping you from home?" Ilsi asked. "Don't you miss your family?"

"It's complicated," Gilly replied. "It's not safe where I used to live."

Gilly was helping Ilsi practice walking with both legs from the cottage to where Crescent slept in the small field of grass. Ilsi was wobbly but getting the hang of it while Gilly stood by in case something went wrong.

"Why, because of the Wall?" Ilsi asked.

"Well there's that, then there's—hey!" Gilly exclaimed. Her hands flew to her mouth as if she caught herself swear. "How did you—?"

"How did I know you're a horrible liar?" Ilsi laughed. "You've got two sisters that I've already met—Reshma and Ophelia. The family resemblance is strong."

"You know Reshma?" Gilly exclaimed. She grabbed Ilsi by the waist and hugged her close. "We thought she was left behind in Tijer."

"She was, but she's now out here looking for you," Ilsi said, folding her arms over her chest. "And it's likely that she's looking for me since I've passed the time we were supposed to meet and keep traveling. Stay close to me and I'll make sure you two are reunited."

Gilly's face pinched as her eyes filled with tears. Ilsi couldn't quite tell if the young girl was happy or sad.

"I'm so happy she's okay," she said. "I've been worried about what the soldiers might've done to her."

"Well, what happened to the rest of you?" Ilsi said. "Your parents? Siblings? I forget how many there are of you."

Gilly chuckled and wiped her eyes dry as she said, "We were taken on a boat and it docked somewhere—I couldn't even tell you where because I don't know the geography here. Plus we were blindfolded and kept below deck for most of the time. We were taken to some camp . . ."

Ilsi could tell this story was hard to tell and put her hands on Gilly's shoulders and brought her in for a hug.

"The Yildirim are terrible," Ilsi said. "No doubt about it."

"I'm so safe here with Giselle," Gilly said into Ilsi's neck. "If I leave I know they'll find me. They'll take me back . . ."

"Would you feel safe with Reshma protecting you?"

Gilly shook her head. "I'm not really sure. You know enough about Giselle to understand that she is very powerful.

Well, for an old lady."

"Just think about it," Ilsi said. "What's the point of worrying about your family's safety if you decide never to be reunited with them?"

Gilly's lips spread into a thin line as she and Ilsi found themselves back at the cottage. Ilsi lay on her back again and thought about her father and wondered what it would be like to finally see him again and know what happened to him.

Maybe tomorrow I should tell her what happened to Ophelia, Ilsi thought, as she limped back inside the cottage.

———◦•◦———

"Giselle, I must ask you something," Ilsi said. She was sitting down and helping the woman pull weeds from her garden.

"Ask away, dear one."

"Do people often have visions in your care?" Ilsi looked at her from the corner of her eye in hopes of catching a reaction. The woman didn't appear fazed.

"It depends," she said simply. "A lot of things happen in that little cottage. It depends on if the person is wounded physically or emotionally. Have you had visions, girl?"

"I'm not sure," Ilsi said. "I've just had the same dream each night and it gets more clear with each night. It's something that happened to me when I was a little girl. What I remember is fleeting—or details that my father shared with me. But what I see is something that no one else was there to see."

"It definitely sounds more important than just a dream," Giselle nodded.

"Did you do that?" Ilsi asked. "I usually never remember

my dreams. But these are so clear. Did you give me something to help me remember?"

Giselle shrugged. "It's my job to give people what they need," she answered. "Those things go beyond bandages and a warm meal. My property happens to be conducive to mental and spiritual healing."

"Can you help me make sense of certain details?" Ilsi said. "Do you interpret dreams?"

"If it's a vision of what you've already experienced, I don't have to interpret. I can just tell you what you need to know."

Before Ilsi could question her, Giselle, used her walking stick to prop herself up and stretched her hand and placed her thumb on Ilsi's forehead between her eyes.

Ilsi staggered backwards; the rush of her past flowed over her like a huge tidal wave. She felt dizzy and sick as she faced Giselle. Her wise and knowing eyes gazed back at her.

"I don't understand," Ilsi finally said, her voice cracked. "What did you do?"

"I can't really do much for you if I don't know what vision I'm working with," Giselle explained. "But the Wall that surrounded your clan was created to protect you from the evils of your day. It was meant to keep your powers secret from the Yildirim."

Giselle noticed that Ilsi was trying so hard to keep her emotions in check. Her face flushed red, and a tear raced down her burning cheeks. The vision of the event shook her up all over again.

"What was so bad in the future that the hooded man and his tribe created that stupid Wall?"

"Calm yourself, child," Giselle said, placing her hands on her shoulders, "What is done is done. That is the danger of looking in the past. What you have seen can never be changed. Besides, the wall—"

"The Wall ruined my *life!* He got *that* part right. What was so bad that he forced me to suffer this way?"

"Ilsi!" Giselle exclaimed in an otherworldly voice and Ilsi suddenly hushed. "I know that this is upsetting you, but you must know what they saw. If you refuse to calm down, it will not help you at all.

"What they saw came to pass. They thought that they could prevent what they saw. The *Understanding* tribe saw the rise of Althod. They saw that he had acquired *Entice* from his brother, Cornelius. However, much to their dismay, he sacrificed his brother to do so. It's unclear if he has acquired *Fortune* yet."

"How does he know where all these people are?" Ilsi mused. "How did he know to find me, and how will he find the others? How do you even know these things even though they weren't part of the vision?"

"I've sensed that with Althod's adopted power, he is able to give fragments of it to his soldiers, and they can pass through walls to find those they seek," Giselle said. All cheeriness and good humor was gone. "As for my knowledge of these things, I've known Althod's beginnings as a tyrant long before you and I met."

"So that's how they first invaded Ravenna," Ilsi murmured to herself. "That's how they invaded Ladala's lands, too. It must be something about those amulets."

"Come, child," Giselle groaned, waving her hand, "I may know a lot, but I am old and tired. I need rest. You keep at it with the weed pulling." Ilsi looked down at the ground, staring at the good soil and budding herbs peeking through. As soon as she could hear Giselle start to snore, Gilly came to join Ilsi in the garden.

"You know when she sleeps during the day," she said, "It's because she's up to spinning tales again."

Ilsi sat in the dirt and stared into space. She was trying to accept the fact that her dream wasn't just a dream, but a real reminder of what happened. Knowing that the Wall was useless anyway against the Yildirim made her blood boil; the Wall was more like punishment rather than protection. And the Sea King . . . he must've known all along about the event or the rift between the two parties, which was why they banished her so readily. *Stay and stink in your water,* Ilsi thought, seething.

Gilly tried again, "What did she show you?"

She knew. Maybe she'd already asked.

"I've had these dreams . . . visions," Ilsi muttered. "Whatever you call things that are supposed to reveal the past in a confusing way."

Gilly thought Ilsi was joking but she soon realized just how miffed Ilsi was at the moment. She sat in the dirt next to Ilsi, hitching up her skirts so they dangled from her knees as she hugged her legs close.

"I made the mistake of asking her about the Wall, too," Gilly said. "I've been here for months and I still don't know everything there is to know about Giselle. I just know that someone with that much knowledge and power is too powerful for the Yildirims."

"Will she fight them?"

"She's an *old lady*," Gilly said, as if that were obvious enough of an answer.

"We need her," Ilsi said, now drawing her knees to her chest.

"I've been sent here on behalf of Lady Ladala to ask Giselle to join our side against the Yildirim. They don't even know what she's made of, but it was worth the risk to send me and Reshma to find her and convince her to be allies with us."

"War is so awful," Gilly said sadly. "Look what it's already done to us."

"I just wonder why Giselle doesn't already help, or why she resists my asking," Ilsi said. "Does she see the future? Has she foreseen something?"

Gilly shook her head. "Based off of past experience, I'm too afraid to ask."

CHAPTER 36

So, it's true, Mama. You know exactly what it felt like. You were brave and you didn't want me to feel alone about Swift. I wonder if people trusted you with their other problems—maybe you knew about Tyk's parents and their worries about him becoming an Animan. What a burden silence is. I hope you'll always be proud of me and know that I won't let your death be in vain. I will help create a world where there are no more walls. A world of vulnerability and trust.

I don't know if you helped me see the past or if it was all Giselle's doing . . . but thank you.

⸺◦◦◦⸺

Ilsi awoke a week from that day, and she mustered the earned strength to be able to walk around without a limp. At that point, Giselle asked the two younger girls to go up deeper into the mountains to collect some items for her—and it would be faster and easier with Crescent's help. Gilly was absolutely delighted when she heard of Giselle's plan, and Ilsi winced at the sudden nightmare of breaking her leg again. She watched Crescent as he practiced flying again, swirling around the cabin. Ilsi hesitantly rode her once more to test Crescent's wing strength, but coming back to the ground was much smoother this time.

Giselle gave Gilly some food and her own weapons: a small bow and arrows, and a small dagger. Ilsi shuddered at the thought of a young, sweet girl using a weapon like that, but she was only five or so years older than her. Plus, she was related to Reshma, Ilsi summoned Crescent back to the ground and Giselle gathered the three for her last words.

"Now, Ilsi. Here's a list of things you must find, the rest I will find here in the forest. Now, you'll be in the mountains and as such there will be wildlife out and about. Just be aware of where you step; the only *creatures* you may have to worry about are Yildirims. Stay on the trails is all I ask."

"Don't worry, Mistress Giselle," Gilly chirped happily, "Ilsi and I will be fine." Giselle gave a small nod and a cheery smile to Ilsi.

The two Ravennans both quickly mounted Crescent, and Ilsi dove under the collar of her shirt for the whistle hanging about her neck. Ilsi sounded the small whistle and could hear nothing but the sound of Crescent's wings beating furiously. Giselle waved goodbye, and her figure became smaller and smaller the higher they went.

Ilsi once again saw the land laid out below her. The sun was shining brightly, a better contrast then her last flight. She immediately saw the Charcoal Mountains looming before them with their peaks hidden by perpetual swirls of clouds.

"See those trees with the leaves already turning?" Gilly said, "We can go there to land. There should be a clearing close by."

Ilsi grinned, finally enjoying the feeling of flying. She sounded the whistle once more, and Crescent made high-speed towards the red and orange slope on the mountains ahead.

Crescent landed at the place Gilly suggested. The mountainside was full with trees bearing red and orange leaves. It was a sight that Ilsi hadn't seen for a long time and it made her smile. Ilsi dismounted and helped Gilly slide to the ground. She looked around. The trees soared high into the skies, and small woodland creatures were scurrying and darting from one tree to the next.

"We need to find the Stone Path," Gilly said, as she motioned for Ilsi to follow. Ilsi smiled. For a small kid, she knew the mountains well. Ilsi motioned to Crescent to follow; the dragon did so, but instinctively hid his luminous white body in the trees a few paces behind them.

Ilsi looked at the piece of parchment she was given. She furrowed her brows.

"A handful of Forget-me-nots, two cups of fire seeds, and a pinch of four-leaf clovers? This sounds like a recipe," Ilsi said. "And it's not like these are amazingly-rare items."

"Not rare at all, but they grow best here," Gilly shrugged. "As a Fire Weaver, I just listen to Giselle." Ilsi nodded in agreement and followed the young girl.

They came to a more barren stretch of land. Ilsi looked around in awe. A few trees stuck out, but the ground was covered in hundreds of bizarre slabs of stone. They stuck out like tombstones, but in all sorts of sizes and colors. They also protruded in odd directions, like they were just dropped from the sky. Most of them came to Ilsi's middle. It was like a sea of large rocks, stretching onto small hills. The path wound wildly around the stones like a snake.

"This is my favorite spot to find herbs," Gilly added.

"Where *are* the herbs?" Ilsi muttered quietly. Gilly didn't respond. Instead, she walked along the small, winding path around the rocks. Ilsi followed suit, and Crescent began gliding from one rock to another. Ilsi silently followed Gilly as she wove around the rocks; Ilsi attempted to look around to see if she could identify them herself.

"I found it!" Gilly called. "There are so many! My lucky day." She raised her tiny fist, which clenched a handful of four-leaf clovers.

"You *found* those already?" Ilsi asked.

"Yes, they're not so hard to find, once you know the right places to look," Gilly stated simply.

"So where is the other stuff?" Ilsi asked.

"I know where the forget-me-nots sprout, so you can be the one to find the fire seeds," Gilly said.

"And *where* exactly would those be?" Ilsi asked, who still had no clue what fire seeds were, or what they looked like. Gilly smiled and crouched down again to search.

"Just keep going along the path, you'll find them on a big tree, you *can't* miss it," she said, her voice muffled a bit. Gilly disappeared again behind the rocks. Ilsi shrugged her shoulders. She beckoned for Crescent to follow suit. He flew curiously behind her.

Ilsi turned and point to the ground as she addressed the beast, "Stay with this young girl." Ilsi smiled in mild surprise as the dragon actually obeyed her and slunk into the trees to watch Gilly work.

"Are you sure that you'll be okay by yourself?" Ilsi called. There came a pause.

"Sure, I've been up here loads of times. I just hope *you'll* be okay by yourself."

Woof, Ilsi thought. *The attitude runs in the family.*

———◦∞◦———

Ilsi found a brick-reddish path that led higher up into the mountains, and she decided to walk up. It was growing darker, and the trees on the mountains blended nicely with the magnificent sunset. Ilsi's boots began to acquire a familiar reddish tint to them.

Then, she then saw something that she had never laid eyes on. An enormous tree stood before her. The leaves were all the deepest and richest red color that Ilsi could imagine. Although they appeared to be healthy leaves, they were . . . *on fire*. It looked like a huge fireball, like the sun. The leaves were all aglow but the fire neither stopped nor spread to the other trees. It was just *burning*.

Bright glowing lights also dotted all over the tree, and its branches gave off an intense heat. The tree reached to the skies and outdid all other trees in its shape and color. Ilsi could feel its warm glow on her cheeks as she got as close as she could.

"The burning tree," Ilsi murmured to herself. "Is this what Berg and his family were talking about?" She smiled and her heart pricked with hope that maybe Reshma or Tyk could be close by and looking for this tree. She tried not to be extremely hopeful, but the thought of seeing them after so many weeks reminded her of how much she missed them.

She didn't dare touch the tree with her bare hands, but instead used her bow and arrow to knock some of the fruit down. Giselle's request was just a handful, so she shot down four or five. They plopped to the ground and held a faint glow like an ember but otherwise didn't spread their heat or flame.

Ilsi ventured closer and saw that once plucked off the tree, they were just round yellow objects about the size of large olives, only aglow, of course.

She began to murmur a difficult spell and dared touch the fruit with her bare hands. The lights in each object suddenly blew out like a candle and became a dull grayish color. Once she was done, she filled a small pouch with the gray balls.

"Hmm, a burning tree that never dies."

She was standing at the foot of a burning tree, trying to contemplate what its purpose was; if it was a home to special creatures, had special powers, or if it was an ill omen.

"Did you get the seeds?" Gilly asked from behind. Ilsi whirled around at the low pitch of the girl's voice.

"Yes, I did," Ilsi said. "I'm no expert but I think I have them—"

"Good, we need to get out of here."

"Where's Crescent?" Ilsi asked.

"Still in the trees by the Stone Path. He won't come down."

Ilsi suddenly heard a branch snap and the low murmuring of voices. She involuntarily reached for her bow. Gilly appeared to have heard it as well. Ilsi and Gilly made eye contact when they heard the sound of footfalls and they ran into the large sea of rocks again and climbed over or swerved before collapsing into a suitable hiding place, each girl picking her own spot.

The two crouched down together behind a set of larger slabs of stone, which seemed to create a wall around them. Ilsi saw their dragon companion and motioned to Crescent to stay hidden in the trees; not like the creature needed warning or encouragement.

Ilsi had no clue who or what was coming, but the rhythmic stomping and clattering gave it all away—it had to be the Yildirims once more.

"Halt, men!" one voice shouted. The area was still.

"I want your group to search this section, and I want you to take your group in that direction. Comb the area and report any suspicions!" the voice shouted. Ilsi heard the rhythmic shuffling of feet going in two other directions away from their hiding spots.

She looked through a small space between two stones. She saw two men off to the side, while all others were scanning the area. There was a man in a thick black uniform and dark gray armor over his chest, arms, and legs. She assumed that he was the head-honcho of this operation based on ornate helmet he held at his hip. The other had a black hood covering the back of his head. She could hear his lower tone very close to where she was hiding.

"We can't afford to mess this up, Reubens," the man in charge said sternly. "Althod would be most displeased if we fail this *diversion*."

"I'm sure that she is here. Were you blind to the dragon flying in the open air?"

"If this becomes another wild goose chase, Reubens, I won't pretend this *expedition* didn't happen. Don't pretend that Althod isn't irritated with you," the man said, scratching his chin and then the back of his neck. "Besides, it seems odd for you to be stalking this girl. What makes her so special that we need to send a troop of men to sniff out *this* one?"

If Ilsi didn't know better, the man's tone gave away a slight betrayal on Reuben's part. The man seemed content with Reuben's plight.

"I've done this type of work long enough to be certain of my abilities, can you say the same for yourself? *Commander?*" Reubens countered, icily. He obviously didn't like being talked down to. His comrade merely shifted his feet and sighed.

"I'm sure you're quite capable, *General* Reubens."

Ilsi's eyes flashed and she tried to stifle a gasp. Reubens was *way* high up in the ranks. Practically bosom buddies with Althod himself. Ilsi leaned against the rock silently. The day was growing darker. She dared not to make a sound; if she remained quiet, she would be safe.

She looked over at Gilly; she was trying very hard to remain silent and motionless. The commanding voice kept ringing throughout the path. The voices and sounds would leave, and then come back. They hadn't come very close to where Ilsi hid quite yet.

"Commander, we haven't found any sign of the girl," a young man's voice said.

The man in armor sighed. "This isn't making my job any easier. Has word from Kains reached us yet?" he asked gruffly.

"Yes, sir. The villagers said that there's an herbal witch in the woodlands surrounding it. They say that she takes in folks from all over the place," the young Yildirim said.

"Well, we'll have to pay this witch a visit, won't we?" The commander said. Ilsi saw the pain of realization in Gilly's face. She looked like she wanted to scream out loud, maybe even call down fire on them, but she held her peace.

"Sir, I've also received word that they've found signs of the

Ice Chanter traitor. They think that he's escaped to Karno," the Yildirim added. Now it was Ilsi who turned ashen white.

"Take your men to see this old witch. As for me, I've going to see that we attend to catching this boy," the Commander said. "Now gather everyone, and we'll leave immediately. This search is getting more and more absurd."

The sound of marching feet soon died away. Ilsi bit her lip as she shook her head furiously. Those men didn't come anywhere near them. They were either dimwits and didn't know how to properly find two young girls, or they knew how close they were hiding and talked loud enough for them to hear.

Is it a trap? Was all of that a show for us? She couldn't do anything. If she wanted to stay alive, she had to sit there and do absolutely nothing but keep silent. She took a fistful of grass and pulled it out of the ground in fury.

After an agonizing hour or two, Ilsi steadily slid down the summit with Gilly, making heavy strides as they were racing back to the cabin.

"Gilly!" Ilsi said. "Let's take the dragon and beat them to it!" Ilsi knew the girl was afraid of being seen in the air, but Ilsi didn't care. They would reach the cottage faster and they would rain fire and ice down on anything that tried to shoot them down from the sky.

"Don't worry, everything will be all right," Ilsi said, drawing the dragon near and helping Gilly scramble up on the dragon's back and scooting herself behind Gilly before taking off.

They flew in silence and angst. Ilsi surveyed the ground

below, just waiting for someone to spot them. The day had grown so dark that she could barely see. If it weren't for Gilly's directions, it would've taken them much more time.

Once Crescent landed on top of Giselle's garden, Ilsi couldn't dismount fast enough. Gilly raced into the cottage and out of sight. There wasn't a sound; the night was calm.

She gingerly brushed the ivy away, and opened the door. Putting a hand to her heart and commanded it to beat at normal pace. There was Gilly, curled up in Giselle's lap like a small child, as they rocked gently in a rocking chair.

CHAPTER 37

The soft glow of lavender candles lit the small cabin. The curtains were closed. Gilly's deep breathing was soft, as she was sleeping comfortably in her bed. Besides the occasional sniffle, she seemed to have calmed down.

Giselle reached for her dark-wooded walking stick, and made her way to her cauldron, her lines of age becoming apparent. Ilsi had just finished describing what had happened in the mountains and what the Yildirim were doing.

"Those ruffians don't know the first thing about finding a runaway," she said, "If you asked me, they shouldn't take advice from those hooligans in Kains."

"Kains?" Ilsi asked.

"Kains. It's the village just outside this forest. It's really small, but full of dodgy people. If you ever come in contact with them, you would understand why I live out *here*," Giselle remarked, whisking away a stray strand of hair from her face. She began taking all sorts of strange objects from a small satchel and stuffing them in jars or paper-wrapped boxes.

"I still have the fire seeds," Ilsi said, "and Gilly gave me the forget-me-nots and four leaf clovers."

"Splendid work, m'dear! Let's see then," Giselle said, clasping her hands together with glee. Ilsi pulled out the three ingredients, which Gilly had wrapped in thin paper. Giselle got right to work and stashed away their precious findings.

"It felt pretty good being in the mountains again," Ilsi said. "I owe it to you and your hospitality."

"That you do," Giselle chuckled merrily.

"Yeah, pretty soon I can leave and hopefully find my friends with Ladala or something," Ilsi said, brightening just at the thought. "Have you considered the offer to come join us?"

They've been through this a few times already and Ilsi's was ready to see this through. Giselle giggled and shook her head.

"It's funny you're asking an old lady like me to be a soldier."

"It's not what I'm asking entirely," Ilsi said, waving it off. "What I'm wondering is if you'll be allies. Ladala sent me all the way out here to find you. We really need your help if we're ever going to win this war."

"I already know I'm not what you need," Giselle said. "Whatever it is you think you need, it won't be enough."

"But they threatened to find you," Ilsi said. "You've already said you don't like them, so why not help us put them in their place?"

"Dear child," Giselle sighed. "Their threats don't bother me at all. The place is pretty hard to find unless you travel by dragon."

"Well, if you aren't threatened by them, why let them win and terrorize and—"

"Because I'm tired of fighting other people's battles!" Giselle roared, spitting harshly every few words. "I've been called to arms so many times for wars greedily started and messily ended!" Her face quaked a bit from the reaction and coughed miserably for a few seconds. Ilsi's eyes bugged out a bit at the sudden rage and she took a step back.

After Giselle wiped her lips with her sleeve, she rattled, "If you want to fight Ladala's fight, I can't stop you, dear child. But I'm done. I've done enough fighting."

"But this isn't just Ladala's fight," Ilsi said. "I want to do whatever I can to give my clan a fighting chance. Does no one out here believe in honor and loyalty?"

"Which ones do you plan to save, hon? The Ice Chanters or the Swift clan?" Giselle returned. Ilsi stopped to think, her brows furrowed.

"What—"

"Or is it the Elven clan? Doing this as a favor when they're fully capable of doing things their way?"

"She didn't make me do anything!" Ilsi countered. "I made my own choice."

"It's always about power, power, power. That's all you people ever fight over. Why not be content with the abilities you already have? I have so much power I don't know what to do with it and I live out here in a cottage just fine!" Giselle rambled, staring at Ilsi's torso or something behind her as if she was muttering to herself.

"Ladala at least wants to use her power to help other people besides her own!"

"I'm sure she can hear both of you with how loud you're both arguing!" Gilly yelled above the two. She came from her tiny bed and stood in between the old woman and Ilsi a head taller than both of them and all three were silent. "Just please be done with this. I don't like the yelling."

After a few minutes, Ilsi spoke first.

"I'm doing this for *me*," she said through terse lips. "What they've done to me is unforgivable. What they've done to my loved ones can never be repaid. The Yildirims must stop and if you know so much, that much you should understand."

She stormed away and into the garden. She felt foolish for doing so; it was already past sunset so the only local source of light was the lanterns lit inside and the crescent moon overhead. She would have to swallow a lot of pride to ask to come back inside to sleep. She looked up as she hugged herself and sighed.

Crescent lurked nearby and settled next to Ilsi. She leaned against him since he seemed open to the idea, plus he was considerably warmer than the chill nighttime air.

She was finished with reasoning with Giselle. Getting rejected by the Sea King was stinging enough, but Giselle made it beyond clear that she wouldn't answer the call when needed. *So what's keeping me here?* Ilsi thought. *I'm healed up and I can travel. I should just consider this a lost cause and find Ladala again.*

———◦◦———

Ilsi's mind was filled with voices, and she blinked a few times. She found herself awake, and it was late morning. She was covered in a thick quilt and she still lay against Crescent's body. She continued to hear someone muttering under their breath.

Ilsi wiped her face free from straying drool and got up to her feet. She went around the corner to see a figure in a familiar cloak standing at the door.

"Well look who it is," Ilsi grinned, instantly recognizing the figure.

The stranger turned and pulled the hood down to reveal herself, Reshma. She held faithful Dash by his reins as her lips curved into a cocky smile and her eyebrows rose. Reshma laughed and the girls embraced.

"How did you even manage to find me?" Ilsi said.

"It took a while. I accidentally took a wrong turn, and I ended up half way to Yling. Imagine *my* surprise!" Reshma explained. "Tyk took off for his protection, so who knows when we'll see him around. But I decided to look around since turning up at our meeting place seemed like it wouldn't work."

"I managed to find this place through sheer dumb luck," Ilsi said, nodding in the direction of Crescent's sleeping form. "Took a tumble in a storm and had to heal a broken ankle."

Ilsi turned to look over her shoulder to say, "Gilly, get out here!"

Reshma immediately locked eyes with Ilsi in shock as Gilly poked her head through the door.

"*Gilly?*" Reshma exclaimed. Gilly just stood there, appalled. The three couldn't think of anything to say. Everyone stood frozen for what seemed like forever. Before Reshma could utter another word, Gilly instantly wrapped her arms around Reshma's waist, and sobbed.

"Please, don't let this be a dream! Please let this not be another dream!" Gilly cried out. Reshma enfolded her arms around Gilly's head, and she bit her lip. She suddenly burst into laughter. She crouched down on her knees so she could touch Gilly's cheek.

"Gilly, it's *me*. It's really me this time. I'm not going anywhere," she said. "What are you even doing out here? With Ilsi?"

"I'm safe here," Gilly said. Reshma used a fingertip to brush away a tear. From the path, Giselle was hobbling towards her cottage. Gilly sprang to action and took the basket the woman was carrying and matched her pace. Reshma turned to see the short old lady and Ilsi cleared her throat.

"Giselle, this is Reshma, she's my very good friend," Ilsi said, pointing to Reshma.

"Enchanted to meet you, m'dear," Giselle said with a toothy grin, shaking Reshma's hand.

Reshma looked surprised again as she said, "You're Giselle! We came all this way to find you!"

"Yes, so I've been told," Giselle smiled as she headed into the cottage. She gingerly took the basket from Gilly and nodded encouragingly before disappearing. Ilsi locked eyes with Reshma and shook her head with a frown.

"I see," Reshma murmured.

———⊸∘⊷———

"We should move on. There's no point in me staying here any longer," Ilsi said later that evening. She sidled up to Reshma during a quiet moment. Giselle and Gilly were already asleep and only a candle or two gave the two friends any light.

"I know you're hung up about the Yildirims in the mountains, but I just got here," Reshma said slowly, bringing her mug of cocoa to her lips, "Give me a few days' rest and I'll give them a good fight if they're truly bent on coming here."

"We're endangering Giselle and Gilly by staying here," Ilsi whispered sharply. They both turned to look at the dimly lit beds. The soft sound of breathing was discernible.

"I can't believe Gilly is here. Can you imagine that of all

places, she's *here*?" Reshma whispered back with a smile. She winked as she said, "You're doing a better job of finding my family than I am."

"That's not the point," Ilsi snapped quietly, "I know she's family, but I don't want to put your sister and Giselle at risk because of me."

"Something is keeping Gilly here and I can't put my finger on it," Reshma said, ignoring the previous statement. "But whatever the Yildirims did to her way back then, I think she's too afraid to venture out again against them."

"I can't imagine she'll be happy let you leave," Ilsi answered. "You're the one that's actually related to her."

"It's a shame Giselle isn't up for coming, either."

"Yes, a pity."

Ilsi waited for a sarcastic retort, but didn't receive an answer. Reshma was asleep on the dining table, her arm propped up on the table by the elbow and cradling her head in her palm. Ilsi sighed and turned to the window. She looked back at her slumbering friend and let out a big sigh.

The Ice Chanter suddenly blew out the small flame of the remaining candle and darkness flooded the cabin.

CHAPTER 38

Rays of morning light poured into the windows. Reshma blinked a few times, and lifted her head from the table. A cold mug lay next to the lone candle. A comfortable quilt had been placed on her shoulders, and she gathered it closer around her. Giselle's bed was neatly made, with no one sleeping in it, and Gilly was still asleep. Ilsi's bed was also neatly made and empty.

Reshma looked out the window and saw Dash grazing outside; it was quiet with just him outside. Giselle came into the cottage and looked up at Reshma.

"Giselle," Reshma smiled. "Good morning. Where's Ilsi?" Giselle turned, and a look of relief crossed her face.

"Oh, you've finally awoken, child," Giselle replied with a raspy voice. "I haven't seen Ilsi for a few hours."

"But where did she go?" Reshma asked. "Why didn't you tell me sooner?"

Giselle said wearily, "Well, I wanted to wait until it was a problem, you see. Maybe she went off hunting, I'm not her granny. But I think she left sometime last night."

"*What?*" Reshma cried. "Why would she do this?"

"You were the last to speak with her, not me," Giselle

insisted. "But she had the look of hero's remorse on her face. That's for sure."

"I need to find her before she gets killed," Reshma said. "She can take care of herself, fine, but nothing good ever comes from being so rash."

"Is it my fault?" a voice murmured. Reshma turned and realized Gilly was sitting up in bed wearing an over-sized nightgown.

"What do you mean, sweet child?" Giselle asked.

"You found me," Gilly began, looking at Reshma. "Maybe she thinks because we're together that you're—"

"Done fighting?" Reshma interrupted. "Ilsi isn't thinking straight. I'm getting my things."

Giselle slipped out of the cottage, not saying anything or looking at anyone. Reshma began taking her sleeping clothes off and hastily putting on her riding clothes. She had barely arrived, so she was only half unpacked anyway. Her mind raced with anger and frustration which made it more difficult to work quickly.

She could feel Gilly's eyes watching her and looked over her shoulder to see Gilly standing there, holding her cape but still wearing her nightgown.

"What's wrong, Gill?" Reshma asked.

"You're leaving," her sister replied, "You just got here."

"It doesn't mean you have to stay," Reshma replied. "We'll likely come back once we're safe. You could come with me if you want. Your choice. I don't think there's anything here for you."

It shouldn't be much of a debate anyway, Reshma thought. *It's either stick with your family or not.*

"Gilly, fetch me some Bergamots. I am tired as an old gray mule," Giselle said from outside. The girl obediently went off in search of the herb, leaving her cloak behind.

What happened to you, Gill? Reshma wondered to herself, as she was left alone in the house.

———◦◦◦———

Reshma suddenly flinched at a loud noise. Gilly was screaming or yelling, or something. Reshma looked out the window to see about five to eight Yildirims flooding into the clearing. They were surrounding Dash, Gilly, and Giselle, who looked like she was in the middle of saddling the horse.

Reshma quickly darted out of the cottage and unsheathed her long sword.

Blades first, fire second.

Before a single Yildirim sword was raised, Reshma flung herself at the soldiers, cutting them down with her sword and flames. Shots of fire erupted from her hands, scorching and igniting weapons. The fire within her was so intense that one unlucky lad fell and rolled around, engulfed in an unquenchable torch.

"Gilly, you shouldn't be here!" Reshma cried over the noise of battle.

"I'm not a child anymore!" Gilly shouted back. "Besides, you're ruining the patch of Arrowroots!" Gilly had one hand around Giselle and the other was shooting fire from her palm as she sang in a pure soprano. Reshma finally created a ring of fire around her sister, the old woman, and their steed—which meant they were protected, but now more Yildirims turned on her.

More came from all directions. Reshma looked around in confusion. *How many were waiting? How many were out there?*

She was suddenly blasted with an electric shock. Someone actually grabbed her by the shoulder as she felt the pain ripple through her body. She fell to the ground, and the grip she had on her bewitched fire loosened. She couldn't hear much; her ears rang. Reshma felt a sharp pain in her side; her body had no desire to rise, but her instincts were screaming at her to grasp her sword and fight.

Two soldiers grasped Reshma by her arms, and roughly pulled to her feet without mercy. They directed her vision towards Gilly. She and the others were surrounded by surviving soldiers.

"Hold your fire!" one called, "unless you want to see your granny shake like a leaf, too." Reshma focused her thoughts and energy on breathing. One of the soldiers standing between those in the scorched ring pointed to a few others and told them to search Giselle's property. Two or three listened and walked away.

"You're coming with us, so move quietly and close together," the soldier holding Reshma said. The soldier, a woman, shoved Reshma towards the others and Gilly took a few steps to catch Reshma and steady her.

Gilly kept looking to Giselle with pleading eyes. She was frightened after seeing her sister flail on the ground and counting how many soldiers were around to guard them. Giselle kept a stern face and placed both her hands on her walking stick with contempt.

"Please, help us," Gilly whispered. Reshma couldn't tell if it was for her or for Giselle, but her muscles were twitching and shaking, so she couldn't do much besides stand in a wide stance. It was better than being on all fours.

"If it's what you wish, child," came the soft reply. She hardly moved a muscle as thick tree roots and vines burst through the ground, exploding through Giselle's garden. Reshma looked up, to see all the Yildirim soldiers were entangled in thick vines. They were flailing their feet and hands to break free, but they were defenseless against the vise-like grip. She held her hand out, keeping her spell steady.

"Hey!" one soldier barked, "Put us down!"

He tried to free himself by casting thunder but felt the full brunt of his own attack. The vine thrashed his limp body around in the air.

"Dearies," Giselle said, speaking to the girls, "you should leave while you have the chance." Gilly looked to Giselle. "Go to the safe place or follow your sister." Gilly nodded and gave her a big smile. She turned her back to Reshma, and broke into a run. She jumped, and suddenly morphed into a falcon. She soared into the sky and disappeared over the trees, much to Reshma's surprise.

"Gilly!" she cried. She didn't waste much time, but instead rushed towards Dash, mounted, and urged him forward and away from the cottage.

"Come on, Dash," Reshma whispered to the steed, "Let's find Ilsi. And Gilly. Hell, let's get out of this place." The beast galloped onward with excitement and power and Reshma held onto the horse's neck for dear life. Giselle was left alone with all the Yildirim soldiers at her disposal. They protested and yelled from a few feet off the ground.

Suddenly she disappeared before their eyes. Her vines uncoiled themselves and slunk back into the soil. The soldiers all fell to the ground and either passed on or stared there, appalled. The cabin had disappeared. The old woman disappeared. It was just the soldiers and a torn garden.

CHAPTER 39

Ilsi opened her eyes to greet the friendly sunlight. Streams of sunlight seared through tree branches, and fresh dew dotted the leaves. She fully came to her senses when Crescent snorted close to Ilsi's face, softly blowing at her hair. She rubbed her hands over her eyes and slowly rose from the area of flat grass that she had been resting on.

She had been out here in the forest for about three days. She had little idea where she was, but she was sure that the mountains were still to her right. She began patting Crescent's neck, as she thought.

A loud abnormal screech stretched its way across the sky, and a flock of birds flew away from their perch. She didn't think much of it; if she was stuck in Beast Forest again, it was one of the friendlier sounds she'd heard.

She decided after a few days of searching that Ladala would keep her people in the forest where they seemed most comfortable. To avoid being seen, she and Crescent walked and slept by day and flew at night. She was looking for any sign that would look like a mysterious entryway. So far *everything* seemed mysterious. And unhelpful.

She knew they were being tracked by her soldiers and wondered if any would swoop down from the trees and finally give her directions or lead her straight to it. At least know she wasn't alone in the forest.

For the next three hours, she made the pattern of riding, stopping, sleeping, riding, stopping, sleeping.

Where am I going? Ilsi thought, looking to the compass. Just when she thought the trees were playing tricks on her and sending her in circles, a bright light shone a few yards before her. Instead of some sort of magical occurrence, Ilsi found that she had finally escaped the forest, and had ridden to a shoreline.

There were a few low hills about, then a sudden drop into the sand. She and Crescent stopped at the edge of the grass. Ilsi looked with interest to the shore. She unfastened her boots, and stepped into the sand. She could suddenly remember the beautiful shores of Ravenna, before it became frozen and barren. She gazed out at the still water, and tried to remember what life was like before the Wall. A soft wind swept around her, tousling her hair and all she heard was silence.

She crouched down, and sunk a hand under the sand, and let it pass through her fingers. She groaned and her other hand combed her hair in frustration. What felt earlier like a burst of inspiration, the next vital move, suddenly felt foolish. *What if I have failed enough times that Ladala won't give me sanctuary? What if our deal is broken?*

She heard a screech. With her feet in the sand, she turned back to look at the forest line. A falcon circled overhead and looked down on her with its pointed beak. It screeched before swooping away.

No sooner, she heard her name.

Ilsi put on her boots again and saw Reshma riding full speed out of the forest and practically into Crescent. She quickly dismounted and huffed towards Ilsi. Before Ilsi could say anything, Reshma closed the gap between them and slapped Ilsi across the face. The sound echoed, and Ilsi put a hand to her cheek. She bent over, as she absorbed the stinging pain of the blow.

"What on *earth* were you thinking?" Reshma shouted, breathing heavily.

"What was that for?" Ilsi cried out, backing away from Reshma.

"Why did you leave without telling anyone?" Reshma asked with fury. Ilsi sucked in her breath, wincing, and threw a deathly glare back.

"I saw how happy you were with Gilly. You've already found some of your siblings and," Ilsi said, chest pounding, "you're getting what you want and I didn't want to muck it up."

"That's no excuse to go away by yourself," Reshma said. "If you want my help—"

"I'm not worth protecting," Ilsi said, shoving Reshma's hand off of her own shoulder, "I'm not worth your family's blood."

"What's gotten into you? Why are you all of a sudden trying to play the hero?"

"Reshma," Ilsi said, standing back up again, putting her hands into fists, "quit scolding me like a child!"

"Did you not stop to think that I might want more than to just find my family—but help you fight back for Ravenna?"

"Look, if I were in your shoes, I'd go looking for my family and go in any direction opposite of the Yildirims, rather than directly towards them."

"Here's a kicker—my brother is a Yildirim, and I watched him attack Berg's family inn. Do I have a choice? You don't just abandon those you care about."

"I'm sorry about your brother," was all Ilsi could murmur.

"I at least know he's alive, that's always a good start," Reshma replied.

"Did Gilly stay with Giselle?"

"She's not here," Reshma said. "She helped me track you and flew off. Yeah, you heard that right—she's an Animan like you. Except a falcon and not on the moon's whim."

"Just whenever she feels like it?"

"There she is!" someone yelled. A few soldiers trickled onto the scene, followed by more. It was a swarm and they were the only two targets.

"What if you're brother is here?" Ilsi asked.

"Attack anyone that doesn't use fire is all," Reshma said through gritted teeth.

"We're fighting?" Ilsi asked incredulously.

"Fight or die!"

Ilisi felt such an immense burning desire within her body. *I won't give up . . . I can't.* The sudden thought surged throughout her soul, and she let out a cry, and charged towards the first opponent. She knocked down a Yildirim with her sword in her fury. fIlsi took a quick glance at Reshma, who was in the middle of a duel with a burly soldier, dodging and taunting him. Ilsi closely avoided a swinging blade in time to save her neck. She blocked herself with her blade, and evaded more attacks. She looked around, and found it to be of no use. They kept coming; there was no end to their numbers.

She was suddenly seized by four or five firm gripping

hands. She flailed and kicked, but the more she screamed, the more Yildirims flooded the scene. Dash whinnied, and Crescent let out a terrifying roar, unlike any Ilsi had heard.

For the first time, she witnessed Crescent fight back. The dragon flapped his mighty wings and hovered in the air for the higher ground and spewed blue fire on the soldiers below. It distracted the soldiers enough that Ilsi was able to throw icicles or punches at whomever came too close.

Is the whole army here? Ilsi thought. She half expected to see Reubens around here somewhere, watching his lackeys do his bidding. Or even Althod, with the surprising amount of numbers.

So many for just the two of us?

Ilsi looked around and was suddenly enlightened. Elven soldiers were also on the battlefield. They were grossly outnumbered, but they were worthy opponents. *They've come to help,* Ilsi thought, flushed with temporary relief. *We're not abandoned.*

She suddenly felt something clash against her face. She staggered back and put a hand to her forehead; fresh blood soaked her fingers. Her vision was hazy; confusion and chaos surrounded her. Her knees buckled as she tried to remain calm. She put a hand to her head and tried to look up. A female soldier took a swipe at her with a thick, spiked club and struck Ilsi in the face again.

She heard Reshma scream her name. Ilsi looked horrified at her hands. They were a sickening sight, blood dripping from her fingers. The soldier roughly grabbed her to lift her up.

"I said capture, not kill!" Ilsi somehow heard above the din. Ilsi recognized the voice as Reubens's. He stood a foot or so away in full, dark gray battle armor and sent lightning through the soldier that just beat her. The woman gurgled and screamed and fell to the ground. Ilsi felt the effects of the attack and felt an unnerving spasm through her body.

Ilsi locked eye contact with Reubens as he approached. He and Ilsi moved slightly away from each other when a tall line of fire blazed between the two. Ilsi turned and was surrounded by fire, the heat unbearably close as her wounds wept mercilessly. Reshma stepped through the fire and crouched down in their sanctuary.

"Ilsi! What's going on? Where are you hurt?" she cried. Reshma put Ilsi's weak arm over her shoulder. She was trying to get her out of this mess. Ilsi wiped blood out of her eyes. It was getting harder to see.

"We need to warn the others," Ilsi said, barely able to speak. "Reubens is hell-bent on my undoing and taking over these lands." Her hands shook mightily as she pried one of the rings from her fingers and dropped it in the sand. Reshma's eyes flashed. The light dulled, and the girls clasped each other's bloody hands.

"If you want to help," Ilsi said, coughing up blood, "Don't give this to anyone but Ladala."

"Why give this to me?" Reshma said. "It's the only thing that actually burns me!"

"Althod will use it like I can," Ilsi said, groping for fabric on her person to tear and use for her head. "Ladala will keep them safe."

"You're not staying here like you're implying," Reshma said. "I won't let them take you."

"People are dying because of me," Ilsi said. "I'll go with them to give you and Ladala time to recoup. You'll get me out of there, I know it."

"Ilsi, you're insane!"

"They'll keep me alive," Ilsi shook her head deliriously.

Reshma shook her head and said, "You can at least put them in this satchel for me." Ilsi obeyed and scooped them up and dropped them in.

Suddenly, Reubens leapt through the flames and tumbled near the girls. They shrieked as he snarled and made a grab for them.

"You are under arrest!" he roared as his hair fell in his face. Reshma kicked at him with fire coming out of her soles and he flinched back. She held Ilsi up to her feet and they escaped the circle together. Ilsi felt the scorch slightly as an extra layer of pain. They staggered and quickly surveyed the scene. The elves were outnumbered and falling back. Crescent had left the scene by then and an Elven soldier was fighting while riding Dash.

"They're retreating," Ilsi breathed.

"And for good reason," they heard behind them. Reubens quickly curved his arm around Ilsi's neck and held a knife to her throat.

"You're not leaving unless I say so," he said in Ilsi's ear. He looked up to Reshma and said, "One wrong move . . ." He didn't have to finish. Reshma backed away with her hands up, a scowl on her face. Reubens motioned his head towards Reshma and shouted for his men to capture her, but they were too late; the soldier on Dash galloped towards them and fought any people coming towards him. He lent a hand and Reshma got on the horse.

"Follow them!" Reubens barked. The soldiers began on foot and on horse to follow the retreating elves, the one on Dash gaining the most speed.

Ilsi stood practically lifeless on the beach, surrounded by soldiers. She was then taken, tied with cords, and brought with the assembly of soldiers. Ilsi's head was bent, as if in prayer, both proud and anxious about her sacrifice.

CHAPTER 40

Ilsi shook her head wearily. She could remember little of what happened after she gave Reshma her rings. She just felt an immense weight push on her shoulders, and she sank to the ground. It was like she was carrying the world on her shoulders and no one offered a hand.

She awoke in a room constructed out of large, dark gray stones. The dark walls created a cool and quiet environment. A few candles and torches lit the room but she couldn't see them clearly due to a cloth draped low over her eyes. She lay on a cot in a long nightshift. As she turned her head from side to side, she realized that thick material swathed around the top and side of her head and made it a bit difficult to see. She raised a hand and realized it was gauze and bandages. She must've been hurt.

After a few shaky breaths, Ilsi tried to call out. Her voice came out as a rasp and a few pathetic coughs. Surprisingly, her thoughts turned to Tyk. For some reason, she needed someone to tell her that he was okay.

A woman in a white worker's gown came to her side and knelt down. Ilsi reached her hand out to feel the woman's dress, just as a way to know she was real.

"Reshma? Tyk?" came her words.

"Drink this, hun," was the reply. The voice murmured in low tones. Ilsi felt a hand cradle around the back of her head and tilt it up a bit. A bowl was pressed to her lips and she swallowed a comfortable and soothing liquid.

"Let's take a look at that wound," came the warm voice. In a few seconds, she was free of the binding and could see more clearly. The woman didn't look her in the eye, but rather looked just above at her forehead and crown of her head.

"Well, you're awake and this wound is slowly patching up," the woman sighed, "So that's better than last week."

"How long have I been here?" Ilsi asked. She gingerly put a hand to the side of her head and didn't feel her hair, but skin.

"Just a few weeks," the woman replied. "Be careful with where you touch. We had to shave part of your hair to stitch up your wounds. Don't worry—it'll grow back."

The woman pulled out a small mirror for Ilsi to inspect herself. The gash twisted its way from her temple to the middle of her forehead. She was sure her nurse had saved her life. Because of that, she liked the woman instantly.

Her nurse wore her hair back in a curly bun and kept as many strays away as possible with a scarf knotted just behind her neck. The woman looked like she was old enough to be someone's mother; Ilsi felt safe knowing someone was watching over her.

"Where are we?"

"You're in a hospital, hun," the woman said giving a reassuring smile. "I work here. I'm watching over you."

Next to the woman's knees, there was another bowl covered with a cloth. She held it in one hand and pulled back the cloth.

She dipped two fingers into the bowl and gently spread a cool salve on Ilsi's forehead. Soon after, the nurse wrapped Ilsi's head with new material. Ilsi smiled and sighed in relief.

The nurse tended to other bruises and cuts on Ilsi's body while the patient silently twirled a precious gem around her fingers that hung from a necklace around her neck.

Snow flurries swayed this way and that as a figure looked at the tips of the Pearl Mountains. He wore a black uniform with a long and trailing black cloak with a fur trim around his neck. He stood out in a balcony, thinking to himself. His hands were folded behind his back, as he looked outward. Suddenly a young soldier entered from behind. He tapped his foot and saluted.

"What is it, boy?" the man replied, turning around. He absentmindedly fingered at his braided red beard.

"Sir! News from base!" the soldier stated monotonously.

"Well?" he barked. The boy shuffled, and gave the man a small parchment. The man read and reread the note and finished with a grunt. He ripped the paper and the pieces diminished at his feet. A small frown formed.

"Another batch of rebels?" the old man asked.

"Yes!" the soldier said, "Many are coming from Charcoal Ridge, sir!"

"And no sign of the girl?" the old man sighed, massaging his forehead. "Speak! I command you to speak!" the old man cried, turning towards the frightened soldier. He became irate when he didn't receive a straight answer. The soldier went pale, and cold sweat streaked his face.

"Y-yes, sir," the boy gulped, "We're pretty sure of it this time. Well, General Reubens is positive it's her."

"Bring Reubens in immediately."

"Already here, my lord," came the reply. Reubens came in the room wearing a blue velvet tunic and black pants. Despite the bruises and cuts decorating his face, neck and hands, he looked like he had a good night's rest and a decent shave. Althod knew something had to be good for the man's face to be etched with that uppity grin.

"I read your report," Althod said. "You look like there's more to the report that I don't know about. Have you recently married?"

Reubens chuckled away Althod's sarcastic joke and straightened as he said, "I have the girl in my custody. After examining her effects, I have discovered that she is the girl that you need to further your plans. She carries a book that resembles a journal. She writes as if to her mother and spills her secrets on each page."

"Where is she?"

"She's in the infirmary. One of my soldiers dealt an almost-deadly blow and so she is resting. She'll be ready to join the ranks within a week."

"Quite the quick healer," Althod grunted. "Has the nurse or healer said anything else of her condition? Any sort of information revealed?"

"They've said that she's taken exceptionally well to the amulet and isn't fully comprehensible," Reubens explained. "She and I will be working close together in the next few months."

"You sound a lot like a cat that likes to play with his food."

"I'm doing this for you, my lord," Reubens said with a bow.

"She'll reveal Ladala's location under your power and she'll have no one else to blame but herself."

"Very well," Althod said. "Bring me word when she reveals something useful."

"As always, my lord."

———◦———

Resting became a daily part of her routine, with the occasional walking around. The nurse let Ilsi roam wherever she pleased. She seemed to have misplaced her mother's journal as well as her rings. *Oh right, Reshma has those. Perhaps she has mother's journal, too?*

Ilsi was very curious about where she was. She knew easily enough that she was in a hospital or healing center, but she wanted to know exactly where she was. Was she close to home? When was Reshma going to come and kill the Yildirim that gave her this head wound? She thought these things while she looked out the windows and saw tall trees with snow frosted over the branches and pine needles. It reminded her of home, except it seemed more beautiful. Maybe because even though there was snow, she could go wherever she wanted.

She even told the nurse that she didn't even need shoes because she knew the perfect spells to stay warm. She offered to sing those spells for the nurse so she could come outside with her without her long coat, but the nurse merely decided to watch instead. She often watched the girl carefully pick her way around the trees in a simple cream dress and a red amulet hanging from her neck. Ilsi would stretch her legs, then come inside to sleep again. The nurse patted her feet dry until they had a pink, healthy glow.

———— ◦≫◦◦◦≪◦ ————

The next time Ilsi awoke, someone held her hand and gave it a pat. She opened her eyes and her nurse beamed down at her. Well, it was more of excitement and nervousness, the way her eyes widened a bit.

"Miss, you have a visitor."

Ilsi sat up and craned her neck to see a man in blue velvet that off-set his charcoal hair and goatee nicely.

"Is he a prince?" Ilsi asked her nurse. The man chuckled kindly and sat on the floor next to her. Ilsi gave him a bemused grin.

"Oh, you're Reubens," Ilsi said.

"He's the one who gave you that necklace," the nurse reminded her. Ilsi instinctively fingered the red gem curiously. It was prettier than her rings.

"You're right," Reubens said. "That's my name. I've spent a lot time looking for you. I'm glad you're feeling much better. My soldier that hurt you has been sufficiently punished."

"I saw you kill her, the soldier I mean," Ilsi said. "You used your Yildirim abilities. I've dodged you long enough to know that tune."

"Why have you run so much?" Reubens asked gently.

"Ladala told me to," Ilsi said simply. "I promised to help her defeat you to protect my clan." She didn't remember any other time where she felt so frank and bold. It helped that Reubens didn't look angry at all. He seemed interested in what she had to say.

"You've been away from Ladala for a long time now," Reubens said. "How is she?"

"I don't know," Ilsi said, confused for the first time since she had been there. "Do elves get sick?" She felt foolish for asking, but Reubens seemed like someone who would know. He chuckled and shrugged.

"I've never seen a sick elf, so your guess is as good as mine," he said simply.

"Hey! You know Tyk, don't you? My friend from my homeland?" Ilsi said. Reubens looked like he didn't follow but wanted to. "I miss him. I'm worried that your soldiers have hurt him. Will you help me find him?"

"He's not among my ranks," Reubens said. "But perhaps you can accompany me in finding him and Ladala. She and I need to exchange prisoners on neutral soil, but I can't really do that unless I know where she is."

"I've been looking for her, too," Ilsi said. "She promised to protect me, but her soldiers weren't enough. I should tell her that she should double her efforts. What use am I if I'm dead?"

Ilsi hoped that Reubens wasn't offended that she still liked Ladala more and wanted to be her ally. But Reubens didn't seem bothered. Ilsi knew that if he was bothered, he wouldn't be so nice to her and help her feel better. Maybe he saved her life, too.

CHAPTER 41

Report for our lord Althod from General Reubens and written in his own hand:

We have been marching in Beast Forest for a month or so. I can't say for sure if we're getting closer to their new location, but Ilsi has somehow found a means to locate where Ladala's people used to be before we invaded and attacked. She doesn't carry the rings you ask for, but she seems to know where to go without them. She probably can't access their new territory without them, but our latest improvement on the amulets seem to work better for our growing numbers.

One improvement especially astounds me. Ilsi still thinks she is her own person and still has control. She's been frank and honest the entire time we've been associates and still keeps her original alliances (so she thinks) but acts and speaks with entertaining bravery. Currently, she is leading us to Ladala in the vain hope of sabotaging us, instead of the other way around. She's succumbing to the influence more than any soldier I've come across. It suggests an insane amount of repressed guilt on her part.

I've been keeping a running record of her behavior, as I know the results fascinate you and it is my duty. Once she has succumbed long enough, she might just even give herself freely to you to further your plans beyond war victory.

We now head north and await any and all further instructions.
Signed your ever loyal servant,
　Reubens

———◦◦◦———

After a couple of months, they'd given up on their quest in the Beast Forest (for now) and planned to tour other smaller forests. During that time, Ilsi—and a surprising amount of her companions—would feel the moon's touch and give into their Animen forms. It's what helped her gain her bearings of the woods. As a human, Ilsi used her compass until she led them to the old city; it was easy to see with the border tarnished and unable to shield their desolate world.

Based on clues left behind, and Reubens' extensive research, they agreed that it was likely they weren't in the same forest and instead decided to migrate north. Everything south was too populated with humans.

On their trek, they came across a town with a familiar name: Cains. Reubens orders were to flush it out to find rebels, seeing as how they lived close enough to Giselle to prove suspicious.

Ilsi had never raided a village or town before. At first it didn't even make any sense to her; if the point of the trek was to find Ladala to establish a prisoner exchange, then why bother waste time by tormenting the locals? She reluctantly followed orders and went with a small band of soldiers and entered Cains stealthily and quickly.

She remembered little about the city; Giselle told her she didn't really like anyone there, which was why she chose to live in the woods.

The first thing she noticed about the place was the thick, depressing cloud that seemed to drape across every rooftop and over every head. No wonder Reubens ordered the attack; the people were bound under ridiculous superstitions that ruled their every-day actions to the point that their lives didn't seem to hold much meaning. Ilsi was sure that had they not arrived, a poor resident might've committed suicide under the buckling pressure.

Ilsi wasn't sure where it stemmed from; she only knew what she overheard from an interrogation. The soldier was kindly showing her how to extract information and also put new information in its place. The soldier told the young girl under his grip that everyone was supposed to gather in the town square in fifteen minutes without any weapons—otherwise the place would be ransacked for rebels. All Ilsi could remember was the young girl—probably Gilly's age—looking up at Ilsi in fear and dread.

The way her eyebrows knitted together . . . Ilsi thought that maybe the girl somehow recognized her as a good girl dressed in bad girl's armor. Didn't she know that things would work out? That Ilsi wasn't seduced by the Yildirim's power? The moment they found Ladala, she was prepared to turn against Reubens— she promised! She would bring her biggest enemy right to Ladala's doorstep and she, Ilsi, Reshma, and Tyk would lead an attack that would make Althod choke.

She just needed time. She needed them to trust her that she was really under this amulet's spell. If Tyk could do this to help Ilsi, then she could do this to help Ladala.

They sent away the frightened girl as Ilsi turned to the soldier.

"Now what?" she asked. The soldier gathered excess rope, wound it up, and tossed the bundle to Ilsi.

"We wait the designated time, give or take a few minutes,

capture any resistance and march off as per our orders." The soldier made it seem obvious and easy. Maybe this soldier has done this type of thing too many times. "Are you up for it?"

"How would I know?" Ilsi murmured, annoyed. She knew very well what a raid looked like—she'd been victim of one already. The question was whether she was ready to do the same thing to a village of strangers that Reubens had done to her own world back on Ravenna. The raid that started this whole mess.

She clenched her fists and braced herself. She could come away from all of this. She planned on appearing merciless when really she would personally ensure no one would get seriously hurt. She'd be in control enough to look heartless but not inflict the same pain.

Moments later, she began shouting at people, holding a torch high above her head. Luckily, the vast majority of people were already huddled and waiting to face their fate. *They see me as a monster,* she thought, *but I will show them that I'm still the hero.*

One by one, thatch houses began to go up in flames and the people there believed their ill fate was due to a scapegoat, the young girl, who was quickly volunteered as a tribute to spare the rest of the people. Ilsi couldn't contain her emotions. *Would they really blame a little girl for all this?* She wondered if her neighbors blamed her for their misfortune. *Did they give her up to be spared?*

She threw down her torch in the main stables. She rode off angrily on her steed with the soldiers in her squadron and left the miserable people and their animals to their own devices. They carried away the unfortunate girl as if a token of what transpired.

—◦◦◦——

Reubens waited with interest for Ilsi's return. It meant they had another village under their territory to use as a base, and they could finally move on to completing their trek. He and about twenty or so soldiers were waiting in a village a day's ride away. After their days in Beast Forest, they usually made it traditional to rest and drink to recuperate.

After a few days, Ilsi arrived on horseback with a young girl riding with her. The soldiers broke formation after saluting Reubens. They gladly dispersed to soak up any time they could to rejuvenate before they continued on the road once more.

"Status report?" Reubens asked stiffly and formally.

"What is there to say, general?" Ilsi said. She dismounted and helped the girl off the horse. Upon reaching the ground, the girl stood obediently at Ilsi's side but clearly wished she were elsewhere.

"How about explaining this girl," Reubens said, gesturing.

"The town is yours, general," Ilsi said flatly, "but the town rejected their own to be spared. She was branded a scapegoat on their behalf."

"Well done then, Ilsi," Reubens shrugged. "You did the job. The child belongs in my jurisdiction. We'll send her away at once."

"Wait," Ilsi barked.

"Soldier?"

"She's just a child," Ilsi tried, quieter. "We may be soldiers but she's far too young."

"Not fit to be a soldier, that's for certain," Reubens said, aware that the girl wouldn't look him in the eye. "Since you successfully led the mission, *you* can decide where she fits best."

She's not going anywhere near him, or any of these Yildirims, Ilsi thought. *They might be considerably well-behaved around me, but I wouldn't put it past them . . .*

"She'll be my assistant," Ilsi said suddenly. "A squire, maybe?"

Reubens nodded, hardly suppressing a grin. "An excellent idea." He saluted her and she returned the gesture before he walked away to join the other men. The girl stood frozen in her spot, a little hunched over as if she were about to be sick.

"Are you all right?" Ilsi turned to the girl. "You haven't eaten a thing." The girl looked at the ground a few feet in front of her and didn't respond. Her black hair was kept back in a scarf just like Ilsi's nurse. It kept the short hairs away from the round, dirty face.

"I know you aren't mute," Ilsi said. The girl could scream when provoked.

"I'm not hungry, my lady," came the quietest answer. Ilsi reached into her pack and gave the girl a few berries and a tiny loaf of bread.

"Please, just eat these," Ilsi said wearily. The girl took the food in her hands and said on the dusty ground. With each bite, her face grew more and more distraught—to the point that tears were streaming down her face.

Rejected by her own. Here among strangers, Ilsi thought. *The girl is a mess. The sooner we find Ladala, the sooner I can help this girl find a new home.* It was the first plan that sounded feasible; maybe the girl wouldn't stay with Ladala—she wouldn't force the girl to do more than she wanted—but at least she would be on the right side of this war.

She absentmindedly fiddled with her necklace. It was then

that it occurred to her that she was still parted from her mother's book. She looked to the sad girl and said, "I have a job for you. Are you full?"

The girl nodded; despite her polite demeanor before, she practically inhaled the food like it might disappear.

"What can I do for you, my lady?" The girl smoothed out her plain dress and held her shawl bravely.

"I need you to fetch me a book," Ilsi said. It belongs to me, but I don't know where it is. If you find it, I'll let you decide your life's fate. As in, you can decide to stay with me and be protected, or I'll let you run away and live wherever you want. But only if I have my book."

"What does it look like?"

———◦◦◦———

By the end of the week, the girl approached her master with breakfast. She carried a basket with a cloth covering its contents. As she pulled out the food for Ilsi to eat first, she placed the book in Ilsi's hands.

"Is this the book?" the girl asked. Ilsi nodded as she flipped through the pages. She put the book down and silently put all the food back in the basket. After she tucked everything carefully under the cloth, she handed the basket back to the girl. Without hesitation, the girl ran into the woods and never came back.

CHAPTER 42

The snow fell considerably the next few weeks upon the Pearl Mountain Valley, which lies a months' journey north of Charcoal Ridge. The white stuff piled on the streets and on the housetops. As if on cue, members of the lower-class went right to work in the dark mornings to clear paths for horses, carts, and chariots.

The people swathed in furs were already about making their purchases and sending caravans out to nearby cities with wealth and produce. Among the haughty and busy folk, there were two figures waded their way through the crowds. One figure stood a head taller than the other, but let the smaller figure guide through the bustle of people.

The taller figure quickened its pace, and walked hastily next to her companion.

"Are we near the place?" Clouds of warm breath billowed in the cold air.

"Patience, Lady. Just a few more turns," the smaller one, also female, answered, and then added with light amusement, "Anxious to be free of the cold wind?"

"You've got that right," the taller one replied, with a small grin.

"Don't fret, milady, we are at the place," the other said, resting a gloved hand on a bronze handle of a large wooden door. She pushed down upon the handle and the door swung inward. A warm rush of air brushed their rosy cheeks as they stepped in.

The room was filled with the scent of roasted meats and cinnamon. The room was dimly lit with a few low lanterns and candles. There were round tables filling the room, some already occupied by others. They were murmuring to their companions in low tones.

The shorter figure went and found a table off in another vacancy separated from the main room. The figure sat, without removing the long hood that hung over her face. She was quickly joined by the taller figure. The main steward caught her eye as she held up two fingers. The thickly built man soon came over with two steaming mugs in each meaty hand.

"Do you drink?" the taller figure asked lightly. "I should've asked for your preferences before sitting."

The smaller one smiled beneath her hood, and drank in the beverage, until she felt it pass through her body.

"It's times like this that I turn to drinking." The voice was childlike but with a hard edge to it. A child growing up too quickly.

The taller one gave a sigh as she pulled back her hood to reveal her kind face. Her pointy ears poked through the sea of brown hair. She kept her cloak fastened tight, but as she moved her arms to remove her mittens, the young figure could notice that the woman was wearing forest green skirt velvet and a simple piece of armor on top of a simple, long sleeved shirt made of thick cotton. A leather strap was strung across her chest, securing a container of arrows and her bow to her back.

"Come, Princess Karachi. Is there any need to conceal your face?"

"Lady Ladala, I can't risk being recognized," the girl answered, shrinking.

"I know how dangerous it was to escape from your chambers, but you are safe with me," Lady Ladala nodded with an assuring smile.

"Let's move to another place, then," the girl said, motioning to the dark corner diagonal from their spot. It was a round table with a dull candle with a thin curtain pulled to the side.

Once they sat down with their drinks, Ladala yanked the curtains closed and darkened their little meeting area. The girl nodded and pulled off her hood and unpinned the clasp at her throat.

The girl looked like she barely entered her teenage years. Her skin was fashionably pale, and she had bright, watery, pale blue eyes. Her hair was powdered pale blue to match her eyes and was twisted in ornate buns that hung at the nape of her neck. Two tufts of hair were expertly curled to frame her heart-shaped face. She was donned in misty blue traveling dress with a silvery, stiff belt was kept around her waist, and it was shaped like a crown.

"My governess will be furious when she realized I've escaped," Karachi said in distress.

"You still have a governess, your majesty?"

"She was once my nanny, but now serves as my bodyguard. She's a woman I trust more than my own blood."

"Then let me get to my point quickly, and we can end this conversation as soon as we must. Karachi, I've come to speak with you about your brother. We must do whatever we can so he is not corrupted by—"

"Do *not* say his name!" the girl hissed, holding her hands up. "It's poison to my ears."

"Forgive me," Ladala said, bowing her head slightly in respect. "But you know of whom I speak."

"Of course."

"I only mean to warn you that you must not let *him* control your brother anymore," Ladala murmured. "Your brother is the king and his undoing will lead to the undoing of your realm. What will neighboring kingdoms do in retaliation?"

"I sought *you* out for help, if I must remind you," Karachi hissed as she whispered. "Seth will refuse me. I'm his 14-year-old sister, he won't listen to a word I say. If he ever cared to hear my opinion, he would ask me where I heard such things, and that man will dismiss them all. I can't move in my own castle. I'm weaponless. What can I do that won't hurt me or my people?" The pointy-eared woman leaned over the table, closer to the girl.

"We need to work together to take out the Yildirims."

"I like the sound of that, but it sounds messy. It sounds risky."

"If you help us find a way into the castle, I can send help. We can make it look like you had no knowledge of the matter. But we still need your resources and support," Ladala said. "I'll ensure you are safe."

Karachi squirmed uncomfortably on her bench. She put her hands around her cup and stared into the liquid.

"If your plan is to use that Ice Chanter girl to help me, it's too late," the princess whispered. "She's already on their side."

"How do you know about Ilsi?" Ladala's question betrayed no emotion.

"We try to intercept in-coming post whenever possible," the princess explained. "Otherwise we know nothing about what's going on. We're left in the dark about our own affairs."

"That must be incredibly frustrating," Ladala answered, putting a hand on Karachi's. "We'll find other ways to deliver messages back and forth for your convenience, Your Majesty."

"Please do," Karachi replied. She thought quietly for a moment then asked, "Why are you so nice to me? You owe me absolutely nothing."

"Our world is far from perfect," Ladala explained, "but I believe independent kingdoms and realms are more balanced than one cruel army ruling everyone."

"So what is our next move?" Karachi asked, smiling for the first time since they met. Ladala leaned over the table and began to explain. Karachi's eyes widened as they continued to converse and exchange ideas. After much conversation, Karachi nodded.

"Yes, I will follow through," she said. Then, she raised her cup and as the two toasted to their plans, Karachi said, "You can trust me, Lady Ladala."

CHATPER 43

One small act changed everything for Ilsi. She went from being in charge of a village raid to residing in a claustrophobic cell. All for reading a book.

When Ilsi asked her young servant girl to find the book, she was glad to have it back. She was able to reread her mother's words, but also her own. It was like partaking of the wisdom her old self wanted her to remember. As if waking from a dream, she realized she was wearing the Yildirim amulet and yanked it off without further thought or consideration.

Suddenly, her thoughts and emotions ebbed and flowed, washing over her like an unrelenting wave. She retained all her memories of the last three months, but the implications were the things that drowned her. She set fire to people's homes. She let Reubens manipulate her. She was the enemy—even though she tried to resist.

She didn't know if this is what they did to anyone who removed their own amulet, or if this was general punishment for any and all disobedience. All she knew was she had a lot of time to think about the consequences while being confined.

Ilsi was kept literally in the dark about where she was, how long she was there, and how long they meant to keep her there. Based on the amount of shoddy meals that were slid into her room, she guessed she was in there for at least two weeks. She analyzed everything by touch and waited for what was coming.

She was half asleep at one point, when she first heard a voice.

"Halt! What brings you here?" the voice said. It was probably the jail guard. Someone was breaking in. The sound of boots against stone, heavy breathing. The other person merely whispered quickly a few words—that part was easy enough because wherever she was, it was almost always dead quiet.

She heard a small yelp and then a loud, reverberating thud. The room fell silent. Satisfying her curiosity, she rose from her corner. Her legs made cracking noise as she stood to look through the barred window of her door. All was dark, save one dancing light before her. It swayed in the air, which meant it must've been fire. It was coming closer to her face. It came with little time near her nose, and she could feel its warmth. The immense brightness dazzled her, and she shielded her face with her hands.

"Is your name Ilsi?" a tiny whisper asked. Ilsi looked up, closed her eyes as she faced the licking flames and held firmly to the bars.

"Who are you?" she whispered back, almost in tears.

"Your rescuer. We don't have much time."

She heard the sound of metal at work, and her door was unlocked. She released her feeble grip on her prison bars and easily slipped past.

"We must hurry. My spell will not last forever," the quiet voice said.

"Who *are* you?" Ilsi tried again. She couldn't see the person, but the voice and movements made suggested the person was shorter and lighter than her.

"I'm a friend of Ladala's. Now let's move already."

That was enough for Ilsi and they moved on. The mysterious figure held Ilsi's hand to guide her. Ilsi was still in a daze, and had no idea where she was. Before she exited, she saw a guard on the floor, immobilized. His face was frozen in a look of shock and horror.

The figure stopped suddenly, and listened tentatively. Two low voices were murmuring just around the corner. The figure suddenly spoke some words again and a light erupted from the right hand, and struck the two bodies. They illuminated and then stood still. Ilsi's eyes widened. The figure showed little care for the victims, but neither did Ilsi. They were Yildirim guards after all.

Soon, the figure took Ilsi's hand once more, and motioned to the door. The figure began pushing at a large black door, groaning under the weight. Ilsi then tried to help, too. First a sliver of light escaped through the crack, and more light shone around the doorframe until the door was open and unleashed the full sunlight reflecting off of snow.

The light blinded Ilsi tremendously. Every time she tried to open her eyes, she immediately had to close them again. While Ilsi was slightly whimpering to herself, the stranger looked around and decided to head for the snowy hills. Ilsi, grimaced once more, as her bare feet touched the cold ground. She suddenly tripped and collapsed into the snow.

"Come on, we're almost there!" the stranger exclaimed. She whirled around and Ilsi finally could see her. She was probably just a few years younger than herself. Her pale features matched the snowy terrain, along with her warm attire.

Ilsi grasped the extended hand, and pulled herself up. She brushed herself off, and she noticed that her fingertips and feet were changing to a sickly red color.

"Where are you taking me?" Ilsi cried wearily. "Who are you? I must know who you are!" Ilsi cried once more, confused and cold. She had been lied to for months and just wanted someone to give her the straight facts for once.

"Once we're hidden, I promise I'll tell you everything."

They were now in a black-wooded forest. They were moving a bit more slowly, weaving between trees and rotting logs. The wind blew furiously and the figure's hood blew back. Ilsi saw silvery-blue hair exposed in the cold air, elaborately twisted about her head into buns at the nape of her neck. The stranger was also wearing ornate earrings. She quickly pulled her hood back up and kept moving. They climbed further into the woods, side-stepping dead branches and trunks. When they reached a more hidden area, they stopped. The figure was satisfied, and turned to Ilsi. She sat down and began rubbing her feet for warmth.

"I think we'll be okay." The figure bent down and gasped, "Your feet! I forgot you didn't have shoes! You must forgive me, I'm such a dolt!"

"Shoes would be nice," Ilsi said, her breath escaping as white puffs from her mouth, "I bet a good spell can take away some of the pain."

Ilsi silently moved her fingertips and whispered soothing words. She motioned for her fingers in a way that looked like they were plucking the coldness from her flesh. The pain subdued and she felt better. She also remembered feeling like an idiot showing off her Ice Chanter abilities to a nurse who had abused her trust.

The girl pulled out a roll of bandages from within her large sleeves. She beckoned for Ilsi to sit down on a rock, and she began wrapping up her feet.

"I'm glad I brought this," the girl said more to herself, "Ladala said I might need this."

"Ladala?" Ilsi asked. "You spoke of her. Is she here?"

"Please, keep calm," the figure said, keeping Ilsi from standing. Instead, she was the one who stood up. She pulled back her hood. Her round face made her look like the perfect little china doll, precious and delicate.

"I am Princess Karachi," she said, "Sister to King Seth of the Pearl Mountain province." Ilsi merely stared at her. It made sense to send someone who performed stunning spells to rescue her, but she wasn't expecting this sort of royal assistance.

"Am I supposed to bow?" Ilsi asked, motioning to her bound feet.

"No, please," Karachi said waving the request away impatiently, "Just call me Karachi. I came for you because my people and I need your help."

"You need help from me? What you did back there shows me you can handle yourself just fine," Ilsi said, almost in dry humor. "I mean, you didn't even send for your own soldiers to do your dirty work to rescue me."

"I don't just do that to people for pleasure," Karachi rolled her eyes. "The magic thing is a long story. But I'm just a princess; if I'm not the king, I might as well be no one—that's how much power I *don't* have."

"Where is your kingdom, anyway? I mean, Your Highness," Ilsi quickly corrected herself. "I don't even know where I am or where you're taking me." She felt weird talking like this with someone younger than her, even if she was royalty.

"You're standing in it," the princess retorted. "We're undergoing a harsh winter at the moment. On clearer days, you can see the mountains up north." She pointed for emphasis. Distant gray figures stood in that direction with low-hanging clumps of clouds overhead. "I'm going to take you to a meeting point where Ladala will fetch you and help you rest up and recuperate. It's after that time that I will need you."

"To do what?" Ilsi said. She was momentarily distracted by the thought of reuniting with Reshma very soon, assuming she was under Ladala's protection.

"My brother is obsessed over—or perhaps possessed by—the Yildirim leader," Karachi said, staring at the snow. "I'm afraid for my brother. The people are starting to become angry and rebellious because of the influx of soldiers. Distrust in the royal family is not what we need. This man will soon turn our own people against us, and we won't be able to do anything. He's using our lands as some kind of base. I think he even lives in the castle. I'm left out of everything, so I couldn't even say for sure. I just know he frequents our castle more than I care for."

"But you're the princess," Ilsi said, perplexed. "Surely you could command your own soldiers?"

"When Seth is king," Karachi said with a harsh sigh and the roll of her eyes, "so I have no say. *He's* in charge. Besides, *I'm* his younger sister. Not even kings will listen to his siblings, even when he *knows* that I'm right. Could you even imagine me planning a rebellion on my own against my brother? He's daft but he's been a good king. It's . . . it's that stupid old man that's messing with his mind."

"I know what that's like," Ilsi murmured. "They put amulets on you and it warps your mind. It's like believing you're the same person you've always been, but your will has been bent to do what he or his men want. I'm sure your brother doesn't mean to be a bad ruler."

"Then you can help," Karachi said, her fists clenched. "You know more about the Yildirims than I or maybe even Ladala. You can help us be one step ahead of them. Maybe even free him of this amulet so he can come back to us."

"We can talk more once Ladala is here," Ilsi shivered anxiously. The sooner Ladala arrived, the more sure she could feel finally severed from those guards.

"I have your things," Karachi said, handing over Ilsi's travel pack. Ilsi grabbed for it and sifted through, recognizing old food, her compass, and her mother's journal.

"I'm so happy, thank you," Ilsi breathed. The journal was earth and oil stained, but everything was still intact. *Reubens must've enjoyed reading this,* Ilsi thought, feeling wave after wave of embarrassment and guilt.

"We made good time. She's anxious for your recovery, so she should be here within the hour."

"Perhaps I can shorten that amount of time," came a hearty voice. Through the black-wooded trunks, the girls could make out three riders trotting towards them.

"My lady!" Ilsi cried, standing up. Ladala's lush green cloak and her dark brown hair were sailing with the wind. Her features were a stark contrast to the wintery landscape. She nearly jumped off the horse to reach them. Ilsi ran fast with her own will and embraced her friend.

Ladala returned the gesture with, "You are so cold." Ladala untied her cloak from her throat and wrapped it around Ilsi. Ilsi didn't know how cold she really was until she met the intense warmth the heaping amount of cloth gave. She took it as a sign that she was really weak and her heart sank at the thought.

"Ilsi, I know this is difficult" Ladala said as they separated, "but we must keep moving. The guards will come after us. That goes for you too, dear princess."

"I'll follow you anywhere, Ladala, if it means getting away from that prison cell," Ilsi answered.

"That's what I plan on," Ladala said, then faced Karachi, "I would advise that you return home a different route than you took here. We cannot afford for them to detect any absence."

As if planned, one of Ladala's riders dismounted and helped the princess onto his horse. The elf then mounted the steed with the princess sitting in front of him.

"Don't worry, milady, my life is the least of my worries," Karachi said, then looked to Ilsi, "I believe you can help. It was an honor to spring you from jail." She smiled slightly as she urged her horse with her heels out of the clearing and out of sight.

<hr>

Karachi gladly pulled her hood up and hid herself among the people once she and her rider discretely separated. It took all of her patience to force herself into a slow, collected pace rather than run wildly back to her rooms.

She looked up, and she saw the large stone castle before her.

The gray stones were white with falling snow. She gazed at an elderly man standing with the king on a balcony. The old man stood in a black cloak. The king listened intently, as his long, wavy brown hair whipping in the wind. He ran a hand over his goatee in stress and tiredness. *He's on* Seth's *balcony,* she thought bitterly. *That old man thinks he owns our kingdom!*

The princess quietly made her way to the same warm meeting room where she and Ladala met to plan. She entered quickly, and made her way back to a small room that was hidden off to the side. She put the hood down, and let it rest about her shoulders. She looked around to be sure she was alone, and she took a candle in a small lantern that hung from the wall. She drew back a long elegant rug that hung on the wall. It revealed a simple wooden door. She quietly opened it, and disappeared from sight.

Her candle guided her small feet up a spiraling staircase. As children, the passageway was used by Karachi and Seth to sneak out of the castle. She came to a fork, where the stairs continued on, and to the right was another door. On the other side of the door were her royal chambers, and if she had continued up the stairs, she would be on her way to the king's chambers.

She hesitated to open the door to her room, because as soon as she approached, she could hear male voices on the other side. An old woman shrieked and something shattered against the floor. Karachi's eyes widened and she held a hand to her mouth. She heard the sound of boots marching out of her room.

"We'll find the princess," a muffled voice said, "She isn't the only one who knows of secret hallways."

CHAPTER 44

"Where are we going?" Ilsi said as she buried her face into the mane of the white horse and winced against the wind biting at her face. She began to feel the rhythm of the horse's gallop along with her own deep breathing. Ladala leaned into Ilsi as she tried to furiously drive the white horse.

"We've got a week's worth of riding, but I'm taking you straight to camp," Ladala replied. "Reshma has been asking for you."

She made it! She's okay, Ilsi thought.

An arrow suddenly whizzed through the air and struck the neck of the horse. The arrow struck true, but came inches away from Ilsi's own neck and she gasped at the realization. Blood soaked the white coat of the horse, and Ilsi's hands. The horse began to stumble and shriek as it flailed and reared. Ilsi could feel the horse going back down and bringing her with it. She could hear the hooves of other horses from behind. Ladala looked back to see splotchy gray horses coming from behind, with Yildirim guards riding upon them. They shook their fists in the air, shouting.

Ladala's other riders reached out for Ilsi. She saw that one was trying to help her off the horse before they collapsed.

"Ilsi," Ladala said, the both of them still riding on the horse, "Get off!"

Ilsi's head felt like mush. She quickly swung her right leg over to her left side. The white ground looked like a blank blur, as she pushed herself off the horse. The riders pulled Ladala off the horse as Ilsi tumbled in the snow. The horse soon after crumpled and gave way. It landed with a great thud to the ground.

Ilsi felt a throbbing pain in her left leg. She had landed on it quite hard, and she winced as she tried to stand. Five enemy riders approached and Ilsi braced herself for the worst.

Ladala and one of her soldiers pulled Ilsi up to her feet and she felt assured that her leg wasn't broken but still under immense pain. Reubens was naturally at the head of the group and stopped his horse just in front of them.

"Another step, and we harm the girl," Reubens warned Ladala, pointing a hooked dagger at her, "And I am under the impression that you would disapprove of my methods." She merely glared at him, the snow blowing through her hair.

"Don't worry about the girl," Ilsi said through gritted teeth. "This snow will someday melt but the spells I cast will never fade."

"Neither will your guilt," Reubens answered, "or have you failed to mention your recent activities as a Yildirim soldier yourself?"

"I'd only feel guilty if I chose to join you," Ilsi spat, "rather than be coerced!"

"Don't be upset because she's the first to resist," Ladala said. "It just proves how false your methods really are."

With that, there were suddenly four arrows taut and trained on the trio. Reubens held up his hand, and Ilsi knew the slightest sign could mean another arrow in the neck.

"You're all coming with me," Reubens said. "If you want to protect your allies, friends, family, whatever, you'll come quietly."

"What if we come loudly?" Ilsi sneered. "Will we get two amulets, courtesy of Althod?" Her memories of the past three months burned in the forefront of her mind and she wanted nothing more than for Reubens to pay for his mind tricks. He returned her words with a Yildirim strike and a strobe of lightning settled on the three for a few seconds before ebbing away. They all sank into the snow, exhausted from the shocks and burns.

"You're kind of like me," he said to Ladala. Ilsi tried to call out or move, but with the snap of Ruben's fingers, two men were quick to gag her and take her away. He still looked at Ladala with a smirk, while Ladala returned it with a frown.

"We're both like major pawns in this game," he said, patting Ilsi's head as he continued, "Always outwitting each other, a jab here, a jab there to defend our own sides. It's too bad I keep getting what I want."

"You haven't won yet," Ladala said, her smooth voice cross, "This isn't finished." She quickly glanced at Ilsi. Before anyone could muster a counter, Ladala grabbed her rider by the arm and the two disappeared. The guards stared dumbly at the ground as the two figures only left a few fresh green leaves behind. Reubens's veins bulged in his neck and forehead in surprise and anger. He swore heavily, and tore at the ground where Ladala once stood. His red-hot eyes shot at Ilsi, as if ready for her to mock him.

"You dare think us cowards, but your leader just abandoned you. I would kill you for your betrayal and insolence, but I have strict orders to bring you in *alive*," he said, very close to her alarmed face. He even pulled out his knife, to prove he was armed for the job. He turned back to his men, and barked, "We still have the girl, let's move out!"

———◦◦◦———

Ilsi wasn't quite sure how much time had passed before she regained consciousness. She was fully awake and aware of her surroundings when she felt a strong grip drag her onto a massive ship. Her wrists were tied firmly together in front of her body. She was alone except for the fleet of Yildirims surrounding her.

She looked up at the gigantic masts and the sails quivering against the wind. The crew loaded supplies on the ship and others pulled ropes with groaning effort while shouting orders and echoing them for others to hear around the docks. She wouldn't mind riding in such a fine ship, except for the fact that it was manned by enemies, killers, and thieves.

After looking around, Ilsi couldn't see Reubens anywhere and didn't know how she felt about that. Without much time to think, the soldiers marched along a long gangplank that led up to the ship itself. A soldier behind her firmly nudged her to follow up and onto the boat.

Where exactly are we going? she wondered. She had half expected to find herself back in her solitary confinement, so it confused her as to the sudden change. *Maybe they still want me to find Ladala's camp. Even though I still don't have a clue as to where it is.* The only thing Ladala said was that it was a week's worth of riding. Why Ladala hadn't just poofed her away like she did with her soldier was beyond her.

Ilsi stepped aboard the ship, and immediately sank to the ground. She felt weak and her stomach did rolls. She shakily got back to her feet, with a tug at the rope from the Yildirim taking her on board. Everything was so hazy and blurry that Ilsi almost collapsed again. She began adjusting to the rocking of the ship but felt noticeably weaker. She was willing to do anything to get herself off the ship.

She was immediately taken below deck. The soldiers shoved her past random men in tattered work clothes, barking orders to clear their way. After weaving through, she felt the soldier's hands shove her into a room. Before she could turn around and protest, the heavy door slammed in her face, and she pounded the door. She saw little use from doing so, but she wanted to prove that she was not pleased at all by this. She could see out a small window in the door; a lamp hung from the wall, giving light to enveloping darkness around her.

Someone then blocked the light from her view. It was a guard, and after the sound of clinking metal, the door opened. She backed away as he slid in a shallow plate of food. The door was shut and locked again, and she was left alone.

She coaxed herself to at least try to eat the food provided— she couldn't see it well in the dark but it tasted like potatoes. She heard a loud holler, and it jolted her. Because she was below deck, she heard all the commotion above her.

The boat started to move steadily; Ilsi knew that this meant the ship was leaving the port. She carefully positioned herself on the ground. She allowed the rocking of the boat to lull her to sleep. She knew this would be a very long ride; she would have a long time to deliberate her options or even just where the final destination would be, but sleeping would hopefully give her the energy she needed to fight whatever was coming her way.

———◦◦◦———

A few hours later, there was a loud knock at the door. Ilsi awoke, startled. The door opened anyway, and the light revealed a Yildirim in uniform. He was stern, stiff and straight in posture. He looked over her, as if he was mechanical.

"The captain orders your immediate arrival to his quarters!" he said. Without her further consent, two other guards came and grabbed her by the arms, and led her out. She tried to refuse and shrieked loudly. She suddenly thought, *What if Althod is the captain?*

"Let me go! Let me go!" she cried.

"The captain wouldn't want you to be late," the guard bellowed, as he turned on his heel and followed the guards and prisoner from behind.

CHAPTER 45

Up on deck, the crew was about their business and tending to their shifts. They exchanged shouts once in a while, but other than that, things were mum on deck. They gradually stopped their tasks as two, now four, Yildirims handled a young woman up a flight of stairs. She was apparently not willing to obey her captors and they could definitely tell that she was not one of them. The crew looked at each other with nervous, bitter glances, and continued on with their work.

A few looked at each other from various points on deck and connected eye contact and knowing looks. When the first mate stopped his glance over the workers below, they nonchalantly tried to get closer to exchange words. One looked worriedly at the direction of the screaming.

"Do ya think thisn' is it?" one said gruffly.

"I dunno, she's a-sure screami' like she tryin' to wake the dead," another answered annoyed.

"They must be sure about this one," a third added.

The fourth one smiled, "I feel sorrier for the guards than for the lass."

They were all identifiable with the Yildirim bolt, but

otherwise, they didn't look like Yildirim soldiers at all. They barely had a uniform to speak of. They looked more like poor fisherman.

One was a really tall, big man. He had curly brown locks, and a small, rounded beard. His build was large and muscular, enough to kill with his own two hands. His muscles pulsed as he worked, and on his right arm was a fairly large tattoo. He grunted mightily as he pulled the sails by ropes.

The second one was a much thinner man. He had short brown hair tucked under a black bandana. He had a coarse chin and a shrewd grin holding a toothpick in his mouth. He sneered at the ones who were shouting orders at him. He took out his toothpick, and spat to the side. He had a small, white, sleeveless shirt on, soaked with sweat. He went about his work assisting the muscular man with the ropes and sails.

The third one was a bit younger looking than the two. He had a clean-shaven face, and dark, charcoal-red colored hair that was pulled back in a small bun at the nape of his neck. He looked to be in his early twenties with a thin face and a sharp chin with a cleft. While others around him were working whole heartedly, he looked tired and bored. He moved sluggishly with the sails along with his comrades.

The fourth had heavily tanned skin, a clean face, and short, curly black hair. He was bent over, scrubbing the deck, and disdainfully looked that the spot where one of his comrades spat. He wore arm bands; his pant legs were rolled up and he walked barefoot. His thick black eyebrows furrowed as he scrubbed. His muscled flexed and relaxed with each motion.

Once the first mate turned and averted his gaze, the four looked at each other and sauntered a bit closer to talk once more.

The youngest, the black-haired one, said softly, "She might be our ticket out of here."

⸺∘⸺

The captain was very impatient. He sat uncomfortably in his chair and tapped his fingers impatiently upon his desk. It was the only sound in his cabin. His mouth was shaped into a thin line as his eyebrows furrowed. His hair was slicked back, and his uniform was pressed and stiff.

He heard a young woman's voice. *Well, it's about damn time,* he thought, his frown deepening. She sounded panic-stricken. He heard a few thuds again the walls, grunts of men and the sounds of her struggling. In due time, the door was swung open, and the girl was thrust into the room, and the door barred behind her. She turned and pounded the door with her fists.

"I would tear you to pieces if I could!" Ilsi screamed, pounding the door, "You just wait! I'll have your necks, you cowards! Damn you!"

"Stop clawing on my door like a wild animal!" the captain barked. Ilsi turned. Her face was pale, her hair in disarray. At first, her eyes were wide. However, her eyes soon relaxed. She let out a sigh, and she allowed herself to slide down against the door down to the floor. She let her limbs sag and relax.

"Oh, it's only you, Reubens," she said calmly with a shrewd smile, breathing heavily. Reubens face drew in more hatred at the calmness of her reaction.

"Yes, it's *only* me," he said, icily, then he stiffened, "Welcome aboard my ship."

"The pleasure's all mine, thanks," Ilsi said bitterly.

"Her name is the *Roaring Thunder*," he continued without a blink. He was still frowning. Ilsi snorted and just looked around the room from her spot on the floor.

"What am I even doing here?" Ilsi said, rolling her head from side to side against the grain of the door. "Was your solitary confinement full to the brim of liars and betrayers?"

"As much as I'm sure you miss it," Reubens answered, still sitting, "you're hardly of use there."

"What are you plans, then?" Ilsi said, bitterly, "I'm still surprised they promote stalkers to captains."

"I'm a general!" he roared over her, red in the face, veins bulging.

"Then shouldn't a *general* be fighting a war?" Ilsi bellowed back. She was half-bracing herself for a sudden electric strike but none came. Reubens seemed hardly half so threatening except for all the war-decorated knives and swords he had displayed on the wall behind his desk; they radiated from his seated figure like the rays of the sun.

"Let me tell you a little something," the general said through gritted teeth and smoking rage, "you might think because you're not in shackles that you're a free woman. You're property of this army and we will do with you as we see fit. The more you think you are in control, the more you damage your cause."

The cabin door swung open, as Ilsi was sent out.

"You are dismissed, Ice Chanter."

<hr>

The men were quietly watching to see what this girl would do next. To their surprise, she walked down the stairs in a huff, leaving the guards to walk quickly behind her. The cabin door slammed, and a loud and long curse came from Reubens's cabin.

Many tried to hold their snickering. They watched as she disappeared below deck. The guards stared at their prisoner walking herself to her room. They stood there dumbfounded, but gave the workers a dirty look as they went back to their original stations.

The workers looked at each other in confusion. They did however hear the sound of a slammed door below deck and a loud shrilling scream of frustration.

"Lover's quarrel?" one of the deckhands asked, answered by a boisterous choir of chuckles.

CHAPTER 46

Ilsi found herself back in her dark room once more. After pouting and muttering for a few minutes, someone dared to approach her room to deliver one thing she hated more than Reubens: a Yildirim uniform. As she examined her own clothing, she realized it was too frayed and torn to last the rest of the journey.

"Why do I even need this stuff?" Ilsi asked aloud. She was growing more confused about her predicament by the minute and didn't trust anything gifted to her by the general. She hastily put on a pair of trousers that bore no emblem (at least in the dark), a cotton work blouse, and a button-up vest—just in case the guards decided to barge in unaware before she was properly clothed. She braided her unruly hair into a small plait that ended just past her shoulders.

In due time, the guards came once more and she was gruffly directed back on deck. One of them tried to grab her arms, but she easily struggled out of his grip and even struck a blow. He looked her in anger, amazement, and then caution. He silently followed behind her as she led the way in a huff. She was not in the mood to allow them to drag her everywhere she needed to go.

When Ilsi was on deck and in the fresh air, the two soldiers darted into their places in front of her, and she was surrounded. They suddenly stopped in front of the shipmates, and they all gradually stopped their work and they looked to the soldiers. One soldier shoved Ilsi so she was in front again with the stiff man who gave her the uniform she now wore.

"Shipmates!" he bellowed. The working completely stopped working to give their attention.

"This lass is your new ship mate. Show her what to do. No funny business. Get back to work." The guards left and Ilsi stood looking around, unsure of what she heard.

"I'm doing *what?*" she said, icily. The stern man glared at her.

"I have strict orders to have you work or talk. I personally think you do enough talking, but obviously not enough for the captain," he said cynically, and continued off. The men snickered, and kept to their work. They all suddenly ignored Ilsi, and she felt like a fool. She decided to walk around, so full of anger and frustration she could feel her insides threatening to explode.

She ventured to take a few steps towards the sailors as though entering a battle arena, just waiting for her first opponent. The men went about their business, and even bumped into her on purpose and laughed under their breath. Ilsi blushed a bit. She then saw a fairly tanned young man, whistling while he was scrubbing the ground. He seemed roughly about her age, so Ilsi decided to kneel next to him, and she grabbed a large brush and began to scrub.

"You'll have to scrub harder than that to get *this* gunk off," he said in a low amused voice, not looking at her. Ilsi looked at him sternly, and without a word, scrubbed even harder. He chuckled slightly. Ilsi faced him again, narrowing her eyes at him, refusing to speak but still let a scowl escape her lips.

"Welcome aboard," he said, looking at the ground as though he was talking to the wood planks. She still didn't answer him.

"Aw, Wren. Always the gentleman!" a giant man said, patting the young man's back, nearly sending his face into the planks.

"Maybe we'll get a little more help 'round here—she needs to put her wild energy teh use!" another called out, taking out the toothpick in his mouth. He wiped his brow with his sleeve.

A large bell rang, and all the men left their duties and filed themselves down a flight of stairs. Ilsi looked around and decided to follow them. She accidentally bumped into one and she muttered a half-hearted apology before moving on.

———<>———

Ilsi soon figured out that the men were off their duties for their evening meals. Ilsi shifted uncomfortably along, ignoring cat calls and snide remarks. Under the main deck was a small area for the workers to eat. Lamps swung to the swaying of the ship and illuminated a few long benches quickly filling up with rowdy men.

A brighter, larger lamp illuminated where the cooks lined up with the food. She held a small bowl tightly in her hands and soon discovered the specialty: flavorless soup. She went along, and one of the cooks took her bowl and filled it to the brim, then handed her a brown mug with a strong smelling liquid. Ilsi looked inside it and looked at the man.

"I don't drink ale," she said quietly but coldly.

"Then don't," he replied, and Ilsi was shoved along. There were tables spread out, and the noise became louder as the crewmen found places to sit. She avoided unwanted stares, and sat at the furthest table away from any of the crew. When she began eating the soup, she realized how hungry she was. She heard the sound of creaking wooden planks, and realized that the young man she helped scrub the floor was standing right in front of her.

"This seat taken?" he said. Ilsi didn't meet his gaze, but she shook her head no, and he returned her frown with a smile and sat down.

"The name's Wren," he said.

"I'm not friends with Yildirims," Ilsi spat quietly.

"Good work, Wren! We got ourselves a good table. No one really wants to sit by the girl," a red-headed man said with a grin, nodding to Ilsi, "No offense to you, miss." Without further consent, three other men sat down and began slurping and talking to each other.

"You gonna drink that?" the large one said, gesturing to her undisturbed cup. Ilsi furrowed her eyebrows and frowned as he still took the drink.

"We should probably introduce ourselves," Wren said, and pointed to the large man with a brown curly beard, "This is Bear. I think it's pretty self-explanatory." The large man held Ilsi's drink up in a gesture of a toast, and took a swig. Wren then gestured to the man with a toothpick in his mouth.

"He's Fox," Wren said, "He sometimes steals some extra soup for us." Fox belched at the mention of his name. The last one, still silent, was leaning back in his chair. His dinner was finished and now he was napping, his cap tilted over his eyes.

"We call him Ape," Bear chortled, "He looks like one, too, eh?"

"Yeah, and Wren here is Wren," Fox grinned. Ilsi rolled her eyes as if she would rather be having a conversation with her soup.

"Well, what's your name, lass?" Bear asked. Ilsi felt uncomfortable all of a sudden. Ilsi looked around the table to find three sets of eyes looking at her, waiting for a response. She looked down at her soup and mixed her contents slowly with her dirty spoon, not looking at them. *I don't owe them anything,* she thought. The others looked at her expectantly and Fox grinned.

"Looks like someone's keeping a secret," he said, slurping his soup with gusto.

"If I were you, I would keep mum," Bear said.

"Then why do you keep asking me questions?" Ilsi asked quietly.

"Quick, Wren," Bear said, nudging him, "say something to get her to like us."

"What, you don't think you're charming enough on your own?" Wren rolled his eyes. He reverted his attention to Ilsi and said, "This may sound weird coming from us, but being friends with the crew is probably your best move."

"Best move for what?" Ilsi said. It was like these mindless soldiers were actually trying to befriend her. It was then she noticed that not a single crew member was wearing a red amulet. She wasn't forced to wear one, either. *What kind of ship is Reubens running here?*

"I assume you're not staring at my chest because it's hairy," Wren said, as if reading her mind. Ilsi blushed in reply. "There's no need for mind control on this ship. We're the defects."

"Wait," Ilsi said, putting her spoon down. "You're rebels?"

"Don't allow yourself to think that we enjoy being Yildirims," Wren said, "I didn't ask anyone to make me scrub those decks." Many grumbles from the other men followed in agreement.

"Of course, many around here don't mind, in fact, a lot of these boys enlisted themselves to get some money outta this," Bear added. Fox nodded.

"'Course we don't blame you fer bein cross with us," Fox said. "Reubens is as crazy as all get out. The Boss ain't so *benevolent* neither. I do't like 'em all that much."

"Can you use Yildirim powers? Shock people?" Ilsi asked hesitantly.

"This here ship is specially designed ter block any and all magic," Bear said. "No lightning, no amulets, no . . . whatever it is *you* can do."

"So what have you even heard about me?" Ilsi said, finishing up her soup.

"That you done pissed off the good captain," Bear grinned. "Takes a special soul teh do that."

"Oh, I could write a ballad on what I think of the good captain," Ilsi muttered.

"I've already got a name for her," Bear said to Wren. "What's you say to *Cat*?"

"It's easier than enduring name guessing-games," Wren said, looking to Ilsi.

"Call me whatever you like," Ilsi said. "Well, I can think of a few things I won't answer to."

"Cat it is!" Bear said as his final word, raising his cup. The men roared with laughter once more. Wren grinned broadly. Ilsi rolled her eyes, but she grinned as well.

"Now you're one of us, lass. It ain't that special, I know. But, it's somethin' to make yeh . . . blend in a bit. It ain't a good idea to act outta th' ordn'ary," Bear said. "Whether or not yer high on Reuben's list."

Ilsi looked around, and no one seemed to be over hearing their conversation. She thought, *This is exactly the conversation I wouldn't want Reubens to walk into.* She sighed as she looked into her bowl, unsure how she ate the unusually-colored contents.

She retorted, "I'm not who they want me to be, but no one seems to care."

Wren looked at her, his brow furrowed. The others fell silent, except for the slurping and occasional belching. The conversation picked up again, but carefully side-stepped anything to do with Ilsi. If anything, they talked about how long they'd been working on the decks and where they considered home. Ilsi jumped at the sound of a clanging bell. Ape looked around lazily, being aroused from his small nap.

"Ape, get up, fool!" Bear said, lifting him to his feet like a rag doll, "This here is Cat. You don't be messin' with Cat and we're makin' sure neither does anyone else." Ape, still unaware of what was going on, waved his hand absentmindedly and filed out with the others. Wren looked at Ilsi and smiled,

"Let's go, Cat. The grime and barnacles aren't about to come off themselves."

CHAPTER 47

So this is what it's like to be a normal person. This is what it's like to not be cursed. In many ways, I've always wanted to feel this way. It seems so much easier than being different and being okay with it. But now I think I've gotten past my childhood worries and insecurities. Knowing that my differences make me stronger helps. I have you to thank for that, Mama. It's what you wanted, isn't it?

———⋘⊙⋙———

During the early evening, Ilsi assumed her place with Wren and helped scrub the deck. She gazed over their work space to see the sun setting slowing under the horizon. Her muscled tightened and screamed for rest, but she would rather her arms fall off than be in the same room as Reubens again. He didn't exactly make for good company.

"Try to move to the left and I'll do the right," Wren said to her, "that way, it'll get done sooner."

"You don't talk the same way as the other men," Ilsi said curiously. "I mean, your accent is a little different." Wren grinned wryly, as he wiped his brow.

"Yeah, this may sound like a bit of a tall tale, but I actually come from an island called Ravenna," he said, not facing her, but gazing towards the sun with a grin, as if with a feeling of nostalgia. Ilsi's eyes widened. She held in her shock by biting her lip and gazing at the ground. *That's impossible,* Ilsi thought. *We were the first ones to escape. How did he do it? Maybe he's trying to get me to talk.*

"I haven't heard of that one," Ilsi lied. "Where is it?"

"Just off the coast of Yling, if you must know. But my accent comes more from my time in Yling. I moved there with my two brothers for work. My master found interest in me, and I was sent to school," Wren explained. "When I was fifteen, I went to go home to visit my parents. I was out at sea. I traveled for days upon days, months. It seems silly to say, but . . . I couldn't find her. I couldn't find Ravenna. It was gone. As if it never existed."

"What do you mean . . . *gone?*"

"Gone, as in disappeared. I traveled back to Yling, and I was laughed in the face. No one believed me that a whole island, along with all the people could vanish out of existence," Wren said with a sullen sigh. Ilsi felt bad for lying; he's been away from home a lot longer than she was.

"I believe you," Ilsi blurted. He looked at her, curiously, and then resorted to grinning again.

"The only one who believes me is a lass," he chuckled.

"I'm a *lady*, kind sir," Ilsi grinned, raising an eyebrow. "Just because I haven't attended school in Yling doesn't mean I haven't a brain to think with."

Wren sat back on his heels and laughed. "You sound a lot cleverer than half of the duds I had to study with."

"How long ago were you even in school?"

"Only a year ago. I'm well into my nineteenth year."

Is he trying to flirt? Ilsi rolled her eyes at the hint of pride in his voice. She wasn't the best guess at age, but she still found it hard to believe the Yildirims recruited so many young people.

"You *can't* be older than me. You're just a bit over my head," Ilsi teased. She wondered if this was what it was like to have a brother.

"*Always* judging a book by its cover, are we?" Wren said, slightly offended. Ilsi could tell this was a sore subject.

"Woah, woah," Ilsi said, holding her hands up in mock surrender. "I'm the right size for my gender and age, thank you much. Is there a spell to make one stretch to be a bit taller? Someone should teach it to you."

"I *could* set your hair on fire at this exact moment if I so wished!" he blurted.

"What, like a *Fire Weaver*?" Ilsi blurted, and she quickly chided herself for saying so. Wren suddenly stopped in shock.

"*What?* Did you say *Fire Weaver*? Do you even have *any* idea what a Fire Weaver *is*?" he said in shock. He was staring at her in awe, dropping his brush. Ilsi used her sleeve to rub her face. He could see a flash of pain on her face, as she tried to hide how emotional she was. She hadn't thought about the Wall in such a long time, it was almost like reliving the moment.

"I was there when the walls went up and we were locked in," was all Ilsi could say. "I'm an Ice Chanter."

Ilsi heard the call for the crew to change work shifts. Half of the men resumed maintaining their large sails, and the other half abandoned their work to sleep. Ilsi was one of them. She wiped her wet hands on her pants, and wiped the sweat off her forehead with her arm. She glanced over at Wren, who was already staring at her, but looked away once they locked eye contact. Together, they retreated below deck. They went through the small eating area into another hallway which led to bunks and cabins. Wren leaned closer to her.

"This conversation isn't over," he muttered.

"Get some sleep," Ilsi murmured in reply. "Can I even trust you?"

"I'm working until I'm free," Wren said. "I don't work for Reubens if that's what you're worried about."

Ilsi nodded, firmly, and Wren disappeared into another room. Ilsi walked down the narrow hallway and into her room.

———◦◦◦———

"Please don't hurt us!"

"Who are you? What do you want with us? Stay back!" another startled voice called out. There was a small candle on a candlestick in the middle of her ill-kept room. Three other young women were huddled together in the far back. Ilsi's eyebrows furrowed. They all somehow looked oddly like Ilsi. On the far left was a tiny frizzy-haired blonde, a girl with wavy hair in the middle and a girl with a long plait to the far right.

"What are you *doing* in here?" Ilsi asked, perturbed. *Reubens, this is one sick joke.* They all quickly stood, as they realized the voice was feminine.

"Just ask those men who shoved us in here like animals!" the frizzy-haired one cried out.

"Hush!" Ilsi said, motioning for them all to sit and relax.

"Who are you?" the girl with the plait asked.

"I'm a fellow hostage," Ilsi said quickly. "You're in my room."

"What are we doing here?" the wavy-haired girl asked shakily, "They just took me off the street and took me into this boat!" The other girls agreed, and asked Ilsi all sorts of questions at once. Ilsi silenced them.

"Please, just calm down. You are on a Yildirim ship. We are all hostages. I do not know where they are taking us. I basically don't know much more than you do," Ilsi said. "Where were you before we set sail?"

"Well, after we were captured, we were taken down below deck," one girl shivered. "Then they just moved us around and left . . . all the other ones below."

"And the captain—have any of you met him?" They all shook their heads no.

"We were told that we were to stay here and wait for them to get us when they land," the one with the plait. After that, no one spoke. Ilsi put a hand to her temple to soak all of this information in. She was in this room, now sharing it with three frightened girls. Three girls that look oddly like her in their own way and apparently were locked up with other people down below deck. Were they all "defects" as the Yildirim crew called themselves? She came to the sure conclusion that Reubens was one sick man.

"Well, it's a pleasure to meet you," Ilsi shrugged slightly. "My name is Cat. At least, it's what people call me here."

"The crew gave you a name?" the plaited-haired one asked.

"It's that or divulge my real name," Ilsi answered. "No way I'm going to be friendly with the people who kidnapped us."

"Should we have names like that, or something?" the frizzy-haired girl asked, timidly, aware she was interjecting at an awkward moment.

"That sounds fine," Ilsi said, "Just about everyone here does, too."

"All right, I pick Mouse," whispered the frizzy-haired one.

"Doe," the plaited one replied.

"Goose," the third one said, quietly and out of place. It was returned with a confused look from Ilsi.

"*Goose*?" Mouse replied, "What kind of name is *Goose*?"

"Well, it's all I could think of! I tried to think of something that starts with a G, since my real name does. How many animals can *you* think up off the top of your head that starts with a G?" she returned, defending herself.

"Let's see, we have giraffe, gopher, gorilla," Doe mumbled with a sly grin.

"I like mine better," Goose muttered.

Ilsi's vision soon adjusted to the faint light and she got a better look at the girls. Mouse looked five years younger than Ilsi. She was much smaller than Ilsi, with short frizzy blonde hair that tickled her cheeks and barely skimmed her shoulders. Her limbs were thin as twigs, and her hair was ruffled and wild, like she just woke up from a fitful dream. Her eyes were beautiful, but her eyes were not green. They were a pretty hazel hue.

Doe was more older-looking with a blond plait hung over her shoulder. It was very long. The girl was huddled on the floor, and the plait was in danger of being stepped or sat on. She actually looked older than Ilsi. The girl instead wore a smug look on her face and the shadows made her cheeks look sunken and thin. She didn't look very pleasant, as if she chose to still be guarded to protect herself. She held her shawl close to her shoulders.

Goose was freckle-faced with long, wavy blond hair passed her shoulders. She still looked a bit perturbed, but she was calmer. Her round cheeks had a small hidden pair of dimples. She, like the others were still wearing their every-day clothes, albeit a bit frayed and wrinkly.

"At least it looks like they provided us with blankets," Ilsi observed, moving the candle to get a better look at the room she stayed in. It seems like the new cell mates brought perks like light and something to cover herself while sleeping.

"What do you think they'll do to us?" Goose asked. "We must've done something to be separated from the others like this."

"I'm trying to figure that one out, too," Ilsi answered.

CHAPTER 48

Ilsi awoke to a soft tap on the door. Ilsi rose quickly and realized that she needed to meet Wren up on deck. She looked about, and the three young women were huddled together, sleeping soundly. Their candle was dull and growing dimmer and dimmer. Ilsi got up to her feet, and opened the door quietly. She peered out, and Wren was already heading towards the stairs. Ilsi took another quick look at the new hostages and quietly headed out. She quietly closed the door behind her.

When she climbed up the stairs to reach the deck, a cool fresh breeze greeted her. She realized how hot it was below deck, and she was glad of the new fresh air. She had barely known the sailors for a day, and they were already greeting her pleasantly like old friends. Bear clamped his meaty hand on her shoulder and gave it a good shake, while Fox smiled with his old toothpick still between his teeth. Ape would smile and wave vaguely, but not as whole-heartedly as the others.

Her eye caught sight of Wren who was already at work. She knelt beside him to begin scrubbing, as Fox, Bear, and Ape were leaving their shift and heading below deck. Ilsi made her way towards Wren and remembered last night's conversation.

Her mood suddenly changed and felt uncomfortable. Wren probably noticed, but he didn't say anything. He merely reached for a brush floating inside a water bucket and handed it to Ilsi. They silently went to work; the only sound was the wind upon the water and the bristles of the brushes moving back and forth.

"There are three more hostages in my room," Ilsi suddenly muttered. "I've only seen them for a few hours and they've nearly driven me insane. And get this—they all sort of look like me." Wren looked back at her.

"Must be quite the party," he murmured. Ilsi folded her arms and sighed.

"I don't know what Reubens wants with me on this ship. Do you even know where we're going?"

Wren gave her an expectant look.

"*Well?*" he asked. "You have a story to share first." Wren snatched the brush she was using and dunked it in his bucket. Ilsi looked up at him, alarmed. He stood there, with his fists clenched and his face determined and still.

Ilsi sighed and nodded. *He has a right to know,* Ilsi thought.

"It happened a while ago," she began, tilting her head up, to look at the purple and pink sky. Wren knelt back down to the ground, attentive and patient. "I was just a little girl. It was my mother's birthday, and I went to her favorite part of the fields to pick flowers. I saw her coming, running so fast towards me.

"She . . . she was screaming, crying. I was so afraid. I tried to reach her, hoping she would comfort me, and everything would be all right. And then . . . ." Ilsi gazed into space; the memory of the wall striking between them flooded her mind, her mother's scream, mingled with her own, echoed in her mind. She looked to Wren, as he motioned for her to continue. She wiped the corners of her eyes, trying to remove any evidence of emotion from them.

"Next thing I knew, there was some transparent wall between me and my mother. She disappeared. The last memory I have of her is beating the wall with her hands, and crying. I decided to run home. My father couldn't break the wall. It was like glass that couldn't shatter. It was wood that refused to burn, or ice to melt. It was just . . . there.

"Basically, the island's been cursed. The wall made the island invisible and inaccessible. The people were separated. They still are," Ilsi said.

"The people?" Wren asked. Ilsi realized that she especially caught his interest, since he was worried about his family.

"Well, the Ice Chanters were separated from Fire Weavers. Where I used to live, the Wall makes the snow fall all the time, but it's bewitched. We can't control it at all. It's now really hot where the Fire Weavers are. It's hard for them to grow anything there, and their water supply is draining," Ilsi explained. He would probably be the only one to care about the actual circumstances.

Ilsi looked up at Wren, his face pinched with worry and sadness. She looked down at the wooden planks again. Then a thought dawned on her. Why did she feel that she could trust him, a Yildirim? *Is Reubens watching me? Did someone overhear me?*

Wren sat on the deck next to Ilsi and gave her a small smile.

"Please," Ilsi said worriedly, "don't tell anyone what I just told you."

"That's a promise I can keep," Wren said seriously. "I won't tell a soul. I won't let a hand touch you." They both nodded to each other.

"Can you finally tell me about why I'm here?" Ilsi asked.

"Well I wasn't sure it was worth it until I knew who you really are," Wren said. "He's after those who has one of the Elite Powers—"

"Elite? You know about all that?" Ilsi asked in surprise.

"I went to school, remember?" Wren said tapping his head. "If you know about it, then could I make an educated guess that you have one of them, yes?"

Ilsi didn't respond, but Wren let out a big sigh and nodded.

"I understand. Anyway, when all four abilities combine into one body, a human body . . . bad things can and *will* happen. That's way too much magic and untamed power for one person. It can consume a person to control them and do . . . unimaginable damage," Wren explained.

"Is this what Althod wants? And what about me? Do I just die, waste away? What exactly is he planning to do?"

"Who knows? It's never really ever happened before. But I have a feeling he might not quite understand this at all, either," Wren said, shaking his head.

"So are we going to see him soon? Are we sailing to him?"

Wren shrugged. "We've been picking up rebels along the way to take them to be recruited. That's all I know for sure. But if Reubens thinks you're someone Althod really needs, then I don't know why it's taking so long."

"And you know Althod's intentions how?"

"They were wired into my brain when I was forced to wear the amulet," Wren explained. "Everyone knows their purpose when they wear one of those things."

"I've spent months wearing that thing and I didn't know of that. I didn't know of any plans," Ilsi spat.

Wren gave her a wary look at the declaration but smartly

chose to respond with, "The plan sounds a bit different depending on the soldier. To some, the plan is to save their own people. To others, it's because they've committed so many misdeeds that this last one might redeem them. What did you feel?"

"I felt like I was too smart for Reubens. I felt like I was supposed to lead him to Ladala, but I thought I was creating an ambush to catch him," Ilsi sighed dully. "I'm not proud of it."

"No one really is," Wren scoffed. "I certainly felt foolish once I got on deck and thought about all the ideas that I thought were mine. It's part of the *Entice* charm; you see what you want to see but in the end, it's all to do Althod's bidding."

"So," Ilsi asked, "how then did you end up tangled up in all of this?"

"Well, you know how I found out the Ravenna was gone, right? Well, I guess I did well enough in school. I ended up being an assistant to a professor, who knew just about everything. I would stay in his mansion of a library for hours. I was so wrapped up in wanting to know the truth. I wanted to know what happened to my homeland. A whole island doesn't just *disappear*, you know.

"I got a small job to work for Yling's prime minister. I spent my time doing research and serving the ambassador for Yling. Then, a few years ago, a whole fleet of ships arrived at Yling's shores, carrying hundreds of those Yildirims. They came and ransacked the whole place. All of us were caught by surprise. The original leader of the Yildirims was in the room with me, *talking* to me. Then, next thing I know, he's on the floor soaked in his own blood.

"His men betrayed him. He was a good man. I always had respect for him and his methods. That is, until they gained a new leader, who turned everything around. They tore up everything in sight, and whatever wasn't damaged was stolen. The library was destroyed. Irreplaceable documents, letters, knowledge, everything was lost.

"And then my fate became the same as others. They captured the whole lot of us and we were taken as prisoners. A lot of them committed suicide. I was sent to be trained. And for all that," he said with a sad smile, waving his brush, "I eventually got this job."

Ilsi was blown away. Her burning hatred for them was ignited again and kindled.

"How awful," Ilsi said bewildered. "I assume Althod was that new leader?

"Correct. I know life isn't always peaceful and perfect, but when Althod showed up, everything has been chaotic since. The Yildirim used to be divided into sub groups. Some were part of a secret police, others spies, or some sailors and soldiers. Now, they just act like a bunch of pirates," Wren said sourly.

"No kidding," Ilsi said with a half-smile, gesturing to the ship.

Wren's words echoes in Ilsi's mind. She quietly continued on with her shift without another word to Wren, who was deep in his own thoughts. She kept scrubbing, up and down, back and forth. She would occasionally look up, to make sure Reubens wasn't watching her. Once in a while, he would stand out on the deck, gazing out at the wide-open sea, talking to other men steering the ship.

He must be waiting, Ilsi thought. *Of course I can work and be up here as I please so he can catch me when I feel safe, just like last time. I can't let him guilt me with all these innocent prisoners.*

Ilsi looked down at her hands, wrinkled from working with the brush.

"What are you thinking about?" Wren said. Ilsi twitched in surprise.

"Oh, just thinking," she said. "Wondering how I'm going to get off of this ship."

CHAPTER 49

Ilsi had changed quite a lot over the past five months. She was just like all the others, skin glistening of sweat, hair matted and greasy, and a little bit of dirt sported on her arms and legs. She was slowly getting used to the idea of working for a certain part of the day and getting broken blocks of time to sleep. She looked forward to the early morning rays of sunshine as the light played of the water like small specks of diamonds.

Her fellow shipmates, Bear, Fox, Wren and Ape, were her closest friends, and they always greeted her like a kid sister. She even felt comfortable around the rest of the crew, and they began nodding politely to her as she passed. Ilsi was referred now as "Cat" and got used to it. She managed to get along with the crew by moving from job to job to help, which earned her immediate admiration. She still had anger and hatred towards the captain.

The best part of this whole trek was that no matter the moon's phases, Ilsi couldn't feel the Animan influence in her. She had long since discovered that magical abilities were muted on the ship somehow; traditional beatings were used to subordinate any smart asses on board. It gave her freedom from the curse she was still adjusting to.

Ilsi however found that the company of prisoners in her room to be torture as well. She groaned with displeasure when her shift ended, because she knew who she would have to put up with soon after. They were never allowed to leave the room; well, they were too scared to attempt to leave, but they were always bored in the meantime. When she would enter, she would be bombarded with complaints, accusations and loads of questions. They argued constantly.

They were outraged that Ilsi was working all day and out and about in the sunshine and fresh air, while they were kept in the dark with nothing to do but simply squint at each other. Ilsi quickly reminded them that there were scores of Yildirims up on deck. None of the girls ever really accepted her explanations or excuses. Since she didn't know why they were there, she didn't feel the need to completely confide in them. To her, it was ironic that she trusted just about every member of the crew (the working ones anyway) more than the girls—or Reubens' use for them.

It seemed like a rather ordinary day, when Ilsi noticed a change in their course of direction. The men working with the sails were ordered to change the angles and to catch another gust of wind. Reubens was barking orders, and steering his ship more to the west than east, their general direction before.

"What's going on?" Ilsi asked Wren. He looked over at her, while she made an effort to give Reubens a dirty look. Wren could sense her general concern when she turned to look at him. Her eyes were bright and determined, waiting for his reply.

"From what I'm hearing, it sounds like we're heading for shore," he said. "For a pretty long break." Ilsi blinked a few times. He could sense her hesitation upon asking why.

"Why are we heading to shore?" Ilsi asked, hiding her concern. Bear, Fox and Ape soon overheard her question and joined the conversation.

"Pickin' up sommore rebels and prisoners, I s'pose," Fox said with a shrug. "Isn't that what we do all the time?"

Ilsi snorted at the response and folded her arms in contempt. They've done that a few times since she'd been aboard. She knew this because for the duration she would be barricaded in her room.

"This ship has room for only so many prisoners," Wren said, daring to glance at Ilsi. Ilsi's thoughts turned to the other hostages in her room. *They don't even know why they're in this ship,* she thought. She shook her head in disgust.

"Well, in a way, that's a good thing fer Cat," Bear said, clamping his meaty and grimy hand on her shoulder, "I was a bit worried 'bout you. Most of the time when they think they've got themselves the girl, we head east," Bear said, pointing towards east, "But I guess that they ain't so sure."

Ilsi felt a bit of guilt, knowing that she had only told Wren of her true identity. She didn't want to tell any more people about herself and her past, and no one felt eager to share theirs. Her friends were like the older siblings she never had, but she felt much safer in their ignorance. Besides, they didn't care. They still stood up for her and watched over her like a sister. No matter if she was a number one hostage or a random girl on the street; they didn't want anything bad to happen to her.

"Will they let me go?" Ilsi asked. The men shrugged sheepishly.

"We haven't been a'lettin go nobody yet," Fox said, looking at his feet. "Not like we'd let anything happen to you first."

"Hey!" a Yildirim called, obviously of a higher rank, "I don't stand here to watch you runnin' your mouth!" The group looked back to see the man who owned the commanding voice and grumbled as their conversation soon disintegrated.

The group dispersed to continue on with their labor. Ilsi knelt down to take her place next to Wren. He looked over at her and he noticed that Ilsi was moving faster and harder than her normal pace. Her face shone with sweat but she didn't care. Her exhaling breath was fast paced. She was pretending to be hard at work, but wheels were turning in her head. Something was on her mind.

"Ilsi, you seem so excited, what are you thinking about?" Wren said with a grin, placing an arm on her shoulder, as if to stop her from vibrating. "No need to be extra excited about our chores." She looked at him with a small grin, and fire burning in her eyes. She leaned over and whispered,

"*Land*, Wren. Land means escape and revenge!"

"*What?*" Wren exclaimed. Wren looked at her, wide-eyed with surprise. "Are you out of your *mind?*"

"Wren, I *know* it sounds crazy and impossible, but I've got to," Ilsi said in a breathless whisper. "Reubens has been playing mind tricks with me this whole time, and it's time to show him that he won't break me."

"And how exactly are you going to *do* this?" Wren said, with a look of worry on his face. "I don't particularly respect Reubens and his authority, but this could end badly. I don't think you want a bigger bull's-eye on your back If you aren't careful, you could get killed, or put any of us at risk in the process."

"Wren, I need your help. You know this ship better than I do," Ilsi said, looking at him, with sheer determination shining in her eyes. Her lips were drawn together in a firm line, her jaw set. They locked eye contact, for what seemed like a long minute, when Wren looked away. A small grin settled on his face.

"How could I resist such authority of a lady?" he murmured quietly, as Ilsi smiled dryly.

"You must understand," Wren began, "a lot of us are willing to help you. I hope you know that. We'll do it out of friendship and all, but we want out, too. I want to get off this ship just as much as you do."

"Is that why you're friends with me?" Ilsi asked, arching an eyebrow. "I know that I'm probably your best chance of ever getting back to Ravenna."

"Because of your Elite powers?" Wren asked. "I don't understand."

Ilsi sighed. "Because of *Swift*, I was able to pass through the Wall myself."

Wren whistled. "I had no idea. But like I said, these men would die for you. At least . . . I speak for myself. If you want to do this plan carefully."

"I hope you know I wasn't planning on leaving on my own," Ilsi said, catching Wren by surprise yet again.

"What do you mean?" Wren asked. Ilsi stopped scrubbing for a moment, and gazed up to look in the direction of Ruben's captain chamber. He stood with his hands behind his back, gazing out to sea. He looked down at where she worked for but a moment with sheer disgust in his face. Ilsi stared hard back at him for a moment and turned to face Wren.

"We've got a few weeks to make this happen. I want to see the look on Reubens's face when not only *I* escape, but every other prisoner on board with me!"

Chapter 50

A pair of cold black eyes gazed across the blue sea. Reubens was pacing, like a hungry wolf about his ship. Everything was going according to plan. Not according to *his* plan, but his master's plan, that is. He looked coldly down at Ilsi. He had seen many prisoners in his day, plenty of torture as well, but he didn't know how to deal with this one. He hated those who didn't fear him. If he had his way, everyone would wear an amulet until their minds were trained to think as one, rather than for themselves.

As for the girl, he knew it. He had encountered her more than once, and despite the mocking he had endured from the other generals, he knew she had to possess one of the Elite powers. He saw the fugitive with his own two eyes in Dove, where the blond-haired maiden used it to escape them, but only for that short time. How else did she get here? He lacked proof besides his passion; his master frowned upon that.

Reubens decided he was going to wait. She would soon prove her true identity and then she wouldn't be his problem anymore.

He turned his gaze from Ilsi and looked closely at Wren. He knew too much for Reubens's liking. His brows furrowed, as he looked more closely at him. His mouth curled into a disgusted snarl. He wasn't gathering enough information, but Wren could fix that. He saw Ilsi look away from Wren and up at him, with a stern, determined look. He met her gaze with a horrid glare. He was thinking, plotting his next moves to be rid of her, once and for all. He looked out to sea. He watched the waves roll in all directions.

"Maybe," he said softly, "Maybe that boy can *really* be of some use."

———◦◦◦———

Ilsi felt tired. Her brain was pulsing with too many thoughts and ideas; they bounced off the inner walls of her skull, and she put a hand to her pounding forehead. She was half way wanting to confine herself in her "cell" and sleep without one word from the other captives, but the other half knew that the "without one word" part wouldn't happen. She went below deck without Wren. When she began walking in the dining area, her body met the feeling of moist steam, as she breathed in the last of dinner's aroma. As she walked around a few of the long benches, she approached the wooden door at the middle of the room. She opened it like normal.

"What are you doing here?" a voice called, as Ilsi jumped in surprise. A pair of sharp black eyes was staring back at her. They belonged to a strange black-haired man.

Ilsi tried to push him away, but his face drew near hers. He held her firmly by the arms to prevent her from leaving. Ilsi grunted loudly, trying to free her arm, but he was firmly tightening his grip the more she struggled. As he held her, he smiled a weird grin.

"I know who you are," he said shakily, his facial features quaking, his eyes maniacally staring at her, "I know who you are!"

"Get off of me!" Ilsi said. She drove her knee into his stomach, and he released her to clutch his abdomen.

Wren, followed by Bear, Fox, and Ape, suddenly came in and they surrounded the injured man. Ilsi quickly decided that she should step back, knowing that the men would take care of the rest. She saw that he had fallen to the ground onto his knees, still grasping his stomach, as his breath came out in wheezes. She felt a tang of guilt, she shouldn't have kicked him, but he had frightened her and that was enough.

"You leave her alone, man," Wren cried, gripping onto the injured man's shirt. Fox pulled Wren off of him, as Wren tried to calm himself down.

"Geta grip, Wren," Fox said, "You gotta get a hol' yoself." Wren stopped, but he looked at the man with pursed lips and gripping, clenching hands. Bear pointed a big finger hard into the man's chest.

"Now you best count blessin's that we didn't give you the ass beaten' you asked fer. You give Cat no more trouble," Bear said in a low rumbling voice, "Or I'm agonna make an example of you."

Bear stalked off, as Fox followed behind him. Ape mindlessly walked behind them both, letting out a long yawn. Wren looked down at the man, who had begun to breathe normally, and was huddled against the wall. Wren took a step closer to him.

"If I see you even *look* at her, I swear, you won't like what's coming for you," Wren said in a low voice, "and that's a promise."

The man scrambled to his feet and went through the door into the dining area. Wren allowed himself to calm down, and to allow his heart to beat at its normal level. He shouldn't have let his anger get the best of him. He turned around, and saw that Ilsi had disappeared into her room. He let out a sigh, and tiredly made his way towards his room for the night.

⤜◦⤐

Ilsi entered her small room, with a hand to her heart. She knew that Wren had promised her that he would protect her, but she didn't understand his full meaning until now. She looked around; the three other girls were lying in her own respective and claimed sleeping area. A single candle was lit; otherwise the room was completely dark as usual. Doe's head became visible, when she suddenly sat up from where she lay. Goose and Mouse rose as well.

"What happened?" Mouse asked timidly, "We heard some men shouting, and when we heard the door open, we pretended to be asleep."

"Oh," Ilsi said with a shrug, "one of the men was drunk." In her mind, she was shaken up because that man looked just like Tyk. She prayed her mind was playing tricks on her, but the thought of a deranged Tyk on board made her feel ill at ease.

"I hate men when they're drunk," Goose said, as if her opinion was necessary. Ilsi smiled, making Doe look rather suspiciously at her.

"You look like you know something," Doe said trying to read Ilsi's face in the dim light. Ilsi suddenly remembered the news she heard today. She began to quietly tell them about the plans to head towards land. Her audience listened intently, hanging onto every word. She then paused. She decided to tell them of a plan that she had devised to escape. In truth, she and Wren had spent considerable time elaborating on what to do, but for now it was safe to leave him out of her story. When she had finished, Doe gave her a suspicious look.

"So, you're telling us that this plan is going to get us *out* of here?" Doe asked quizzically. "Just like that?"

"You mean," Mouse said, in a wistful manner, "we won't be prisoners anymore?"

"Yes," Ilsi said, "if we work together, we can help the four of us, *and* all the other prisoners that are elsewhere on this ship."

"But how do you know that it's gonna work?" Mouse whispered.

"A little bird told me so," Ilsi said with a mysterious smile. "Are you with me?"

CHAPTER 51

Ilsi silently followed behind Wren further below deck; it was dark and quiet. The sounds of snores coming from the sleeping crew covered the sound of the squeaky floor planks as they sneaked by. She felt her forehead. The humidity was making her sweat in nervousness. As they continued on down the way, the two felt the sudden heat from the adjacent kitchen. They quietly swung the double doors out. They came into the dimly lit dining area. Ilsi let out a sigh of relief. Neither the cook, nor anyone else was present. Wren turned and the candlelight was etched in his face. He put a finger to his lips to remind Ilsi to stay quiet.

The pair edged on, and came to large staircase. Moonlight spilled its eerie light upon the steps, and the sounds of working men were audible from above deck. Wren motioned to her that it was safe to continue on. Ilsi silently inhaled, and shakily followed.

Wren stopped quietly before a wooden wall. It was secluded in the shadows of the stairs. As arranged, no one was guarding the area. He was barely visible, but Ilsi could see his outlined figure with her eyes now adjusted to the darkness plus the candle.

He stretched his hands in front of him, and pushed on the wall with his palms. The wall gave a lurch, and it shifted forwards. He pushed the wall to the right, and it slid quietly to the side. Ilsi barely breathed as Wren disappeared in the darkness. She quickly followed so she could follow the quivering candlelight.

She commanded her feet to shift forward, and she sluggishly followed her friend deeper and deeper into obscurity. *Why is it even so dark down here?* Ilsi wondered. It seemed like any of the common areas had some kind of light source for warmth. They walked down a narrow hallway. Wren opened yet another secret door with extra care. She knew this was when she went first, not Wren. She stepped in and stood immobilized as she heard the secret door slide back into place. She felt a warm hand hold her own, and she exhaled, knowing it had to be Wren. He gave her hand an extra squeeze and she felt braver.

Ilsi suddenly smelled an awful combination of sweat, bodily waste, and death.

"Is this the room?" Ilsi whispered her voice small and scratchy. She heard a couple of crackling noises; Wren lit an oil lamp hanging from the wall and he held the bright lamp to his face. He looked solemnly at her and nodded. He motioned for Ilsi to walk with him, and he shone his light before them. Ilsi walked only a few steps, only to have the sudden desire to turn around and vomit.

Prisoners. Women sat everywhere, all chained together. Their prisoner garb, old tattered dresses, loosely hung on their figures. The stench intensified, to the point Ilsi was certain she couldn't forget it. The sound of low murmurings, shifting weight, clanking of chains swelled. Scared, bruised and sunken faces turned to look at her. She could see in their worn and empty eyes that they didn't know what to think of her.

Why are there no men? Ilsi thought. *Why target women that look like me? Reubens, you're sick.* Ilsi turned when Wren tapped her shoulder. He had the same confused look on his face; she could tell that he was just as confused and disturbed as she was. But they had to keep going. Their plan was only half completed.

The lantern was placed on the ground next to Ilsi's feet. The warmth of Wren's body vanished, as he took a few steps away from her. She heard the sliding door open and close again. After the door was closed, the voices around her rose to a whisper. Ilsi knew it would be a long night. She sunk her hand into a small pocket in her tattered pants, and pulled out a worn piece of cloth. She unfolded it to reveal an ancient-looking brass key. It had completely lost its shine, but it still did the job.

Ilsi picked up the lantern, and began walking about, crouching down to unlock the shackles of her fellow cellmates. They began to sigh and moan. They breathed out words of relief. Whispers flooded the area as others passed on what was going on. Ilsi felt satisfied, when she had helped unlock all of the chains on their hands and feet. She made sure to tell them what she was doing and that they shouldn't be afraid. Many of them thanked her in languages she didn't understand. She wondered where they were from and how long they were here.

She felt like she was at least releasing herself from the guilt thrust on her. Soon, these women could return to their homes, and possibly make Reubens look like a major fool. This plan, whether it worked or not, was well worth the gratitude shining in each of their faces.

Ilsi suddenly felt a hand clasp her forearm. The light of the lamp revealed a young girl's face. It was Mouse. She was part of the plan, too. She and the others sat together, trying to put on brave faces. Mouse seemed more frightened then when they first met.

"He will come back, won't he?" her voice cracked in question. Ilsi blinked and nodded. Once Ilsi felt confident that everyone knew the basics of the plan and what she expected of them, she found a spot to sit. She held her knees to her chest and tried to sleep sitting up against the women—a common sleeping position choice in the cramped space—and Mouse put the light out.

⊸∘⊶

The sound of the secret sliding door woke Ilsi up from her half-sleep. She flinched, as the women around her roused from their sleep. She and the others felt tense. *Who's there?* She saw a small flickering light. As suddenly as it shone, a hand covered the small flame, and then the hand pulled back to reveal the light. She sighed. It was Wren's signal. As the light came closer, she arose to meet it. Without prior thought, she flung her arms around his neck in joy and relief. She had hardly slept and had no way of tracking time. She had almost thought he forgot about her or was deterred from following through.

"Everything's ready, Cat," he whispered in her ear.

She nodded and sighed. She turned to the other prisoners; all were awake now. They now knew the plan. In the darkness, the second phase of the plan began, as dark black pieces of armor were dispersed to all of the prisoners. It seemed to take an eternity, but Ilsi was forlorn when Wren had to leave. He would be in trouble if he was missing from his duties. Ilsi's heart sank when the small light finally disappeared.

Ilsi awoke the next morning. She felt uneasy. She could hear the men above deck, shouting and stomping about. They were near land; a whistle was signaling to the men on deck and those on shore it seemed. Ilsi felt herself being carried along with the tide until she could somehow feel that the ship had finally stopped. From inside her soul, an uncontrollable urge— an unbridled emotion—began to surge throughout her body. Her body gave off so much heat, combined with the heat and anticipation from the others and her armor; it was like humidity after a hot summer rain.

Suddenly she heard what she was waiting for. She didn't see him, but she could imagine a Yildirim at the top of the main stairs, standing erect as he shouted,

"All soldiers on deck, pronto!"

With great haste, a prisoner opened the secret door and it released beams of light. Some women around Ilsi held up their hands and gave muffled groans. Ilsi stared into the light unmoving. It was beautiful sunshine. The women assembled themselves together, and filed out of the room. They went through the small hallway and through the final secret door. Other soldiers, obviously the real ones, filed out and intermingled with the crowd of prisoners, but they didn't seem to notice. Ilsi wasn't in front like she wanted to be. In the middle of it all, she was nowhere to be seen. As according to plan.

CHAPTER 52

Reubens sat in his cabin. His face was stone cold, and didn't show an inkling of emotion. His was wearing his fancy uniform. He wore a starched black long-sleeved shirt and pants, with a small captain's cap on his head. Over his clothes and boots, he wore a long black leather coat with a belt securing the coat close to his waist. He just had a knife and a whip at his hip. A large, deadly bolt stretched across his shirt.

The Yildirim general sat with strange instruments of measurement scattered across his desk. A large map was stretched out over his workspace. He worked with impatience during the early morning. He jabbed his map with his index finger over the map, directly on top of the coast of northern Yling. He bit his lip with agitation. He thought to himself when suddenly, one of his officers approached.

"General!" the man said, accompanied by salute.

"Go on, man," Reubens barked back.

"We are ready to dock at your word," the man said. Reubens rose from his seat, and he left his cabin without acknowledging the officer. The sea's soft breeze brushed his cheek, but he paid no heed. The timid soldier followed after him. He could see the horridly busy docks ahead of him. He sighed with annoyance.

"We're going to need some soldiers," he muttered. He turned to the officer, "Summon the soldiers and have them ready on deck, now." The edgy officer nodded and quickly saluted. He quickly went down the stairs and below deck. The *Rolling Thunder* pulled closer and closer to shore. There were already men with the Yildirim symbol across their uniforms waiting for them. The men on deck quickly reacted to Reubens's orders, and a long plank was prepared to allow passage off the ship. Reubens suddenly turned.

The sound of thudding feet reverberated around the ship. Organized marching force of Yildirims emerged from below deck. Each had stern expression as they marched mechanically off the ship, with Reubens at the lead.

Six months at sea, he thought to himself. *Let's see what's become of them.*

———◦◦◦———

Ilsi tried to hide the smirk on her face. The workers on deck had a mixture of disappointment and worry on their faces. They all stood, clad in their Yildirim uniforms, even though she met them as humble seamen. She caught sight of Wren among the crowd. He looked especially worried. She knew that she would never see him again and her future's outcome was up in the air. They exchanged nods, and Ilsi walked on. She began sweating with anticipation and sighed heavily.

In a few steps, she would be the old Ilsi. Suddenly, her whole body ached to confirm her suspicions. She was officially off the ship and she stepped on land. She almost faltered and collapsed, but she kept her composure. She realized it was the feeling of having her powers and abilities back. She noticed the soldiers around her experiencing a similar rush.

Her blood surged with new excitement. She recognized the docks well enough—Yling! She was a less than a week's journey away from home! It felt good to know she was so close to freedom. She stared ahead, and she saw Reubens, staring back. She was tempted to smile, but she knew it would spoil everything. He stared at her, and moved his gaze elsewhere. Even *he* did nothing to stop her. She smiled to herself. *Perfect.*

Ilsi proudly went forward, certain that her escape was secure. She didn't even know where the original soldiers lay and where the false ones were. She hoped they would be brave enough to save themselves once they were far enough away.

She looked down at her own image. Despite her bad opinion about the uniform, she was glad that she, the prisoner, was clad in one herself. Once Reubens sent them into the city to do his bidding, and once they reached to their respective posts, the women knew to simply . . . disappear.

The army marched in time through the markets in silence. Other civilian sailors and traders kept their distance and made sure to do their business without a fuss.

It seemed so perfect. So many major roads spiraled out of Yling that all of them led safely to the prisoners' homes as far as Ilsi knew. She could find Sebrah again, and hopefully restock before her new quest. She needed to find Reshma and get back her rings. She smiled to herself in triumph. Things were starting to finally turn out. She could escape with the clear conscience that not a single prisoner suffered any longer aboard the *Rolling Thunder* in her name. In fact, things looked better than she ever planned. Once Reubens was deep enough into the city, there was no one left to stop Wren and the others from disappearing as well.

Suddenly, Ilsi stopped in her tracks. A huge lightning bolt struck a nearby building with a mighty rumble. The building shook mightily. People around her fled in terror. Lightning was striking buildings like rain.

Everyone ran, including the soldiers. More cracks of thunder, again and again and again. Their systematic, rhythmic march suddenly unraveled and they ran in chaos.

Ilsi prayed that her fellow prisoners fled with their new chance; she never got hers. Ilsi was struck. She stood immobilized and she dared not to look behind her. She lost control of her nerves and began to twitch and convulse on the ground like a fish out of water.

"Thought you could outrun your destiny?" a familiar voice called. Ilsi's shoulders would have slumped if she had the control to do so. It was Reubens. He was behind her, and she could imagine his triumphant yet smug grin.

"Did you *seriously* think I was that stupid? No one except me sees you for what you really are. I could care less what you planned on doing by helping the other prisoners, but your future is entwined with mine," Reubens said wickedly. *Blast!* Ilsi wanted to say, *How did he know? HOW DID HE KNOW?* She began to panic, praying that the others were fleeing in safety.

"That's not the way to propose to a girl," called a familiar voice. The tingling sensation left Ilsi and she could lie still on the ground. She smiled as she turned to lay on her back. Sebrah.

Sebrah stood with her proud shoulders back. Her attire was like a swirl of red crimson. Her clothes weren't ragged, torn or frayed like the ones she wore on their first meeting. They were fine and magnificent. Her long, dark blonde hair was tugged and twisted into one long braid that looked like a lethal whip. She had a long, loosely fitted shirt tucked into a pair of brown pants. A large crimson jacket hung from her shoulders. The tail of the jacket swayed about her thighs. She was still decorated with daggers of all shapes; that never changed. With the rough year that had come and gone, she looked older. She looked like she was exiting her twenties and entering her thirties. She was still strong.

"Why don't we leave the lass out of this? You're mine, Reubens," Sebrah said, her determination dripping from each word.

"I thought that was you, Sebrah. I see you're flaunting the treasures the government is giving you," Reubens followed tartly.

"All in a day's work," she returned with venom. "Shall we continue bickering with words, or have you forgotten how to fight with your fists?"

Ilsi tried to shake her shoulders back and forth or even wiggle her toes, but the only thing she could do was breathe in her current stasis. Reubens stepped in front of her with his back turned towards her. Instead of freeing Ilsi like she wanted, he reached with his right hand for his long whip and with his left for his curved dagger.

It was decorated with the haunting symbol of the bolt at the hilt, and it looked like an expensive gift given to him for his status. Sebrah merely chuckled to herself. She crossed her hands in front of her and each hand gripped a sword of fine steel. There was a long screech as she unsheathed the two weapons.

"Are you sure you remember, or must I remind you?" she said, with a cocky smile.

"I don't need schooling from a civilian," Reubens countered. He lunged at her, but she blocked his attack by shoving her two blades at him in the shape of an X. She merely laughed at him. They lunged at each other again in their attempt to beat the other to the ground.

These two must have some kind of history, Ilsi thought. *Reubens must have a bad habit of fighting women.* She was slowly regaining feeling in her hands and it felt good. It had been a while since she even hummed a tune, but it came back like learning to walk. She warmed up her throat and pointed her fingers weakly at Reuben's feet. Long shards of glassy ice shot up from the ground and Rubens performed fancy footwork to avoid getting skewered. He turned around and held out his whip threateningly.

"Stay down!" he shouted. He flashed his whip in her direction, but someone blocked her way. Bear stood in the way as the whip curled around his muscular forearm. Reubens actually had to look up at him. He looked equally confused and horrified.

"Only cowards attack a woman on the ground," Bear grumbled. Ilsi felt hands grip her arms and someone lifted her to her feet. Wren and Fox were quickly at her side. Bear had no weapons, but took a few steps towards Reubens. He held his fists up and clenched them. Reubens still held his dagger and took a brave lunge towards Bear. In return, the sailor gripped Reubens by the wrists to prevent his blade from going anywhere near him.

"Can you stand on your own?" Wren murmured quietly to Ilsi. "Bear will hold him off as much as he can."

"I was shocked," Ilsi said. "It made it nearly impossible to move." Her legs bent awkwardly with her knees facing towards each other. She could only feel her ankles and feet at the moment.

"Help me carry her to safety," Wren said to Fox and he nodded grimly. They draped Ilsi's arms around their shoulders and lifted her up by her thighs. She gripped with her fingers as much as she could as they walked her away as quickly as possible.

"He's not lookin' so good," Fox said, turning to look over his shoulder. "Some of the troops are coming in as backup. It's just Bear and that crazy braid lady there to fight the soldiers.

"They've called for reinforcements," Wren grunted under Ilsi's weight. They were taking her into town and over the cobblestone streets.

"Put me down between one of the buildings or something," Ilsi said. "I'll crawl for help while you get Sebrah and Bear out of there."

"Bear knows what he's doing," Fox said. "He knows to duck out when there's too many of them. I see him heading south. Hopefully into the forest. The hell if they ever find him in there."

"Where are you taking me?" Ilsi asked her head lolling and leaning against Wren's.

"Stay with us," he warned. "We're meeting up with other dissenters. We'll get you out of the city in no time. Promise."

CHAPTER 53

Try as she might, Ilsi couldn't move her arms. Her blurry vision came into focus. She found that she was face down, lying on the ground. Her arms quaked, as she used them to rise to her feet. She bent over to brush the dirt from her clothes, to realize that she was still dressed as a fake Yildirim.

She felt a sudden swaying motion. She suddenly leaned too far to the direction of the sway, and collided into a wall. She rubbed her shoulders at the pain and moaned to herself. When her vision came back to her, she became surprised and afraid. She was in a cell. The walls felt moist to the touch. The bars that served as the door to her cell looked grimy and ill kept. Despite that, she gripped the bars tightly, and shook them mightily as if her own strength would cause the whole prison to collapse. The swaying motion moved her to the left, and she shakily stumbled in the same direction. She felt tears sting her eyes. She was not only in a prison, but she knew that it was aboard the *Rolling Thunder*.

Blast, she thought, *what happened?* One moment she was on Wren's back on her way to freedom and then the next moment, she's back aboard the ship. She sighed. *At least the other prisoners escaped safely. I'd rather face Althod myself than let another girl suffer in my place.* As if on cue, she heard a quiet stirring sound. Ilsi suddenly jumped at the slightest sound. A weak and feeble voice made itself audible.

"Cat?" it called out. It was the voice of a girl. She saw a small figure trying to stand. The girl was small, but the cell's lack of height even made her bend at the neck to get a good look at Ilsi. Across a small hallway, two cells over, was the figure of Goose. She gave a feeble smile. She had a Yildirim uniform on as well, and her face was dark from soot and dirt.

"Cat? I knew it was you," she whispered, her voice cracking a bit.

"Yeah," Ilsi said, her voice hoarse, too. "Why are you here? Where are we even?" Goose made a sad smile.

"The night before our escape, I awoke, and found that Doe was creeping out of our room. I didn't think it was fair that she got some fresh air, so I went after her. I was spying on her, so I made sure that she didn't see me. She went up a secret stairway, close to where the other prisoners were kept, and she went through a trap door. I stayed just under the door to hear what was going on, because I heard strange voices," Goose explained in a whisper.

"What I heard made me surprised. Doe was talking to another *man.* She told him your entire plan of escape. I was absolutely shocked. I fled down the stairs and back to our room before Doe found out. I thought that when I met you in the women's cell to get the fake uniform that I would be safe. Somehow, Doe somehow found out that I had overheard their conversation, and they made special effort to make sure I didn't escape before I could tell you . . . about how she lied to us and betrayed us."

"*What?*" Ilsi said in disbelief, "We could've all been *free*, all of us! Why did she snitch on us? Why would she *do* such a thing?" She rattled the bars again in anger. No wonder Reubens knew. She knew it was too good to be true that he would allow her to roam above deck unlike the other girls. He was watching the whole time, both above and below deck. He set up spies to find out her plans. She thought it would work, and now her careful planning laid there on the cold ground in shreds.

She sunk to the ground. She tried to remember all that she said around Doe that she could've told Reubens. She felt like kicking herself. She realized that she gave away Wren as her ally helping with the plans. She put him in danger. Now he was certain to pay for her foolish tongue. The whole point was to get revenge on Reubens and it looked like he was smarter than she thought. Now, she got one of her friends, perhaps her other Yildirim friends, all in trouble.

"Ilsi," Goose said in her whisper, trying to get her attention again, "What's wrong?"

"My other friends that helped us escape will now be punished for this."

"You did your best. It's not your fault that Doe decided to betray us. That is out of your hands. Besides, would you like to know who helped Doe betray me?"

"Who?" Ilsi asked, wondering how worse things could become.

"Your friends were captured when we all escaped. Thanks to that man, Ape."

Ilsi's jaw dropped. Another traitor. He was there the whole time, listening to their conversations. He was supposed to help the other men to stir up some kind of diversion in case something went wrong aboard ship. She didn't talk to him much or know much about him, but she trusted him. She was still thinking of dark thoughts, when she heard Goose sink back to the floor of her cell. Ilsi suddenly felt exhausted, too. She looked back at her dimly lit cell, wondering how she could comfortably sleep.

While she was thinking, she heard a new stir. It was much closer to her cell. It was the cell directly in front of her. Through the bars, she saw a dark figure bringing itself to its knees. It was a man. He rubbed his eyes, and brushed his thick black hair away from his eyes. He looked directly into Ilsi's eyes. Ilsi's eyes widened. His did as well.

"It's really you," he said, his voice croaked.

The man came closer to the bars. With one hand he gripped a bar tightly, the other he used to reach out to her and she did the same. They were able touch hands. *It was Tyk.* Ilsi was suddenly filled with an indescribable happiness. She was so happy to see him alive.

"Have you been on this ship the whole time?" he asked quietly, giving her hand a tight squeeze.

"I don't know," Ilsi said, puzzled, "I was on the *Rolling Thunder* for half a year. I think. Is that where we are now?"

"No," Tyk said. "I've been on that ship a time or two. This is different."

"How can you tell? How did you even get here?" Ilsi asked, her stomach clenching.

Tyk let go of Ilsi's hand, and used it to grip the bar by his face. He sat there, thinking. He bit his lip, as if in deep thought. His thick eyebrows furrowed. He looked frustrated.

"They kept me in here during my Animan phase. It was embarrassing to say the least."

"Tyk, were you on the *Rolling Thunder* with me?" Ilsi asked quietly.

"No. I was fine until I heard about what happened to you. I ducked in and out of the ranks to hear any news. It was easier than I thought. I just came in uniform to one of the little camps and no one said anything about it," Tyk said, "I didn't want to go back, but I couldn't find you anywhere, so I knew that you would run into them sooner or later. You caused quite the ruckus. I made sure I was there to help when the ship docked in Yling. But, Reubens must've saw it coming."

"He sees a lot of things coming," Ilsi replied bitterly. "I bet Reubens indirectly made it easy for you to come back to lure you here in his elaborate trap."

"It sounds like you're blaming yourself for something I chose to do on my own."

For a while, the two said nothing. Ilsi could only hear the boat creak as it swayed from side to side.

"I hear you're famous around here," he said with a smile.

"You think?" Ilsi said, dryly, "I'm the only girl, Tyk. I thought there were women in the ranks, so I don't know why it's such a surprise."

"No, I mean a lot of the men talk fondly of you," Tyk said, grinning furtively, "and practically all of the prisoners escaped. Did you do that?"

"Tyk—"

"I bet that made Reubens turn a shade of green," Tyk tried to smile.

"Don't you see? He let that happen," Ilsi said, gripping the bars and shaking her head. "I thought I was doing something for good, but he didn't care what happened to the prisoners. He just cared about my failure. I know of at least one person who didn't make it off besides me, so what if there's more?"

"Ilsi," Tyk said, "wasn't it worth the risk?"

"Yeah . . . I suppose," she answered defensively. She didn't feel like arguing, but she still felt guilty about Goose. Not to mention angry with Doe and Ape.

"Were you okay on the ship?" Tyk said, "No one pushed you around, did they?"

"Well, Reubens didn't exactly make it fine dining and feather-fluffed pillows, but I'm fine," Ilsi said, with a small smile, "I—it was actually . . . enjoyable."

"Enjoyable? Yildirims?" Tyk asked sarcastically, nodding at her fake uniform, "You're not planning on joining are you?"

"I already have, and I've already left," Ilsi muttered. "Another one of Reubens' doings. But it was nice living without magic for a while. The soldiers couldn't hurt me and Reubens couldn't really prove anything, so it had its advantages. It was like a time of freedom."

"You got off once, you'll do it again," Tyk said.

"It'll work with extra help," she said, very quietly, "Where's my Yildirim allies when I need them?"

"You've got me for now," Tyk said. He softly kissed his own fingertips and held out his hand towards Ilsi. Her fingers grazed his before she brought his fingers to her own lips. "Is that enough?"

"Plenty."

CHAPTER 54

Mama, I wish I could say that running into Tyk is a relief. However, I'm having that sinking feeling. Like something is about to go terribly wrong. I've escaped enough sticky situations to know when I'm about to walk into another one. Except this feels much, much worse. If you don't see any more entries here, you'll know why.

———⟡———

While Ilsi was dreaming she heard talking. At first the voices were quiet and incoherent. They were like flies buzzing in her ear, so she swatted them away. However, someone clutched her wrists and held them firmly to the ground. She suddenly woke up. Someone was trying to pin her to the ground with their hands.

"Hey!" she exclaimed, struggling. She saw two darkened faces close to hers. Their faces were hidden in cloak hoods.

"Stop! Let me go!" Ilsi cried. She leaned back and kicked as hard as she could with her legs. She knocked one back and surprised the other. She tried swinging her body to smash the other against the wall. It worked momentarily.

"Hurry!" one of them cried. They struck her between the

shoulder blades and tied Ilsi's hands behind her back while she was in shock from the blow. Ilsi began screaming for help. Tyk bolted up from his sleep. His eyes went wide and he began banging on the bars.

"Let her go!" he exclaimed, "Stop it! Stop it now!" One of them struck him violently, and he fell back in his cell. Ilsi was still squirming and struggling to get free.

"Tyk!" she cried, concerned for her own safety and for Tyk. One of them yanked her by the hair and she screamed. They dragged her out of the cell and up the steps to the prison's exit. Goose screamed after her.

"Get your hands off of me!" Ilsi said, viciously biting one of their hands. He yelped and struck her across her face. She reeled in shock. She felt another blow on the back of her head and she sank into black darkness.

—⊷∘⊶—

Ilsi lifted her face from the floor and tasted blood on her lip. She noticed she was lying on silken carpet. Her eyes widened and she tried to pull herself off the ground. The lights around her were hazy, so she blinked a few times to try and clear her vision. She sat on the floor and realized she was still in uniform. She flung the cape and armor away with anger and disgust. She was clad in a long-sleeved shirt, black trousers and black boots. She pulled herself into a criss-cross sitting position and she clutched her head and moaned. Her back and head were throbbing in pain.

She stared at the carpet again and it came into focus. It was lavishly patterned and it looked very expensive. She was sitting in the middle of a very ornate room. A large chandelier hung from the ceiling and it was lit with hundreds of candles. The tiny flames flickered a bit, casting shivering shadows on the walls. Large printed violet tapestries hung on the walls, nearly covering them up completely. There were low, long couches backed against a large window. The curtains were closed, but she could see barely any sunshine, so it had to be late in the evening.

Suddenly, someone opened a door behind Ilsi. She flinched and scrambled to her feet. It hurt to fully stand. After long days of sitting and standing with a bent back, it proved painful for her to stand straight. She heard a low chuckle. A woman entered the room. She wore a long, flowing violet dress that matched the drapes all too well. Her sleeves were cut down the middle, revealing pale flesh. The ends gathered at her wrists. Her head was covered in a veil that wrapped around her neck, but Ilsi could see dark black hair poking through. She was very pale; her milky white hands were clasped in front of her dress and she wore a wry grin. She wasn't very attractive despite her ornate dress.

"I see you're finally on your feet," she said, her voice low. Ilsi guessed the woman had to be twenty years older than her.

"What do you want?" Ilsi asked, clenching her fists. The woman merely grinned with an arched eyebrow.

She motioned to one of her couches and asked, "Care to sit down?"

"I'd rather stand," Ilsi returned, icily, "I haven't been able to stand for days. That's what happens when you're jailed for no good reason. I assume it was your doing?"

"Yes and no," the woman said, thoughtfully pacing the

room, "I understand it was hard to . . . *retrieve* you in the first place. Reubens wasn't the least bit pleased to see you gone."

Ilsi was genuinely concerned. "Where am I then?"

"You're in my private apartments. Reubens was on his way to deliver you to the chief Yildirim himself. I made sure that didn't happen," the woman said, staring into Ilsi's eyes, "That sounds a bit like a favor, doesn't it?"

"Perhaps," Ilsi said coldly, "but I'm sure you didn't do it to help me. So no, that's not a true *favor.*"

"Aha," the woman purred, "I see you're not it the mood for dawdling."

"What do you want from me?" Ilsi asked again, clenching her jaw, slowly losing patience.

"I want information," the woman said, "a secret." She stared at Ilsi, holding her arm out in front of her, pointing at her throat. Ilsi suddenly grimaced, and her eyes bugged out. Her throat was constrained and she could hardly breathe. The woman didn't flinch.

"What is your most unique ability?" the woman intoned, her eyes glazed white. Ilsi tried to scream, yell, or use another spell to counter her, but no words came, except, "I can conjure *Swift!*"

The pain suddenly left her, and she held her throat in terror. Her strangled words echoed wickedly within the room. The woman used some sort of spell that forced people to tell the truth. The woman put her arm down and smiled. Ilsi put her hands to her throat as she breathed heavily.

"Music to my ears," the woman said.

"You're a . . . horrible person," Ilsi said, her voice grated. "Why would you do that?"

"Dear girl, I wanted to make sure I found the right person," she said without emotion. "Now that I know who you are, I can introduce myself. My name is Emiliya, otherwise known as Althod's daughter."

———⊙∘⊙———

"You're his *daughter*?" Ilsi exclaimed.

"Yes," the woman said indifferently, "It's quite lovely, isn't it? Bet you didn't think a monster could be a father."

Ilsi suddenly felt fuzzy and sick.

"What else do you have in mind for me, Emiliya?" Ilsi murmured, "I told you what you wanted to steal."

Emiliya just grinned as she quickly raised her hand to cast another spell, but Ilsi quickly countered it with a deflecting spell. She created a shield of ice and the spell somehow whizzed back towards Emiliya. The pale woman started holding her neck, her mouth wide in agony. Her eyes went cross and they bugged out. She tried to wheeze or stop the spell, but the spell immediately worked its charm.

"I never wanted to be close to him because of his rotten plans. I hate him! He's such a fool! He doesn't even know that I have *Swift*!" she cried out, then began choking. She collapsed on the floor, free of the spell. Her veil came loose and fell to the floor. Ilsi's eyes widened in fright. The woman silently sobbed on her carpet. Her short and untidy hair looked as if cut by a jagged, dull sword. Her hair covered her eyes as if ashamed.

"You're father doesn't know?" Ilsi asked quietly. "Isn't our powers passed down by blood?" Ilsi had always secretly hoped to find someone else of her clan, but wished it didn't happen like this.

438

"Of course he doesn't know," Emiliya retorted, refusing to rise, "If I revealed it to him, he wouldn't care if it was me; he would sacrifice me willfully to follow through with his plans."

"What does he plan to do with our powers?" Ilsi quickly asked.

"I don't know," Emiliya replied quietly. "I overheard only a little bit, but enough. He never talks to me, he doesn't even let me see him. Ironic that it's probably the reason I'm still alive." Ilsi shivered; Althod wasn't just about collecting people for their abilities; it seemed like he was only interested in the abilities.

"Althod . . . he couldn't be so cruel to sacrifice his own *daughter*," Ilsi said as Emiliya turned to face her.

"I wouldn't be so sure of that. You don't know my father."

"So why did you bring me here? Why did you stop Reubens from taking me to Althod?" Ilsi said, adding coldly, "I would've taken your place and save your skin if what you're telling me is true."

"Do you *actually* think that I plan to let my father succeed?" Emiliya said bitterly, "I plan to be the reason why he *fails*. I want to take away his future like he took mine."

"Why does that still not sound like you will let me go?" Ilsi dared to ask. Emiliya rose to her feet, wiping her face with her sleeve. She stared grimly at Ilsi. "Think about it. It would only frustrate him even more if I were to escape and rally more allies to take care of him. Not to mention, I have a bit of a score to settle with Reubens myself. What if I helped you disassemble his whole army?"

"No. I'm afraid I can't let you go," Emiliya said, hollowly. "I plan to purge everyone who ever possessed *Swift*." Ilsi gulped, her mouth went dry.

"Yes, my dear," Emiliya said, with a maniacal look in her eye, "I plan on ending you like I have with so many of our brother and sisters. Once there are no more of them out there, my precious father will have no one to sacrifice and it will leave him ruined. Then, as soon as I see him sick with anger and rage, I'll finish the work by killing the last person with *Swift*, me."

"You can't do that," Ilsi said, quickly, "I didn't come this far to get killed by *you*!"

"Don't be fooled, dear," Emiliya smiled wickedly again, talking in a high, whiny voice, "I've done it loads of time, I promise to make it quick. I must admit, if you didn't have *Swift*, I would fancy you to be an excellent friend."

There was a sudden change to her appearance. Ilsi definitely could tell she was insane and poised to kill. She had no idea what kind of power Emiliya could possibly know; the woman didn't draw a weapon. Emiliya suddenly sent her hands flying, calling upon another spell. Ilsi fell to the floor, as the spell flew past her. It accidentally zapped a nearby lamp and it exploded against the wall. Ilsi rolled to the side, avoiding another spell.

"Come now, dearie," Emiliya said, "You're only delaying the inevitable."

One thing Ilsi knew was that Emiliya wasn't an Ice Chanter, and that made Ilsi grin. She scrambled to her feet, and deflected another on coming spark. Something behind her shattered. She sang a difficult spell and directed it at Emiliya's body, just as she was about to cast some other spell. Emiliya was suddenly frozen in her place. Her face was wrought with anger, twisted in rage as all her fingers were fanned out. Emiliya was covered in ice and powdery snow like a scary ice sculpture.

Ilsi stared at her odd creation, then at her hands. Ilsi suddenly took her golden opportunity and pushed the sculpture over with all her strength. It fell mightily as shards of ice spewed everywhere. She waited to for the satisfaction of watching the pieces fly before she fled. She didn't know where she would go, but she knew that she was escaping and she was still alive.

CHAPTER 55

The hallways were lit by large sconces. It was a bit hard to see in front of her, so she took a sconce off the wall and held it close as she navigated. *Am I in a castle?* she wondered. If this was Emiliya's personal apartments or chambers, she wanted out. Who knew who else she spent her time with.

It was bad enough that Althod wanted magic from other people, but Ilsi thought it was sick that he thought more of his power and glory more than his own daughter. She suddenly felt a sudden pang of emotion. She felt guilty for turning the woman into ice, but it seems like Ilsi had wandered into a world of kill or be killed.

Her thoughts were interrupted by the sound of shuffling of feet. So far she hadn't encountered any guards, and she was worried that they were crawling all over the place, waiting for her. She clenched her right hand; they would end up as ice sculptures if they tried to take her again. She ventured farther and came to a corner.

She was met with a large, bright light; a lantern. She held her hand out, but she felt someone hold her by the wrist. It was firm, but also reassuring. A dark face met hers, etched in shadows that flickered from the lantern's light.

"It's not a good idea to be here, lassie," a familiar, deep voice murmured. Ilsi smiled brightly. She slung one arm around Wren's neck and gave it a grateful squeeze.

"What are you doing here, Wren?" Ilsi whispered excitedly. She could hardly contain her excitement and relief. "I thought you were kidnapped because of me! How did you escape?"

"It doesn't matter now," Wren whispered back, "but I'm here to get you out of here." Ilsi could see Wren's face better with the lantern's help. His face looked tired, his eyes glazed a bit. Ilsi could only assume she looked the same. It felt like a long time since she ate a decent meal and had a good night's rest.

"Let's get out of here and help the others," Ilsi replied. "Some of our friends didn't make the escape and Emiliya the devil woman might have them somewhere. I don't really know. Do you know where we are? Is there a dock close by?"

At first Wren didn't respond. Then, he said, "Let's hurry, before the guards come."

Ilsi nodded vigorously in reply. She followed Wren as he ran the way he came. Dozens of thoughts whirled through her mind. She had so many questions to ask Wren. She wondered how he was captured, where he was, or how he escaped. She realized it was dangerous to stand around and chat when they needed to get themselves to safety first before they could help anyone else. She was just grateful that Wren somehow found her and knew the way out. It was good to see a friendly, familiar face.

Her brows suddenly furrowed. *Wait, how* did *he know I was here? How would he know these hallways?* As if Wren sensed this doubt, he took her hand gently and said, "C'mon, we're almost there."

Ilsi pulled away. His hand was really cold, almost freezing—even to Ilsi. He was right; there was a long, dark curtain in front of them. It was outlined and etched with bright light from the other side. Wren lifted the curtain and disappeared through. Ilsi had no idea where it led, but she went through without much hesitation.

She entered a large, brightly lit room. It was a huge ballroom, with a huge chandelier in the middle. She was standing on a raised level and a grand staircase was right in front of her. The floor was polished to the point that Ilsi could see her reflection. The large rectangular room had two double doors across the floor that mirrored the entrance where she stood.

Wren stood before her. His eyes were wide, cloudy and gray. He was wearing the same clothes he wore the day he met her, tattered, frayed and worn. He stood quietly in the middle, and Ilsi ran to catch up with him. He stood there, staring off into space without blinking.

"What's wrong?" Ilsi asked, waving a hand within his trail of vision. It was as if he went stiff like a statue.

She heard a muffled shout from outside. The yelling announced a squad of Yildirims. They created a blockade by circling around Ilsi and Wren and holding up large black shields. Their insignia crackled over the crest. It was like being in the middle of a huge thunderstorm.

"Wren," Ilsi cried, "help me fight them!"

"I'm sorry, Ilsi," Wren said, hollowly, "I can't."

"What?" Ilsi exclaimed, confused. For a second, she wondered if he was back to wearing an amulet, but he had nothing around his neck. Wren suddenly began to shake violently. His hollow eyes rolled back and his head snapped back. He collapsed like a fallen puppet; he fell violently and didn't stir.

"Wren!" Ilsi screamed. She bent down to help him. He felt corpse-cold. Ilsi rolled him onto his back and saw the truth. He was dead. She used her strength to roll him over, but she found no wounds, scars, dried blood, anything. Ilsi stood up slowly, and backed away from him in horror. Wren acted like the brother she never had, and to see him dead with glazed eyes gnawed at her heart.

"Not you, too," Ilsi said, her throat tight and sore. She was confused, but still aware of all the eyes on her, so she swallowed her grief and stood over Wren's body, prepared to fight the soldiers away. If things couldn't be worse, someone entered the circle, by pushing the Yildirims aside. It was Reubens himself.

"I knew there was something about you two," he said, curling his lips into a smile. Ilsi stood, defending Wren's body, facing Reubens.

"What did you do to him?" Ilsi uttered through gritted teeth. "You murderous bastard." Reubens merely clucked his tongue.

"You trusted him so *easily*," he murmured, looking at Wren, "You were just so *eager* to tell him everything about you. It was almost too easy to keep secrets from you, *lassie*."

"What do *you* know about him that I don't?" Ilsi said tersely.

"The only thing *worth* knowing—he is one of the few who possess *Fortune*," Reubens said, with a hint of gloating in his eyes. "Althod handled him quite well."

"Then," Ilsi whispered, looking again into Wren's empty eyes, "who was I talking to? No magic can bring back the dead." Althod seemed bent on reaping people for their abilities. What use did he have for the husks? She felt ready to vomit.

"You are under arrest," Reubens said. "You can think about how you'll ask Althod himself so you'll know what is coming for you."

With this reply, Ilsi lunged furiously at Reubens. She suddenly jumped on him and pushed him to the floor and began punching his face. He barely defended himself.

"How *dare* you!" Ilsi screamed loudly, continuing to punch him, "What more could you possibly want from me?" She enunciated each word with blows to his face. Ilsi was about to send another flying fist, but Reubens readily grabbed her by the wrist. She tried to pull back, but Reubens twisted her wrist. His lips curled into a wicked smile when he saw Ilsi's scar and made an audible laugh. Ilsi freed herself, but Reubens didn't care. Blood came from his nose and his face was blotchy with blue and purples hues, but he still grinned wolfishly. Ilsi backed away, holding her wrist protectively.

"I saw you that day we captured your friend in Dove. Don't make the mistake of thinking I can forget a face. Your presence here is proof enough that you have Elite powers to escape your squatty island."

Ilsi clenched her fists angrily.

"You probably thought that I had no clue—that I was stupid, huh?" he asked, not waiting for a response. "Of course, I followed you to get proof."

"Althod didn't believe *you*?" Ilsi asked, sarcastically. "Althod must have no faith in his generals."

"Shut up," he retorted, then slapped her across the face with sparks dancing between his fingers. "Our Lord Althod doesn't act on assumptions. Besides, I know enough about you that would make it easy to suspect you." Ilsi raised an eyebrow. *This guy makes Althod look normal.*

"You must be proud. Rise to the ranks to general and your claim to fame is being a stalker. Should I clap for you?" Ilsi asked bitterly. If she were to die, might as well get in the last word.

"Don't waste your breath," Reubens snapped, unsheathing his dagger, "You forget your place."

"For heaven's sake, Reubens," Ilsi murmured, "I don't flinch at little shiny pieces of metal anymore."

Reubens lunged at her, twirling the dagger in his grip so he could stab downward. Ilsi lunged, too. She grabbed his wrist and held firmly.

"What do you think you're doing?" Reubens said, pointing his dagger at her forearm flesh. "I can command all these soldiers to subdue you with the slightest signal. You've lost the battle and we've barely begun."

Ilsi looked into his eyes and began singing softly. It was slow, mournful, and reached to a few low notes. Where she gripped his hand, his flesh turned sickly white and spread to his fingers, turning the tips purple and they stuck to his dagger. He cried out in surprise and pain; his hand was completely frostbitten.

He pulled his arm back, but his hand became heavy enough to crack and fall off his wrist. His eyes gaped in horror at his fallen hand and dagger and then stared in alarm at his stump of a wrist. His old hand shattered into pieces like an expensive vase.

"My . . . my," he murmured, "That was my spell hand."

Ilsi stared at her callused and dirty hands. She locked eyes with Reubens. He was terrified.

"You are a monster," he whispered.

"Coming from you?" Ilsi said, "I'm an Ice Chanter." She suddenly lunged for him and shoved him to the side. She held up her hands and they glowed brightly. The Yildirim soldiers who had witnessed their brief scuffle drew back in fright and gave her space. She sprinted towards the only exit. She still held her hands out as a warning to anyone who tried to threaten her.

"You *fools!*" Reubens screamed, still cradling his handless arm. "I don't care if she uses her black magic on you, I command you to seize her!"

Ilsi shoved the doors open and found within her the spirit to run. The boots she wore as a part of her Yildirim costume proved advantageous. She looked to the ground and realized that she was running on snow. She looked up and gazed in surprise at the Pearl Mountains. Their tips were invisible, covered in fog and clouds.

"After her, faster!" she heard Reubens scream. She ignored the landscape for a moment and ran for her life. She ran through the streets, making random turns, dodging stray dogs and avoiding any Yildirim that might cross her path. She panted heavily, but she found strength to continue the escape. She didn't know which city she was in exactly, but she knew that she could orient herself once she found decent shelter. She would find Tyk and disappear in Beast Forest until further notice.

Her mind went ballistic and her stomach churned when she stopped abruptly at the end of an alley. If they were still on her tail, they would soon corner her. She quickly looked around for an escape route and saw a town inn sign swinging in the frozen winter air. There were soft lamps lit in and outside, so Ilsi pushed the door quietly and was embraced in warm air.

It was hazy and smoky when she stepped in, but she could hear low, drunken murmuring. She saw a private room off to the side and decided to step in. She sat alone at a wooden table. She couldn't keep still as she tried to wrack her brains for a way out of her mess. They would find her any minute, and it wouldn't be difficult to find a blonde girl running around town without wearing suitable and tasteful winter clothing. She massaged her forehead and sighed heavily. *I can't go about freezing off limbs or running away,* Ilsi thought to herself. *I can't hide anymore.*

CHAPTER 56

Ilsi flinched when someone whispered her name. She heard it again and this time whirled around to meet a pair of cloudy gray-blue eyes and silvery-blue curls. She reached out to hug Princess Karachi, and felt much better when her figure wasn't frozen cold like Wren's.

"Where have you been?" the young princess whispered nervously. "I heard from Ladala that you didn't make it safely back to her territory."

"I've been all over," Ilsi sighed deeply. "We were ambushed. She left, I was taken on a ship, escaped, got recaptured, then a freaky woman captured me to kill me, I escaped, got ambushed by Yildirims, escaped, and now I'm here," Ilsi said quickly. Karachis eyes widened.

"You've been gone for almost a year and yet here you are in my kingdom," Karachi said. "Things have gotten worse here. You really should leave as soon as possible. Go anywhere. Althod has taken permanent residence in our castle."

"What about you? Isn't this inn a strange place for a princess?"

"Not when I need to get out of the castle. Ever since you broke out of jail, I've been watched constantly. Someone must have suspected me or something. I blink and someone knows about it. Seth isn't himself anymore. He's sick all the time and he's bossing me around more than he used to," Karachi said motioning to her ornate rug on the wall, "I use this passage way to break free every once and a while. Or hope to hear what's actually going on outside."

Ilsi parted her lips to speak more, when she heard a table turned over, glass shattering, cursing. The princess chewed on her lip nervously, looking around her.

"His soldiers are looking for me. Go!" Ilsi said, motioning to the secret passageway. Karachi picked up her skirts while Ilsi held the rug back to open the secret stairway. Karachi soon disappeared and Ilsi was alone. A dozen Yildirims or so broke down the door to the room Ilsi was in and she flinched as wood chips flew everywhere. They formed a semi-circle around her, blocking the exit and drew their swords, their faces impassive. Reubens elbowed his way through, his handless arm bandaged up tightly.

"Consider your options, woman, because you have none," Reubens said, frowning. He motioned for her to leave the cramped room and out in the open. She held up her hands, but only to comply rather than threaten. Behind the rug, Ilsi heard a reverberating, shrilly scream. She moaned. She wasn't nearly surprised to find that Karachi was caught and a Yildirim pushed her back through to the tiny room to join Ilsi. She scowled.

"With one word," Reubens threatened, "You either come with us, or watch as the soldier spills her blood. Your choice, of course."

Ilsi stood motionless. "You wouldn't dare murder the king's sister."

Reubens blinked at this, but stood his ground. Ilsi looked at Karachi, who trembled bravely at her side. A soldier held an arm around her throat and pointed the tip of his sword at her throat.

"You will regret this act of treason," Karachi breathed. "My brother may be dull in the head but this is not your land to rule."

Before anyone could react, another batch of soldiers burst in.

"That woman is under arrest by order of our Lord Althod," the lead soldier shouted importantly. He approached with iron shackles and they clanked in his hands.

"State your rank, man," Reubens turned coldly. The soldier was ready to grab Ilsi and clap the shackles around her wrists, but Reubens stood in his way. "As your commanding general, I will not ask you again."

"I come at Althod's bidding, General Reubens," the soldier responded, unshaken. "She is to come with me to negotiate the exchange of her life to set her Ice Chanter friend free. If she comes quietly and obediently."

At that, Ilsi wanted to vomit.

"I'll go," she croaked, holding her arms up and close to each other. "But you must allow the princess to walk unaccompanied to her chambers. Unharmed."

"I knew that if the lad wouldn't work, your compassion and guilt for others would turn you in," Reubens muttered. He grabbed the shackles from the soldier and clapped them on Ilsi's wrists himself, stump and all. He motioned with his remaining hand towards her, and the twelve Yildirims surrounded Ilsi.

"Go where it's safe, princess," Ilsi said, gesturing to the tapestry with her head. Reubens shoved her by the shoulder towards the open door and she stumbled forward. She didn't dare turn around, but heard the rug swish back and forth and Karachi trip up the stairs in a frantic escape.

———◦◦◦———

Ilsi thought that she would cry, but there wasn't a tear left in her eyes; there was just sighs escaping her mouth into the freezing air. Since Ilsi was thought to be extremely dangerous, she wasn't touched or closely approached by any of the Yildirims. They feared her no matter what Reubens said. Twelve or so soldiers formed a circle around her and held up magic-reflective shields, all with their insignia in the middle. Ilsi looked towards the front where Reubens led his band of soldiers towards a large black castle. At his side was Wren, who appeared unshaken and unharmed. Ilsi's expression hardened. Walking or not, he was dead; and Ilsi felt totally ashamed that she believed it was the true Wren for a second.

She looked up towards the looming castle and blinked away the snow falling into her eyes. A cold, half frozen moat defended the castle. The frozen entrance cranked to the ground and the troop walked across the moat. Once they entered, she shook her shoulders to get rid of the snow on her clothes, and her guards flinched, holding their shields at the ready. Ilsi produced a sly grin and rolled her shoulders back and clenched her fists just to keep the soldiers in the circle even more nervous.

Thunder rolled in the skies, laughing at her from the gray heavens. Ilsi looked at her bound wrists in a bit of nervous energy. She gasped when Reubens threw open the large doors in front of them.

"My liege," Reubens called with a grin, "I have returned." His proud gait was apparent through his large stride; his boots clicked rhythmically across the stone floor creating the only sound. He produced a small, triumphant grin as he bowed deeply before his leader.

"Can't you see I'm having a conversation with an invited guest?" a raspy voice returned. A slightly built man was standing with his back towards Reubens and his band of soldiers. His hands were clasped behind his back. His hair was red and short, combed back. His attire was all black, a cape with a large lightning bolt displayed on its folds. He seemed unaware of the large gathering. His attention was drawn towards something far more interesting.

He was staring at the king's throne. He stood on a navy blue rug that ran up a few steps and under the king and queen's thrones. A girl was chained tightly to the queen's chair, her hair poorly trimmed.

"Reshma," Ilsi stammered under her breath, recognizing her instantly, "what have you done to her?"

She looked much different than the last time Ilsi saw her. She couldn't even remember how long ago that was. Her hair was knotted and wild; it was cut in jagged angles, as though she cut it with her dagger. She was darker; she had seen more sun. Her long sleeves were torn off and her attire was discolored, dirty. She was staring in mixed surprise and anger.

"My lord, this is urgent," Reubens began. "I have brought the girl as requested." The man turned and Ilsi stared into the face of the one who ruined her life. His right side of his face was ugly, red, blotchy. It looked burned and scarred. His right eye shone brighter than his left; a yellow, glass eye. The other half was slightly wrinkled. He looked at her and scowled at Reubens.

"You're just wasting my time yet again," he muttered darkly. "One of my other generals has already brought me the woman I require. You may stay to watch, but you waste my time doing so."

"My liege, I beg your pardon," Reubens countered, slightly nervous. "I've got her, the one you actually need. Sir, if you just examine my report, I have solid evidence—"

"Get out of my sight before I dismiss you," the man barked, then turned towards Reshma, "Pay no mind to this fool, my dear, you have to excuse his utter uselessness."

"Please! Just give me this last chance," Reubens cried, too desperate. Ilsi couldn't help but smirk.

"Fine then," Althod sighed, "Bring over your prisoner and we'll compare and contrast. If she isn't who you say she is, I will take more than just your position. Even though I see you're armed with just one hand."

"Y-yes, my lord," Reubens said, and impatiently motioned towards his men, and they pushed Ilsi towards the throne. Reshma looked darkly at Ilsi. Ilsi stared back, wondering how Reshma got there and how she could get them both out alive. Nothing seemed possible; guards and soldiers were everywhere. She grunted as she was shoved by a Yildirim shield to ascend the steps and stand by Reshma.

"Ah, there we are," Althod sighed, bored. He stared at the two, uncomfortable to be standing next to each other. Reshma scowled and frowned deeply and returned Althod's yellow-eyed stare.

"Reubens, bring me your evidence immediately," Althod called. Reubens quickly handed a large roll of parchment. The man clenched the parchment tightly as though he really wanted to crumple it up like garbage.

"She should have one of Ladala's rings on her person, sir," Reubens responded.

"You mean these?" Althod said, holding a tiny ring between his thumb and middle finger, "My prisoner has two." Ilsi's eyes widened. He held them without them burning him, just as if it were made of common metal.

"Yes, I know, sir," Reubens said, "But I have seen this girl use her powers with my own two eyes! I am an eye-*witness*, my liege!"

There was a pause in the dry air. Althod closed his eyes and his eyelids fluttered. He let out a long sigh, and Ilsi crinkled her nose a bit. She wondered if by gross irony she would be released. She erred on the side of caution. Althod raised an eyebrow and gestured to Reubens.

"During our raid in Dove, I saw her pass through the wall, my lord. You only gave us that ability with our Yildirim armor, but she did it all on her own," Reubens said, urgency lining his voice, "I have witnesses as well. That girl you're questioning is an impostor, sir. I've never been so sure about anything in my life, sir."

Althod looked darkly at Reshma. He stepped towards her and clenched her chin and cheeks in his hand.

"You told me you had a companion as you were escaping the island?" he asked, ripping his hand away from her face, leaving red imprints on her skin.

"Of course, I couldn't do it alone," Reshma mumbled, "But I've never seen this girl before. It disgusts me that this man has brought her here. We were to have a *private* conversation, if I remember correctly."

"Are you referring to our deal?"

"I promised to help you once you removed all your soldiers, Althod," Reshma answered, curtly.

"She addresses you by your *name*, sir?" Reubens practically squeaked.

"Yes, we were having a private chat long before you paraded in," Althod returned, "I know the perfect solution to our little mystery."

Althod merely flicked his pointer finger and everyone could hear the shuffling of feet and shouts and grunts from the corridor. Five Yildirims dragged in a very angry, shouting figure. Ilsi felt like her lungs squeeze in her chest. Her eyes opened wide and couldn't look away.

Tyk stood, breathing heavily, trying to yank himself free. His clothes hung loosely around his figure, and his hair was just as wild as Reshma's, only he sported dark scruff on his chin. He looked exhausted, drenched with sweat; criss-crossed red welts lined his shoulders and back. The men chained him to a far-off wall, with his hands being raised above his head, and his neck chained in place. He shook miserably, avoiding Ilsi's eyes. Ilsi suppressed the urge to vomit.

"The experiment is simple," Althod explained, "Whoever knows this man is obviously the one I'm looking for. No questions."

For a few minutes, not a muscle moved. Ilsi breathed heavily, no apparent plan was coming to. Reshma looked to Tyk, her eyes bright, and Tyk looked back, grunted under the strain in his arms. Ilsi saw this exchange and her tough, violent shell crumbled. She couldn't see Reshma's life replace her own. If fighting her friend would set things right, she had no choice. Everyone but her deserved a chance to live.

Suddenly, Ilsi and Reshma began humming and singing a few non-magical scales to warm up. Reshma was shaking, setting her chains aflame. Reubens stood back, frightened. When the chains burned and disintegrated, Ilsi froze Reshma's feet to the floor, and Reshma waved her arms wildly to keep her balance. Ilsi made a run for it, making sure to freeze other soldiers to the ground, too. Suddenly Reshma sang out a spell and created a circular wall of fire around Ilsi. The crackling, roaring fire around her deafened all other noises.

Ilsi stopped in her tracks and wondered how she could get through. Her ice would melt pathetically under Reshma's angry conflagration. *Why is she doing this?* Ilsi thought wildly, *Why is she preventing me from helping Tyk?* Ilsi thought back to Althod's challenge. *Why are we fighting? This doesn't solve the little riddle. How does that narrow down who is the one with* Swift? In a split second, she heard the horrific roar above the crackling sound of flames. Ilsi, sweating under the smoke, followed by coughing and sputtering, realized what was really going on.

"SWIFT!"

CHAPTER 57

From Tyk's vantage point, he could see Althod patiently sitting on the king's throne and whispering to one of his guards. The guard nodded, and signaled to his comrades. They struggled to keep two wildcats connected to their chains. They were much larger than Tyk thought they should be. They look starved, angry, and deadly. Tyk began grunting and trying to break his shackles. His throat was dry and his energy was low; could he freeze the shackles off?

Althod looked ready to set them free as he pointed towards Tyk and promptly put his hands behind his back. The impatient beasts roared ferociously and broke free of their chains. They shook their heads, their collars still around their thick necks. They ran together, snapping their jaws towards Tyk.

As Tyk tried to get Ilsi's attention, the girl was momentarily stuck inside Reshma's ring of fire. Tyk knew he wasn't going to get any sort of immediate help. He screamed as the first pounced and sank his jaws into his calf. Screaming, he strained to look at them, to move away, or save himself with a spell. He was pinned too closely to the wall—he couldn't move or resist their attacks. He felt their powerful claws scratching at his pants and shirt and felt pain tearing up and down his body.

He thought he heard Ilsi scream. However, the deafening roars of the beasts stole his attention as they clawed at his flesh.

"Ilsi!" he cried.

As if coming to his bidding, she zoomed out of the fire ring and into the wall next to him, her chest heaving uncontrollably. The beasts suddenly collapsed, and Tyk let out a cry of relief. Ilsi dropped a dagger as it clanged loudly on the ground.

Reshma gradually stopped attacking her icy prison and instead looked up at Tyk and Ilsi. It smelled strongly of rank, dead carcasses. Ilsi furiously cast a strong ice spell and crushed the shackles that held Tyk's arms up. Tyk fell onto Ilsi and she barely kept him from toppling them on top of the dead animals.

"I've got you," Ilsi murmured shakily. Tyk replied with a kiss on her forehead.

"Guards, bring them here," Althod said lazily.

"Let me out of this!" Reshma roared, burning everything in sight. Reshma was still stuck in Ilsi's ice and she couldn't move forward, but she was trying to melt the ice anyway. She waived her hands and fire spat everywhere. Her powers did nothing and it made her angrier. The guards tried to approach the Fire Weaver, and at the last moment, Ilsi waved the spell away.

Reubens quickly motioned with his head towards Reshma and a few soldiers ran towards her. Her throbbing throat sang out in a haunting alto solo as she flexed her muscles. Blue fire suddenly erupted from her hands and lit them brightly like two mighty torches. Her feet were also aflame. She threw her head back and a torrent of fire spewed out of her mouth like a dragon.

The handful of soldiers rightfully kept their distance at the sudden explosion. Reshma's fierce eyes flecked with fire. She used her feet to kick aside a few of the magic-reflective shields that came too close. She violently threw punches and kicks with swift accuracy. Every one of the soldiers fell to the ground, clutching themselves where they received major burns.

She pounded the ground with her fists enveloped in flames and sent a circular wave of fire around her, destroying everything in its path. The other soldiers shuddered in fear behind their shields and Althod held up his hand calmly to deflect her flames.

Tyk and Ilsi stared in horror. There were small heaps of ashes strewn across the stone floor. The only thing that protected them was a shield of ice they created together.

Reshma took in a deep breath and opened her mouth, spewing fire from her throat towards Althod. Althod raised his hands and cast lightning sparks out of his hands. He shoved his hands forward as if to push his power and sent the whirlwind of fire and storm back at Reshma. The flames naturally glazed over its maker, but the shock fizzled over Reshma's body and shook her frame. She shook unnaturally and collapsed on the ground.

"Take her back to the throne," Althod said to a soldier, motioning to Reshma. Smoke rose from her body. Ilsi's eyes glazed over with tears. Reubens, shocked at everything that happened so quickly and suddenly, looked around and realized there was one soldier besides Reubens alive to command. He bowed slightly and dragged Reshma onto her feet and back to the throne. She had no energy to fight back, and sat limply in the chair, shackled.

"My liege!" Reubens cried, approaching his master and bowing. "It pleases me deeply to serve you."

"You pig," Ilsi muttered darkly, struggling under Tyk's weight.

"Yes, I appreciate your faithfulness. Now if you excuse me,

I have matters of importance to attend to," Althod said and casually flicked his hand towards the door.

"But sire," Reubens squeaked, "I found the last person you need!"

"Yes, and?"

"Sire, don't I deserve *anything* for my tireless service?" Reubens said. He sounded like a starved man.

"Reubens, I owe you nothing, now please go about doing your job," Althod interjected. Reubens' eyes went glossy; his face flushed in shame and humiliation as he left the throne room with a half-hearted bow. He gave one last scowl to Ilsi before closing the door. Althod, not even slightly phased, turned to Ilsi and sighed.

"You have disposed my soldiers," Althod said, gesturing to the floor. "If you want this woman to live to see another day, I would suggest coming over here."

Ilsi set her jaw and helped Tyk shuffle slowly the few yards it took to approach Althod. She still gave him wide berth. She wanted to *Swift* herself and Tyk out of here, but she wouldn't dream of leaving Reshma there captive.

"Why are you doing this?" Ilsi asked tersely. "You want me, don't you? Why bother wasting your abilities tormenting everyone else around you."

"I can tell Ladala has been filling your head with lies," Althod answered. "She has been fooling you to think I want to control our known world."

"Is that really true? Forgive me if I can't imagine the reason why my protector would lie to me more than you have to your men. Why should I trust you when you are responsible for the death and enslavement of my clan and other cities? It's because of you my mother is dead!" Ilsi cried.

"Oh, don't include me in tribe squabbles," Althod tisked. "I didn't create that wall."

"It was made to keep people like you out," Tyk grunted.

"Had you come quietly, you would've spared yourself and others a lot of the heartache," Althod answered, his eyebrow arched, waiting for a rebuttal.

"Don't listen, Ilsi," Tyk warned, quietly.

"He can't *really* be the brains behind your brawn. Don't you see? They have their own plans for you, and they intend on keeping you happy only to help them reach their own gains," Althod said, smoothly. His yellow eye flickered with curiosity. "No one else but me really understands and respects your amazing abilities.

"My dear, this isn't about manipulation, this is about *progress*," Althod said, "I have researched, studied, and meditated longer than your time spent on this earth. In my searching, I have discovered a way to heal our planet and rid itself of corruption. Unfortunately, I'm the only one willing to do what it takes.

"I could be the ultimate sacrifice and heal this world of its sickness, pain, and agony, and in return be granted the power to live eternally," Althod said, shaking his fist, "Ilsi, with your power, I could finally unlock the way to doing such. Your reward would far surpass what Ladala or any other meddling creature could offer you."

Ilsi didn't blink the entire time Althod spoke. Her eyes were fixated on Althod's golden eye. As he spoke, all she could think about was her father, friends, and allies. In her mind they were all visible in her mind and they were looking to her. They were looking for a leader to deliver victory. They looked sad; as if they were sad to see Ilsi go, but they nodded to her.

It's your destiny, their eyes said. *We will honor you and your sacrifice.*

She squeezed her eyes shut, willing the vision away.

"No, Althod, I know this trick," Ilsi growled. "I won't sacrifice myself to you and your own wishes. Your plans could never take my pain away, and it certainly couldn't bring my dead mother back. I could never forgive you, nor believe your silly lies!"

"Your brave words sting me just a bit, but your permission wasn't exactly a requirement," Althod said. Ilsi looked around and realized that she was standing an arm's length away from Althod; she had left Tyk on the steps and she didn't even realize it. He was still telling her to stop listening to Althod. Reshma was still quiet and heavy.

He then pointed his fingers and cast a spell in a low, bass voice. A deep purple glow suddenly surrounded his hands and he shoved his hands forward towards Ilsi. A beam erupted from his hands and shot towards her direction.

Ilsi recoiled in shock. The beam shot her directly in the heart.

Instead of collapsing to the ground she remained standing, with her arms outstretched and her feet apart like a star. Her head flew back, as she felt something whooshing around her and tugging at her chest. Her heart throbbed with pain and she had a hard time breathing.

The air around her sucked out her breath and she couldn't inhale any air in return. She panicked and tried to scream, but couldn't hear her own frantic pleas.

Just when she thought her eyes would roll back and pass out, her chest inflated to normal size and she took in big gulps of air. She felt much better, to the point she felt more awake, and there was nothing to worry about. She finally collapsed on the floor, but falling to the ground felt like floated on air. She couldn't quite put her finger on her concerns, but thought that after a long sleep, she would remember. But sleep would come first.

———◦◦◦———

"ILSI!" Tyk screamed.

Ilsi sprawled against the floor. Blood trickled from a nasty cut on her forehead. Her head shifted weakly, her eyes half open. She didn't move. Tears streamed down Reshma's empty face, as she weakly struggled against the grip, her wrists bleeding. Tyk could crawl towards Ilsi's body without being deterred. He looked into her empty face and put a bloody hand to her brow.

"No, no," Reshma whispered, her head hanging heavily. "This isn't happening."

Althod rested his arms after holding them out and took a few deep breaths. He swayed his head from side to side like a ferocious animal; his face became more wrinkled and scorched than before, but his grin made his face even uglier. The castle walls began shake and everyone could feel everything rumbling.

"As you both shall see," Althod said, facing Tyk, "I believe you will find this girl's end far more graceful and merciful than your own." He neared Tyk, unsheathed a long sword, and held it at Tyk's throat. Tyk breathed heavily, his eyes full with anger, a flicker of yellow.

"You coward! Killing a woman," he raged under his breath.

"You make it *too* easy for me to destroy you," Althod exclaimed, pulling Tyk's face closer to his own face and sword, "That's what traitors get."

Althod loosened his grip on Tyk and walked away. The

rumblings became more evident. Ilsi's body shifted with the rumbling.

Tyk gritted his teeth. It was hard for him to control himself any longer. He felt wicked, wild; the beast was somehow coming alive. Tyk let out a blood-curdling scream, as he buckled under insanity and fell back to his knees.

He clenched his shoulders as he felt the pain in his spine. Fur covered his flexed and shaking limbs. His clothes couldn't hold their stitching and tore like wet paper. Long claws scratched at his face as he felt the pain of his nose elongate into a fierce snout. Tyk the wolf was ravaging, his fur standing up as he bore his lengthy teeth. He snorted and roared like a lion.

"You didn't know I could transform you, didn't you? Didn't think I'd discover your devilish secrets? With Ilsi's powers, I can meddle with yours, too. You're going to have to get used to this—this isn't another one of your *phases*," Althod said, still not facing him. He turned around and bellowed a spell aloud. Tyk as a wolf shrieked and whined as he transformed into an even more vicious creature.

He was much larger and demonic, ugly with matted fur and long fangs. His fur was splotchy as though he was covered in mud. His back arched and he scratched at himself violently. Reshma stared in horror at the scene before her. The creature looked up at Reshma with hunger, but Althod gestured towards the exit. The beast instead sped out of the room, barking at anyone who came near him.

The room was silent again, except for Tyk's growls, still audible throughout the corridors. Althod turned his gaze towards Reshma, who used her strength to keep her eyes open and her head up.

"Don't you feel the cosmos shifting? I can already feel it."

"Shut up," Reshma returned hollowly.

"It's a pity I couldn't work with you like you so boldly offered," Althod said, gripping her face with one hand, "but I am afraid your business is faulty and worthless. It was rather valiant of you to try and protect this girl—Ilsi is her name? However, it was a grave mistake to lie to me." She was about to protest, when suddenly he raised a hand to the strike. A zap of green light, and Reshma disappeared from plain view.

"No! You can't do this! You will destroy everyone, everything will die!" Reshma's voice cried out.

"I believe I just did. I have done the impossible, my dear. I can control *Entice*, *Understanding*, *Fortune*, and *Swift*. I have learned to take people's souls, and permanently transform people into vicious animals and invisible nobodies."

Althod, still facing the deceivingly empty chair, flicked his hand upwards by the wrist and the shackles broke and clattered to the ground.

"I would suggest you find a good spot to observe what is to come," Althod said. "You will likely not outlive my plans for humanity."

CHAPTER 58

From miles and miles away, wind rippled across fields of grass like waves of the sea. Ladala ran quickly towards the middle of her camp. Her long brown curls spun wildly in the wind around her head like an angry storm cloud. She wore dark pants and riding boots under her deep forest green commander's uniform. Her light green skirt swished around her calves and the sun reflected off her proud brown breastplate. She wore a long-sleeved white shirt under the armor that clung to her hands and wrists. She held a protective helmet under the crook of her arm.

She ran and signaled her messengers clad in armor to rally her troops. Her troops yelled in harmony to meet quickly, clanging their armor together to meet their commander. Ladala found her horse and quickly mounted him in order to gain height above her soldiers. They circled around her with their spears, arrows, crossbows and swords. Ladala's black horse trotted around in nervousness. Ladala raised her bow and called for silence.

"Listen, my warriors!" Ladala cried. "Now is the time for us to battle mightily and bravely! The humans, the Beasts, and our troops are once again forming an alliance to fight to protect our lands, our families, and preserve all else that we hold dear!"

"Hoo-ah! Hoo-ah!" her troops agreed. They knocked their breast plates with their armored arms.

"Look towards the skies my warriors! They are changing!" Ladala said, "Look towards the trees, the good soil and the streams! They are changing!"

"Hoo-ah! Hoo-ah!"

"Look to the poor, suffering earth! How she wishes to be well again!" she cried, "Look to the west! The islands are starting to sink, and poor Ravenna cannot flee! Look to the Pearl Mountains and the lava erupting over the inhabitants! Look to the Beast forest, how the animals flee and die! Look to the coasts and how they flood with angry seas! The whole world is suffering because of the wickedness of one man!

"We hoped and we prayed this day would never come, but now we must fight to survive! We will *not*—we will *never*—surrender or falter!"

"Hoo-AH! HOO-AHH!"

"My lady!" a voice cried from the crowd. The soldiers made way for a young man dressed in higher ranks than the other soldiers. His face was hard to discern with his full helmet shielding the bridge of his nose and all of his face, save his mouth, eyes and jaw line. He knelt respectfully quickly and touched his left shoulder with his right fist. He kept his eyes from her gaze.

"My lady, my group is ready for your command," he spoke.

"Excellent, proceed to leave at once," Ladala said.

"We are ready to leave faster than a heartbeat," he said, then looking directly at her, "We won't rest until our duty is fulfilled."

"You have my trust and full confidence, Basim," Ladala

said. "You can turn this all around, I know it."

He motioned to his men and two soldiers parted from the rally to follow him. The soldiers looked to the sky. Above them, a large dragon ascended and climbed into the skies. His pearly, sparkling blue scales sparkled in the light like a gypsy's crystal ball. Then a lone soldier riding the large creature saluted to those on foot.

Ladala smiled brightly and joined in the chanting.

"Hoo-ah! Hoo-AH! HOO-AAAAH!"

———◦∞◦———

"Mistress Giselle, I'm worried about Reshma," Gilly said quietly. It was raining and they were standing outside to feel the coolness drench their skin.

"I would be, too, my sweet," Giselle answered, hugging her shoulder, "but she's alive."

"Really?" Gilly asked hopefully, her toes clenched the wet mud. "How do you know?"

"I can feel it in my rattling bones, little one," Giselle said.

"What about Ilsi? Do you think she's all right?" Gilly asked. She stared into Giselle's eyes after a pause. Giselle's features softened and rain fell down her cheeks like teardrops.

"The worst has happened, Gilly," Giselle whispered, "This isn't the end, it's only the beginning, now."

"And it seems so quiet now," Gilly mused sadly. "Are we just going to sit here and wait?"

Giselle stared off, deep in thought.

"I see that I must take Ilsi's invitation," Giselle murmured. "I will help Ladala's side in my own way, and in my own terms. I know that's what you wish."

Gilly brightened. "What changed your mind?"

"Well," Giselle paused. "I want this world to still be beautiful and good. For you and your future kin."

Gilly smiled. She knew this meant that she would hear more news about Reshma.

"It's a pity," Giselle said, "we probably won't see our chrysanthemums by the time they bloom. Boo, what bad luck."

<hr/>

Sebrah looked over her small, ill-kept hut before leaving. She had a small knapsack with foodstuff, and extra clothes. However, that wasn't much of a concern to her. She tightened her belt and checked her twin daggers at both hips, secure. Each boot had a hidden dagger. She had a dagger strapped to each wrist and forearm, four deadly edges. Two poison darts were stuck in her hair disguised as hair ornaments. Two hefty axes were strapped to her back, plus she had another bag filled with more poison darts and a bow to shoot them with. She hefted a crossbow and tried to decide where she would hold it. It seemed there was nowhere else, so she threw it over her shoulder and picked up her bag. She turned around and remembered; she left her helmet on her bed. She fastened it quickly and checked that her other armor was secured.

She kicked open the door and shut it again with her heel once she was outside. Once leaving her hut and with all her choice weapons, she looked like all the other soldiers leaving their houses and bidding their families good-bye. She followed behind her troop, waving and displaying yellow flags. She already felt a bit of heat from her full armor and helmet, but she grinned under her helmet. She had been waiting for this battle, and she prepared for victory—just like the good old days. Once the soldiers formed larger ranks, they began singing old familiar war songs and Sebrah joined in; she knew them all perfectly.

⇒◦⇐

Charcoal Ridge slowly fell asleep under the crescent moon's soft glow. The traffic on the streets slowly disintegrated and a few quiet wanderers found their way into the large, recently repaired inn. There were lights in all the windows and the smells of soup, bread and meat drew weary and fatigued guests inside. A large crowd of people were standing at a large desk where they were directed towards the last few available rooms or towards tables where a young man with fiery red hair smiled and greeted them.

He worked swiftly and expertly, rushing to and from the kitchen with hot steamy plates of food. There was a table of people waiting for him to assist them and he made her way over. Berg wiped her hands on his apron tied around his waist and made his way to another busy table. It was his evening to bus tables and he was almost done for the evening. Everything felt normal in town except for the heavy and stifling presence of Yildirim soldiers.

Berg perked up and listened intently and noticed that the guests by the window were pointing outside in curiosity. He suddenly heard lots of screaming from outside the inn. Berg suddenly changed direction and waded through the people towards the exit.

"Berg, take care of your tables!" his father called, "I can't have you rudely ignoring them!"

"Fa, I'll be back, give me a moment!" he called back and leaned outside the door. He could see figures running free in the street. Many of them were screaming and running as fast as they could. Once his eyes adjusted to the darkness she could see that they were women of all ages. Their hair trailed in the air like full sails and they were shedding Yildirim armor like snake skin.

"What the—" he breathed. They weren't screaming with fright, they were shouts of acclamation. Doors lined along the street opened wide and light spilled out onto the sands. Mothers and fathers, brothers, and sisters raced into the streets and snatched them into their arms and never let go. Fathers kissed his daughters's damp hair while mothers tightly wrapped shoulders with a shawl and gave loving embraces.

Berg leaned against the post with his arms folded. Dozens of guests shoved him to the side to make way and towards the young girls just as excitedly as the girls running into their arms. Berg felt someone grab her shoulder tightly.

"What is all that screaming for?" the innkeeper said. "It's louder in here, Berg. Get to the tables."

"Look!" his wife called, clutching his sleeve excitedly, "Look at them! Isn't that Etta's girl?"

"Ma, I have to go!" Berg called, then untied his apron and wadded it up and left it on a messy table. He squeezed through the doorway amongst the crowd leaving the inn. His mother grasped his hand quickly before Berg was swept too far by the current. His mother looked at him earnestly, confused and worried. "Ma, I'll come back. I'll be all right."

Someone in the inn boasted that he would celebrate by buying drinks for everyone and the room filled with cheers for their returned women and daughters. Berg slipped out the door and into the night.

"Karachi, come to the looking glass," an elderly voice called meekly. The young princess stared out the window, watching the snow drift endlessly to the ground below. With another reminder, she finally arose, gathered her massive skirts, and walked silently to an ornate mirror to sit in a small chair. A small old woman gently pulled the pins out of her hair, and long curls fell and bounced one at a time like small waterfalls. Karachi stared at the mirror with empty, emotionless eyes. Her mouth played in a line as she waited for her newest governess to finish. She was planted by the Yildirim leader after her beloved and life-long governess was killed.

"Enough of the sighing, dearest," the elderly woman requested, as she gently combed the princess' long curls. Karachi said nothing in return, but slightly jerked her head at the motion of the woman's tugging.

"Thank you," Karachi breathed when the woman was finished. "Today has just been a trying day." The woman smiled slightly and silently walked away. Karachi still stared at her face without so much of a twitch; a blink here or there was all. She had felt that way since Ilsi was captured in the inn.

She finally washed the thick, expensive powder and makeup off her face, rubbing her eyes. She stared at her normal complexion; her skin was three shades darker without the white powder that made her look pale as milk. She then arose and someone came and helped her undress from her large gown. Her hips seemed to expand and relax from the load of her dress. Someone guided her to a small, expensive bathtub as they washed the bluish silver powder from her hair, revealing raven black curls.

The princess slipped into a warm bed gown, and she slid into a long furred robe that enveloped her entirely. Her servants left her and she walked soundlessly back to the window to stare at the large window. She swiftly and silently began braiding her own hair into a long plait down her spine. As she got towards the end to her long hair, her brows furrowed softly; she didn't have anything in her hand to tie around her hair to keep her hair braided. She arose and walked towards her nightstand and rummaged in the dim lamplight for a ribbon. She quickly and expertly tied it in place before her hair fell out of place.

In the silence she heard a large, rhythmic whooshing sound. Her head spun around and her braid whipped onto her back in response. It was a loud, beating noise just outside her balcony window. She gathered her robe close around her and edged close towards her window.

Suddenly, two dark figures jumped and landed atop her large balcony. They crept silently towards the princess and bowed deeply. She returned the bow with one herself. She could hear men shouting, coming from her front door and she turned and jumped at the knocking and clambering. She looked back at the figures, two young soldiers. Just behind them were two other soldiers astride a large dragon, silver and twinkling in the moonlight. The princess smiled, revealing a pair of snow boots on her feet under her nightgown.

Just then, her door broke down and guards rushed in to attack. Karachi edged towards the window, casting spells on the soldiers as they approached. They froze in mid-stride with anger and alarm etched in their faces. Before long, Karachi had to leap before more came. She ran towards the dragon and the soldiers lifted her to safely sit on the dragon's back between the four of them. The helpers swiftly jumped up and the dragon shrieked slightly as they flew away from the balcony. She gripped excitedly to the person in front of her, as the guard behind her made sure she was secure. She looked down at her dark, gloomy home and then smiled at the guard behind her.

"Finally," Karachi breathed.

Thank you so much for reading this book! Please leave a book review on Amazon, Goodreads, or wherever you bought this book. It helps other readers find me and hopefully be obsessed with me.

To stay updated on part two, you can find me at Wit & Travesty, you can sign up for the newsletter, or you can find me on social media:

Instagram: @whit2ney
Twitter: @witty_whitters
Facebook: Wit & Travesty

About the Author

Whitney O. McGruder has been plotting to become a published author ever since she wrote her first Sailor Moon fanfic in middle school. She earned her BA in English with a minor in editing in order to make this dream a reality. Fifteen years after the fanfic, not only has she finally published her debut novel, but she's a savvy full-time editor and the co-owner of Wit & Travesty. She also freelance edits, plays Pokémon Go and RPGs with her husband, dyes her hair pink, collects nerdy clothing, and otherwise has no chill. She lives happily ever after with her author-husband, Travis, in Utah.

Acknowledgments

Oh my days, my shoutout list will probably be the longest one ever—there have been so many of you throughout the past two decades who have helped me finally publish this novel.

First off, major thanks and kisses go to Travis, who became my friend because I told him I was writing this book. This book is available to the world just 14 years after the day we met. Thank you for being my first beta reader and for assuring me that I could do this.

Thank you, Mom and Dad, who still bought me books, notebooks, laptops, and my education—knowing I wanted to be a writer and having no idea what I was actually writing. You taught me to approach my dreams with a realistic plan and so far so good!

Thanks to my younger brothers—Jordan, Justin, and Nicholas—for also being supportive even though some of you aren't super into books. It's fine; you'll end up in upcoming novels. Major thanks to the rest of my family for being so loving and patient while they've been kept in the dark.

Big hugs for Emily Bates for performing all the formatting for this book. You came in and saved me during a stressful time.

Thank you Hannah Ratliff for being a treasure of a friend and a very important and helpful beta reader. I won't be debuting any gender-confused dragons any time soon thanks to your clever eye.

Lindsey Penugula, thank you for being the first beta reader to kick me in the pants. Jonathan Baker and Jessica Hancock, thank you for being a part of the best writing group ever devised. Thank you as well to Brittany Olsen and Ari Velez (and her little family) for helping with additional beta reading and letting me talk your ears off.

Then there's all the in-person and online friends I've made. Oh my days, there are so many of you! I specifically must thank Kara Jorgensen, Angelika Offenwanger, Caitlin Jones, Kate M Colby, Amanda Richter, Louise Bates Ayers, and Teralyn Mitchell for being amazing fellow-writers. Most people said that I could publish this book, but since you have all done this already, I trusted your words of encouragement a bit more.

Lastly, if you've ever told me you'd read this book or wrote encouraging messages to me, THANK YOU. I've met you through work, the internet, church, and school—as I am friendly AF. If you let me sign your book, I can write something more heartfelt. But for now, know you are all amazing and significant to me.

Made in the USA
San Bernardino, CA
31 October 2018